THE STREET OF BROKEN DREAMS

Summer 1945. The nation rejoices as the Second World War comes to an end but Banbury Street matriarch Eva Parker foresees trouble ahead.

Whilst her daughter, Mildred, awaits the return of her fiancé from overseas duty, doubts begin to seep into her mind about how little she knows of the man she has promised to marry. Or are her affections being drawn elsewhere?

Meanwhile, new neighbour, dancer Cissie Cresswell hides a terrible secret. The end of the conflict willbring her no release from the horrific night that destroyed her life. Can she ever find her way back?

Under Eva's stalwart care, can the two young women unite to face the doubt and uncertainty of the future?

THE STREET OF BROKEN DREAMS

Summer 1945. The nation rejoices as the Second World War comes to an end but Banbury Street matriarch Eva Parker fore- sees trouble ahead.

Whilst her daughter, Mildred, awaits the return of her fiancé from overseas duty, doubts begin to creep into her mind about how little she knows of the man she has promised to marry. Or are her affections being drawn elsewhere?

Meanwhile, new neighbour, dancer Cissie Cresswell hides a terrible secret. The end of the conflict will bring her no release from the horrific night that destroyed her life. Can she ever find her way back?

Under Eva's stalwart care, can the two young women unite to face the doubt and uncer- tainty of the future?

TANIA CROSSE

◆

THE STREET OF BROKEN DREAMS

Complete and Unabridged

MAGNA
Leicester

First published in Great Britain in 2019 by
Aria
an imprint of Head of Zeus
London

First Ulverscroft Edition
published 2021
by arrangement with
Head of Zeus Ltd
London

This is a work of fiction. All characters,
organisations, and events portrayed in this novel
are either products of the author's imagination or
are used fictitiously.

A catalogue record for this book is available
from the British Library.

ISBN 978–0–7505–4878–6

Published by
Ulverscroft Limited
Anstey, Leicestershire

Printed and bound in Great Britain by
TJ Books Ltd., Padstow, Cornwall

This book is printed on acid-free paper

In memory of my dear ballet mistress
Miss Doris Lightowler Knight
And, as ever, for my darling husband
You waltzed away with my heart all those years ago
And we're still dancing together half a century later

SPECI ▓▓▓ ADERS

THE ULVER ▓▓▓ N
(registered ▓▓▓)
was establis▓▓▓ r
research, dia▓▓▓ ses
Exampl▓▓▓

- The ▓▓▓
  Ho▓
- T▓ ▓▓▓ at
  O ▓▓▓ or ▓ ▓▓▓ ren
- F▓▓▓ reseal ▓▓▓ ye disea▓▓▓ and
  treatment at the Department of
  Ophthalmology, University of Leicester
- The Ulverscroft Vision Research Group,
  Institute of Child Health
- Twin operating theatres at the Western
  Ophthalmic Hospital, London
- The Chair of Ophthalmology at the Royal
  Australian College of Ophthalmologists

You can help further the work of the Foundation
by making a donation or leaving a legacy. Every
contribution is gratefully received. If you would
like to help support the Foundation or require
further information, please contact:

THE ULVERSCROFT FOUNDATION
The Green, Bradgate Road, Anstey
Leicester LE7 7FU, England
Tel: (0116) 236 4325

website: www.ulverscroft-foundation.org.uk

Prologue

May 1944

She stared up, motionless, at the dark, cold arc of the sky. A dead, three-quarter moon struggled overhead, peering between banks of grey mocking cloud and spilling its liquid silver glow over the bomb site. She couldn't move, pinned by shock to the rubbled ground and broken bricks beneath her, eyes trained on the ether that hovered above, every detail searing into her memory forever.

That stretch of her nightly journey home always made her stomach clench with uneasiness. Five minutes' walk from where she got off the last bus, she turned down the long street that was no longer a street. Once upon a time, it had been a continuous terrace where people and families had lived and played, a pleasant, tree-lined road opposite a small London park. But since the bombs had come, it was an empty void, the site only partially cleared, tottering walls propped up to make them safe until the bulldozers moved in. The burned-out beams were like black skeletons against the sky, and in the darkness, the ruins were but a tangle of shadows where writhed the ghosts of those who had perished in the blasts.

Tonight, though, had been different. The wondrous reverie that swirled in her head had been but mildly interrupted by the kerfuffle as she'd waited on the platform at the back of the bus. As it drew to a halt at her stop, a large figure had crashed down the stairs from the upper deck. It had landed in a heap by her feet. In the gloom of the blackout, she'd just been able to distinguish the shape of an American forage cap. And by the smell of alcohol that wafted around the fellow, he'd clearly had far too much to drink.

'Sorry, ma'am.' An instant later, the silhouette of a second GI had followed down the stairs and hauled his inebriated compatriot to his feet.

'Best get him home, sonny,' the bus conductor, an older man, had said with a mixture of disgust and sympathy. 'Best thing's vinegar and a raw egg — if yer can find such a thing,' he ended with a grimace.

The girl had waited while the sober GI dragged his companion onto the pavement before stepping down off the platform herself. While they staggered away down the road, she'd paused to let her eyes focus in the darkness. She'd tipped her head skyward and a beam of moonlight had fallen across her face as the clouds parted for a brief moment. At least it wasn't utterly pitch-dark and she should be able to grope her way along the familiar route home without any trouble.

'Hey, little lady, d'ya want a ciggie?'

The lurching voice at her elbow had made her jump. She'd known who it was before she'd even turned her head. The gust of cigarette breath laced with beer and whisky fumes had fanned her nostrils, and she'd pulled back with a shudder.

'Put that out!' she'd retorted as he'd waved a lit cigarette in front of her. 'That's all it'd take if there was a bomber overhead.'

'But there ain't no bombers — '

'Yeah, give me that.' The other soldier had suddenly appeared and, easily grabbing the little white stick with its glowing tip from his friend's hand, had ground it out under his foot. 'My apologies again, miss. He gave us the slip. Come on, Chuck. Let's get ya back.'

The second chap's voice was deep and sonorous, and the girl couldn't quite make out his accent. It was American, yes, but there was something else mixed in with it. Casting a quick, disdainful glance in his direction, she got the impression in the glimmer of moonlight that he was dark-skinned. Ah, that might explain it. There were plenty of black GIs in the US Army, after all.

But she wasn't going to hang around to find out if she was right. She'd set off down the road, rolling her eyes in annoyance as she heard the drunk GI's voice raised in protest.

'But look at her! She's a little beauty. And she's got spunk. Ya saw her face in the moonlight. Ain't she the prettiest thing ya've seen all night?'

'I'm surprised ya can see anything at all, ya're so pie-eyed. Time to sleep it off, I reckon. Now, come on!'

The sober Yank had grunted in exasperation, and when the girl dared to risk a furtive look over her shoulder, she saw he was half dragging his stumbling pal away — thankfully in the opposite direction. Well, that was a relief! Within moments, she'd forgotten all about the incident as she'd made her way through the unlit streets, and she slid back deliciously into the glorious fantasy. It hadn't been a fantasy, though, had it? It had been

3

real.

As she'd turned the corner and began to walk past the bomb site, for once, she hadn't feared the eerie tentacles of the dead that seemed to reach out for her in the dark. The grandiose, emotive tones of Wagner's Overture to *Tristan and Isolde* rang once more inside her skull, filling her head so that there was room for nothing else. The new, much-heralded *pas de deux* had been a triumph, the tumultuous applause reaching into her soul. This was what she had dreamt of, strived so hard for, all of her young life. Her male principal dance partner, Sean, had smiled at her so proudly as he had shown her off to the audience, standing back with a slight bow as she dipped in a curtsey again and again. The stiff netting skirt of her tutu had bobbed up and down as she accepted the bouquet that was presented to her and picked up the individual flowers that were thrown onto the stage.

The enchantment of the intertwining of music and ballet, her most beloved form of dance, still burned in her heart as she made her way home, the magic rising like a fountain in her breast and lifting her soul to some mystical heights. The street and the darkness melted away and her very being was lost in some other place where grace and movement reigned.

She wasn't sure how or when the sensation came over her that she was being watched, dashing her other world to smithereens. Only seconds later, she began to hear footsteps behind her. Was she being followed? She quickened her pace, heartbeat suddenly racing. It was probably just some innocent passer-by, someone she knew even, hurrying home. But she didn't like the way the footsteps were speeding up, getting closer.

She forced herself to turn her head but without slowing her pace. She was shocked and alarmed to make out the form of what could only be the drunk GI lumbering after her. Though he didn't seem so drunk now. He was a big man with a long stride, and though he was unsteady, he was gaining on her.

'Leave her be, Chuck!'

She saw the other one, then, loping along some way behind, bent double and clutching his stomach as if he'd been on the end of a hefty punch.

'Ya know I like a bit of spirit in a girl!' the first soldier roared in reply. 'It'll be fun having her, and ya ain't going to stop me!'

'Run, miss, run!' the second soldier called out with a gasp as he tried in vain to catch up.

She didn't need telling twice. She turned her head forward again and fled. She knew she was fleet of foot, fast, her muscles strong. The devil would never catch her! The gap was widening as she flew along now past the bomb site, and soon she'd be among the labyrinth of narrow backstreets she knew like the back of her hand. She'd lose him in seconds. He'd never be able to follow her in the blackout, and she'd be safely indoors, leaving him lost and defeated in the dark.

Nearly at the surviving houses, heart thundering, breath burning in her lungs, her foot caught on a paving slab that had been cracked and lifted in the bombing raid that had obliterated the street. She felt herself falling, but it happened so quickly and she couldn't stop it. She put out her

5

hands, but pain seared through her ankle before she made contact with the pavement, her palms stinging as they slapped on the ground. She knew the man would be on her in a trice. She had to get up and run on. She tried desperately to scramble to her feet, but the agony scorched up her leg and into her head. A sickening dizziness clouded her consciousness and darkness closed in.

It was the pain as her back scraped on the jagged ground that brought her to her senses, and she knew she was being dragged into the bomb site. The next instant, the soldier's heavy body was pinning her down, and she twisted her head as she tried to avoid his slobbering lips.

'So ya won't give us a kiss, eh, honey?' he mocked, and began noisily licking and nuzzling her neck.

She thought she was going to vomit. She struggled, arms flailing. But he caught her wrists. He was so *heavy*. She did the only thing she could. Hawked up some saliva and spat in his face, hoping the surprise would give her the chance to escape.

It didn't. He stopped. And then he laughed. A sound of pure evil. Then a giant hand slammed across her cheekbone, sending her head reeling. Her senses stole into nothingness, and she lost time. A few seconds, perhaps.

By some miracle, she felt the great weight suddenly lift from her. She forced her eyes open. Silhouettes in the darkness. Shouts. Thumps and crashes. Thuds as blows landed. The two men were fighting. Her chance to flee. She must! She scrambled to her feet, but her ankle gave way and she yelped as she landed on her knees. *Pull herself up again, ignore the agony. Limp, stumble back towards the pavement.*

A cry behind her. She turned her head, oblivious to the tears of desperation dripping down her cheeks. One of the men, she wasn't sure which, was falling backwards, crumpling to the ground like a puppet whose strings had suddenly been cut. The other stood over him for a moment in a gloating stance, then viciously kicked the inert figure over and over again.

A terrified whimper escaped from the girl's throat. Dear God, it was clear who was who! She hobbled on, too drenched in fear to look back. She wanted to close her eyes, blot it all out. But she could hear his heavy footsteps lurching over the debris of the bomb site. She knew it was coming. But it couldn't, *mustn't* be real.

Before she could reach the pavement again, she squealed as he caught her arm and swung her round. The stench of drink and cigarettes attacked her nostrils again, and she lashed out, fighting like a wild cat. But he grabbed her shoulders, almost lifting her off her feet, and flung her down on the ground.

She couldn't breathe, utterly winded, her mind falling into some dark hole. She was helpless as she felt him drag her further back into the site again, where, in the blackout, no passer-by would ever see. She tried to struggle, but he gave that demonic laugh once more. Grabbed her hair, tearing it from her scalp, and thumped her head back hard on the ground.

She saw stars. Couldn't move. Half blacked

7

out. Consciousness came in waves. She knew he was lifting her skirt, pulling off her knickers, but it was unreal, like a nightmare where everything is disjointed and doesn't make sense, and her limbs were limp and didn't respond to any message her stupefied brain tried to send them.

It was only when the pain ripped up into her body that she was snapped back to her senses. It was so intense that, for a second or two, her mind was stunned and oblivious to all else. Then she realised what was happening, and the horror and humiliation speared into her. She opened her mouth to scream, but a sweaty, iron hand came tightly over her face. She was suffocating, gasping for breath, the fight to stay alive greater than the terror of the monster thrusting into her. She felt herself passing out. The end had come. And she welcomed it.

'Ya leave her alone!' was the next thing she heard, the outraged voice of the other GI, the one she believed was black, who'd been knocked unconscious and kicked for good measure.

'Too late,' came the smirking reply. Laughing, nauseating.

Just above her. His weight no longer pinning her down, though the pain still burned inside her.

'What! Ya don't mean ya've . . . ? Ya filthy bastard!'

'Now don't ya go mentioning this, ya dirty nigger,' the other voice, from further away now, threatened. 'One word an' I'll put ya on a charge, an' it won't just be for insubordination. In fact, I'll say it was you who did it. That'll get ya hanged an' ya'll regret ever openin' ya mouth!'

'Jeez, what the hell've ya done? Ya can't just leave her — '

'She was asking for it, walkin' alone at this hour. So come on. An' not a word or ya'll regret it!'

All went quiet then but for the scuffling of feet. Somehow, the girl found the will to lift her head. She could just make out the silhouette of a taller man dragging the protesting, struggling outline of the other soldier away down the deserted street. Footfall fading. Then silence. Her head fell back and she sank down into soft, comforting blackness.

The music, the gentle harmonies, the crescendos, were playing again, she was dancing, spinning, her body moving with such grace, her arms floating. But her foot wasn't working properly. She couldn't do it. Sean frowned at her and she shook her head . . .

She was staring blindly at the moon. Not a sound. Not a breath of air. What was she doing there? And then she tried to move.

Her entire body seemed racked with pain, reality flooding back with all the might of a sledgehammer. Falling, her ankle on fire. And then she remembered. The men. Yankee soldiers. And she knew what had happened as something struck deep inside her like an arrow.

The brutal howl that escaped her lungs and cut through the still night was that of a wounded animal. And it wasn't just the physical pain. The degradation, the shame, the vile humiliation of the heinous act that had been committed against her. She wanted to scream it away, rip it out of her. But she couldn't. It was all a blur, but it had been done, and couldn't be undone.

Oh, dear God, it was a nightmare. Couldn't be real. Mustn't be real. But she knew it was. With a tearing moan, she curled up on her side and waited for it all to go away.

1

April 1945

Evangeline Parker passed the Duke of Cambridge on the corner and turned into Banbury Street. Ooph, it was good to get home! She'd been queuing for what seemed hours for the week's rations of tea, sugar, tinned food and what have you at the grocer's, and then again for the few days' rations of meat at the butcher's and whatever fruit and veg was available at the greengrocer's. She didn't have the luxury of one of those things she believed were called a refrigerator. Just a lead-lined box with a marble shelf and a metal-mesh door to keep the flies out. So, at the end of the week, she'd have to queue all over again for fresh supplies for the weekend.

For all that, what did she have? From the butcher's, a pig's trotter — that her husband, Stan, liked but she could never stand — one kidney and a couple of slices of ox liver. There hadn't even been any bacon or sausages available, and Old Willie would never have lied to her about that. She'd lived in the little backstreet near south-west London's Battersea Park for virtually all of her fifty-nine years and had been a faithful customer and, she hoped, friend for most of her life, feeding her own growing family on his meat and nobody else's.

Thank goodness spuds and bread weren't on

ration, even if the latter was the horrible, grey-coloured National Loaf. She'd managed to get their due ration of tea, sugar, butter and margarine OK, but the few ounces of cheese had come as a bright orange colour rather than the normal mousetrap, so she hoped it was going to be edible. Add to that a selection of vegetables — carrots, turnips and spring greens but sadly no onions — and their ration of tinned fruit, peas and spam, and somehow she'd have to feed her family on that for the next few days.

Not that there were so many mouths to feed these days, what with only two of their six offspring living at home. The eldest two, Kit and Gert, were both married and had long flown the nest. With a lifelong passion for trains, Kit had left grammar school at sixteen to work on the railways. Now he was the sub stationmaster at a place called Edenbridge Town in Kent. For a rural station, it was incredibly important freight-wise, and had been even more so during the war. As a railway worker, Kit had been exempt from conscription, for which Eva thanked the Good Lord. Railway lines had been obvious targets for German bombers, of course, but a couple of bombs exploding near the Edenbridge lines at the beginning of the raids had been the extent of any danger. So Kit and his wife, Hillie, daughter of Eva's best friend — ah, how she still missed poor Nell, though she'd been dead ten years or more — and their two little ones had been safe throughout the war.

As she puffed up to her own front door, her arms weighed down with the precious shopping,

Eva glanced along the street to the little terraced house, a few doors down, where Nell had lived and suffered at the hands of her brutal husband. She'd been well out of it, poor love, for over a decade, but Eva swore she could still see her sometimes, waving with a forced smile, putting on a brave face. All the dreadful things that had happened belonged to another time, a previous, sad story, but Eva would never forget them.

Sadness tugged at her big, warm heart as she let herself into her own home. Number Twelve, where Nell and her family had lived, was empty yet again. When both Nell and her husband had died, the eldest daughter, Hillie, had moved back in to take care of her five younger siblings. Then when she had married Kit, all seven of them had gone to live together in Kent, and it had been some while before the house was re-let. A Mr and Mrs Goldstein had eventually moved in, an elderly Jewish couple who'd seen which way the wind had been blowing and had thankfully got out of Germany before Hitler had done his worst. Thank Gawd they had. The concentration camp of Bergen-Belsen had recently been liberated, and the horrific stories of what had gone on there were so evil and despicable that they were beyond belief. As it was, the Goldsteins had lived out their lives in relative safety in Banbury Street. Old Abraham had been widowed the previous year, and Eva and Stan had done their best to console him. But he'd literally pined away before their very eyes until he'd passed away just two weeks ago.

As they'd left no family, Eva had taken care of

everything and, to her surprise, had discovered that the old man had left all he had to her as thanks for her kindness over the years. Not a huge amount of money, but some expensive jewellery that she kept under lock and key. There was what she believed was called a Hunter watch, worth a pretty penny on its own, three eighteen-carat gold rings, one with a huge diamond almost the size of a farthing, and some brooches, bracelets and necklaces that even Eva's untrained eye could see were the real McCoy and not just paste. She'd never seen anything like it. Should be in the Tower of London with the Crown Jewels, she'd joked to Stan. But, for the time being, she didn't quite know what to do with it all and somehow felt she could make the most of it when the war was over. For now, it was locked away in the little strongbox Abraham had kept it in, hidden beneath the floorboards with a heavy sideboard on top.

Sighing now as she dumped the shopping bags on the table among the debris of breakfast — such as it had been — Eva untied the scarf that hid the curlers in her hair. After all, you couldn't let standards drop just because there was a war on! She'd never been able to afford a perm, although maybe she could now with her little legacy, but old habits die hard and she didn't want to waste even a penny. So the curlers still went in every night and didn't come out until just before Stan came home from work. She might not be the best housekeeper in the world, nor the best cook, or anything else for that matter, but she loved her Stan and always wanted to look her best for him.

The last six years had taught her that. You never knew what was round the corner, so best to make the most of every minute.

Ah, good. The gas was working, and she could make herself a nice cup of tea. The third time she'd used the same tea leaves, but you got used to that. She'd be blooming pleased when this war was over — which it looked like it might be quite soon — and things could get back to normal. Ah, just think of it. No more rationing, no more blackout. No more fear. What bliss!

Just as she was pouring the weak tea into the chipped mug — she'd rinsed it under the tap in the scullery but it still had a brown tide ring in the bottom, but never mind that — a small sound from the hallway caught her ear. Her spirits lifted as she plodded back towards the front door. For, as she'd hoped, an envelope had landed on the mat. She recognised the writing before she stooped to pick it up. Oh, goodie! A letter from their eldest daughter, Gert. Neither of them had been any use at letter-writing before Gert had married and moved away, but they had learnt!

Now, Eva settled down in the old armchair with the stuffing hanging out and the springs gone so that it wasn't comfortable any more, but she couldn't bring herself to throw it out just yet. It had been her mum's. And while the chair was still there, Eva felt as if Old Sal was still there, too, even though she'd been gone some ten years or so. Silly really. Sometime soon, she'd promised Kit, when the war was over and you could get something better than Utility Furniture, she'd let him buy her the new one he wanted her to have. She could afford to get one herself now, of course, but it was still a case of letting go.

Tearing open the envelope, Eva unfolded the letter. Only one sheet, but paper wasn't always easy to get hold of. And Gert had filled both sides, keeping her writing small even if it wasn't very neat. It would keep Eva content for a good few minutes as she deciphered the scrawl.

Dear Mum and Dad, Milly and Jake,

Hope you are all well, and no more flipping doodlebugs coming your way. Doesn't look as if there'll be any more, does it? They say old Adolf's beaten. Let's hope they're right. I know I'll be relieved, what with Rob out in France. He said in his last letter it's really only mopping up the last pockets of resistance, but you never know. It was bad enough when he was wounded out in Sicily. He mightn't be so lucky another time. I just want him back home and working his old regular hours at the bank.

Eva's mouth twisted with rueful sympathy. It was all anyone wanted, wasn't it, to have your loved ones safely back home? Gert had done well when she'd married Rob. They'd moved out to a pleasant Surrey suburb called Stoneleigh, where a whole grid of semi-detached, mock-Tudor houses had been built over a huge area. The front gardens were twice the size of Stan and Eva's back yard, and many of the back gardens were a hundred feet in length!

Gert had 'improved' herself since her mar-

16

riage and had even trained herself to speak the King's English much better. But she was still the same old Gert, with a heart as big as the ocean, which was why Rob had fallen in love with her. They'd produced three bouncing sons in quick succession before war had broken out and Rob had gone off to fight. Though boisterous and unruly as they'd grown, the boys nevertheless had hearts of gold just like their mum, and Eva was as proud of them as she was of her other two more reserved grandchildren, Kit and Hillie's son and daughter.

Have you heard from Gary recently, Milly?

The letter went on, and Eva could imagine her eldest daughter's face creasing with compassion for her next youngest sister.

Must be so hard for you with him still out in the Far East with the Japs refusing to give in when it looks like the war in Europe could be over very soon. So keep your chin up, girl. And what about you, Jake? Have they accepted you into the Fire Service yet? You've been a runner for them all this time, so they should welcome you with open arms. I know you want to do better for yourself and you can't wait to leave Price's. I know I couldn't when I worked there. Don't know how you can still stand it, Dad, after all these years. Still, I suppose you're in the sawmill, which is different. You two been to any good footie matches together recently?

Eva felt a little nick in her heart. Stan had worked at Price's massive candle and soap factory down the road beside the river since he'd come back from the first war. Gert had worked there, too, in the candle-packing shed, until she'd married Rob. When war had broken out again in 1939, the family had agreed it would be better for Stan and Eva's four younger children to go and live in relative safety with Gert and Rob in Surrey. However, in the summer of 1941 when the Blitz appeared to be over, Mildred and Jake had both insisted on returning home to London. Mildred had left school in 1940 and had been working in a shop on Stoneleigh Broadway ever since. Back in Battersea, she'd again been a shop assistant until she turned eighteen and was conscripted to work on the buses, which, to her delight, she found she much preferred. Jake had only just left school in the July of 1941, and Stan had got him his very first job at Price's. It wasn't ideal for him, but with the war on, everyone had to put their ambitions on hold.

And then, on 13th July 1944, at a quarter past ten in the morning, a V1 rocket had landed on Price's, and Eva would never forget it.

Several of these massive flying bombs had attacked the area in the previous month, coming, without warning, at any time of day or night. It had been the Blitz all over again, or even worse. At least the explosive and incendiary bombs in the Blitz had been small by comparison, and were dropped by waves of enemy planes, the air-raid sirens warning of their approach so that you at least had time to seek some sort of protection

18

in a shelter. But although the sirens went off occasionally, these new self-propelled, pilotless bombs came mainly undetected until it was too late, instilling a permanent fear into you as they cruised stealthily through the air before dropping onto their target, obliterating everything in sight. They made a droning sound like a massive insect, which was why they'd earned the nickname of buzz bombs or more usually doodlebugs. It was said that if their roar cut out when it was immediately above you that you knew you'd had your chips as they'd simply plummet out of the sky. By the end of June 1944, seventy to a hundred V1s had been reaching London every day.

Amazingly, though, up until that July day, there'd been relatively few civilians killed in the local area, despite all the terrible destruction the V1s had caused, though tragically it was a different story in other parts of London. Even when Price's had bought it, only two workers had perished. *Only two.* That was how you'd come to think, Eva winced.

The factory's pump house had been hit and fire had spread to the tons of oil and turps and animal fats, which had gone up like a tinderbox. Burning liquid had oozed out into the Thames, where seven barges had been moored, waiting to unload their cargoes of paraffin wax, and they'd been damaged, too. The sky around had been black with choking smoke, and when Eva had run out onto the street at the massive explosion that had shaken the house even at that distance and word had eventually come through that it was Price's that had been hit, she'd been numbed with ter-

19

ror, as if the very flames that were starting to rage through the factory had set her veins on fire with fear as well. Her Stan, and their younger son. It had been Jake's seventeenth birthday. Surely fate wouldn't be so cruel as to take him on the day he'd planned to go out to celebrate with his mates that evening?

As it happened, both her men had been safe, but Eva would never forget the trembling that had consumed her so that she hadn't been able to think straight. Her head had been reeling as she'd panted through the streets, still in her slippers, as fast as her wobbling legs would carry her, almost collapsing and wheezing as if her lungs would burst by the time she got to the factory.

The sight that met her eyes had made her sink down on her knees. A sea of fire against a black dome where the summer morning sky should have been. And then, among the chaos and the noise and the deafening crackle of leaping flames, she recognised two familiar shapes battling together with the force of the stream of water spurting from one of the many fire hoses that were blasting into the inferno. Eva's heart had almost stopped beating, such was her relief. Of course. Both Stan and Jake were ARP wardens for the factory, and Jake was a runner for the fire brigade, though this wouldn't be the first time he'd actually helped tackle a blaze.

Now Eva shuddered at the horrific memory and forced her attention back to Gert's letter. Was there news of her two youngest children, Trudy and Primrose, who'd also been evacuated to

Gert's in 1939 and were still there? Ah, yes. Gert mentioned them next.

Trudy's still doing so well at the Grammar, so she wants to stay on here till she finishes when she's eighteen. Me and Rob don't mind, and it's been good company for me while he's been away. She's a bit busy with her schoolwork at the moment, but she sends her love. Primrose can't wait to get home to you, though. I still think it makes sense for her to stay here until the end of term, then she'll be leaving anyway as she'll be fourteen by then, of course. No scholarship for her, but we can't all be clever clogs, can we? I'll miss her help with the kiddies, mind. She's always been very good with them.

A tingle of pleasure rippled down Eva's spine at the mention of her grandchildren. Proper handful, they were! She wondered how they'd turn out when they grew up and hopefully calmed down a bit. Would they inherit Rob's diligence and the intelligent side of the Parker family, or take after their happy-go-lucky mother?

Eva was so pleased and proud, though, that, like her elder brother, Kit, Trudy was really clever and could even go on to university in time. Blimey, that'd be something. A first in the Parker family. Even Kit hadn't done that. But Eva was secretly happy that the very youngest of her six children, Primrose, wasn't as bright, and so would be coming back to Banbury Street when she turned fourteen in the summer. At least Eva would have three of her children at home to love and care for.

21

She knew she'd never been the shiniest penny herself, and the family home was probably the most chaotic and disordered on the street, but she'd do anything for anybody, like a huggable teddy bear that people turned to. She'd done her bit for the war, too, joining the WVS. A lot of them were middle-to upper-class women, some of whom had sneered down their noses at her London accent and the way she managed to make the uniform look unkempt.

'Look, you stuck-up cow,' she'd said, putting one particularly obnoxious woman in her place, 'the tea what I serve from my urn is every bit as good as yours, and I serve it with a sympathetic smile and a kind word, which is more than what you do.'

'That's right, darlin',' a builder, covered in dirt and dust who'd been digging in rubble all night to rescue survivors, grinned triumphantly, and his mates had all cheered in agreement. 'You tell 'er!' And since that day, she'd been treated with far more respect.

She wasn't on duty again until Thursday, but thankfully there shouldn't be so much to do. The last of those terrible V2s to fall nearby — the size of trains and even worse than the V1s if that were possible — had been back in January, a dreadful business when seventeen people had perished in an explosion further down York Road from Price's. And though the bloody things had brought appalling death and destruction to other parts of London since then, there'd been none for almost a month now. The Allies had liberated virtually everywhere in France, Belgium and the

Netherlands and destroyed all the missile launch sites. With any luck, they'd driven the Germans back so far that they couldn't even launch the flying bombs from aircraft either, which they'd taken to doing as a last resort. So there shouldn't be any more V1s or V2s suddenly appearing overhead. Eva certainly prayed not.

Almost afraid to get her hopes up after so many years of fear, she turned her attention back to her daughter's letter. Gert had signed off with lots of love and kisses, but there was an almost illegible P.S. squeezed in at the bottom.

So sorry to hear about Mr Goldstein. Has anyone else moved in yet?

Eva sucked in her bottom lip. She hadn't told Gert about her legacy from the old man yet. Only Stan knew about it. They'd agreed to keep it a secret until after the war, and then Kit might have an idea about what to do with the jewellery. After all he had connections with all sorts of trades through his work. Or their old neighbour, Charles Braithwaite, who'd managed the jewellery and fine gifts department at the local prestigious department store, Arding and Hobbs, before he was eventually promoted to senior manager. He might know how best to deal with them. But for now they'd have to wait and see.

As for Number Twelve, Eva was sure it wouldn't be long before new tenants moved in. After all, with so many houses bombed during the Blitz and then being destroyed by these wretched flying bombs, people were desperate for places to live. So Banbury Street would have some new residents very soon, and Eva would have more chickens to take under her generous wing.

2

Eva heard the front door open and the sounds of Mildred bringing in her bicycle and propping it against the wall in the hallway. A moment later, Mildred breezed into the back room.

She threw her London buses uniform cap onto the table next to where Eva was chopping the carrots and turnips. Unpinning her hair, the girl shook her head and her auburn curls sprang out in a frizzy halo.

'Hello, Mum. You OK?' she asked, flopping down onto one of the kitchen chairs.

'Yup. You had a hard day? You look knackered. I'll just get your dad's trotter on the gas and then I'll make us a cuppa, fresh tea leaves and all.'

'Yeah, hard shift,' Mildred yawned. ''Specially the early morning. People trying to get to work and school or what have you. Thank Gawd I've finished for the day. Me feet are killing us. Here, tell you what, mind, a horse and cart just turned into the street behind us. Thought it was the coalman come early, but it had bits and pieces of furniture and that sort of stuff on it. I reckon it's the new people moving into the Goldsteins' old place.'

'Really?' Eva wiped her hands down her stained apron. 'Wonder who they'll be? Better go and say hello. Make them feel welcome.'

'Give them a chance, Mum,' Mildred chuckled. 'They're not even here yet. At least, they wasn't a minute ago. Expect they had to catch a bus and it was late. Usually are, and doesn't I know it. There's too many what rants and raves at me as if it's my fault!' She rolled her eyes dramatically. 'But I remind them there's a war on, and they should be glad there's any flaming buses at all.'

'Maybe not for much longer.' Eva jabbed her head emphatically as she plonked the teapot down on the table so hard that the brown liquid slopped out of the spout and ran down to make yet another mark on the well-worn wood. 'The war, I mean. Could be over any day. Turn on the radio for us, would you? Can never get the hang of tuning the thing meself.'

'Yeah, OK. Just a minute. I hope it's over soon, too. Be about bloody time.' Mildred gave a long, satisfying stretch, leaning back in the chair with her arms above her head. 'To think I was still a schoolkid when it started.'

'And now you're a wise old woman,' Eva teased. 'All of nineteen years old.'

'Well, it's made us feel a lot older. Especially with Gary fighting somewhere out in the Far East. Without the war, we might've been married by now. But I do enjoy me job on the buses, and I mightn't have got the chance without the war. Might have ended up working in that bleeding factory like Gert did. Oh, thanks, Mum,' she said as Eva pushed the chipped mug of tea towards her.

'That bleeding factory, as you put it, kept your dad in work all his life and food on your plate,' Eva reminded her.

26

'Yeah, I know.' Mildred paused to light a cigarette and drew on it deeply. 'Wonder what'll happen to it after the war? With part of it destroyed by that V1 last year? I mean, I know they was up and running again ten days later, but it wasn't easy, Dad said. And if the gas and electric ain't gonna be interrupted by Hitler's bombs no more, will people want so many candles for emergencies and what have you?'

'Oh, I don't know. Candles are still cheaper, and people like them for Christmas and birthday cakes and things. And churches. So hopefully it'll keep your dad going till he retires. Got a few more years yet, mind. And what with him having paid into Price's pension scheme most of his life, we'll be able to manage OK.'

Eva bit the inside of her lip. *And with her little legacy.* She didn't like keeping it a secret, but she'd promised Stan she would. For now, anyway.

'Oh, this a letter from Gert?' Mildred asked, spying the already dog-eared corner of the paper sticking out from under the old chopping board. 'Can I read it?'

'Course. And while you do, I'll just pop out and see if the new people have arrived yet.'

'Well, take your curlers out first, Mum,' Mildred grinned. 'You look like something from outer space. Don't wanna frighten them to death before they've even moved in.'

'Cheeky monkey!' Eva admonished, grinning from ear to ear as she gently cuffed her daughter around the head. Nevertheless, she duly removed her curlers before quickly dragging the hairbrush

27

that resided on the mantelpiece — clogged with hair — through her unruly waves. She even paused to take off her pinny — her jumper wasn't *too* grubby underneath — and withdrew her aching feet, bunions and all, from her slippers and wriggled them back into her shoes.

Leaving Mildred reading Gert's letter, Eva went out into the street. Excitement bubbled in her stomach as she stepped straight onto the pavement since the houses on that side boasted no front gardens. Or at least, you could hardly call the few inches of ground beneath the bay window of each front room a garden, in her opinion. It was a short terrace as London terraces went, consisting of only nine little houses. But then it was a short street, part of a grid of roads set at right angles to each other, more or less, that had been built towards the end of the last century, or so Eva believed. She vaguely remembered they'd been relatively new when she'd come to live there as a small child with Old Sal and her dad. Before the old devil scarpered, that was, leaving his wife and little daughter to fend for themselves! What a lot of water had gone under the bridge since then.

The houses opposite were much grander, particularly the first four that dated from some time earlier than the terrace. Each boasted a semi-basement for the servants — not that any of the residents had servants nowadays — with what were known as area steps leading down to a separate servants' entrance. A short flight of stone steps led upwards from the pavement to each main front door and there used to be railings along the pavement to stop anyone falling down into the 'area'. They'd all been taken away to be made into bombs or planes or something, but it was rumoured that doing this all over London had been a complete waste of time as it turned out they were mainly made of the wrong metal! Now there were just stumps along the pavement, although some people had made an effort to fix up some sort of makeshift barricade for safety's sake.

The remaining houses opposite were slightly less grand, with no semi-basements and with the front doors on street level. They were, though, a lot posher than Eva's terrace, with tiny front gardens. All the houses on that side also had decent back gardens as opposed to the claustrophobic yards on Eva and Stan's side.

Eva paused for a moment, surveying her little domain, her chest swelling with pride. She might have lived in one of the humbler dwellings almost all of her life, but she considered she was queen of the street. Matriarch, her Kit had proudly pronounced her. Eva liked that word. It made her feel like royalty, although Kit had explained that it meant a motherly figure. And Eva supposed she had acted like a mother to almost everyone in the street.

Take Number Three opposite. The hoity-toity Braithwaites had lived there for some years, considering themselves superior to their neighbours until Gert and Hillie had secretly befriended their down-trodden daughter, Jessica. But the barriers had eventually been broken, to a certain extent, at least. If not exactly bosom pals, Eva had become friendly with the Braithwaites, even the wife,

Hester, who was more stuck-up than her husband, Charles.

The Braithwaites had eventually moved up the ladder to a posh apartment in a fancy block. But it was to Eva that Hester had turned for consolation when Jessica had been with her dentist husband in his native Nigeria when war had broken out and had been marooned there ever since with Hester's two grandsons. And again, when Arding and Hobbs, where Charles was employed, had been bombed and Hester was terrified for his safety, it was to Eva's door that she'd come running.

Meanwhile, a Miss Chalfont had moved in after the Braithwaites had left — a school teacher who was also acting as caretaker for the brewery that owned those first few houses as well as the pub on the corner. A pleasant but self-reliant woman, busy with those of her pupils who hadn't been evacuated, she was happy to pass the time of day with Eva but was always scuttling about on some errand.

And then, soon after the Blitz began, a Mr and Mrs Hayes had moved into the upper rooms of the house, having been bombed out of their previous home. They had a little daughter, Lily. Must have had her quite late in life, Eva considered. And why Lily hadn't been evacuated, Eva had never discovered.

Tragically, John Hayes had been killed on ARP duty the previous year as a result of a V1, and Eva had helped poor Ellen pick up the pieces of her life.

A few doors down in one of the more modest houses lived a family almost as chaotic as the

Parkers. It seemed the Smiths were equally as unfortunate, as they'd had several relatives who'd also been made homeless by the Blitz. They'd all come to squeeze in together and muddle through as best they could. Eva had sometimes given them a hand when they'd needed it, too. A bit of washing here and there, or, on a few occasions, she'd given them some of the precious kindling Stan brought home, useless leftovers from his work at the sawmill at Price's factory. And Eva had given them all an open invitation to call in for a cuppa.

It had been the same with the Goldsteins. On their arrival, the elderly couple had spoken little English, and when they'd talked to each other, it sounded like gobbledegook to Eva. But when others on the street had been wary of them, Eva had embraced their presence, especially when they'd managed to convey their sad story to her. 'That there Hitler is as much their enemy as he's likely to be ours,' she'd explained to the neighbours back in the years before the war when nobody had known quite what a monster the man with the funny little moustache and even funnier haircut was likely to become. It was through Eva that the sympathy of others had come to join hers, especially as the horrors committed against the Jews by the Nazis had become more apparent.

But now the Goldsteins had lived out the rest of their lives in relative peace — if you could call the Blitz and the more recent V1 and V2 attacks relative peace. And coping with all the other deprivations the war had brought. And now new people

31

appeared to be moving into Number Twelve —
whether a family or just a couple, Eva had yet to
find out. But she was determined to make them
feel welcome in their new abode. Besides, she
liked meeting new people. It was part of life's rich
tapestry, as far as she was concerned.

Just as Mildred had anticipated, the horse and
cart had come to a stop outside Number Twelve.
An older man in a flat cap and an old jacket
darned at the elbows was starting to unload, with
the help of a boy just as poorly attired. Eva tutted
to herself. At least someone had made the effort to
patch them up. It was taking make-do-and-mend
a bit far, but they probably couldn't afford new
clothes even if they had enough coupons, which
they probably didn't. No doubt, they'd sold any
clothing coupons they had on the black market.
But Eva was pleased to see that at least the horse
looked well cared for.

A couple of dining chairs not much better than
Eva's already stood incongruously on the pavement, although the man and his lad were struggling
to lift down a heavy armchair which would put
Old Sal's dilapidated thing to shame. As she shuffled up, Eva noticed there wasn't a great deal on
the cart, mainly old greengrocer's boxes used as
packing cases and a couple of battered suitcases
among some odd bits of furniture. But then she
knew Number Twelve was let partly furnished, so
it already had the basics.

It was as she reached the items dumped on the
pavement that Eva noticed an old pram on the
back of the cart, its large wheels a bit rusty and
its coachwork scratched and dented. Oh, did that

mean it was going to be a young family with a baby? Maybe a wife who'd got preggers again when her husband was on leave and couldn't wait for him to come home for good when the war was over, which mightn't be long now. Oh, how exciting! Eva could take them under her wing if they didn't have anyone else to help. She missed having little ones around her, and none of her grandchildren lived near. She wouldn't intrude, mind, if her new neighbours didn't seem to want her friendship. She might have a generous nature, but she'd hate anyone to think she was a busybody!

'Here, lady, yer ain't got a key ter this place by any chance, have yer?' the carter's rough voice jolted her from her thoughts. 'I ain't got time ter hang around waiting. Time is money. Got uvver customers waiting, see.'

Eva shook her head. The man's brusque manner had spoilt her reverie. She did still have the key Abraham Goldstein had given her, but she'd taken an instant dislike to this fellow. Besides, how would it look to her new neighbours if she opened up their new home to this chap who was probably a stranger to them? She'd give them the spare key when they turned up, of course, explaining why she had it. That would be a good excuse to introduce herself.

'Sorry, no, I ain't got one,' she lied, and had to bite her lip as the man rolled his eyes in exasperation.

But then she saw his expression lighten as he looked past her back down the street. 'Oh, never mind,' he growled. 'Here they come. What took yer so long?' he shouted, raising his voice.

Eva at once turned round and had to quell her surprise at the little group walking towards her. She'd expected a youngish woman carrying a baby and with a few other children in tow, judging by the state of the pram. And maybe accompanied by some other adults who'd come to help her. But what Eva saw was very different.

As they came nearer and she could see their faces more clearly, Eva judged that the woman leading the band was maybe in her mid-forties. She was the one carrying a bundle that Eva guessed must be the baby, and not the young girl walking by her side as one might have imagined. The girl was carrying a string bag in each hand, and there was something about her that captivated Eva's attention for several seconds. Was it the graceful way she held herself, her long, swanlike neck? She was a beauty and no mistake, and even though she wore a baggy old cardigan over a loose-fitting dress, Eva could see that her limbs were long and slender.

Eva reluctantly dragged her gaze away from the girl to the two men walking behind. One was young, twenty or so at a guess. Like the girl, he was tremendously good-looking, and Eva could see a strong resemblance between them, so she assumed he must be her brother. But unlike the resigned expression on his sister's face, the lad was wide-eyed with curiosity, his head swivelling on his neck as he gazed this way and that, taking in his new surroundings.

And then, once again, Eva quickly had to hide the look that wanted to show itself on her face as shocked sympathy flooded into her generous heart. The other fellow might be twenty years older than the woman carrying the baby, although perhaps his strained face might have aged through suffering. A crutch was tucked under his right arm, although as they drew level, Eva could see that this wasn't quite the case. The crutch was buckled with straps over his shoulders and around his arm, which ended in a hook. And instead of a foot protruding from his right trouser leg, she could see the end of a wooden stump. No wonder it had taken the family longer to get there than the impatient man with the cart had anticipated. The poor fellow, who was clearly missing his right arm and leg, could only walk slowly, and his family, or whoever they were, weren't going to leave him behind.

Eva instantly respected them for that, and she pushed past the removal man, smiling as broadly as she possibly could.

'I take it you're our new neighbours?' she beamed. 'Welcome to Banbury Street. I'm Eva Parker and I live at Number Eight. Anything you need, just knock.'

3

The woman's green eyes creased at the corners as she smiled back at Eva's welcome. 'Thank you. That's very kind, so it is.

Bridie Cresswell. Shake your hand, I would, only I can't,' she nodded pleasantly, using her eyes to indicate the bundle she was carrying.

Eva's grin broadened as she absorbed her new neighbour's friendly attitude and the fact that she clearly hailed from the Emerald Isle. But there was another matter that filled Eva with delight as well. 'Oh, a baby!' she exclaimed, peering down at the tiny face swathed about in a shawl. 'Can I have a hold?

Your arms must be aching something rotten.'

'So they are,' Bridie Cresswell agreed, moving the said limbs forward to relinquish their precious cargo into Eva's eager hold. 'The baby's called Jane, and this is my daughter, Cecily,' she added, indicating the girl at her side, 'but we all call her Cissie.'

Eva dragged her gaze from the infant in her arms. 'How d'you do?' she asked Bridie's elder daughter, who replied with a half-smile as she nodded in greeting but spoke not a word, as if she'd rather not be there. Perhaps she was shy and needed some encouragement, so Eva said brightly, 'You look about the same age as our Mildred. I'll have to introduce you.'

'That'd be good,' Bridie answered, almost as if

covering up for her daughter, Eva felt. 'My husband, Ron, and our son, Zac.'

Eva glanced towards the invalid with just time to exchange broad smiles with him before the handsome young man stepped forward and held out his hand, seemingly not noticing that Eva couldn't shake it because she was holding his baby sister.

'Pleased — to — meet — you,' he said with slow deliberation, and the penny dropped with Eva as she moved her face into the most open, welcoming expression she could muster. It had crossed her mind that it was unusual to see a lad of his age on the streets and not in uniform. He could have been home on leave, of course, but most of the men in the forces still wore their uniforms proudly when out and about. It struck Eva at once, though, from the way he spoke, that Zac Cresswell wasn't quite all there, the poor lad.

'Here, you lot, stop gassing, will yer?' a sharp voice cut in over Eva's shoulder. 'I ain't got time ter waste even if you have. Who's got the key, or d'yer want us ter leave everyfing on the pavement?'

Eva had to bite her lip to stop herself from giving him the length of her tongue but distracted herself by cooing down at the baby as Bridie produced the key and marched up to the front door of Number Twelve.

'I'm sorry we took so long,' Eva heard Bridie apologise. 'Had to break our journey to collect the key from the landlord's agent, so we did, and missed the next bus. And my husband can't move so fast, of course.'

'Hmmph,' the carter grunted irritably, since he

37

couldn't argue with that, could he, Eva considered with satisfaction. 'You gonna show us where yer want everyfing, then?'

'As best I can — '

'Well, if it ain't in the right place ter start, don't expect us ter move it. That strapping lad o' yers'll have ter do it.'

Eva couldn't believe the affrontery of the man, but it probably wouldn't do to interfere. Her new neighbours wouldn't be too happy if the fellow took offence and indeed dumped all their belongings on the pavement as he'd threatened. Of course, if he hadn't been paid yet, he probably wouldn't, but often these sorts of chaps demanded payment up front. But, either way, he seemed an unpleasant character, and better not to upset him. Eva wondered why the Cresswells had employed such a brute, but maybe he came cheap and they didn't have much money. And with the war on, and petrol even for businesses such as removals still scarce, perhaps he was all they could find.

Eva watched as Bridie disappeared inside the house she herself knew so well and propped open the front door so that the obnoxious removal man and his sullen boy could start bringing things inside. Eva turned, drawing a breath to engage in conversation with the other members of the family, but got no further.

'I'll take her now,' the girl — Cissie, wasn't it? — all but snatched the slumbering infant from Eva's arms. 'She'll sleep better in the pram.'

'Oh. Erm, yeah, of course,' Eva muttered in surprise as Cissie settled her baby sister in the battered old pram that had just been lifted down from the back of the cart.

'Sorry, not a very good introduction.' Ron Cresswell appeared at Eva's side and, balancing on his crutch and remaining leg, held out his left hand. Eva found it difficult to shake but hid her awkwardness as the gentleman went on,

'Good of you to come out to welcome us.'

'Not at all,' Eva beamed back, taking an instant liking to the stranger who appeared relatively well-spoken, just as poor Nell had been. 'Like to think I can be a good neighbour to everyone. Hope you'll all be very happy here.'

Before she could say any more, the young man came up and hovered by his father's side. 'What — shall — I — do, Dad?' he interrupted in his slow drawl. 'Can — I — go — inside — and — have — a — look?'

'Of course, Zac. Only don't get in the way.' Ron gave a wry smile as his son loped off. 'Things haven't been easy of late,' he admitted in a low tone, instantly warming to Eva's kind personality. 'And poor Zac finds change hard. We were bombed out, you see. That doodlebug in Islington last Boxing Day.'

'Blimey!' Eva couldn't contain her gasp. It had been a terrible affair with seventy-odd dead and many severely injured. Everyone in London knew about it.

'Yes.' Ron's face was solemn. 'We were lucky to escape with our lives. And we were thankful for that. But we've been pushed from pillar to post ever since. We've begged, borrowed or stolen most of what you see on the cart,' he made a wry attempt to joke. 'You can't imagine how relieved

39

we are to have found somewhere permanent to live at last. Maybe life will settle down again now.'

He threw Eva a rueful glance, which she returned with a sympathetic smile. Fate had been particularly cruel to this family, and it simply wasn't fair. Eva was trying to think of something suitable to say when Bridie Cresswell emerged from the house again.

'Sure, I'm sorry about that. Isn't the man about as rude as they come, but he was all we could find at short notice.'

'Well, I can see you've got your hands full,' Eva sympathised, relieved that the awkward moment was over. 'But when you've got your stuff inside, don't worry about finding the kettle. Come into me for a cuppa. Number Eight, remember? I'm not the tidiest on the street, but I'll give you the warmest welcome.'

'Sure, I'm likely to take you up on that!'

'Really kind of you, Mrs Parker, didn't you say?'

'It is. But call me Eva,' she grinned back. 'And if you need any help, just call. Our Mildred's back from her shift, and my Stan and our Jake'll be home from work later, and they'll be happy to lend a hand. But I'll leave you to it for now, and maybe see you later. You know where we are.'

And giving them all her generous smile, Eva took herself back home to Number Eight.

* * *

40

As Eva went inside, sidling around the bicycle, Mildred was coming down the stairs from changing into her civvies. 'Well?' she asked, her eyes sparkling with a teasing light.

'Have you managed to frighten them off?'

'Enough of your cheek!' Eva laughed back. 'Come into the kitchen and I'll tell you all about it. Shall I top the pot up?'

'Nah, I'm all right, thanks, Mum,' Mildred answered, following Eva into the back room and sitting down at the table. 'So, spill the beans, then,' she urged.

'Well.' Eva lowered herself onto one of the wooden chairs opposite her daughter, eager to report back. 'They seem a real nice family, but my, do they have problems.'

'All the better for you to mother them, then,' Mildred grinned. But then she lifted an enquiring eyebrow as her mum's forehead beetled into a frown.

'Well, unfortunately, when I say problems, I really mean it,'

Eva said, pursing her lips. 'For a start, the poor dad's missing an arm and a leg.'

'What?' Mildred's eyes opened wide in sympathy. 'Oh, crikey. Oh, I'm so sorry, Mum. I feel a bit ashamed now. I know how you like to take people under your wing, so I thought you was just exaggerating.'

Eva shook her head. 'Wish I was. Really nice chap, mind. Ron his name is. Had a bit of a chat with him. Seems they was bombed out by that bleeding doodlebug what fell on Islington, and this is the first proper place they've found to live

41

since.'

'Blimey, they *have* had more than their fair share of bad luck, ain't they?' Mildred was aghast. 'And was that how he lost his, what did you say, arm *and* leg?'

'Nah, he wouldn't have recovered that quick, love. Strikes me he's a lot older than his wife.' Eva nodded her head pensively. 'Could've been some sort of accident, I suppose. But I reckon he's even a bit older than your dad, so he could've been wounded in the first war. And I'd guess it brought them down in the world if they've come to live here. He talks a bit more proper like. Not *really* posh, but a bit like poor Nell did. Mind you, what with the Blitz and then the V1 and V2s, if you've lost your home, there ain't many empty houses around and beggars can't be choosers.'

'And if you're right, they must be living on a war disability pension, so they wouldn't exactly be rolling in it, would they, poor sods?' Mildred scoffed with bitterness as she helped herself to a Rich Tea biscuit. 'So what about his wife, then?'

'As I say, she's obviously a lot younger, 'cos she's just had a nipper.'

'Oh? So how old d'you reckon she is, then? Here, you are sure they're . . . well, married like?'

'Oh, yeah. Seem a very genuine family to me,' Eva assured her. 'She's Irish, a really warm person. I'd guess she's well into her forties.'

'That's a bit old to be having a baby, ain't it?'

Eva shrugged. 'Not really. It happens sometimes. I was forty-two when I had Primrose. And look at Ellen across the road. She must've been forty-six if she was a day when she had little

42

Lily. And it's not Bridie's first. That's her name, Bridie. Which makes things easier. They've got two grown-up children and all, you see. A girl, quite a fairylike thing, about your age. Seems a bit, I don't know, not exactly aloof. More keeping herself to herself, maybe. But you can understand that after all what they've been through. I said you and her ought to become friends.'

'Oh, thanks, Mum!' Mildred rolled her eyes. 'She don't sound my type. And I'm not like you. I can't make friends with just — '

'Yes, you can. And you are like me. Only you doesn't know it yet. And there's a boy. A bit older than her, I'd say. Only he's a bit simple. I mean, he talks, but it's all sort of slow, as if he's not quite all there. And he seems a bit sort of . . . ' Eva paused to search for the right word. 'Childlike, I guess you'd say. Such a pity. Really handsome lad. But you can see why he's not in the forces.'

'You wasn't kidding when you said they've got problems, then,' Mildred considered. 'But they've come to the right place if they need someone to lend them a hand.' She reached across the table and squeezed her mother's hand proudly.

Eva felt a blush flaring into her face and patted her own cheeks to hide it. 'Well, I invited them to call in for a cuppa once they've finished unloading their stuff. So give us a hand to spruce this place up a bit, will you? Can't have them come in here when there's spud peelings all over the table, can we?'

'Gawd, you must be impressed with them!' Mildred chuckled. 'Never bothered you before!'

'Well, it's good to make an effort once in a while — '

'Once in a blue moon, more like.'

'Cheeky!' Eva grinned. 'I only want them to feel welcome, that's all. So take that washing off the clothes horse and take it upstairs, would you? Must be aired by now. Don't want them seeing our bloomers, do we? And I told them your dad and Jake would give them a hand when they get in from work if they need it.'

'Talk about offering other people's services!' Mildred laughed as she stood up. 'Don't know what you're gonna do about the smell of Dad's trotter, mind.'

'Nothing I can do about that,' Eva grimaced. 'Takes ages to cook and he'll want it for his tea. Just don't you light up another fag. Good job it's a nice spring day and I've got the window and the scullery door open, getting rid of the stink of cigarettes.'

Mildred wrinkled her nose as she sniffed the undies she was gathering off the clothes horse. They did smell a bit. Her mum would've done better to leave them on the line in the back yard even if the sun had completely gone from it now. But even outside, washing got to smell of coal smoke from all the chimneys around — when you could get hold of any coal, of course. Mind you, it was spring now, so it didn't matter as much if you couldn't. It was just the local factory chimneys that were producing the coal smuts now that left dirty marks on your clean washing and made it smell. She supposed she couldn't blame this flaming war for that, but she'd be glad when it

44

was over and you could keep warm in winter and have decent food on your plate — and without having to queue for hours for it! But perhaps it wouldn't be long before peace was declared. In Europe anyhow.

Her heart flipped over as the image of her Gary out in the Far East somehow flashed across her mind. It sounded exotic, with dense, steaming jungle, strange creatures and beautiful flowers. Amazing — if there wasn't a Jap hiding behind every tree, waiting to stick his knife in your guts. She'd seen it on the *Pathé News* film clips at the cinema. Gary was on submarines, however, moving stealthily about on or under the water. Mildred shuddered at the very thought of being trapped like that beneath the waves. But it also meant that she could never know exactly where he was and the whole idea terrified her.

Mildred's older brother, Kit, had managed to buy her an atlas and she'd seen where places like Borneo and the Philippines were in relation to China and the dreaded Japan, and everywhere in the area the Japanese had overrun. But, unlike her brother, who had an inborn sense of geography which he needed in his job dealing with rail freight going in all sorts of different directions, Mildred was apt to get overwhelmed by all these strange places. Her geographical expertise only extended as far as the London bus routes so that she could advise passengers on their journeys. The Far East was a jumble to her. All she knew was that without flying to the moon, it was about as far away from Banbury Street as a human being could get, and the idea of her Gary being out there was something she tried very hard not to think about.

She sighed weightily as she ran upstairs with the washed items of clothing, hurling her worries aside. You'd go blooming mad if you thought about it all the time. She'd been seventeen when Gary had gone off to war. Too young to get engaged and they hadn't known each other long enough, her mum and dad had protested. But they'd made their pledge anyway. She'd loved Gary then. And she couldn't let him go off to war feeling rejected. But she hadn't seen him for so long, she sometimes wondered if she'd even recognise him, let alone still love him. But, for the time being, she was pushing her doubts to the back of her mind and most definitely keeping them to herself.

Well, at least this new family coming to live in Banbury Street would give her something else to think about. She couldn't wait to meet them, even if the girl didn't quite sound her cup of tea. But she liked people in general, which was perhaps why she enjoyed her work so much. Perhaps she wasn't so unlike her mum after all!

4

Watching the empty removal cart trundle away down the street, Cissie Cresswell jiggled the baby in the pram to settle it back to sleep. She'd learnt over the past couple of months that was what you did when an infant's feeding time wasn't due yet and the bundle of matinee coat and bonnet was beginning to wriggle. Let it wake too early and you'd only get cries of hunger. The time to play and let the tiny creature start learning about the new world it had been born into was when it was armed with a full stomach and a clean, dry nappy, not when it was howling its head off.

Once Cissie had bounced little Jane about sufficiently to rock her into slumber again, she manoeuvred the pram over the threshold and into the narrow hallway of their new abode.

It wasn't easy, with the carriage being a wide, old-fashioned affair suspended between massive wheels. God knew where her mother had purloined it from, and Cissie didn't really care. The contraption had seen better days, its coachwork scratched and dented, and the solid rubber tyres worn and slightly shredded on the edges. But beggars couldn't be choosers and they'd been lucky to acquire one at all, her mum had said when she'd proudly appeared with the battered article.

Cissie carefully navigated it along the hallway, trying not to wake its potentially screaming occupant, or damage the walls and skirting boards.

Not that it really would have mattered. The place was clean, but it was dark and dingy and a bit of a dump, nothing like their previous home, which had been just as small but light and airy and welcoming. The woodwork in this new house was badly chipped, the walls a sickly mustard colour. The whole place needed a lick of paint to freshen it up — if such a thing was obtainable — preferably in nice bright colours. Perhaps her dad could have a begging word with the landlord, although the rent wasn't excessive so it could well fall on deaf ears. But sometimes people were sympathetic towards her dad. He had, after all, given half his body at Passchendaele in the last war and obviously hadn't been able to work since. If he'd only given half his body, and not half his mind as well, things mightn't have been so bad. But, as it was, her dad suffered in every way possible.

Cissie compressed her lips in rebellion as she squeezed the pram into the front room. It would be nice and quiet in there for the baby, who would hopefully sleep on for another half-hour before demanding attention. The parlour was to be Cissie's bedroom and, later on, they would be moving down one of the single beds from the back room upstairs. In order to accommodate it, a small sofa facing the fireplace — left by the previous tenants apparently — would need shifting into the bay window. It was just as well it fitted, as Cissie needed a clear space for something else as well. But they wouldn't be doing any rearranging of furniture just yet, and for the moment, baby Jane could snore and snuffle on undisturbed.

Cissie tiptoed out of the room and, silently

closing the door, went into the downstairs back room that, together with the scullery that led from it, served as the kitchen. Her mum was standing by the table, deciding where to keep all her pots and pans, crockery and cutlery that Zac was unpacking from half a dozen or so old orange boxes. Ron had managed to persuade their former greengrocer to give them to him free of charge, and they would break up into good kindling wood afterwards.

'Sure, it's just as well we don't have a lot,' Bridie was declaring, turning a prettily decorated, bone-china jug over in her hands. 'The people before left a lot of stuff behind and it's far better quality than anything we have. Look at this,' she said, holding the jug towards her husband. 'There's a whole little tea service in the cupboard. Wouldn't you be thinking they'd take such a thing with them? So you be careful, Zac, not to drop anything that's not ours in case they come back for it,' she concluded, dipping her head at her son.

'I — won't, Mum,' the young chap promised. 'You sure — they're clean?'

'Well, they look spotless to me, but you can wash them all again later if you're careful,' she smiled indulgently. 'But first won't we make the beds so at least we'll be all ready to lay our heads down tonight. And so Jane's still asleep, is she, Cissie?'

'Yes, I managed to get the pram in the front room,' Cissie informed her with a deep sigh. 'Bit of a squeeze, but maybe she'll stay asleep a while longer.'

Bridie quizzed her daughter with a raised eyebrow. 'Well, let's get on while we can. We'll bring the bed down for you when she wakes up, and when she's been fed, maybe we can pop along to that nice lady who came to say hello.'

'Eva Parker she said her name was, didn't she?' Ron put in mildly from his armchair that fitted nicely beside the fireplace.

'She did so. And it'd be rude of us not to accept her invitation. So come on, Zac, move yourself,' Bridie ordered, bustling out into the hall. 'You can help us make up the other beds upstairs.'

Zac obediently followed his mother through the door and Cissie dutifully went to join them, but her father's low voice made her pause in her step.

'It's at times like these that I feel so useless,' he murmured, lowering his eyes to the hook at the end of his right arm. 'Your mother's such a practical person, taking care of everything, that sometimes I don't think she realises just how stupid I feel.'

Cissie turned back into the room, her heart aching for her poor dad, and laced her arms about his shoulders. 'Well, I think it's just as well she's so capable. I don't know where we'd all be without her.'

'Hmm.' Ron nodded with a wry grunt. 'And you are happy with everything we decided?' he asked hesitantly. 'Our move here? A new start? The *big fib*?'

Cissie's lips firmed into a line. 'Not entirely,' she admitted in little more than a whisper. 'But I knew Mum had her heart set on it. And she was so amazing when . . .' she faltered. But then she nailed a confident smile on her face. 'We'll make a go of it, Dad, really we will. There's a lot to sort

50

out, but we're going to make a new life, just see if we don't.'

She dropped a kiss on his balding head and made for the door. He watched her go, his eyes misting over. His darling daughter was so strong in her own way, despite what she'd been through. But he prayed to God she could be as strong as she thought she was. For surely their future was as uncertain now as it ever could be.

★ ★ ★

Eva drew in a sharp breath. 'Ah, there's a knock at the door. Probably them. Now, do we look tidy enough?' she asked, eyes sweeping over the hastily cleared and wiped table.

'Cleanest I've seen it in years,' Mildred assured her with a deep chuckle. 'Now don't keep them waiting on the doorstep.'

'Would I do that?'

Nevertheless, Eva paused to pull off her dirty apron and stuff it in a drawer before she strutted off down the hallway. Mildred watched her go, shaking her head in amusement. Without her two youngest to mother, her mum relished taking under her wing those less fortunate than herself, and it certainly sounded as if this new family came into that category.

Mildred could hear muted voices along the passage and, a few moments later, her mum came back into the kitchen, holding open the door for her guests.

'Do come in,' Eva invited them. 'There's just about enough seats for everybody.'

Mildred's face blossomed into a brilliant smile as the visitors sidled around the table. 'Hello, I'm Mildred, Milly for short,' she introduced herself, beaming at a short, well-set woman with striking green eyes and thick black hair wound into a victory roll. In her arms she carried a tiny baby whose starfish hands patted its mother's chest as its eyes wandered vacuously over its new surroundings.

With the woman's arms occupied, Mildred didn't offer her hand in greeting but continued to smile broadly instead. Then she nodded at the tall young man following his mother. Mildred felt her heart dance a little jig, for just as Eva had described, he was incredibly handsome and his generous mouth broke into a glorious grin as he gazed at her.

'And I'm — Zac,' he drawled, confirming Eva's opinion that he wasn't quite 'all there', but pumping Mildred's hand up and down nonetheless. 'Pleased to — meet you. And this is — my sister — Cissie.'

Mildred turned her eyes on the young girl bringing up the rear and paused to take in what she could only describe as a vision of loveliness. Her slight frame filled Mildred with envy, and she moved with such grace, head held high on her long neck, that she appeared to be floating. She was as beautiful as her brother was handsome, yet a smile barely flickered across her lips as she acknowledged Mildred's welcome.

'Ron sends his apologies.' Bridie's Irish brogue broke over Mildred's thoughts like summer rain on a drought. 'It's been a bit tiring for him, so it has. I'm Bridie, by the way,' she said, turning to

Mildred. 'It was so kind of your mammy to invite us for a cup of tay. Can't stay long, mind. Got a lot to do, so we have.'

'Yeah, I understand,' Eva beamed. 'Can I have another hold of the baby? Give your arms a rest. Cor, she's awake this time,' she crooned, taking little Jane from Bridie. 'Mildred'll make the tea, won't you, love? Hello, little one,' she cooed down at the infant. 'I'm your new Auntie Eva. So how old are we?'

'Seven weeks,' Bridie told her proudly. 'And such a good little soul.'

'Ah, hear what your mummy says about you?' And then, turning to her new friend, Eva prompted subtly, 'A big gap between her and your others.'

She noticed Bridie flick a furtive glance towards her elder daughter, probably because she didn't like talking about such things in front of her, Eva assumed. But then the Irishwoman seemed perfectly happy to answer the question Eva had hinted at. 'Sure, she came as a bit of a surprise,' she admitted with an open smile.

'That's the best way. Six I had altogether. But your husband told me you was bombed out by that doodlebug what fell on Islington. You could've done without that, you being preggers and all, on top of everything else.'

'You couldn't have spoken a truer word. But we survived and here we are.'

Eva and Bridie appeared to be hitting it off, so Mildred left them to talk and stepped into the scullery to light the gas under the kettle. It had already boiled once so it wouldn't take long. Mildred wasn't sure whether to use fresh tea leaves for

53

their guests but decided to compromise by using the same ones as earlier, plus just half a spoon of new ones from the week's ration.

Everything was already set on the table, and as she carried through the teapot — being careful to shut the door and keep the smell of her dad's simmering trotter to the minimum — Mildred considered how she could break the ice with Cissie Cresswell. She wasn't quite sure if the girl was painfully shy or just utterly aloof. Or maybe she was so fed up with all that had befallen her family that she simply felt cut off from what was going on around her.

'Shall I pour?' Mildred offered as jauntily as she could. 'Does everyone want tea?'

To her amazement, Zac picked up one of the mugs from the table and scrutinised it thoroughly.

'Is this — mug clean?' he demanded, his frown deepening as he almost lowered his nose into said object.

Mildred blinked in astonishment. What a cheek! She had actually picked out the best of her mum's crockery and made sure it was far cleaner than normal! She glanced sharply across at her mum to catch her eye, but it was Bridie who came to her rescue.

'Of course it is, Zac,' she told her son with a half-reassuring, half-chastising smile. 'Doesn't he have this thing about cleanliness,' she explained, with a look in her eyes that pleaded for understanding. 'Sure, we're used to his ways, but they can be a bit embarrassing, if you know what I mean. Loves to keep everything as clean as a whistle, so he does.'

'Well, you can come and clean my house whenever you want, lad!' Eva laughed, her chins wobbling up and down. 'Never seem to have time for housework, me. What with all the queuing for food, and I do me shifts with the WVS. And what about you, Bridie? Was you able to do anything before this little one came along?' she asked, stroking baby Jane's button nose.

'I'm a fully trained nurse, so I am,' Bridie replied, nodding her thanks as Mildred handed her a mug of tea. 'That's how I met Ron. Lost his limbs at Passchendaele in the first war, and I was working at one of the army hospitals in Calais. I travelled back to Blighty with him when he was well enough, and, well, one thing led to another.'

'Oh, saints alive, you must've seen some terrible things out there,' Eva gasped, sincerity trembling in her voice. 'I was at home with our eldest, Kit. Just a nipper then. And our Gert came along in the spring of 1915, so I didn't do nothing in the first war. And I was lucky. My Stan came home in one piece. So that's why I wanted to do me bit this time round.'

'So did I,' Bridie told her, sipping her tea. 'I gave up nursing to marry Ron. You have to if you get married, and he still needed nursing at home for some while anyway. And then I had Zac and Cissie, so it was years before I could go back to work. Couldn't work in a proper hospital, of course, being an old married woman, so haven't I been working in an old people's nursing home instead. Until Jane was well on the way, of course,' she added hastily.

Mildred had been listening intently, as eager to

learn as much about their new neighbours as possible. But her mum and Bridie were getting on like a house on fire and it felt awkward listening in on their conversation. So as Zac seemed to be content inspecting everything around them, she turned her attention to Cissie, who was sitting as still as a rock, eyes riveted on her hands which were clasped in her lap.

'What work d'you do, then, Cissie?' Mildred asked brightly, praying she'd get an answer from the taciturn girl. She was relieved when Cissie looked up and met her gaze with large, hazel-coloured eyes.

'None. Not at the moment, that is,' she admitted sharply, as if daring Mildred not to question her.

'Oh?' Mildred, surprised again by another member of this strange family, was not to be put off, however. 'How old are you, then?'

'I'll be nineteen in August.'

'Oh, well, I'll be twenty in October, so not much different from me. Only you look younger, you lucky thing. But . . . ' Mildred hesitated as she wondered whether she should ask or not, but decided she would anyway. 'Ain't you been conscripted, then? I've been on the buses ever since I turned eighteen.'

'Oh, yes. Well, not exactly conscripted, but it's still part of the war effort. The work I do is partly funded by CEMA.'

'CEMA? What's that?'

'It stands for Council for the Encouragement of Music and the Arts,' Cissie explained almost curtly as if Mildred ought to know. 'A bit like

ENSA. You know, entertaining the troops. Only this is for civilians. It's mainly for taking culture into factories and so forth. Poetry, art, music, plays. To keep up morale at home, that sort of thing. But I work for a rep company and our producer wangled some sponsorship from them.'

'Oh, I see. So you're an actress or a singer or something?' Mildred's blue-green eyes widened with excitement. 'Cor, our Jake'll be interested in that. Loves singing, he does, and he plays the guitar.'

Cissie's face seemed to close up like a clam. 'No. I'm a dancer,' she said, and Mildred thought she detected bitterness in her voice, although she had no idea why she should feel aggrieved. 'Only I damaged my ankle a while ago and it's not strong enough to go back yet.'

'Oh, Gawd, I'm sorry,' Mildred answered with genuine feeling. Poor girl. That explained it. That was the last thing you'd want as a dancer. No wonder Cissie was so down in the mouth. 'But d'you think you'll get back to it soon?' she asked, hoping that by showing an interest, she could draw the other girl out of her shell. And she *was* interested. She could see how Cissie would be a natural dancer with her slight and elegant physique. 'What sort of dancing d'you do, then?'

'Oh, all sorts. It's a variety theatre, so it can be almost anything. A lot of tap and chorus line. Character stuff. To things like Gershwin's 'Fascinating Rhythm' or 'I've got Rhythm'. Audiences love Spanish flamenco, the tarantella. Tango. The can-can —'

'Oh, I know that one!' Mildred butted in

57

with enthusiasm, since she had no idea who Gersh-whatever-his name-was might be. But at least Cissie seemed to be opening up as she spoke about what was evidently her passion. 'All high kicks, ain't it?'

'Well, yes, sort of,' Cissie actually chuckled. 'But we have great singers, too. And sometimes we dance to them. Semi balletic. To some of Vera Lynn's songs sometimes, or maybe something like 'S'Wonderful, S'Marvellous' — '

'Suppose that's Gersh-thingy, too, is it?'

'Gershwin. And yes, it is,' Cissie smiled, making Mildred feel like top dog for having guessed correctly. 'But my real love is pure classical ballet. Our dance master choreographs to mainly popular classical music, but he sometimes puts a more modern interpretation on it. A bit like the Ballet Rambert. So people who think ballet is just soppy with girls in tutus and men prancing about in tights can see it's not like that at all.'

'It sounds flipping amazing,' Mildred breathed.

'Oh, it is. You'll have to come along one evening.'

'Cor, I'd like that. But I'll wait till you're back performing yourself.'

Mildred bit her lip as she saw Cissie's face cloud over. Idiot. That was the wrong thing to say. They were getting along so well and now she'd put her bleeding foot in it. Of course the girl would be upset if she couldn't be performing because of an injury. But before Mildred could think of anything to rescue the conversation, Bridie stood up, taking the baby back from Eva.

'Well, we must be getting back,' she announced with an appreciative smile. 'Lots to do before we

58

can crawl into bed tonight. Thank you so much for the tay. Very kind of you, so it was.'

'Not at all,' Eva beamed in reply as she began showing her visitors to the front door. 'We hope you'll be very happy here, even if you are a long way from home.'

'Well, it's the best place we could find, and we felt we wanted an entirely fresh start.'

'Yeah, I can understand that. And remember, if you need anything, a bit of babysitting maybe, you know where we are.'

'Sure, I can see you're going to be a good neighbour to us. Thank you so much. Zac, say goodbye now.'

'Good — bye,' the young man said obediently, and as they all stepped onto the pavement, he began heading in the wrong direction.

Mildred noticed that Cissie caught her brother's arm and gently turned him round. 'No, this way, Zac,' she said softly.

'Oh, silly me,' he grinned. 'It's because — it's new.'

'Come on then.' Cissie waved to Mildred as they walked down the street. 'See you again soon,' she called.

'Well, I'm thinking that went well,' Bridie said to her daughter in a low voice once they were out of earshot. 'We stuck to our story and I reckon they believed every word.'

'Yes, I believe they did,' Cissie mumbled under her breath.

'And I reckon if Eva believes us, she'll make sure the whole street does, too. So don't you worry. Everything's going to work out fine, so it is.'

Cissie drew her prettily bowed mouth into a knot as they went inside their new home. She prayed her mother was right. And she had warmed to Eva and Mildred Parker, despite herself. But she'd need to keep her distance if she wanted to keep the secret. For some while, at least. Pity. But that's what everything — the whole family's sacrifice — had been about. And she couldn't risk ruining it all.

It was all because of her, after all.

5

'We're home, love!' a male voice called from the hallway, and a moment later, the door to the back room was flung wide and two men in working clothes walked in.

Eva had propped open the scullery door and glanced across from stirring a pan of vegetables simmering on the stove. 'Hello, Stan, love!' she beamed, lifting her face for the daily evening ritual of receiving her husband's kiss on her cheek.

'Jake, love,' she greeted her son as well. 'Had a good day, both of you?'

'Yeah, fine, ta. Same as usual, anyhow,' Stan answered, pouring two mugs of tea from the pot Mildred had just placed on the table and handing one to Jake. 'What about you two? Shift OK, Milly?'

Mildred, though, scarcely had time to nod before Eva abandoned the dinner preparations and plodded into the kitchen.

'Interesting day, anyway,' she declared. 'Queued all morning for food, but then there was a letter from Gert. And then, later on in the afternoon, a new family moved into Number Twelve.'

'Oh, yeah?' Stan lifted an eyebrow as he sat down. 'And no doubt you went straight round to introduce yourself?' he teased.

'Course she did,' Mildred laughed, watching her mum colour. But Eva's embarrassment didn't last long.

61

'You'll be relieved to know they're a real nice family,' she informed her menfolk. 'We won't get no trouble from them.'

'I can see Mum wanting to help them.' Mildred now took over the conversation. 'She's already had them in here, giving them a cup of cha. The dad didn't come, mind, so I ain't met him yet. Mum did, though.'

'Yeah, nice fella. Bit of a cut above us, I'd say. But let me tell you all about them.'

Eva plonked herself down in one of the kitchen chairs and proceeded to relate all she had learnt about the Cresswell family in an uninterrupted stream. When she finally stopped to draw breath, she gazed at her husband and son with a look of satisfaction at her knowledge glowing proudly on her face. But they all knew she was the kindest person on earth. To others she might appear a bit nosey, but she only had other people's best interests at heart and if anyone had a secret to hide, Eva's lips would be sealed as if stuck together with glue. The past had proved that beyond a doubt. And if this new family needed any help, Eva would certainly be the one to give it to them.

'Well, I'll look forward to meeting them all in due course,'

Stan announced. 'Maybe I can have a good chat with, what did you say his name was, Ron, poor sod? 'Cos I was in the first war meself, he might want to talk about it, and I always think talking about things helps. But just now, me stomach thinks me throat's been cut, so how long's this dinner gonna be?'

'Bout quarter of an hour. Not long enough for you to read the sports section of your blooming paper,' Eva chided as Stan glanced longingly at the scanty newspaper he'd dropped on the table.

'What about our Gert's letter, then? Have I got time for that?'

'Yeah, all right. It's behind the clock on the mantelpiece. Don't say a lot, mind. But they're all OK.'

Stan reached up to retrieve the envelope and then, sitting back down at the table, pulled a battered packet of Player's from his pocket and lit up a cigarette.

'Mum wouldn't let me have a fag once she knew the new family might be coming round,' Mildred complained. 'Had to open the window wide and then keep the scullery door shut to keep out the pong of your trotter.'

'Mmm, yeah, thought I could smell it. My favourite!'

'Huh, you can keep it,' Jake finally managed to get a word in edgeways. 'If that's all that's on offer, I'd rather go without any meat altogether and just have veg.'

'What, like Woolton pie?' Mildred joked, taking the mickey out of the famous recipe put out by the wartime government. 'Can you really enjoy a pie what don't have no meat in it?'

'Yes, and why not?' Jake wanted to know. 'Doesn't bother me too much, does meat. And neither of you should be smoking indoors anyway. It's a fire hazard.'

'Oo-oo-oo,' Mildred mocked. 'Just 'cos you

don't smoke. Yet, little brother.'

'No, well, I've seen enough fires never to want to start one by smoking some silly little white stick,' Jake pouted defensively.

'Good job you ain't never been in the forces, then,' Mildred pointed out. 'Gary says they hand fags out like sweets in the Navy. Or like sweets used to be before they was put on ration.'

'Wonder how long it'll be before we start getting rid of rationing when the war's all over?' Jake considered grimly. 'Going to take some time for things to get back to normal, I reckon.'

Mildred contemplated her younger brother as he went back to swallowing his tea while it was still hot. As he'd matured, he'd become more and more like their elder brother, Kit. He might not have gained a scholarship like Kit, but he was very intelligent and seemed able to understand things beyond Mildred's comprehension. And like Kit, he'd naturally developed a more grammatical manner of speech, possibly because he, too, loved to read. The similarity didn't end there. A lanky youth, Jake had recently started growing broader of shoulder, and his hair had lost its reddish tinge and turned a rich dark brown. Although, unlike Kit's which had always been dark like his father's, Jake's hair had retained a coppery glow in certain lights. Kit would always be the strikingly handsome one, but Jake wasn't far behind. He'd make someone a good catch, Mildred considered with concealed pride.

'War's got to end first,' she grimaced, bringing her thoughts back to their conversation. 'It's a bit like being in limbo, ain't it? We know we've won, but they still ain't given in yet.'

'Yes, odd feeling, isn't it?' Jake pulled a wry face. 'But I reckon we're on the brink. In Europe, anyway. Hitler's beaten. Churchill must reckon so, or they wouldn't be about to turn the street lighting back on. And there's been no more doodlebugs lately. Don't suppose there will be any more now. But I reckon things'll drag on in the Far East for a while yet. The Japs don't seem ready to surrender just yet.'

'Well, at least they've never dropped any bombs on us here,' Eva observed as she started bringing in the dinner, and father and son had a friendly race to get out to the outside lav in the back yard.

By the time they came back in and washed their hands at the scullery sink, Eva had already served out.

'Get your chops round that, then,' she instructed.

'Thanks, Mum.'

'Well, tell us more about this family,' Stan said, sawing his knife through the thick skin of the trotter. 'He's Ron and she's Bridie, but what did you say the kids' names are?'

'Zac and Cissie,' Eva informed him through a mouthful of kidney. 'And the baby's Jane. Quite a looker, the girl, Cissie,' she went on, catching Jake's eye and winking at him. 'But she's a bit — now what word would our Kit use? Oh, yeah, I know, taciturn.'

'Oh, she's OK once you get talking to her,' Mildred voiced her own opinion. 'I think it's just 'cos of what they've been through. Get her talking about her passion, dancing and music, and she seems happy enough to chat. That's what she

65

does for a living, you see. A dancer. Only she's hurt her ankle so she ain't been able to work for a bit.'

'What sort of dancer?' Jake asked, his sapphire eyes lighting with interest.

'Variety,' Mildred told him, eagerly anticipating his response. 'She likes ballet best, but she does all sorts.'

'Wonder if she's any good.'

'I'd've thought so. She's built like a fairy, very pretty and, well, she just moves like a dancer. I thought you'd be interested,' Mildred nodded knowingly. But then she went on with a cheeky grin, 'Not that me little brother's interested in girls. Never even walked out with a member of the fairer sex, have we?' she teased.

'Oh, shut up. I'm not even eighteen yet.'

'I was engaged to Gary when I was seventeen.'

'That was different. He was going off to war. You probably wouldn't have got engaged otherwise,' Jake retorted. 'Anyway, I've never found a girl I was interested in.'

Eva raised an eyebrow and was just about to break in and stop the light-hearted argument when Mildred went on, 'Well, you might be interested in Cissie, what with you liking music and your playing and singing and everything. It'd be something you'd have in common. Sort of.'

But Jake had already calmed down and shrugged mildly as he cut into the cube of liver on his plate. 'Well, if she's as pretty as you say, she's probably got a fellow already.'

'Afraid I dunno. Didn't ask. But with most of the fellas away fighting, maybe she don't. So

66

this could be your chance. Your destiny!' Mildred grinned. 'Anyway, ain't you curious to meet her? Might be sooner than you think, 'cos Mum offered your and Dad's help this evening. She told them to call round if they needed it. To move furniture or whatever. Not that they've got much. It was lucky dear old Abraham had some decent stuff what was left. And then there was the kitchen table and beds what came with it before.'

Eva had been eyeing cautiously the banter between her offspring, and now her gaze snagged on Stan's. Mildred had been teasing her brother, and Eva had been wondering if she should say something to stop her doing it again? But it seemed the conversation was already taking a different tack so she didn't need to.

'Yeah,' she joined in instead. 'And Bridie was relieved when I told her nobody'll be coming back for any of the stuff left in the kitchen. She could really do with it. Abraham would've been pleased it's gonna be put to good use. Oh, Gawd,' Eva suddenly gasped, putting her hand to her mouth. 'I forgot to give her Abraham's spare key. Be a dear and take it round after dinner, Milly, would you, if they ain't come to ask for any help before then. And you can go with her, Jake, and offer your assistance,' she finished triumphantly.

Jake said nothing but turned his attention to spearing some overcooked spring greens onto his fork as casually as he could. But curiosity was frothing inside him. He rather liked the sound of this Cissie despite some of the things his mum and sister had said about her. She

67

must enjoy music and take it seriously just as he did. Secretly, although he felt nervous about it, he couldn't wait to meet her.

6

Mildred knocked gently on the front door of Number Twelve and threw Jake a cheeky smile. Her brother had shown some reluctance to accompany her, but she knew that, deep down, he was curious about their new neighbours, especially Cissie. It always seemed odd to her that Jake was happy to play his guitar and sing for anyone — he performed once a month at the Duke of Cambridge on the corner — and yet he was actually quite reserved. But sometimes she wondered if he didn't hide behind his not inconsiderable talent and that it gave him some small amount of confidence when he was performing.

Her train of thought was interrupted as the door opened and Cissie herself stood there, looking as if she was ready to challenge the world. But her face softened and her mouth curved into a cautious smile as she saw her new friend.

'Oh, hello, Mildred,' she said politely, but made no move to invite them in.

Mildred hesitated slightly. She knew the house so well, both when the Goldsteins had lived there, and before that as a child when it had been the family home of Kit's wife, Hillie, and Eva had been best friends with Hillie's late mum, Nell. It felt strange to Mildred not to be going inside as it was almost like an extension of her own home.

Cissie's just standing there made Mildred feel awkward and she was grateful that she had an excuse to have called. 'Me mum forgot to give you this. It's a spare key,' she said, holding out the said item in her palm. 'She used to look after the old couple what used to live here. But obviously she don't need it no more.'

'Oh, thanks.' Cissie took the key from Mildred's hand with a quick glance beyond her visitor to the youth standing behind. But she said nothing and Mildred felt she needed to prompt the conversation forward.

'This is me brother, Jake,' she introduced him, standing to one side.

She watched the expression on Jake's face and smiled to herself. He nodded at Cissie, his lips set in a line but his eyes bright and shining. Oh, yes. She could tell he found Cissie interesting at the very least, and he held out his hand.

'Pleased to meet you,' he said steadily. 'You must be Cissie. Mildred's told me all about you. Well, that is, obviously she's just met you, too, and doesn't really know a lot about you, either. But, anyway, welcome to Banbury Street,' he concluded, and Mildred had to suppress a groan. Got his knickers in a twist there, didn't he? Not helped by Cissie scarcely touching his proffered hand before snatching her own behind her back as if his fingers had been red-hot coals.

Mildred felt she had to come to Jake's rescue. 'We was wondering if you needed any help? You know, moving furniture or something. Jake'd be happy to lend a hand, and our dad, too, if you need it.'

She waited while Cissie's eyes shifted indoors along the hallway behind her before turning back to the two young people on the doorstep. 'That's very kind of you,' she declined politely and yet somehow evasively, in Mildred's opinion at least. 'But there's heaps of other stuff to do, so if you don't mind . . . '

'No. Course. We understand, don't we, Jake? We'll let you get on. But if you need anything, you know where we are.'

'Yes, thank you. And thanks for bringing round the key. It'll save us getting another one cut.' And so saying, Cissie all but shut the door in their faces.

'So, what d'you think of her, then?' Mildred probed as she and Jake covered the few yards back to their own home.

Jake pulled a face as he shrugged. 'Well, she's really pretty, just like you said. And I can imagine her as a dancer. But she's not that friendly, is she? Unless . . . ' Jake faltered, shaking his head. 'You don't think she's hiding something, do you? She seemed almost, I don't know, nervous. As if she didn't want to let us in in case we saw something they don't want us to see.'

Mildred blinked at him in astonishment. Had Jake observed something that she hadn't? Well, come to think of it, he could be right. But it proved he *was* interested in Cissie, and Mildred jabbed her head at him with a half-teasing, half-encouraging smile.

'Well, little brother, you'll have to work your charms on her to find out, won't you?' she grinned. And opening the front door to Number Eight, she skipped jauntily inside.

★ ★ ★

71

Cissie shut the door as quietly as she could and then, turning round, leant back against it for a moment with her eyes closed, waiting for her rattling pulse to slow. She knew they meant well, but their new neighbours couldn't have chosen a worse time to call. She'd barely given them a glance, and of course . . . She'd maybe have to be a bit more careful on the next occasion she met Jake Parker. It wasn't his fault he was a young man, after all.

Taking a deep breath, she put the key on the hallstand that had been one of the items left in the house and scurried along the passageway to the back room and the crisis that was going on there. The day had already been too much for her father, and when Zac had dropped the tin opener on the floor with a loud clatter, the memories had come streaming back.

Shells were exploding all around him, splattering mud in filthy, blinding showers, and his friends were falling as gunfire mowed them down, their bodies juddering as every bullet burst into their flesh and they screamed and writhed in the stinking morass. Cissie had seen photographs of the first war when she'd been at school. It must have been hell on earth to have been there. Worse. Unimaginable. Just like being trapped on the beaches of Dunkirk, or being part of the invading forces on D-Day as wave after wave of fine men were slain like sitting ducks, even if it was successful in the end. Or fighting in the desert or the jungle, on land or sea or in the air, or anywhere else involved in this second terrible conflict that looked at last, thank the dear Lord, as if it would be ending soon. But her poor dad's own personal hell had been at Passchendaele and it would dog him for the rest of his life.

When she opened the door, her dad was still cowering in his armchair, trembling so violently that the chair legs were clacking on the uneven quarry-tiled floor. Ron was curled up as well as he could with his false leg, his one arm and the hook folded defensively over his head. Zac was backed against the far wall, lips caught between his finger and thumb in remorse at having triggered his father's terrors but still not really understanding although he'd witnessed it so many times before. Bridie was attempting to pacify her husband, but every time she lightly touched him, he ducked away further as if it was making things worse.

'I can't do anything with him,' she despaired as their daughter came back into the room. 'Can you try, Cissie, dear?'

Cissie nodded, biting on her lip. It appeared a particularly bad episode, and sometimes when her dad was like this, they just had to wait until it passed. But it broke their hearts to watch him suffering and they always tried to coax him out of it if they could.

As Bridie went to comfort Zac, who was mumbling tearfully that it was all his fault, Cissie dropped on her knees beside Ron's chair, being careful not to touch him and instead uttering soothing words. 'It's all right, Dad,' she crooned, her voice light and tender. 'It was all over a long time ago. You're home now and safe.'

She watched and waited while his shaking eased slightly and he appeared to be paying attention. She started singing then, very softly. She knew her voice was nothing compared to the singers they had in her repertory company, but it wasn't bad. As she began almost to whisper 'The Teddy Bears' Picnic', a favourite song he'd liked to sing with her when she was younger, Ron slowly turned his head to look at his beloved daughter. She nodded and smiled at him encouragingly between breaths, and his lips twitched as he gradually joined in, and both their voices increased in volume until they reached the end of the song.

Ron blinked his faded, watering eyes at her as they lost that faraway look. 'Oh, dear,' he mumbled. 'Have I been away again?'

'Yes, Dad. But you're back with us now,' Cissie confirmed, sympathy smouldering in her eyes.

'Oh, I'm so sorry. Silly old fool. I didn't mean — '

'It's all right, love. We're all here, safe and sound, so we are.'

Leaving Zac, who was also calmer now, Bridie opened her arms wide, and this time, Ron was happy to sink into her embrace. Bridie gazed over his shoulder at Cissie and mouthed a thank you at her.

'Who was that at the door just then?' she asked softly.

'Oh,' Cissie answered, since she had temporarily forgotten all about their visitors. 'It was Mildred and her brother. Jake, I think his name is. Came to ask if we needed any help and to give us a spare key. Apparently Mrs Parker used to look after the old couple who used to live here.'

'Yes, that's right. She told me, so she did.'

'Well, anyway, I managed to send them away.'

'And they didn't ask — '

74

But just then there was a wail from the adjoining room.

'Oh, saints preserve us, there's Jane woken up again and it's not time for her feed yet. You'll need to fetch her in,' Bridie said, her arms still tightly about her husband.

Cissie turned towards the door with an exasperated sigh, knotting her lips as she reached for the handle. They really could have done without a baby adding to their troubles. And Jane was more than half the problem, wasn't she?

7

'Hey, love, have you heard?' Stan asked excitedly, bursting into the kitchen as he and Jake arrived home from work the following Monday. 'They say they've repaired the minor bomb damage to Big Ben and they're gonna light it up tonight! First time in nearly six years.'

'Yeah, I know!' Eva beamed back, her round cheeks ruddy with joy. 'It was on the radio. Wonderful, ain't it?'

Her smile broadened even further as her eyes scanned her husband's and her son's jubilant faces, and inside her ample bosom, her heart dared to take a little leap. Those six years had seemed an eternity: from watching her four younger children go off to live with their big sister in leafy Surrey and then the first items going on ration, through the Blitz that had raged through London as well as other cities throughout the land and the bomb that had fallen just yards from Banbury Street — making Eva believe the end had come as she and Stan huddled beneath the stairs — to the flying bombs that had once again terrorised the capital as Hitler had attempted to crush the British bulldog spirit — but without success.

Eva knew her family had been lucky — or maybe blessed. The nearest any of her loved ones had come to immediate danger was when Price's had been hit. But in the end, all of her own had survived without a scratch.

Eva had lived through two world wars, for that was what they were. Could it be that after all this time lasting peace was on its way? She scarcely dared think it and tried to quell the euphoria that was simmering inside her, just itching to erupt.

But then Stan, her beloved Stan, stepped forward and took her hands. 'Really looks like it could be over, don't it?' he said, his dear, wrinkled face serious, as if his thoughts were echoing hers. It was a time for joy, but it was also a momentous event and the solemnity of it weighed on both their souls. Eva could feel moisture collecting in her eyes as they both paused to remember. Eva had no other family, but Stan had lost a nephew early on, their son-in-law had been wounded but was now with the army in France, and Mildred's fiancé was still fighting the Japanese.

But just then, Jake's voice interrupted their moment of reflection. 'We thought we might go up to Westminster to see it,' he announced, brimming with youthful exuberance. 'I was just a kid last time I saw it lit up. Bound to be loads of people there. You want to come, Mum? It'll be a moment of real history. Something to tell your grandchildren,' he concluded with a teasing wink, since she already had five of them.

Eva blinked at her son and the grin returned to her face.

'Yeah, why not?' she laughed, infected by Jake's enthusiasm.

'When we've had tea and cleared away. It's baked spuds and a tin of baked beans. Mildred don't finish her shift till late tonight but hers should stay hot enough in the oven even if it is turned off.'

'Probably as well she can't come,' Jake commented wisely.

'You know, with Gary. It's going to be hard on everyone who's got someone still out there, or who's lost someone.'

Eva and Stan exchanged knowing glances. Thoughtful was their Jake, despite his youth. An old head on young shoulders.

But then he'd witnessed so much of what no man should ever have to see — let alone a young lad — when he'd been a runner for the fire brigade and ended up helping to tackle fires and rescue survivors — and the not so lucky — from collapsed buildings. Forbidden by law for someone so young, but it happened often enough, and now he was approaching the age when he could join the service officially. The fires he had dealt with hadn't been as intense or widespread as during the Blitz, but individual flying bombs had wreaked a just as terrible destruction, only on a more confined scale. But apart from the obvious tragedies, Jake had relished the physical challenges of firefighting and the sense that he was doing good. He'd also said how he admired the knowledge and experience of senior fire officers and could see himself carving a proper career in the brigade. Whereas at Price's, the prospects weren't good, and he had doubts about the company's future anyway.

'Well, move out me way and let me see how the spuds are doing,' Eva chided, breaking her train of thought as she bustled out to the stove in the scullery. 'And we can leave a note for Milly.'

'Notice how your mum said we'll have to clear

away before we go,' Stan winked at his son when Eva was out of earshot. 'She wouldn't have worried until recently. Reckon she wants to impress our new neighbours if they call round unexpectedly.'

Jake tossed up his head with a light laugh. 'Hasn't improved her cooking, mind, has it? Well, at least this is a meal she can't spoil. The spuds won't be ready yet I don't suppose, so I'm going to have a play while I'm waiting.'

'Leave the door open, son. You know we like to hear you. Put us in the mood for celebrating.'

'Yes, OK, Dad,' Jake said, disappearing into the front room that had been his alone since he'd returned from his sister, Gert's. Once upon a time, as a little boy, he'd shared it with his grandmother and younger sister, Trudy, while then-baby Primrose had still slept in her cot in her parents' bedroom upstairs. But nowadays it was strictly his own male territory, and his most precious possession, his prized guitar, was propped in the corner.

'What d'you fancy, Dad?' he called through the two open doors. '"White Cliffs of Dover"? A lot of our brave lads should be seeing those again before too long.'

'Nah, something a bit brighter than that,' Stan called back.

'OK.' Jake perched on the stool he'd managed to buy. It was 'Utility' of course, stamped boldly on the underside of the seat. Plain and simple and requiring minimum materials. But that didn't matter. It was perfect for sitting on and playing his guitar, and he was grateful to have been able to acquire one at all.

He bit his lip thoughtfully as he tuned the strings. Something jolly. He'd been introduced to playing guitar on folk and Irish music but had developed a natural ear for picking up all sorts of tunes, and now his repertoire was broad and varied.

Ah, I know, he thought to himself. And strumming a couple of chords, he broke into 'Would you like to Swing on a Star?' from the film of the previous year, *Going My Way*, singing his way happily through all the verses. By the time he came to the end, it had certainly put him in a light-hearted mood for the trip up to Westminster. He heard his parents clapping from the next room, and decided to regale them with his lively and comical rendition of 'When I see an Elephant Fly' from Disney's *Dumbo*, a film he knew his mum had loved. But after that, he went on to one of his favourite, more mournful songs, the traditional Irish 'Last Rose of Summer', his voice rising and falling in gentle waves.

Half an hour later, there was movement in the kitchen and Eva announced that dinner was ready. Potatoes and beans were indeed served out on the table, with a pot of tea to wash them down. They ate hungrily, since it was the last food they'd get until morning, chatting as they munched.

'What time d'you think we need to leave?' Stan asked between mouthfuls. 'Gets dark about half nine, don't it, with this double British Summer Time? Pretty parky outside, mind. Bit like winter again, and after that glorious weather we had a few weeks ago.'

'Depends if we're gonna walk or try to catch a bus,' Eva said hopefully.

80

'Let's walk going, anyway,' Jake suggested, 'and see for coming back.'

'You could do with the exercise, Eva, love,' Stan observed with a teasing wink. Although in fact, after five years or so of rationing, his plump wife had lost a considerable amount of weight, reminding him more of the slim figure she'd possessed before her six pregnancies.

'You can go off people, you know!' Eva grinned back. 'For that, you can wash up. And while I get ready, Jake, why don't you pop along to Bridie's and see if any of them want to come with us? It'd be a nice gesture.'

'Oh.' Jake tried to disguise the fall in his voice. That would mean asking Cissie, wouldn't it? Well, she was really attractive, but he'd been a bit put off by her cold attitude when they'd taken the key round and he wasn't in any hurry to see her again. But he knew better than to try and dissuade his mum when she had her heart set on something, so he gave as casual a shrug as he could. 'OK, if you really want,' he answered and, retrieving his work jacket from the back of the chair, made his way to the front door.

He sucked in his cheeks as he stepped along the pavement and, knocking at Number Twelve, waited patiently for an answer, praying nobody would come. But it was only a few moments before Bridie opened the door and her face creased into a welcoming smile.

'Ah, you're Eva's son, Jake, aren't you?' she beamed as if greeting a long-lost son. 'I recognise you from the photo on your mammy's mantelpiece. Won't you be coming in?' she invited him,

81

walking back down the hallway and making him feel obliged to follow her into the kitchen, where the two men and Cissie were sitting at the table. They had evidently just finished their meal, too, although Cissie was dandling baby Jane on her lap — not that she looked too happy about it.

'Look if it isn't Eva's Jake,' Bridie announced. 'Jake, this is my husband, Ron, and our son, Zac. So what can we be doing for you?' she went on as the men nodded at him in greeting.

He noticed that Cissie barely glanced his way.

'Oh, well, expect you've heard they're lighting up Big Ben tonight,' Jake said, trying to hide his reluctance. 'Milly's on lates, but Mum and Dad and me are going up to see it, and Mum wondered if you'd like to come with us.'

He stood for a second or two, mentally crossing his fingers that the unseasonably cold weather might put them off. But his heart tumbled when Bridie's face lit up.

'Sure, that's kind of her,' she declared with a broad smile. 'But there'll be big crowds so it'd be difficult for Ron, and then there's the babby. But I'm sure Zac and Cissie would love to go, wouldn't you now?' she prompted, turning to them.

'Oh, yes — please!' Zac's handsome face bubbled with excitement.

But Jake saw Cissie's expression cloud over. 'Oh, Mum, we shouldn't leave you,' she protested. 'It wouldn't be fair.'

'Nonsense,' Bridie replied. 'You don't want to disappoint your brother, and you couldn't expect

82

them to take him on their own. So, when are you leaving, Jake?'

'In about half an hour. But are you sure you want to come? It's turned bitterly cold.'

'Sure they do,' Bridie insisted, and Jake inwardly sighed.

'We'll wait for you to call, then,' he said, hoping Cissie might protest further. But she didn't, so forcing a smile to his lips, he made for the door. 'See you later, then. I'll see myself out. I know the way.'

The Cresswell family all smiled and nodded and watched him go. But the moment they heard the front door close, Cissie turned on her mother, exasperation burning on her face.

'Why did you say that, Mum?' she demanded. 'I really don't want to go.'

'No, you really need to start getting out again,' Bridie insisted. 'Doesn't she, Ron? And you'll be in good company, so you will. Jake seems a nice young man, and you'll come to no harm with his parents there as well.'

'But what about Jane?'

'Sure, you've never bothered much about her before, so don't try using her as an excuse now. Can't I be managing her on me own for a few hours? Now go and tidy yourself up a bit while I get Zac ready. Put on those nice slacks you used to wear and your best Fair Isle cardigan. And you'll need your winter coat. I've moved the buttons back.'

'Yes, Mum.' Cissie gave a deep, reluctant sigh, lifting her eyes to the ceiling as she laid the baby down in the drawer that was serving as a cot. She adored her mother, but there were times when she could throttle her. Like now. For what had Bridie let her in for?

8

'Are you all right walking all this way? With your ankle, I mean?' Jake enquired, grateful to have some topic of conversation to cling to, since somehow he and Cissie had fallen behind Stan and Eva, who, not surprisingly, was mothering Zac in her own inimitable way.

'Yes, I'm fine, thank you.' Cissie's tone, Jake noted, was polite and calmer as she spoke. 'It's a lot better than it was. The walk will probably help strengthen it up.'

Jake glanced sideways at her. He sensed she was more relaxed now and that the walk was doing her good in more ways than one.

'So does that mean you'll be going back to work soon?' he asked.

'I sincerely hope so,' she snorted, and Jake detected bitterness returning to her voice. 'Mum can't work because of the baby, obviously. Which means Dad's the only one with an income and that's his war disablement pension, which is pitiful. So we really need my wages as well. I'm working on my ankle every day, so hopefully it shouldn't be long now.'

'And what about Zac?' Jake dared to suggest. 'I can see he seems . . . to have problems, if you don't mind my saying so. Is he able to work at all?'

'Oh, yes. If it's the right job. Give him something repetitive to do and he'll do it to perfection. For hours. It suits his condition. And no, we don't

85

mind talking about it.' Cissie surprised Jake with her sudden openness. 'Not to people who understand. It's those who don't and mock him for it who make us angry. He can't help being how he is.' Cissie glanced up at Jake and he caught the flash in her eyes. He had the impression she could be quite the tigress, despite her petite size, and he was thankful when she gave him a grateful smile. 'But I can see you and your family seem to understand,' she said, jerking her head to the three adults walking in front of them.

'Yes, Mum's a born carer,' Jake agreed somewhat proudly as Eva evidently said something that made Zac laugh. 'She should've trained to be a nurse like your mum, but she had no chance of a decent education, and besides, she met Dad and had Kit quite young. That's my elder brother. He's married and lives in Kent. His wife used to live in your house many moons ago.'

'Oh, yes?' Cissie sounded genuinely interested and Jake felt he was beginning to break the ice with her.

'It's a long story. I'll tell you some time,' he promised. 'But you were saying about Zac. Was he . . . born like it, or was it an accident or an illness or something?'

Cissie shook her head sadly. 'Poor thing was born like it. Mum says he seemed OK, placid, developing fine physically. As you can see. But he still wasn't showing any signs of talking by the time he was three. Mum and Dad just thought he was a bit slow and would suddenly catch up. But he never did. Not properly. And I was already on the way. I sometimes wonder if I hadn't been

86

and they'd realised then that Zac had a problem, whether they'd have ever had another child in case it turned out the same. And then Jane wasn't planned, of course.'

There was something wistful in her voice and when Jake caught her eye, he said with a shy smile, 'Well, I'm glad they had you.' He held her gaze for a moment and then wished he'd kept his big mouth shut at the expression that came over her face. Oh, Lord, what had he said? Perhaps it was because she was already spoken for and, like Mildred, had someone in the forces she was worried about. 'So, d'you have a sweetheart somewhere?' he asked nervously as he didn't want to upset her.

She faltered in her step and literally shrank back from him, eyes wide in a face that had instantly drained of its colour, making Jake think that maybe she'd *lost* a young man in the fighting. But then she virtually spat, 'No!' her voice trembling with something — was it fear? Jake blinked at her in astonishment, quite taken aback with her reaction. But before he could think of anything to say, she appeared to recover herself and went on, 'I've never had time. And I've only ever been in love with my dancing.'

'Oh. Oh, I see,' Jake stammered, since he didn't know how to respond to her odd behaviour. And then his own creative nature came to his rescue. 'I can understand that. Especially doing it professionally. I play the guitar and sing. That's my passion. I could do it for hours on end. It must be the same for you with your dancing. Tell me, how did you get into it?'

They'd crossed over Albert Bridge and were

making their way towards Westminster along the Chelsea Embankment.

The light was rapidly fading from the sky and already the Victorian lamps were beginning to glow like misty haloes in the dusk. Jake couldn't help thinking how pretty and romantic it looked, all the more so because it was an unfamiliar sight, it being only the last few days that the government had considered it safe enough to turn the street lights back on. What a feeling of release, of unfettered joy, was just waiting to burst out the minute they had the word the war was definitely over. Wouldn't it be wonderful to share the unsurpassed elation, Jake considered, with a girl in his arms?

Glancing at Cissie, he had the most overwhelming desire to take her hand, to feel a tingle as his fingers met with hers. But he knew it was a stupid idea and crushed it from his mind. There was something about Cissie he couldn't fathom and he sensed that any physical contact would be the last thing she wanted.

She did, however, seem happy to engage in conversation. 'Oh, I've danced all my life,' she answered with a shrug. 'I went to a little ballet school in a hall when I was four and I loved it. And then when I was about seven, I used to stay on to watch the tap class after mine. I begged Mum to let me go to that as well, but she could barely scrape the money for the ballet classes. And then, one day, the teacher got me to join in the tap for free. Mum was mortified, but the teacher said — oh, dear, this sounds a bit boastful — but she said I had real talent for dance and should be given every opportunity. Mum just had to pay for the one ballet class, but the teacher gave me two private ballet lessons a week for free, and the tap. She said if she could train me well enough to get a scholarship to the Sadler's Wells Ballet School, it'd be reward enough. But then the war came along, and that was that.'

'Oh, that was a pity. But you must've kept on dancing somehow.'

'Oh, yes. I was evacuated to a town in Devon called Tavistock and I went to a dance school there. Hardly Sadler's Wells, but it was good, and I learnt all sorts of different types of dance, just as I would have done at the Sadler's Wells School. It wasn't free, though, and Mum had to find the money. But by then Zac was more reliable — for various reasons, he wasn't evacuated, you see — and Mum was able to go back to work. I came back to London when I was fifteen, when the Blitz seemed to be over, and I could have auditioned for Sadler's Wells then. But they were being sent all over the place, entertaining troops and factory workers and the like, living in digs, having to sleep on trains. Well, I didn't fancy all that. But then I found out about the company I'm with now. They do move around a bit, but only in London, in town halls or small theatres. So . . . ' She appeared to hesitate slightly before continuing, 'I can usually get home to Mum and Dad at night. So here I am. Apart from my ankle, of course,' she seemed to finish as an afterthought, almost as if she'd forgotten about it.

Jake had been listening patiently to Cissie's story, quite enthralled if the truth be told, imagining what it would have been like for him if he'd been a professional performer with his guitar. When she came to the end, he, too, had more or less forgotten about her ankle.

'And are you sure it's OK walking so far? Say if it's not and we'll catch a bus or a tram or something.'

'Oh, yes, of course.' She appeared to force a reassuring smile to her lips. 'Just a few more weeks and I should be back.

I might have to start back in the chorus till it's fully strong again, though.'

Jake raised his eyebrows in pleasant surprise. He still sensed Cissie was holding something back, but he was definitely warming to her — and she to him, he'd like to think. Maybe the reticence that had quashed his initial attraction to her was melting and they could get to know each other better.

'Were you one of the main dancers, then?' he asked in awestruck admiration.

Even in the deepening dusk, he saw a dark hue flush into her cheeks as she blushed and gave an embarrassed nod. She must be good, then, but too modest to say so.

'I'd love to come and see you,' he said, but at that moment, Zac stopped and turned round to them.

'Cissie!' he called nervously, his eyes wide.

'Yes, it's all right, Zac, I'm here,' she reassured him, stepping forward to take her brother's hand. 'Right behind you. I'd better stay with him now it's dark,' she said briefly to Jake.

Jake nodded and hurried to catch up with his parents instead. The streets were getting crowded as they approached Westminster, the distinctive shape of the Houses of Parliament a massive shadow against the murky, cloud-covered sky. It seemed that thousands of people had come to witness the reillumination of the iconic symbol of the British spirit that had seen them through the most horrific of times. There were both men and women in uniform, but hundreds of civilians, too, all jostling to get a view, and Jake was glad the tower of Big Ben was of such a height that everyone would be able to see. The mass of people was becoming so dense that it was difficult to keep their little group together. And when a wave of movement surged through the multitude, Jake wasn't the only one to become separated.

His heart gave a painful thud, for suddenly he couldn't see Cissie, and he was overwhelmed by a protective urge. She probably stood at little over five foot and was so slight, she could easily be crushed. For a moment or so, he was really worried, but all at once she reappeared at his side, her face torn with worry.

'I've lost Zac!' she screamed above the clamour of the thousands of voices. 'He'll be terrified!'

Jake knew he had to do something. Recent memories of when he'd helped the fire brigade after flying bomb attacks came to his rescue. *Keep calm and don't panic. You can't help if you're in a state yourself.*

'Stick with me,' he instructed, taking Cissie's arm. 'We'll find him.'

She glanced up at him and he saw trust in her eyes — trust he hoped he could justify.

He ploughed his way through the crowds, calling out a repeated, 'Excuse us, please! Looking for a lost child!' with the same authority he'd used when trying to bring help through a crowd watching a bombed or burning building.

Cissie seemed to accept his white lie without questioning.

'He can't have gone far,' he tried to reassure her, raising his voice above the noise, and he felt her fingers tighten desperately on his arm.

Jake kept raising himself on tiptoe to see over the heads of the crowds. Fortunately he was tall, but Zac was even taller. It wasn't many minutes before Jake spied a figure, hat knocked askew in the crush, one hand over his head and his other thumb plugged in his mouth as he turned frantic circles.

'I've got him!' Jake shouted at Cissie, dragging her through the throng and not taking his eyes from Zac's petrified figure.

'Here, get out the way, you moron!' someone was mocking Zac as they finally reached him.

'Yeah, who let you out of the asylum?' another youngster, not in uniform and probably about the same age as Jake, was jeering as he spun Zac round so the poor lad became even more disorientated.

Jake couldn't believe what happened next. Before he had a chance to do anything himself, Cissie broke away from him, and giving one of the chaps making fun of Zac an almighty shove, she elbowed the other viciously in the ribs.

'Just you leave him be!' she yelled.

Pulling Zac away, she glared defiantly at the two startled bullies who'd begun to back away. Jake caught them exchanging glances and while one of them stared back at Cissie with his jaw dangling open, the other raised his hands in submission.

'Blimey, she your girl?' he blurted out to Jake who had one hand each on Zac and Cissie, trying to direct them away from any more trouble. 'Good luck ter yer, mate. I wouldn't want 'er. Bloomin' little spitfire.'

Jake didn't answer, but his eyes snapped at both men over his shoulder as he dragged Zac and Cissie away through the crowds. Zac looked a lot less worried now, asking in his slow drawl when Big Ben was going to light up. But Jake could see that Cissie's face was still tense, ready to give anyone else the length of her tongue. He decided it was an occasion when discretion was the better part of valour, so he did nothing as his sharp eyes searched out his parents. Besides, a peculiar sensation had come over him, locking his brain in unwanted confusion as the stranger's words whirled in his head. Cissie his girl? Well, there was no denying he was attracted to her. She was a beauty, and when they'd been talking on the long walk up to Westminster, she'd opened up to him quite pleasantly. But the fellow was right that she could be as sharp as a razor, and Jake still felt there was some mystery about her. He wasn't sure whether it intrigued or deterred him. But yes, overall, he considered he did quite like the idea of Cissie being his girl. Not that he imagined there was any chance of it!

'Oh, there you are! We was so worried when we got pushed apart!' Eva cried, relief written on her face. 'You all OK?'

'We lost Zac for a few minutes, but we're all right now,'

93

Jake answered simply, not wanting to go into detail. He didn't want Cissie reacting again and relating their little contretemps with the two men, although he could see she was concentrating now on keeping a tight grip on her brother.

'Thank Gawd for that.' Eva nodded her head up and down, her lips bunched. 'So how long before they turn the lights on? It's flipping gloomy down here and cold enough to freeze your arse off. And I've had enough of being squashed in the crowds, too. Perhaps it wasn't such a bright idea to come, after all.'

Yes, Jake was beginning to wonder the same thing. It was all right for him and his dad, both being tall and strong. But for his mum and Cissie, who were both short, it must be quite daunting. Once again, Jake experienced a need to protect Cissie — even if she could probably take care of herself by all accounts — but he also felt a responsibility towards Zac, especially as he'd been the one to go round to their house and invite them to come with them!

But, glancing up, he could just see the hands of the giant clock in the sky coming up to the hour and, a moment later, the seething multitude magically hushed as the bells rang out their familiar prelude. And then, on the first stroke of the hour, a faint glimmer behind the four faces of the clock grew in intensity and finally reached its old, proud, luminous glow. Such a cheer went up from the thousands of throats that it was deafening, and people began jumping up and down and hugging each other in jubilation. Victory, peace, they must be nearly there. What rejoicing there would be when the end was finally announced!

Jake realised that someone had started singing, and voices all around were joining in. For Jake, there was no better way of expressing emotion than in song, and his own tenor tones were soon added to the general cacophony. Cissie glanced up at him, her hazel eyes warm with delighted surprise, doing something unexpected to his heart before he sang out even more lustily than before.

They stayed a little longer, caught up in the general euphoria, but Stan and Jake both had work in the morning. As soon as the pressing crowd began to thin, they started to make their way home. Zac was turning his head round as he walked, trying to look back at the illuminated faces of Big Ben, grinning from ear to ear.

'Someone looks happier now,' Jake observed, using his eyes to indicate Zac.

'Yes.' Cissie smiled up at Jake, making his chest squeeze.

'Thank you for bringing us. And for looking after us.'

Jake returned her smile, relieved that the outing had been a success after all, and was about to say it had been a pleasure, when Stan turned round to them.

'Looks like the bus queues are as long as your arm,' he grimaced. 'D'you want to wait, or are you up for walking home?'

Jake glanced down at Cissie and saw her puff out her cheeks. 'Might as well walk, if that's OK with everyone else.

What about you, Mrs Parker?'

'Oh, do call me Eva. But I'm fitter than what

you think. But I thought you had a bad ankle, ducks?'

'Oh.' Cissie appeared to correct herself. 'I have, but it feels fine, so I'm happy to walk. We can always catch a bus later if need be.'

'Sounds like a good plan to me,' Jake agreed. 'So which side of the river d'you want to go? The way we came, or over the other side?'

Was it his imagination, or did his heart do a little jig when Cissie looked up at him and smiled. 'The way we came. It's prettier, don't you think?'

Oh, yes. That suited Jake just fine!

9

Eva's chest collapsed as she released a sigh of frustration and leant back in the chair, her heavy eyelids closing. If truth be told, her blooming legs were aching from the walk up to Westminster and back the previous evening. It had been a wonderful experience, mind, almost magical, despite it being so cold for the time of year. As if things really were starting to get back to normal, even if in general terms they weren't. For here she was, poring over their ration books and points coupons, trying to decide what the flipping heck they were going to eat for the week.

Rations were easy. You just took everything you could — provided your grocer had it in stock. With sugar and preserves you could manage with less, but everything else was essential: half a pound of fats, a quarter of bacon, two ounces each of cheese and tea and one measly egg. The fat ration might sound reasonable, but if you needed sandwiches to take to work all week it soon went, and then the whole of the rest of it went into pies and dumplings and the like to fill a working man's stomach. As for milk, four adults in the house meant a total of eight pints a week, one delivered each weekday by the milkman from his horse and cart, with three on Saturdays to tide them over the weekend, which it just about did.

It was the points that were the nightmare, currently six each per week, a total of twenty-four for the family, and then you had to choose what to use them on. But to make it more difficult, all was measured in pounds weight. It was easy enough when it came to things like rice or macaroni or dried fruit — not that Eva would buy the latter very often as just one pound used up sixteen points — but how much did a tin of soup or fruit weigh? At least a tin of baked beans weighed exactly a pound, so you didn't feel as if you were being cheated. It counted as three points, and eked out between the four of them with a large baked spud each, it made a decent, filling meal. But they'd had it last night, and though they would doubtless have the same before the week was out, Eva didn't feel it was right to have it two days running.

As for meat, the system was so complicated that Eva had never entirely been able to fathom it, especially with the allowances changing all the time. Thank Gawd she had Old Willie to advise her. She trusted him implicitly, and although they mainly lived on offal and cheap cuts of meat, occasionally something more tasty came their way. Mind you, it was a mystery to Eva when Willie announced that she could have them! Whether or not he was involved in black marketeering, she didn't know. But if he was — and it wouldn't surprise her — she was happy to turn a blind eye if it meant a little variety on their plates.

Oh, her poor brain needed a rest. Maybe she'd put the kettle on and make herself another cuppa with that morning's leaves. She was getting too old for all these shenanigans just to keep their stomachs satisfied! But before she could stand up, Mildred waltzed into the room, pinning her uniform cap on

98

her rebellious curls.

'I'm off now, Mum,' she startled Eva by interrupting her mum's chain of thought. 'By the looks of you, you'll be in bed when I get home off me shift.'

'Oh.' Eva blinked her eyes wide. 'You ain't got time to look at the points coupons, have you? I can never make head nor tail of them.'

'You've managed all these years!' Mildred chuckled. 'Best just go down the shops and see what's there, first. And no, I ain't got time, I'm afraid.'

'Oh, pity.' Eva was crestfallen, but then her expression perked up as she said, 'You've only got till Sunday on lates, ain't you? And then you've got a few days off, so you can go and see Cissie. She don't know no one round here, and I reckon she could do with a bit of cheering up. Mind you, she and Jake was chatting away last night,' Eva finished with a knowing wink.

'There you are, then. But I expect she'd rather some girlie company, so I don't mind popping round. Might even persuade her to come out with me and me friends from the depot. But I must be off. Can't be late. See you, Mum!' And plonking a kiss on Eva's curlers, Mildred flounced out of the kitchen. A few seconds later, the house shook as she slammed the front door closed behind her.

Eva took a deep breath, letting her lips vibrate like the coalman's horse as she let it out. She pushed the ration and points books away. She'd come back to them later. But for once in her life, she didn't really fancy another cuppa. Her eyes wandered listlessly about the room and came to rest on the tumble of red, white and blue material she'd dumped on her old mum's chair. Perhaps it'd be more fun to get on with her sewing.

It was so confident that German surrender was imminent that, in anticipation of widespread victory celebrations, the government had announced that you wouldn't need to use your clothes coupons in order to buy material to make bunting. Patriot that she was, Eva had been delighted when she'd been able to spend a few bob on half a yard each of the three different colours of coarse calico, plus several yards of tape. Now she gathered everything up and, sitting back down at the table, began to ply her needle. She wasn't all that good at sewing, but it didn't need to be very neat, and as long as it didn't all actually fall apart, it didn't matter. Bunting for a street party was hardly the same as a dress for the queen, after all.

Eva edged a rough, single-turned hem about the edges of a blue triangle she'd cut out the previous day, using large, uneven stitches. Just to stop it fraying, she told herself. When she finished, she picked up another. Red this time, just for a change. But her mind was restless, butterflies starting to flap about in her stomach. This was all very well, preparing for vast celebrations, but what if it all went wrong? What if the war dragged on for weeks more? Months? What if Hitler managed to rally his forces and fight back? After all, you really didn't *know* anything, did you? Just what you was told in the papers or on the wireless. And what if Mildred's Gary got himself killed on the other side of the world as he fought on against the Japs?

Eva put down the scarlet triangle and, leaning her elbows on the table, rested her chin in her hands. She was starting to feel old. Weary of the constant battle. The first of May, spring on the way, not that you'd think it from the weather. The war was supposed to be drawing to a close, and she should feel bright and expectant, but here she was, sitting on her tod, stitching soppy little bits of material. She needed company. She wouldn't have any until Stan and Jake got in from work. She wasn't even on WVS duty that week. They'd been told there'd be plenty to do as the troops came home, but if and when all was back to normal and presumably the WVS was disbanded, what then? She'd need something to keep her occupied, make her feel useful.

She couldn't wait for her Primrose to come home from living with Gert, but in the meantime, she supposed she could always get on a train and go and visit Gert or Kit. Yes, maybe she'd do that one day. But . . . Oh, how she still missed Nell, even after all these years. Her bosom pal. Dear Nell who'd lived at Number Twelve. Eva got on well with all her neighbours, but it had never been the same as her relationship with Nell. There was Ellen across the road at Number Three, for instance. A lovely woman of a similar age to herself, though apt to be a little more reserved. Eva could pop across to her now for a chat, but then she remembered that Ellen always went out early on a Tuesday afternoon to do her shopping before she collected Lily from school. And with all the queuing you expected to do, she'd probably gone out ages ago.

Number Twelve. Of course. A grin spread across Eva's face and she felt her short-lived depression lifting. Yes, she'd take herself and her sewing round to Bridie's. It might not suit her new neighbours, of course, and she might have to come back, but it was worth a try.

Grabbing her shopping basket, she stuffed all the sewing into it and made for the door. She'd need her coat, even if it was May. But as she stopped in the hallway to shrug into it, she remembered she still had her curlers in, as usual. In the old days, she'd have happily gone round to Nell's with a scarf tied over them. Not that it hid the curlers properly. But perhaps she should make an effort, so she slipped back into the kitchen and took them out, roughly pulling a hairbrush through her frizzy mop. She glanced in the old mottled mirror over the mantelpiece. Her crowning glory was neither a crown nor glorious, but it would have to do.

When she knocked on the front door of Number Twelve, she was pleased that it was Bridie who opened it. The stout Irishwoman's face broke into a welcoming smile.

'Eva!' she cried in delight. 'Won't you be coming in? It's as cold as the Galtee mountains in winter, so it is.'

'Oh, ta,' Eva answered as she stepped inside.

'Come through to the back. I was just about to make up the babby's feed, so I was. Can't feed her myself. Having a babby at my age is one thing, but the good Lord made it so that I couldn't feed her myself, so she's on the bottle. You can give it to her if you like.'

Pleasure sparkled in Eva's heart. 'Yeah, I'd love

to, ta. Love babies, me. Me grandchildren are that much further away, so I don't see so much of them. But I'm hoping Mildred'll give me some and stay a bit nearer. And Jake, too, in his time.'

'Does Mildred have a young man, then?'

'Yeah, she has. Didn't I mention it? In submarines in the Far East, so all this here talk of victory in Europe is blooming hard on her.'

'I'm sure it is, the poor soul —'

'Oh, that's nice music.' Eva hesitated by the closed door to the front room. Through it wafted the dulcet, lilting tones of an orchestra playing a beautiful waltz. 'It's classical, ain't it?'

'Sure, isn't it Cissie practising her dance?' Bridie explained. And then, oddly, she seemed to usher Eva swiftly past and into the kitchen. 'A new gramophone and some records were the first things she saved up to replace after we were bombed out.'

'Oh.' For some reason she couldn't quite fathom, Eva felt slightly awkward as Bridie closed the kitchen door behind them as if wanting to shut the music out. Eva gave a mental shrug. Oh, well, none of her business, she supposed, and turned her attention to the occupants of the room. Ron was sitting in his armchair, cradling baby Jane in what remained of his left arm, while crooning to her and tickling her tummy with his right hand to stop her crying while she waited for her bottle.

'Hello, Eva.' Ron looked up to greet her with a smile. 'What can we do for you, or is it purely social?'

'Hello — Mrs Parker,' Zac slurred as he came in from the scullery. 'Nice — to see you.'

103

'You, too, ducks,' Eva nodded. 'And remember it's Eva.'

'Oh, that doesn't — seem right.'

'OK. Well, make it Auntie Eva if you like. But I was wondering if your mum's any good at sewing? I'm making some bunting for when we have a street party, but sewing ain't me strongest point, so I thought we could make it together. Only if you wanted to, mind.'

'Sure, that'd be grand! Wouldn't I be making some myself if we had any spare cash to buy the material? Is that everything in your basket? Zac, make room for it on the table while I see if Jane's milk has cooled enough. I promised Eva she could feed her, Ron.'

'Righty-ho. Well, here she is, Eva,' Ron said as Eva put down the basket. 'It's good to see a friendly face. Thanks so much for coming round.'

Eva felt as pleased as Punch to take the baby, gazing down on the tiny, rosebud face. A few minutes later, Jane was guzzling noisily in her arms while Ron directed Zac in cutting out triangles of material, and Bridie expertly hemmed them round with small, neat stitches. Soon, all four adults were chatting away as if they'd known each other all their lives.

Eva was as happy as anything as she fed the baby. She felt in her bones that she and Bridie were going to be such close friends, just as she had been with poor Nell for all those years. Before things had become so dreadful with Harold. Eva had sat in this very room with Nell on so many occasions. The poor woman's ghost still lingered in the walls. But now life had, at long last, come

full circle, and Eva felt that peace was coming —
in more ways than one.

★ ★ ★

'Cissie, love, it's far too soon.' Deep lines of concern were etched on Bridie's face as she shook her
head at her daughter. 'You've been practising all
afternoon. Sure, it'll do your insides no good, all
that bending and twisting. You need more time to
recover.'

Cissie stared at her mother as she used a towel
to wipe the sheen of sweat from around the low
neck of her leotard, and then twisted her head in a
desperate circle, making Bridie's heart tear in two.

'You don't understand, Mum,' the girl moaned
from between clenched teeth, her eyes closed
tightly in a maelstrom of pain. 'It's only when I'm
dancing that I feel free again. Clean. That I can
escape for just a short while from what happened.
Concentrating on the steps takes my mind off it
all.'

Her voice was a thin, anguished wail as she
opened her eyes again, a pleading grimace on her
lovely face. The chasm of despair widened, and
just as she felt herself about to tumble into its
crippling depths, Bridie stepped forward, arms
open to envelop her darling girl in all the love and
sympathy and support a mother can. Cissie wept
against her with brutal sobs as memories of that
horrendous night ripped through her mind, and
she wanted to scream as the horrible, empty terror screwed down inside her yet again.

At last, her tears began to weary and Bridie

held her close, patting her back and all at a loss, since her own grief at not being able to comfort her child was unbearable.

'All right, love,' she consented, murmuring into Cissie's shiny, dark hair that was sleeked back from her face into a bun at the nape of her neck. 'But don't overdo it. You've done enough for today. All the time Eva was here. I think we've sewn enough bunting for the whole of London, so we have.'

Cissie sniffed hard, drawing the back of her hand across her nose. 'Is that what you were doing, making bunting?'

'It was so. And, God willing, we'll be making use of it very soon.'

'But that won't change what happened to me.' Cissie's torn emotions took flight once more. 'It won't take it away, will it?'

Her eyes were fierce and defiant, snapping with anger, and Bridie's face folded with compassion. 'No. But neither will it bring back all those fine young men who've lost their lives. Just like it won't bring back your daddy's arm and leg. You've got to find a way forward, love, just as he did. We had Zac and we had you. And maybe one day,' Bridie dared to suggest,

'you'll take comfort from — '

'No! Never!' Cissie spat, her outcry spiked with bitterness. 'She'll always be half — '

'But you agreed not to abandon her to an orphanage. Sure, even the Good Lord wouldn't know what would've happened to her, then.'

'I know what I agreed! But I'll never, *ever* do anything but despise her. And I *have* found a way forward. My dancing. So please, Mum, leave me alone. I just want to do a bit more pointe work and then I'll stop, I promise.'

She gave Bridie a peck on the cheek, and turned back to the gramophone. Bridie felt a heavy, sinking sigh in her chest as strains of Liszt's 'Liebestraum No. 3' filled the front room again, and Cissie returned to the chairback she was using as a *barre*. Bridie closed the door quietly behind her, a great, grey cloud hanging over her. Sweet Mary, would her poor dear daughter ever find peace again? She would pray for her at Mass on Sunday, as she always did. But, to be honest, Bridie wondered how Jesus, Mary and Joseph, and even the Good Lord himself, had ever allowed such a dreadful thing to happen to her Cissie in the first place.

★ ★ ★

It was later that night, Tuesday the first of May, that Bridie tapped lightly on Cissie's door.

'You awake, love?' she whispered, pushing open the door a crack.

'Yes, Mum,' came a small voice from the bed pushed up against the far wall. And as Bridie stepped across the bare boards, Cissie went on, 'I'm really sorry for being so rude earlier.'

'Sure, you've no need to apologise. But I thought you'd want to know this. It's just been on the wireless, so it has. German Radio has apparently just announced that monster Hitler is dead.'

Cissie at once sat up in bed. 'You sure, Mum?'

'My ears didn't deceive me, so. And they repeated it. That fellow with the strong, clear

107

voice. Stuart Hibberd, I think.'

In the light that filtered through the open door from the hallway, Bridie saw her daughter's eyes open wide. Could she detect a glimmer of hope there?

'Does that mean . . . it's all over?'

'Not officially, love, I don't think. But it can't be long, can it?'

Though Cissie said nothing more, Bridie could sense her cautious relief. Feeling encouraged, she dared to perch on the bed next to her, leaning towards her with the infant in her arms. Baby Jane was awake but thankfully not crying, her bright eyes searching about her instead.

'I was just about to feed her and put her down for the night. You wouldn't like . . . to give her her bottle, would you?'

The hint of a smile lifted the corners of Cissie's mouth. 'I know what you're trying to do, Mum,' she said gently. 'But no, I wouldn't. But it is good news, isn't it?'

'It is so. Now goodnight, love. Sleep well and God bless.'

Bridie rose to her feet and, padding out into the hallway, used her free hand to shut the door softly behind her for the second time that day. But at least this time there was hope for everyone, and Bridie's heart rejoiced for that.

★ ★ ★

The following evening, even more good news was reported. Berlin had finally fallen to the Russians, and the German Army there had surrendered at three o'clock in the afternoon that same day. It also emerged that Mussolini had been shot and killed a few days previously, on the twenty-eighth of April, and the next day, the twenty-ninth, the Italian Army and the German Army in Italy had also both surrendered.

The world was beginning to heal, so it was, Bridie thought, crossing herself each time an announcement came through. But would Cissie's soul ever be mended again?

10

'Here, Mum, d'you fancy a walk in the park when we've had this?'

It was the Monday a week later, and Mildred was sitting in the kitchen with her mother, sharing a frugal lunch of bread smeared with a little of the home-made piccalilli Eva had bought at a WVS fundraising event. With the change-over from late to early shifts, and having recently filled in for a colleague who was ill, Mildred had a few days off work. But none of her friends was free, and she was somewhat at a loose end.

Eva's face fell. 'Oh, sorry, love, didn't I say? I've been asked to go into the WVS Centre this afternoon. We're sorting through a load of second-hand clothes we've collected for people what's not got much 'cos of the war. 'Specially kiddies' stuff, the way they grow so quick. And people what lost everything in the bombings. Thought I'd see if I can get some bits for Bridie, for the baby 'specially.'

'Yeah, must be a struggle for them with only one measly income and so many mouths to feed. But didn't Gert give you some baby things on Saturday?'

'Certainly did.' Eva smiled proudly at the generosity of her eldest daughter when she and Stan had taken the train out to Stoneleigh at the weekend. 'Said she's gonna make sure she don't need them no more when Rob comes home from the war. She's got the old playpen you lot had in the loft, and all. I'll offer it to Bridie when Jane starts crawling. But Gert gave us so much other stuff, we couldn't carry no more on the train. And the playpen'd probably be too heavy, anyway, so we'll have to wait till Rob can get his car back on the road.'

'It'll be strange, won't it, to see private motorcars all over the place again?' Mildred mused. 'We're so used to just buses and trams and taxis, and the odd posh car what's probably to do with something official.'

'And I expect the horse and carts'll start disappearing again, like they was before the war. Reckon we'll still have the milkman and the coalman, not forgetting the rag-and-bone man, with their horses, mind. For a bit, anyway,' Eva commented, cramming her last piece of bread into her mouth and washing it down with a gulp of weak, lukewarm tea. 'But till we know for sure the war's over, we shouldn't be counting no chickens. Well, time I was getting me uniform on,' she declared, getting up from the table. 'So, what you gonna do this afternoon?'

'Dunno, really,' Mildred sighed. 'All me friends are on shift, so I'll be on me tod. Not that I mind that much. None of them are really close friends. Weather's a bit better, so I might go and stretch me legs in the park.'

'Why don't you see if Cissie'd like to go with you?' Eva suggested as she made for the door.

'You're determined her and me are gonna be friends, ain't you, Mum?' Mildred chuckled, shaking her head.

'Well, she seems like a nice kid underneath. Just needs bringing out of her shell.'

'Her shell? When she can get up on stage and dance in front of hundreds of strangers?'

'Sometimes people what's shy are hiding behind their talent,' Eva declared wisely. 'Anyway, you ain't got nothing else to do this afternoon, have you?' she decided for her daughter, bobbing her head up and down as she left the room.

No, she hadn't, Mildred agreed under her breath as she cleared away the remnants of the meal — not that there was a crumb left, but the jar of piccalilli had to be stored away, and Mildred took the crockery out to wash in the scullery sink. As she did so, she heard her mum call out, 'Bye, love. See you later!' and after Eva closed the front door none too quietly, all suddenly seemed uncannily silent.

Mildred finished her task and then sat back down at the table, wondering quite what to do next. She did fancy going to the park, even if it wasn't quite the same at the moment, with a lot of it dug up for vegetables, and other reminders of the war so apparent. The two hundred acres or so of Battersea Park had been the family refuge, almost like a second home, all of her life. She remembered fondly the countless afternoons spent running wild there as a small girl, Jake always kicking his football around, no matter what the season. They often went there with Hillie, now Kit's wife, and her brother and sisters. If they were lucky, they were treated to an ice cream or a trip on the boating lake. But it was free to visit the aviaries or peer through the wire fence at the deer enclosure or listen to the concerts at the bandstand. The ones at Christmas, held by the Sally Army and just as dusk was falling, were magical.

Mildred had missed the park when she'd been evacuated to Gert's. There was what was called a rec just round the corner, and a ten-minute walk took them to huge Nonsuch Park, over the other side of which was the grammar school Trudy was doing so well at. But it wasn't the same. Mildred had been particularly miffed when in May 1941 she'd missed the United Services procession that had started in Battersea Park, headed by the bands of the Royal Marines, the Canadian Highlanders, Battersea Fire Brigade and Battersea Home Guard. Mildred liked a bit of rousing military music. Her mum had described it all to her at a later date, but it wasn't the same as being there.

Oh, yes. Mildred loved the park, as did all her family. A restful haven from city life. She felt she was a Londoner through and through, but the parks, not just Battersea but Hyde Park, Regent's Park, Green Park and the like, all of which she'd got to know when she'd returned to Banbury Street and started working on the buses, were part of that way of life. And she couldn't imagine herself ever living anywhere else.

But perhaps it would be a trifle mean not to call on Cissie and ask if she wanted to go with her. The family had only been in the street a few weeks and appeared to keep themselves to themselves. So Cissie was probably feeling bereft of female company of her own age. And so, with a reluctant sigh, Mildred used the outside lav, retrieved from her room a scarf with which to twiddle her wayward hair into something resembling a victory roll and wriggled into her coat.

It was Cissie herself who opened the door to Number Twelve a few seconds later, although Mildred was relieved to see Bridie padding up the hallway behind her, dandling the baby on her hip. The Irishwoman was so much more open and friendly than her reserved daughter and gave Mildred a broad smile.

'Won't you be coming in?' she invited her genially.

'Well, actually,' Mildred hesitated, questioning her decision to call, 'I'm just going for a walk in the park and I wondered if you'd like to come with us, Cissie.'

'Oh. Well, I —'

'Course she would!' Bridie declared. 'Could do with a bit of fresh air, so she could. Tell you what. I've just fed the babby and was about to put her down in the pram, so you can take her with you. I'll just tuck her up while you get your coat on, Cissie.'

While Bridie disappeared into the front room, Cissie raised her eyebrows at Mildred. 'Sorry about Mum,' she apologised in a low voice. 'She can be a bit pushy.'

Mildred's face spread into an amused smile. 'Mine, too. She's gone off to her WVS duties, but it was her idea I asked you. So we've got that in common.'

'What, pushy mums that mean well?'

'Yeah,' Mildred couldn't help but chuckle and felt that perhaps she'd found a kindred spirit in

Cissie despite herself. 'So we'd better not disappoint them, eh?'

A minute or two later, the pram had been manoeuvred over the threshold, the baby grizzling as she settled, and the two girls set off down the street. Mildred wondered quite how they'd get on, but to start with, they had to contend with crossing the wide, busy junction into Cambridge Road. Mildred watched Cissie frowning down into the pram, clearly willing her baby sister to drop off to sleep. But by the time they'd negotiated the other difficult junction across Albert Bridge Road and through the open, ornate iron gates of the Sun Gate entrance into the park, not a peep was coming from the pram and Jane's eyes were firmly shut.

'All quiet on the Western Front, then?' Mildred whispered in a jocular tone, trying to lighten the atmosphere.

Relief was written all over Cissie's face as she turned to Mildred with a half-smile. 'Thank goodness, yes. I never realised what noisy things babies can be for something so small.'

'Yeah, but it must be lovely to have a baby in the house. And she's so cute. I vaguely remember me littlest sister, Primrose. She didn't half have some lungs on her, too, mind.' Mildred grimaced at the memory but felt herself relaxing. 'Puts you off having kids, don't it?'

'I'm certainly never going to have any!'

The extreme vehemence in Cissie's words took Mildred aback and she wasn't quite sure what to say to that. But it only took her a second to gather herself together. 'Yeah, well, I suppose being a

115

dancer, your career'd be over the minute you had kids. But, I dunno. Guess I'll let the future take care of itself when Gary gets home. Assuming he does, of course.'

Cissie glanced at her sideways as they walked along the pavement that bordered the carriage drive in the park. 'Must be hard for you when the war in Europe's over. At least as far as we know.'

'Yeah, it is. Hard, I mean,' Mildred answered, brushing all thoughts of Gary aside. 'But I'll be as happy as everyone else when they tell us that we've definitely got peace in Europe.'

'And it can't be over soon enough for me, and then all the Yanks can go home.'

Cissie said it with such bitterness that Mildred's lips pursed into a knot. All the Americans she'd ever met, mainly on the buses, had been polite and good-natured, even if some had been a little forward. So had Cissie had a bad experience with a Yank? Her face had certainly turned the colour of thunder. But Mildred didn't want to pry, so she said jokingly, 'Yeah. Overpaid, oversexed and over here, as they say. But we wouldn't have won the war without them.'

She saw Cissie lift her shoulders in an acrimonious shrug and thought perhaps she ought to change the subject. Her eyes wandered over the flower beds beside them, where tulips and primroses nodded in front of shrubs in full spring bloom.

'Have you been to the park before? Pretty, ain't it? Especially this time of year. Before the war, they always used to spend a lot more time and money on it. Loads of colourful bedding plants

116

me sister, Gert, told me they was called. She got all into gardening when she got married and got a place of her own with a big garden. Out in the Surrey suburbs. Before that, she didn't know no more about plants than what I do.'

'I don't know much about them, either,' Cissie admitted, 'although I do like them. And perhaps they'll go back to putting in more, what did you say? Bedding plants? When the war's definitely over. It's a bit like me being with CEMA. Did Jake tell you? It's like ENSA, only for entertaining factory workers or civilians. But it's not so well known. Keeping up morale at home, that sort of thing. And I reckon we're going to need a lot of that, even when the war's declared over. Things aren't going to get back to normal just like that. And for some of us, it'll never be the same again.'

Cissie's voice had dropped to a whisper, and Mildred sucked in her lips in an expression of sympathy. Her heart went out to anyone who'd lost their home, although there were far worse things, of course. But she considered it was better to keep her mouth shut and said instead, 'Well, I'm sure the park'll be the same again eventually. Over there, the fields are all dug up for vegetable allotments, but I expect they'll be grassed back over at some point. And then there's the air-raid shelters what they dug out. Not gonna leave blooming great holes for people to fall into and break their necks, are they? There was a couple of V1s landed in the park last summer, but no one was hurt them times, thank Gawd.'

'Did you get many flying bombs this way, then?'

'One fell on Price's. On Jake's birthday last

117

year. Ten o'clock in the morning. Frightened the life out of our poor mum. Thought Jake or me dad might've been killed. But only two bought it, which was pretty amazing.'

'Two too many,' Cissie murmured.

'Yeah, course. Worst we had round here was when one landed up Lavender Hill one afternoon. Nearly thirty died that day. That was last summer, too, only after the one at Price's. The nearest doodle we had was, I dunno, end of November maybe. Fell on the corner of Cabul Road. That's only a few minutes' walk away, so could've been us. And then the last one was just off York Road down the other side of Price's. End of January, that was. Seventeen dead. Terrible. But I don't need to tell you that.'

'No. But let's hope it really is all over now. Feels really strange somehow, doesn't it? Waiting for the news. As if it's not real. Especially when we've lived with the war for so long.'

Cissie tipped her face towards Mildred and gave a friendly if rueful smile. Mildred felt an easy warmth spread through her. Talking to Cissie was beginning to feel like chatting to an old friend. She was so pleased she'd been swayed by her mum's encouragement to call on her. Perhaps her mum was right and she was a chip off the old block at befriending people, after all.

They took their time, making a long circuit around the roads and paths in the park. Mildred pointed out where a barrage balloon had once been anchored. Like a blooming grey elephant wallowing among the laurel bushes when it was waiting, half-inflated, her mum had reported.

And then there was the anti-aircraft battery on the athletics field.

'Manned by the Home Guard,' Mildred explained almost proudly. 'And they was active when we had them raids last year.'

'Well, let's hope all that's behind us now. I just wish we knew for sure, even if Hitler is supposed to be dead.'

'Yeah. Know what you mean. And then you and your family can really start a new life in Banbury Street. Actually, we was talking about you all the other day. Jake said Zac's looking for a job, but you said he needs something repetitive and not too difficult. Well, he and Dad was thinking. Would you like them to ask at Price's? Something like the night-light wicking house. It's where most boys start off, so they'd likely be younger than him. But the work's really easy. Expected to get through a lot each day, mind.'

Cissie's face lit up optimistically. 'Sounds like just the sort of thing Zac'd like. And not too dirty, presumably? He doesn't like dirt. He was conscripted once to work in a factory, but with all the oil and the dirt, he virtually had a fit. So the medical board ended up exempting him from any war work altogether, just as they should've done in the first place.'

'Oh, dear. I didn't realise he was that bad,' Mildred sympathised. 'But he needn't worry on that score. A bit of wax might rub off on your hands, but no, it wouldn't be dirty.'

'Oh, well. Let me have a word with him tonight.'

'Righty-ho. The woman what's in charge of Personnel is Gert's sister-in-law. Been in the offices at

Price's for donkeys has Belinda. Since way before the war. That's how they met, 'cos Gert worked there, too, once. They was friends and then Gert met her brother and hey presto! Anyway, Belinda worked her way up at Price's till she was in charge of Personnel. Married but never had no children, you see. Mind you, I'm not sure how long Price's'll last. What with gas and the electric more or less back to normal with no more bombs fracturing the mains and what have you. I mean, who's gonna want candles?'

'Candlelight's pretty, though, isn't it? People will always want it for various occasions. And birthday candles to put on cakes.'

'Which won't need flipping pretend cardboard icing once we can get hold of sugar again!'

Mildred chuckled aloud at the allusion to what had become a standing joke throughout the war. Cissie joined in her laughter, and Mildred began to think that she and Cissie really could become good friends. So that when they finally arrived back in Banbury Street and they paused to say goodbye outside Number Eight, Mildred asked her what she was doing the following day.

'I'm off work tomorrow as well,' she explained, 'but all me friends are on shift.'

'OK. Well, why don't we see what the weather does?' Cissie suggested, and Mildred was delighted to see that her beautiful if pinched face seemed so much brighter than when they'd set off earlier that afternoon.

'Yeah, good idea. See you tomorrow, then. We'll think of something to do together even if it's raining cats and dogs,'

Mildred grinned and watched Cissie pushing the pram further along the pavement towards Number Twelve. Letting herself into her own house, Mildred felt herself fill up with pride. She'd clearly cheered Cissie up and felt sure they were going to become good friends, just as her mum had wanted.

★ ★ ★

'It's OK, then, if I take some things for me new neighbours?' Eva asked as she helped sort through the pile of donated clothes at the WVS centre. Throughout the war, she'd mainly been involved with mobile canteens, moving at short notice to wherever they were needed, but she was always willing to lend a hand with anything. 'Mind you, the way me uniform's falling apart, I could probably do with a few things meself!' she joked.

Eva had joined the WVS right at the start of the war. Once the children had gone off to live in relative safety at Gert's house, she'd hated the idea of sitting at home, twiddling her thumbs. When uniforms had become available, even if she'd had to pay for most of it herself and use some of her clothes coupons, she'd applied for her certificate of eligibility and had worn her official clothing with pride ever since. So it was no wonder it was looking a bit worse for wear as it had been covered in dust from bomb sites and splashed with tea and soup almost relentlessly during the Blitz and later whenever she'd been involved in the results of the flying bomb attacks. But even though she hadn't taken the best care of it — how others had managed to keep theirs looking so smart was a mystery to her — she felt like the bee's knees when she wore it, far better than the mere armband that usually had been the only thing available to new recruits in the last couple of years.

'What did you say their name was?' the centre organiser asked, ignoring Eva's frivolous remark. She wasn't centre organiser for nothing, and couldn't bear humour, especially from someone like the Parker woman! 'I'll add them to my list of needy families.'

'Cresswell. Bombed out at that terrible business at Islington, poor souls. Only don't go putting their name on no list. I don't know how they'd feel about that. Don't think they'd want to be seen as no charity case.'

'All right. I understand that. But, Cresswell, you say?' The organiser's brow folded into a deep frown. 'I helped out at Islington. I happened to be visiting a friend who's the centre organiser for that area, so I went along to help out with the victims. I don't remember that name. It's rather unusual, and I've got a good head for names.'

Eva gave a casual shrug. 'You can't have heard every name, and you know what it's like in them situations. Blooming chaos. And they was none of them actually at home at the time, thank Gawd, or they'd probably have been killed. So that's probably why you didn't hear their name.'

'Well, yes, that would explain it,' the woman conceded, though reluctantly it seemed to Eva. 'So do take some items for them, but only a fair amount. There are other families on my list, too.'

'Yeah, course,' Eva agreed. *Her* list, eh? Not *the* list. Eva gritted her teeth as she nodded her thanks and then went back to helping her fellow volunteers sort the clothes into piles according to age, size and gender.

But as she worked, Eva began to wonder. Bridie and her family had always glossed over any details about what had happened in Islington. And yet, if it had been her, she'd have wanted to relate chapter and verse. It'd be human nature, wouldn't it? And they said they'd been pushed from pillar to post and were glad to have found somewhere permanent to settle, at last. But surely the authorities would have rehoused them by now if they had no relatives they could go and stay with, especially with Ron and Zac's conditions, and Bridie having been pregnant at the time? And wouldn't they have settled somewhere nearer to home, anyway? Eva had never been to Islington, but she knew it was somewhere north of the river and she remembered Mildred saying at the time that the bomb was about seven miles or so away. So why had they moved so far? The lack of houses caused by the bombings was probably no worse there than around Battersea, and you'd have thought they'd have wanted to stay in an area they knew.

Or — the thought made Eva snatch in a gasp — perhaps they weren't on the list because they weren't actually from Islington at all? Had they been lying all along? And if so, why? What was their secret?

Eva was curious, but she didn't care if they'd come to Banbury Street for some other reason. She liked them, and she was sure that, whatever it was, it was through no fault of their own.

She would tuck the thought away and forget

about it. It was none of her business. She wouldn't mention it to a soul, not even to Stan. She knew there were some who thought she was a busybody, but she wasn't. She just liked people. Found them interesting. And she knew how to keep a secret. She'd kept Nell's for eighteen years, until Nell had asked her to reveal the truth. So she could keep Bridie's secret, whatever it might be, too.

11

Juggling the baby in one arm and attempting to eat her supper using the other hand, Bridie glanced around the table. Zac, who always had a good appetite despite his lean figure, had just finished his plateful and was drinking down some water.

'Zac, love, can you be taking Jane so I can eat my food before it gets stone cold?' Bridie asked her son.

'Of course, Mum,' Zac grinned amiably, so totally at ease that there was no hesitation in his speech. He found his baby sister a delight and reached out his arms to take her. He made some silly, gurgling noises at her and she rewarded him with her gummy little smile.

Cissie pressed her lips tightly together. She couldn't see what the fascination was with this wriggling being that seemed to need attention almost every minute she was awake. Either that, or she was screaming her head off for her bottle. They had the wireless on, although heaven knew why they'd bothered. You could barely hear it from Zac's mindless cooing and the baby's tiny grunts of contentment.

'So what did you talk about with Mildred on your walk?' Bridie asked between mouthfuls.

'Oh, this and that,' Cissie answered casually. 'She told me more about her family and we talked about the war and this sort of limbo we're in. Expecting it to be over any day but not believing it until we're told for sure. You know, that sort of thing.'

'So you got on OK, then?' Ron wanted to know.

'Yes, Dad. Very well. In fact, we're going to see each other again tomorrow. Oh, I nearly forgot. Zac, she asked if you'd like Jake or their dad to see if there'd be any work for you at Price's. The big candle factory down the road where they work. Apparently, their sister's sister-in-law is in charge of Personnel.'

'A factory?' Zac's eyes flashed in alarm. 'Wouldn't that — be dirty? Like — last time?'

Cissie shook her head. 'Apparently not. Not if you're in the right department. I specifically asked Mildred if — '

'We interrupt this broadcast with a newsflash,' a clear, steady and expressionless voice from the wireless sliced into their conversation.

All four adults instantly froze. Cissie felt sure her heart missed a beat and then lunged forward at twice its normal rate. Stomachs clenched, and the world seemed to stand still as they waited. Trembling, alight with expectation. Was it good news? What they'd all been waiting for? Oh, come on!

It felt like hours but was in fact only seconds before they were put out of their misery. Germany had surrendered unconditionally at two forty-one precisely that morning at Rheims in France. The war in Europe was over. Tomorrow was to be a public holiday. Victory in Europe Day. Church-ill would be broadcasting to the nation at three o'clock in the afternoon, and the king would be speaking later in the day. And Wednesday was to be another public holiday, VE Day plus One.

They sat. Numbed. Time fractured as the news sank in. The bombings, the fear, it was all over. After nearly six years, it didn't seem possible.

And then the taut threads began to slacken.

'Oh,' said Bridie without moving her lips.

'O-oh,' said Zac, not quite sure what to make of this evidently stunning news.

But it won't change what happened, Cissie considered in bitter silence. *I've still got to live with it for the rest of my life.*

'It's . . . it's over,' Ron stated quietly as the news at last began to seem real. 'At last. After all this time.'

It was Bridie who moved first. 'Jesus, Mary and Joseph,' she declared, crossing herself. And a few seconds later, she sprang up and cried, 'It's over!'

As Bridie went round the table, hugging all her family, relief gradually began to percolate into Cissie's heart. But if it hadn't been for the war, she wouldn't have . . . She felt stifled and shot out of the room, out of the house and into the street. She needed to breathe . . .

She ran out into the road. It was instinctive, the knowledge that no motorised vehicle would come down it. For some moments, she stood alone, staring up at the evening sky, turning, the buildings spinning a crazied dance in her head. And then she began to hear muffled voices, as if coming from some faraway planet.

The whirling slowed, the houses slotted into place again as if they had never moved. The voices grew louder, began to make sense, and the world became reality once more. And there was Mildred, running towards her, grabbing her hands and jumping up and down, her face one joy-crazed grin.

'It's over, Ciss!' she cried, waltzing her new friend round in a circle before running off to embrace others, leaving Cissie dazed.

More and more people were emerging through their front doors, kissing and hugging each other, strangers to Cissie and her family, who now all stood on the pavement behind her. But such was the whirlwind of exultation charging through the gathering crowd that it wrapped itself around Cissie's bitterness and began to drive it away.

'I can't believe it!' It was Jake now who'd taken her in his arms. A man. She wanted to push him away, but he held her tightly, gazing down at her with such elation radiating from his face. Then he lifted his head sharply. 'Hear that?' he questioned. And then, raising his voice, he called, 'Quiet, everyone! Listen. Church bells!'

Neighbours shushed each other as everyone cocked an ear. Indeed, church bells! Ringing out the peace. Cissie listened, too, and then met Jake's gaze as he beamed down at her again, bursting and ready to release his demented joy.

'Come on! Let's conga!' he cried.

He turned his back on her and, holding her hands so firmly on his waist that she couldn't pull away, he took three steps forward and kicked out on the fourth beat, yelling, 'Ah, yi, yi, yi, yi, yi, YI!' repeatedly at the top of his voice. At once, Cissie felt hands on her own waist and, panicking,

128

glanced over her shoulder. But, to her utter relief, it was Mildred and not another man, and Eva and Stan had fallen in behind their daughter. In moments, it seemed as if the entire street was joining in, with the exception of just a few who were unable to, such as Ron, and Zac who was still carrying baby Jane.

Cissie was jostled this way and that. But she was *dancing*. The one thing that could be her salvation. Oh, Jake, thank you. She tried to keep to the simple steps, but it was impossible with the long line lurching, drunk with happiness, as people stumbled about, laughing, not caring, just alive with one thought: it was over. Cissie found herself caught up in their elation as they went up and down the street. It didn't matter that they were most of them strangers. They all shared one huge emotion, the explosion of joy. And Cissie felt it creep into her own being, too.

The line snaked its way up to the Duke of Cambridge on the corner, then turned round and wobbled up to Stanmer Street at the opposite end, where residents had also spilled out into the road, whooping and shouting with sheer euphoria.

The conga began to break up at last as souls were so bursting with delight that they sought other ways to release their pent-up relief that had waited six years to escape. More embraces and kisses as a riptide of excitement swept through each and every heart. Cissie and her family found themselves being introduced to all of their new neighbours. They might have wanted to keep to themselves, but it was going to be impossible, especially under Eva's wing! And somehow it didn't matter any more. Everyone was so ecstatically happy that they were welcomed with open arms, and nobody was ever going to guess at their secret. All had been in the same boat, sharing the same fears, and now they would share the same joyful relief.

'That's Mrs Hayes and her little daughter, Lily,' Eva pointed out to the newcomers once the initial hullabaloo had died down enough for her to make herself heard. 'They live at Number Three.'

'Yes, sure, didn't they pop over to say hello the other day,' Bridie told her with a smile. 'Nice lady, and what a lovely little girl.'

'Did she tell you poor Mr Hayes was killed on ARP duty last year?' Eva asked, lowering her voice respectfully. 'And have you met Miss Chalfont? She lives at Number Three, as well, in the basement. School mistress she is. And then, at Number Five, you've got the Smiths and their little girl, Jeannie, what's Lily's best friend. And loads of relatives what got bombed out, too. Oh, but if you'll excuse us, I need to talk to people about the street party what we've been planning. Come on, Bridie, you need to come with us. Good opportunity for you to get to know people.'

Cissie's face stretched, quite overwhelmed, as Eva whisked Bridie away. But, a second later, both Jake and Mildred were at her side again.

'Mum roping your mum in, too, I see,' Jake chuckled, half embarrassed.

'Well, of course Bridie'll wanna be involved, won't she, Cissie?' Mildred chided him. 'That's the whole point, ain't it? Everyone mucking in together. And I can't think of nothing better to bring us all together than peace after all this blooming time! Tell you what. I bet it's gonna be like nothing what you've ever seen up the West End! We gotta go!'

Mildred's face was gleaming, stars dancing in her eyes as they moved expectantly from Cissie to Jake and back again. But Cissie was looking hesitant and unsure. Jake noticed her expression, too, and leapt to her rescue.

'Why don't we celebrate with our families tonight, and then go up the West End tomorrow?' he suggested. 'Best of both? We can go up The Mall and that. I bet you the King'll come out on the balcony of Buck Palace. Wouldn't it be great to see that?' he asked, his cheeks glowing with excitement.

'Thank Gawd I've got tomorrow off,' Mildred declared with a sharp sigh. 'It might be a flipping public holiday, but they'll need the buses and what have you running just like normal.'

'Yes, it'll be heaving!' Jake agreed delightedly. He could see Cissie still seemed reluctant, but he couldn't let her miss out on this historic moment. She'd done something to him he couldn't quite explain, and he wanted to share the experience with her. 'We'll look after you, I promise. But maybe not bring Zac this time. Remember how he was when we went up to see Big Ben.'

He was gazing down at Cissie, his brow rucked into an expectant frown as if he would burst if she refused. Bless him, Cissie thought, he didn't realise how he was trying to drag her from the empty world she had retreated into, and she felt

131

as if she was being rent in two. Half of her wanted to go, but the other half wanted to keep quiet and safe. Last week when they'd gone up to see Big Ben reilluminated, the crowds had frightened her in a way she hadn't anticipated. What if *he* was there? What if by some vile coincidence she saw *him* again? She must take a grip on herself. What were the chances of that? And if Zac didn't come with them, Jake really could look after her. And she did trust him in that way. So, losing herself in his kind, handsome face, she slowly nodded.

'Fantastic!' he grinned back.

An instant later, Mildred had enveloped her in a bear hug and was rocking her from side to side as she asked, 'Right, what we gonna do for the rest of this evening, then?'

As her embrace slackened, Cissie managed to extricate herself and stood for a moment, bewildered and astonished at her own decision. It felt as if some kernel of peace was unfurling inside her. It would take time to open up and blossom, but perhaps these good, down-to-earth people would help her find a way out of the darkness. Perhaps the move had been worthwhile in more ways than one!

12

'What you doing with that, love?' Stan enquired the following morning as Eva was carefully measuring a little of their margarine and cooking fat ration into a bowl.

'Arranged it last night,' Eva explained. 'Everyone in the street's gonna give what they can spare of everything. And then some of us are going over to Ellen's to make whatever we can, jam tarts, sausage rolls — well, made with minced-up spam, anyway. She's a bloody good cook is Ellen, and she's got one of the biggest kitchens in the street. Bridie's coming, too, so it'll be a nice way for her to get to know some of the other women better.'

'What about the baby, if Cissie's coming with us?' Mildred demanded, hoping it wouldn't mean her new friend couldn't come with them after all.

'Oh, Ron and Zac are looking after her, and Bridie'll only be across the street if she's needed.'

'Maybe I'll call into them later on, then. Take a jug up to the off-licence at the Cambridge when it opens and get some beer to take with me,' Stan winked wickedly. 'Best way to get to know someone is over a pint.'

'Typical man!' Mildred groaned. 'Here, you nearly ready, bruv? I just need to put on me lipstick. Been saving me last stub of Caribbean Sunset just for this, I have.'

'No need to tart yourself up,' Jake teased. 'What would Gary say?'

'Gary ain't here, is he?' Mildred reminded him playfully, dismissing all thought of Gary from her head. 'There,' she announced, stepping back from the old mottled mirror over the fireplace as she rolled her now crimson lips together. 'How do I look with me Union Jack scarf on me head?' she continued to preen, patting her springing curls that poked out beneath their patriotic halo. And then she chivvied good-naturedly,

'Come on, hurry up. Let's hope Cissie's ready on time.'

'Doesn't matter if she's not. Haven't got one of your buses to catch, have we?' Jake laughed as he trotted out of the room in his sister's wake. 'See you all later. And don't forget Mr Churchill at three o'clock!'

'Won't miss that for the blooming world!' Eva called after them.

A minute later, Jake had to stifle a gasp when Cissie opened the front door to Number Twelve. She was wearing a dress he hadn't seen before, short, puffed sleeves with a Peter Pan collar around her slender throat, a tight bodice with a white belt accentuating her tiny waist, and a skirt that caressed her slim hips. But, most of all, his admiration was caught by her glossy hair, part of which was caught up on her head with red, white and blue ribbons, while the rest hung down her back in a smooth curtain of silk. So many women either had their hair twisted into a victory roll or cut short and permed, but you didn't see long locks flowing freely like that too often. She looked so stunning that it took Jake's breath away. And so vulnerable that he wanted to protect her there and then.

'You look . . . lovely,' he gulped. And noticed her eyes dart at him warily.

'I'll just get my coat,' she murmured.

'Nah, you won't need it,' Mildred interrupted. 'It's turned really warm this morning. Just bring a cardi.'

'Oh, if you're sure,' Cissie answered and, a second or so later, reappeared with a pretty Fair Isle cardigan Jake had glimpsed beneath her coat on the night they'd gone to watch Big Ben return to life. She looked a proper picture, Jake thought to himself and felt proud that he'd be spending this momentous day with such a beautiful girl — almost as if she was his sweetheart.

He and Mildred waited patiently while Cissie called her goodbyes to her family, and then a few steps brought them to the end of the street and Battersea Bridge Road, which, not surprisingly, was busier than ever. But instead of pedestrians beetling along, heads down as they went about their weary business, the atmosphere was jovial, everyone smiling and nodding at each other and calling out, 'Wonderful, isn't it?' to total strangers.

'Right, where shall we go, d'you think?' Mildred asked, though from the looks of her, she'd go anywhere, Jake mused happily to himself.

'Let's head up to Piccadilly,' he suggested. 'We can go through the park, then over Chelsea Bridge and cut up through Victoria and round the back of Buckingham Palace. And then we can walk inside Green Park on our way. Hopefully it won't be quite so crowded if we go that way,' he explained thoughtfully, remembering how Cissie

135

had resembled a frightened rabbit when he'd first suggested their outing the night before. It seemed odd after the way she'd stood up to those two bullies who'd been taking the mickey out of Zac when they'd gone up to Westminster. But maybe she had actually been so scared that she'd reacted like a demon herself? 'What d'you think?' he asked the two girls by his side. 'We've got all day, so we can take our time. Stop in the parks for a rest. 'Specially if your ankle starts hurting, Cissie. And, Milly, you know all the bus and tram routes if we need them. So, good idea?'

Cissie and Mildred exchanged glances and nodded. So they made their way across to Battersea Park, which, Cissie noted, was so much more appealing in the warm sunshine than it had been the previous overcast afternoon. The brightness was spangling like diamonds on the raindrops that had collected overnight on the thick leaves of the tulips everywhere, so that the flower beds resembled glittering carpets of gold and yellow, orange and scarlet.

'Did you hear that awful thunderstorm in the night?' Cissie was prompted to ask, remembering how it had woken the baby, who was only just starting to sleep through until six o'clock in the morning.

'Couldn't flaming not,' Mildred scoffed, since catching up on sleep was paramount on her days off. 'It was like another bloody air raid. Only it was fantastic to know it wasn't.'

'And it's cleared the air so we've got this glorious day today,' Jake put in, a smile fixed on his face, he was so enthralled to be out with Cissie

136

again — as well as the obvious. 'Glorious in more ways than one!' he crowed.

'I bet it put the dampers on the revellers; it came down so heavy,' Cissie went on, feeling more relaxed as she joined in the conversation. 'They say the crowds went mad in the West End last night.'

'Some of them were probably too drunk to notice the rain,'

Jake laughed. 'But I promise you I will remain utterly sober. Who needs to get drunk on beer when you can get drunk on happiness?'

And on having such a good-looking girl by your side, he thought to himself, his eyes swivelling to gaze down on Cissie. She looked up at him, smiling shyly, it seemed. And his heart took wing. Both his mum and his sister might want to do a bit of matchmaking, teasing or otherwise. But now that he was getting to know Cissie better, perhaps he didn't mind so much!

'I wonder if they'll start on the second phase of the power station soon, now the war's over,' he thought aloud as they reached the far side of the park. The skyline in the direction of central London was dominated by the cathedral-like edifice whose two chimneys towered up behind the buildings in Queenstown Road. 'Isn't it great to be able to say that? The war's over.'

'Flipping is,' Mildred agreed, 'even if Japan's still going on.'

'So what's the second phase of the power station supposed to be?' Cissie asked.

'Virtually doubling in size. With a second chimney at either end. It'll make a huge difference to the electricity supply. And with no more bombs to disrupt it either, things'll start feeling civilised again.'

'Yes, it wouldn't be the first time the lights went out in the middle of a performance,' Cissie grimaced. 'Somewhat ruins it if you're suddenly plunged into darkness.'

'Yeah, I can imagine. Had it happened at the flicks. Blooming annoying if you never get to see the end of the film.'

'More important than that, it'll make a difference to our light industry,' Jake went on knowledgeably. 'I'm not sure how wide it'll spread from here, but it'd help the factories up the East End if they've got a more reliable power supply. Those that weren't completely destroyed in the Blitz, of course. It'll all help the country get back on its feet. I suppose armament factories will go back to making peace-time type products. After all, the government'll want to provide jobs for all the men being demobbed.'

'Oh, my Gawd.' Mildred stopped in her tracks, utterly horrified. 'You don't think I'll lose me job on the buses, do you? I'd hate to have to go back to working in a shop or something like what I did before!'

'It's possible, I'm afraid, sis. There was some talk last year about businesses being obliged to give men back their jobs if they wanted them.'

'Oh.' Jake watched as his sister's face fell for just a moment before she perked up again. 'Well, I'm not gonna let it spoil things. It ain't every day you celebrate a flaming world war being over!'

Despite her enthusiasm, Jake heard the catch in

her voice near the end of her words. The world war wasn't over yet. Only the war in Europe. Nobody knew that more than Mildred, and Jake had to admire his sister for forcing it to the back of her mind, just as she had the prospect of losing the occupation she loved so much.

'I suppose I'm lucky having a job I'm passionate about,' Cissie chipped in. 'And you can't replace female dancers with male ones.'

'Well, they'd look a bit silly in them things, you know, with the fluffy skirts!' Mildred chortled with mirth.

'Tutus, you mean? Yes, I suppose they would,' Cissie smiled back. 'Although it's the talent that counts, and the build. My partner, Sean, he's really slight, but he's incredibly strong. He mightn't look so daft in a tutu. He's Irish, like Mum. That's why he wasn't conscripted, of course.'

'You going back to work soon, then?' Mildred enquired.

'Yes, I reckon the beginning of next month. I'm doing a few hours' training every day to strengthen up my ankle.'

'Talking of work, did you speak to Zac last night? D'you want Dad or me to ask at Price's?' Jake asked helpfully.

'Oh, yes, please. But it must be something clean.'

Cissie glanced up gratefully at Jake, although he noticed the tiny muscles in her forehead twitch with concern. The way she cared for her brother touched his heart, and he'd also noticed a couple of times how she kept an eye on her poor dad, too. The more he saw of her, the more he liked her.

But though she was becoming more friendly, there was still something reserved about her, a barrier he had the feeling would never come down.

'Well, I'm gonna burst if I don't do something to let off me steam of happiness!' Mildred declared theatrically as they left the park through Chelsea Bridge Gate and came out onto Queenstown Road. 'Race you across the bridge!' And, her eyes sparkling with challenge, she suddenly raced forward.

Jake and Cissie exchanged amused glances and then as he saw Cissie's eyes dart after his sister, Jake's face broke into a grin. An instant later, they were off in pursuit, dodging the other pedestrians on the bridge's pavement and laughing as they ran. Nobody minded seeing these young people larking about on such an important day. An old couple, hand in hand, smiled at them as they scooted past, for they could see the young lad was probably coming up to conscription age and yet now wouldn't have to go and fight unless the conflict with Japan dragged on. Women with children, too, were only too glad the war was over and to witness youngsters playing the fool in their jubilation.

'Mind your ankle,' Jake warned as they weaved about in their headlong rush.

'Yes, I'm being careful,' Cissie assured him.

They were only seconds behind Mildred and easily caught her up as she stopped at the far side of the long bridge, panting as she leant over to look down into the water that twinkled in the sunlight.

'Not as fit as you thought, eh?' Jake chided,

140

though he was breathing heavily himself. To his amazement, Cissie was the least affected of them all. While tiny beads of sweat dotted his sister's brow, Cissie appeared as cool as a cucumber and not in the least out of breath. Her few hours' training a day, as she put it, must be far more strenuous than he imagined to build up her stamina like that. And, for some inexplicable reason, he felt his chest swell with pride.

As they continued up towards Buckingham Palace, the crowds became more dense and the triumphant atmosphere was electric. Jake felt he could smell celebration in the air, and he could almost have shouted out his delight at sharing it with Cissie. But he felt there was no point in allowing himself to become too smitten with her.

They crossed along behind the palace gardens and into Green Park. A street vendor was selling little Union Jacks on sticks and Jake waited patiently in the queue to buy them one each, proud to make a gift of one to Cissie — although she protested that she'd pay him back as soon as she was working again.

The sun was getting stronger and Jake insisted they had a rest, sitting on the grass beneath the shade of a tree. All around them, people were celebrating, singing and dancing, and children were playing games of tag, while a group of young boys were running about with arms outstretched pretending to be aeroplanes.

Along the pavement, men were working with cables and loudspeakers, testing out a tannoy system that was apparently going to cover the entire city. The first tune that was playing as they got it

141

to work was 'Don't Sit under the Apple Tree', and Jake couldn't resist joining in at once, raising his eyebrows at Cissie as he sang. Mildred also began belting out the words, but Cissie seemed content just to listen.

'You've got a lovely voice,' she told Jake to his utter embarrassment when the song came to an end. 'And you said you play the guitar, as well.'

'Blooming good at it, too,' Mildred nodded, bringing a flush to Jake's cheeks.

'Not really,' he insisted bashfully. 'I just strum along. I learnt from a neighbour of Gert's when we all went to live with her and her hubby when the war started. I don't think it's something I'd ever have thought about otherwise. Other than kicking a football around with a few mates from school, there wasn't much else to do. And then I heard their neighbour playing at a little get-together and I just loved it. He was kind enough to give me lessons for free, and when I came back to London, he gave me one of his guitars.'

'Gosh, that was kind of him.'

'Certainly was. I was just fourteen then, and I'd never have been able to afford one myself. Or even get hold of one, probably, with the war. And it's a really good one. So going to live with my big sister had its compensations.'

'She's OK is our Gert,' Mildred reprimanded him.

'Yes, I know she is.' And then turning to Cissie, he winked, 'She and Milly are like peas in a pod, both in looks and character, so I've got to say that, haven't I? But it was all right for Mildred. She only had to share with our two youngest sisters.

142

Might've been a squeeze as it was a smaller room, but I had to share with Gert's three boys, and proper noisy little rascals they are! So, as soon as it looked like the Blitz was over, I couldn't wait to get back home.'

'And now the war's completely over.' Cissie found herself giving a contented sigh. 'Well, here, anyway. And it should be in the Pacific soon, too.'

'Wouldn't be so sure about that,' Mildred snorted. 'Look at the way they're resisting on that island. Okinawa, ain't it? The Japs know they're beaten, but they won't bloody well give in. But I'm not gonna let that spoil today,' she forced herself to brighten up. 'You two ready to move onto Piccadilly?'

'Yup. You OK, Cissie?'

'Oh, yes. My ankle's not hurting at all,' Cissie smiled back, and when Jake sprang to his feet and politely held out his hand to help her up, she took it gratefully.

The music from the string of loudspeakers followed them as they sauntered towards the very heart of London. Their progress became slower as more and more people were squeezed onto the streets. Sensing Cissie's apprehension, Jake linked her arm through his and held tightly onto it with his other hand. She seemed to hesitate for a moment, but then he felt her grip on him tighten and she held onto him like a limpet. As well she might, since it was impossible to fight the surge as the crowds overspilled the pavements and spread out into the roads.

All manner of vehicles were inching their way through the pedestrians. A horse and cart packed with Australian troops plodded past, the occupants waving and cheering. A pony and trap, its driver and passenger with a large Union Jack draped across their shoulders. Civilians and figures in uniform sat astride beer barrels in the back of an open lorry, whooping and shouting. Other conveyances of all shapes and sizes with grinning faces poking out of windows. It was utter bedlam, the noise of so many raised voices thunderous, one deafening cacophony of unleashed joy shared by so many and topped by the jolly music blasting out over the public address system.

When they finally shouldered their way into Piccadilly Circus, it was jam-packed with revellers. The central fountain, boarded up for protection throughout the war and with its statue of Eros's twin removed, was acting as a precarious perch for some who, in their elation, had dared to climb it. Others had shinned up lamp posts to get a better view of the teeming multitude. Buses, advertising Schweppes, Hovis and Wrigley's on their sides, were attempting to crawl through the impenetrable human wall, constantly sounding their horns in vain confusion.

'Cor, I'm glad I'm not bleeding working today!' Mildred managed to yell above the chaos.

'You are tomorrow, though!' Jake shouted back with a grin. 'And it won't be any different!'

Beside him, Cissie had been enjoying herself until now, despite feeling a little nervous of the congestion. But the old fears were starting to clamp down inside her as she was physically crushed in the seething mass of humanity. She could see nothing but other people's backs hemming her in and panic was taking hold of her. She must gather enough strength to ask Jake to spirit her away before it overwhelmed her.

And then, by some miracle, a small space opened up in front of them like the parting of the waves. 'Knees up, Mother Brown' was blaring out over the loudspeakers, and a small group had started to dance — doubtless knocking others out of their way in the process. But Cissie could suddenly breathe again as several young women with Union Jack scarves on their heads, just like Mildred, were twirling about, linking arms with sailors in their distinctive, white-edged navy collars. Changing partners and whizzing round again.

Before she knew it, a uniformed soldier, fresh-faced but for a disfiguring, recent scar across his cheek, had grabbed her arm and dragged her into the dance. Round and round she went, passed onto the next, everyone hopping up and down, laughing, grinning. Totally innocent. Jake's face flashed before her as he, too, cavorted about, and then Mildred, grinning from ear to ear. The music penetrated Cissie's soul and she felt safe inside again. That unique sensation when she danced of being whole, of being *her*, in control, returned, and she threw herself into the frenzy, singing, a warm gladness filling her very core.

The tune ended, but was instantly followed by 'The Lambeth Walk'. She was off again, swaying her shoulders, her natural grace and flair not going unnoticed. People had stopped to watch her, for while many a young man that day was trying to kiss as many unknown but willing girls as he could, a few had been attracted to this lithe,

145

graceful figure that was moving so fluidly to the music.

'Hey, give us a kiss, honey!'

The words shot through her like a dagger. The same words as . . . She was pulled off balance and into the arms of a brawny GI, his forage cap askew above his immaculate uniform and his face grinning inanely as he brought his mouth down towards hers.

A storm of terror, of the memory, raged through her, blood spinning fast in her head. No! This time, she wasn't faint from pain and knocked half unconscious. She was *her*, she was strong. Her eyes snapped with ferocity as she lashed out against him, fighting in his hold.

'Get off me!' she screamed like someone possessed.

At once, she was freed. The fellow backed off, hands in the air and surprise written all over his face in clear letters.

'Sorry, lady, I-I didn't mean to offend,' he stuttered.

Jake had heard Cissie's cry. He could see the soldier was standing there in shocked embarrassment, other bystanders watching now. Jake felt he had to do something, though he wasn't sure what, and elbowed his way through. When he did, he saw Cissie's eyes were wild and enormous, and her face as white as a sheet as she stood, transfixed and staring at the man.

'Sorry, mate, it's not you. She had a bad experience with an American, that's all,' was the first thing that came into his head.

'Oh, I'm sure sorry for that. I apologise,' the

Yank stammered, doffing his cap. 'And I apologise for whatever it was my countryman did. Makes me feel ashamed. We Americans are meant to be good and wholesome.'

'Apology accepted,' Jake said levelly. 'Cissie?'

'Yes, I'm sorry, too,' Cissie's white lips somehow managed to articulate.

She flinched as Jake's arm came about her shoulder, but she didn't resist. She felt such a fool now, drawing attention to herself over an innocent gesture. And Jake hadn't been exactly off the mark with his 'fib', had he? She was grateful, though, for his support. And then Mildred was there, too, her face wrinkled fiercely.

'What the hell's going on?' she demanded, glaring at the Yank. 'You ain't hurt me friend?'

'No, no. Cissie had a funny turn, that's all,' Jake answered quickly before Mildred could draw any other conclusion. 'I think it's all the crowds. Let's see if we can get something to eat. I reckon she's a bit faint from lack of nourishment, to coin a phrase. OK, Cissie?'

Cissie nodded, unable to find breath for any more words as Jake gently led her away. She glanced over her shoulder, mouthing another apology at the innocent American who gave an understanding smile and a half salute. With Mildred bringing up the rear, they battled out of the main crowd and went in search of a British Restaurant. The government had set up nearly three thousand of these communal canteens throughout the country in whatever premises were available, run by volunteers such as the WVS so that they could offer inexpensive meals off ration. They had been a life-saver for many, especially those who had been bombed out of their homes.

When the happy threesome eventually found one of these establishments, as was to be expected, it was heaving and they had to queue for a place at one of the long trestle-tables. But once they were seated and had collected from the counter cottage pie and peas for sixpence each — not that there was any other choice — they were able to resume a proper conversation.

Jake poured Cissie a glass of water from the jug on the table and pushed it in front of her. 'Here, drink this,' he commanded. 'They say you can feel funny if you don't drink enough.'

Cissie nodded, and gratefully drank down the entire glass in one go before Jake refilled it. 'I'm so sorry,' she muttered, and Jake saw tears collecting in her eyes. 'I've spoilt your day.'

'No, you haven't,' Jake insisted. 'It was the crowds and then dancing when you hadn't had anything to eat or drink for some while. You're so petite, you haven't got room for reserves like the rest of us.'

'And it's turned so warm,' Mildred added. But she'd been mulling over the lie she'd caught Jake telling the GI. Was it a lie, though, or had he guessed correctly? 'But . . . is that what happened to you?' she asked gently. 'You said something yesterday about Yanks and wanting them all to go home. *Did* you have an argy-bargy with one of them? I mean, you don't have to tell us if you don't want to.'

Cissie's face drained of any colour it had and she blinked back at Mildred, unable to speak. Oh, dear God, no! They mustn't find out! But the horror of that night, the darkness and the pain, reared up inside her again. She tried to swallow it down, but it rose up in a tidal wave and her shoulders heaved as she began to retch.

'OK, OK.' Jake and Mildred were immediately one at either side of her. 'Deep breaths, in and out.'

She obeyed helplessly, her head swimming, a blind haze misting her vision. But slowly the nausea passed and the restaurant came back into focus.

'Better?' Jake's voice quivered with anxiety, and Cissie nodded, taking in another deep breath and letting it out in a long, steady stream.

'I really am sorry,' she murmured. 'I think I drank the water too quickly when I was so thirsty. That's all it was. Really. And that fellow, he just took me by surprise. I've never . . . well, I've never been kissed by a man, and it was just a bit . . . alarming. With all the crowds and everything.'

'Oh, is that all?' Mildred puffed out her cheeks. 'And a pretty girl like you ain't never been kissed? Well, I never. But you feeling better? You gonna be able to eat this now?'

Cissie studied both their kind, smiling faces and relief washed through her. That had been a close one, but she seemed to have put them off the scent. They were good, trustworthy people, mind, and a trickle of contentment had begun to flow hesitantly through her veins in their company. 'Yes, I'm beginning to feel quite hungry, actually.'

'Well, don't eat too quickly,' Jake advised, tucking into his own meal.

'And then what shall we do?' Cissie asked, neatly changing the subject.

'Up The Mall to Buckingham Palace, I reckon,' Jake suggested, digging his fork into his food. 'If you think you'll be OK, Cissie? There's bound to be thousands of people. We'll be packed in like sardines. But wouldn't it be fantastic to see the King come out on the balcony?'

'Yes. Yes, it would,' she agreed.

'I'll hang onto you, I promise.'

'And I'll be on your other side. Nobody'll get past me in a hurry. I'm used to giving people what for on the buses, me, if they misbehave!'

Mildred's words were spoken in such earnestness that they brought a smile to Cissie's lips, the incident with the GI all but forgotten. If only she could forget that *other* incident as easily. It was unlikely she ever would, but could she move forward with her life? A tiny voice inside was whispering that, with the unwitting support of people like Jake and Mildred, perhaps she could.

Time alone would tell.

13

They ate their lunch at a leisurely pace, and when it was over, retraced their steps to Piccadilly Circus where the giant Bovril and Schweppes Tonic advertisements had been illuminated on the Atlas Assurance Building, something else that hadn't been seen for nearly six years.

'Give Trafalgar Square a miss, shall we?' Jake suggested as they ambled down Haymarket. 'Unless you fancy cooling off in the fountains?' he joked.

'Yeah, with a hundred other people and your clothes going all transparent when they're wet?' Mildred snorted. 'Nah, let's go straight to The Mall. You ever danced in any of the theatres round here, Cissie?'

'No, but I'd love to. It'd be a dream come true.'

Oh, she was feeling so much better again. Almost normal, the dreadful, aching bitterness drifting away. With her new friends taking care of her, she felt she could relax and start enjoying herself.

They turned into Pall Mall, still swarming with celebrating hordes, but more bearable, until they took a left down Marlborough Road. As they came out into The Mall, not so far from the palace, they could barely move for the thousands of exuberant merrymakers, waving flags and yelling in abandonment. The roar of so many cheering voices was ear-splitting, the only coherence being the music that continued to be bellowed out from the tannoys.

Suddenly, as if by magic, the uproar began to die down and an extraordinary hush settled on the assembled multitude. Anyone who was still talking was instantly shushed, and Jake held up his hand to tap his watch. It was just coming up to three o'clock.

In moments, Winston Churchill's familiar, stentorian voice boomed over the loudspeakers, and everyone fell voraciously on his every word. He gave brief details, confirming what they already knew. In the early hours of the previous morning, German High Command had surrendered to the Allies and the Soviet High Command. The agreement was to be ratified that coming evening in Berlin, and hostilities would end officially at one minute past midnight that night, although the ceasefire had already been sounded all along the Front.

The revered Prime Minister went on to say that although that day they were enjoying their own celebrations, they were not to forget the Russians who had played such a huge and vital part in the victory. Mr Churchill then reverted to the habitual rousing rhetoric the country was used to hearing from him, rhetoric that had carried the nation through the bleakest days of the Blitz and the darkness beyond. A brief summary of the war followed in the most eloquent of language, and they were told that the evil-doers had now surrendered. Japan, though, remained unsubdued, and the task both at home and abroad must now be completed. Britain must continue to fight for the cause of freedom, and Mr Churchill concluded with an inspiring, 'God save the King.'

The adored voice of the nation's hero died away and a gasp of emotion rumbled through the gathered host as the 'Last Post' sounded, and then every pair of lungs joined in the National Anthem, before such a cheer as the world had never heard before swelled up in the warm afternoon air.

Cissie felt buoyed up by such jubilation, her heart touched by a sense of peace and freedom as she kept beside Jake, who was threading his way across the broad avenue and into the park, where the crowds were less dense. The revelling went on at a slightly more sedate pace, civilians and men and women in all different uniforms joining in the jollifications together. This time when a GI wanted to kiss her, Cissie mentally braced herself. But he merely brushed her cheek and went on to be lost in the crowd. Cissie breathed again. Was a little part of her beginning to heal? And all because of the kindness of Jake and Mildred.

They stayed in the park for hours, finding a quieter spot over on the far side of the lake. They sat and talked, laughed, got to know each other better. Cissie felt that she could only have celebrated better if she'd been on stage that night, but that would come. The incident with the American wasn't mentioned again. What had happened to her on that terrible night could not be undone, but perhaps with the friendship of such good people, she could learn to live with it. And perhaps she could start to look forward, just as Churchill had said the whole nation must.

They heard the King's speech being relayed at

six o'clock, and intermittent, distant roars as thousands shoehorned themselves in front of the gates of the palace whenever the royal family, including the two princesses, Elizabeth and Margaret, appeared on the balcony. With double daylight saving, dusk would be late, but Cissie, Mildred and even Jake were beginning to tire, and Mildred had an early shift to work in the morning.

'Let's just go back to the palace and see if they come out again before we go home,' Jake suggested. 'It mightn't be quite so crowded now, and it'd be a pity to miss it.'

'Yeah, all right. But I don't wanna wait too long,' Mildred told him.

They weaved their way back across St James' Park. People were spilling onto the grass from The Mall, building a bonfire with the park deckchairs. It seemed somewhat overindulgent, but who was going to stop them?

As they neared the palace, the area was slightly less manic now. They managed to climb the steps up to the Queen Victoria Memorial to get a better view and begin their vigil. But their patience was soon rewarded as another fanfare of cheering swirled through the air when the King and Queen and the princesses appeared yet again. From that distance, the figures were tiny and it was impossible to see any detail, even of what they were wearing. They could just about make out the waving arms, but what an experience to witness anyway, and with the yelling of the crowds all around them! And then, to the utter delight of the watching multitude, Winston Churchill stepped out onto the balcony as well — at least they guessed the additional figure was the Prime Minister from the deafening roar that exploded into the air.

'Mum'll be disappointed she missed this!' Mildred cried.

'Well, I'm sure you'll enjoy telling her all about it!' Jake shouted back to make himself heard. 'It'll be something to talk about for generations.'

The noise around them was tumultuous, and watching Jake and Mildred frantically waving their little flags and cheering for all they were worth, Cissie joined in. She, too, would relish telling her family all about it. For it was a moment she would never forget.

The hullabaloo eventually died down, the balcony now seeming empty again, and the crowd began to thin out a little.

'D'you think they'll come out again?' Mildred asked.

Jake gave a small shrug. 'I don't know. They must've come out more than half a dozen times, so that's probably it. It's getting late and people are starting to move away. I don't know about you, but I'm beginning to feel it's been a long day. How about you, Cissie? Are you ready to start making our way home?'

'It's been fantastic, but yes, I am. Thank you so much. I certainly wouldn't have had the confidence to come on my own. And it's been wonderful sharing it with you two. But I am really tired now.'

'Well, it'll take us a while to get home, even on public transport. The buses and trains are going to be packed, but it suddenly seems a long walk back.'

'Best foot forward, then!' Mildred grinned.

They set off, almost drunk with elation and weariness, smiles pinned on their faces. Jake glanced down at Cissie. He wondered quite what had triggered her reaction with the GI that morning, but he wasn't going to press her.

'Here, ain't that Princess Elizabeth over there in the WRAC uniform?' Mildred suddenly interrupted his thoughts. 'And Princess Margaret with her?'

'Surely not?'

'Well, I dunno. If they can do their bit for the war, maybe they wanted to mingle with the crowd and managed to get permission. Be a shame for them to miss out on all this. Bet you any money it'll be in the papers tomorrow that they was allowed out.'

'Well, maybe you're right,' Jake agreed. 'But for now, I think we should be heading home.'

They decided in the end to make use of the transport system anyway, even though it was so crowded. When they finally turned into Banbury Street, utterly exhausted, they found bunting strung between lamp posts and across the street ready for the street party the following day.

'It'll be mainly over by the time I get back off me shift,'

Mildred grumbled.

'Not sure it'll be my cup of tea,' Jake decided. 'More of a women's and children's thing. Think I'll be calling on some of my mates from work. See what they're doing for the day.'

Cissie's heart fell. Oh, she hadn't realised, but she must have been looking forward to the party.

Especially if she could sit next to Jake. When she was with him, she was beginning to feel a strange release from the darkness.

'Well, have a nice time,' she said, fixing a smile on her face. 'And thank you both so much for today. You don't know what it's meant to me.' More than they could ever imagine, she thought to herself.

They wished each other goodnight and went off to their relevant homes. Cissie went straight inside and closed the front door, but as Jake and Mildred turned into Number Eight, a big blackout blind, followed instantly by a second one, heaved its way outside. A pair of hands was visible around each one, and as the first one was launched onto the pavement, Eva's body appeared behind it.

'Well, we won't be needing them things no more!' she declared as Stan threw his out as well. 'Gonna break up the frames and have a bonfire at the end of the street tomorrow night. You two have a good time, then? Now, go on, Stan. Go and turn on the lights inside and let's see what our house looks like all lit up!'

She stood back, arms crossed determinedly over her grubby apron. You'd think her little house was a palace, Jake considered, and yet there was his mum in her curlers and slippers. He just couldn't help but burst out laughing.

* * *

'Now don't you go disappearing off to your pals before you help set things up,' Eva admonished

157

the following morning as Jake got up from the table after eating his breakfast — such as it was. 'I need you to help move tables and chairs out into the street for those what can't do it themselves, and anything else what needs a bit of muscle. No point having a strapping son if you can't make use of him now and then.'

Despite her chiding tone, there was a strong element of pride in Eva's voice, and Stan threw his son a surreptitious wink. 'The brewery's giving us several quart jugs of beer that'll be a bit heavy for some of the women to carry, so you can help fetch those, too. Pity you won't get to drink any of it, mind,' he teased. 'I know there ain't many of us men, but we'll have got through it by the time you get back.'

'Perhaps I won't stay long with my mates, then,' Jake replied, equally as jovial.

'Yeah, do come back early.' Eva stood up, jabbing her head at him with a wistful smile. 'We're kicking off at twelve, so Milly'll miss the first couple of hours or so. Would've been nice to have at least one of me kids there for the start.'

'Yeah, 'specially as your mum's done most of the organising,' Stan agreed.

'Well, I'll just stay for the very start, then. And when I get back, I'll come and play my guitar out in the street to make up for it.'

'Oh, would you, love?'

'Be happy to. Oh, is that rice pudding for the party?' Jake asked, eyeing up the large, chipped enamel dish on the table, the congealed contents of which looked thick enough to put a knife through. 'Probably need two of us to carry that outside,

158

too,' he grinned wickedly.

'Cheeky devil!' Eva flapped a handy tea towel around Jake's head, and he laughed as he pretended to fend her off.

'Right. If you want this table outside, we'd better get it cleared.'

They all set to work. Outside in the street, the bunting that had been put up the previous day, zigzagging overhead between lamp posts, fluttered in the light breeze. Neighbours were hanging out of upstairs windows, calling instructions to each other as they strung Union Jacks and more bunting across the front of their houses.

The Smith family, swelled by their resident relatives — grandparents, aunts, uncles, cousins — had spilled out of Number Five. Even Eva, who'd brought up six children in their two-bedroomed house while she'd had Old Sal living with them as well, wondered how on earth they all fitted in the one house. Among them were two adolescent boys who were known to get up to mischief. But Jake roped them in to lining up the tables and chairs in the middle of the street as he and Stan helped to carry them outside. Given jobs to channel their energies into, the boys proved quite useful and kept coming back to ask what they could do next.

'Morning, Jake.'

He turned round, and there was Cissie, smiling a little shyly at him despite having spent the whole of the previous day together and looking just as lovely. Jake gulped, almost wishing he hadn't said he'd meet up with his workmates. But he didn't want his attraction towards her to appear too obvious. He

159

had the feeling after that odd incident yesterday that he would need to tread very carefully.

'Hello, Cissie,' he beamed back at her. 'Smashing day yesterday, wasn't it? Did you sleep OK last night, or were you still too excited?'

'Come on, you two, no time to chat. Work to do.'

Jake was actually glad of his dad's joking reprimand, though he pulled a face behind Stan's back and then grinned at Cissie as he went back to the task in hand. Either tablecloths or old sheets were laid on the assortment of tables, which were then set out with crockery and cutlery. Vases with little flags standing in them ready for waving later on were placed along the tables at intervals.

Miss Chalfont had obviously purloined some supplies from her school and was busy keeping the younger children occupied with making hats, crowns for the girls and tricorns for the boys, although the latter were made from newspaper. A couple of women sported Union Jack aprons, and everyone was dressed in patriotic colours as best they could. Stan even wore a red, white and blue tie Eva had cobbled together for him from the offcuts from the bunting. It was a mess, but he hadn't the heart to refuse to wear it.

Finally, the food was brought out. A complete hotchpotch of whatever everyone could spare. Lots of sandwiches with just a smear of margarine and fish paste, or a wafer-thin slither of cucumber from an allotment or American tinned spam. The 'sausage' rolls, jam tarts and other cakes — sweetened with grated carrots to save sugar — that the cooking party had concocted the previous morning in Ellen's kitchen. Eva's rice pudding, several jellies and even a trifle, though where some of the ingredients for that had come from, Eva couldn't guess. Probably the black market!

They'd decided to keep separate at one end the jugs of beer donated by the brewery — Eva noted that Mrs Smith had her beady eye on that rather than the two bottles of port that had mysteriously appeared as well. Then there were bottles of lemonade and Tizer, and jugs of milk and water, whatever people had been able to get hold of. A few of the adults had volunteered to walk up and down, refilling the children's cups and generally keeping an eye on things.

'Right, everyone!' Stan shouted, clapping his hands to gain everybody's attention above the happy clamour. 'Children, take your seats, and adults gather round behind. Photograph time!'

It took a few minutes to organise, and then Ellen produced her late husband's Brownie camera and took several formal photographs. Stan noted a tear in her eye. He guessed she was remembering how her husband loved taking pictures, and he patted her shoulder to comfort her.

'I'll use the rest of the roll on informal shots,' she told him with a watery smile.

'Yeah, you do that, Ellen,' Stan said softly, and then he raised his voice again. 'OK, before we start, God Save the King!'

'God Save the King!' everyone chorused enthusiastically.

It was spontaneous, but Jake began to sing. At once, the whole street, apart from the very small children, joined in the National Anthem. And

161

when it was over, the walls of the houses reverberated with three ear-splitting cheers. And then another three when someone shouted out in praise of Winston Churchill.

'Right, I think we can begin now!' Eva declared.

Everyone dived in. This mightn't exactly be a banquet, but it was the best they'd seen in six long years.

'Well, I'm off now, Mum,' Jake said to Eva as she turned — as had many of the women — to go inside and brew a pot of tea to bring out.

'OK, love. And thanks for your help.'

'Have a wonderful time, and I'll see you later.'

Eva waited to watch her son turn out of the street. She thanked the Good Lord for this day. Jake would turn eighteen in a few short weeks, and if the war hadn't ended, he could well have been conscripted to go and fight. She shuddered at the thought, a cold iciness trickling through her veins. For what if she'd lost him?

She mustn't think like that. It was over. This street party was proof of that. She turned back to observe the festivities, much of which she'd organised. There were sixteen houses in the street, and with all the displaced relatives of the Smith family, they'd counted nearly seventy people. Mrs Duncan from next door whose husband was away in the army had three young children. The older couple from Number Sixteen.

The Gamlin sisters from Number Seven. The list went on. And there were Ron, Bridie with Jane, the only baby, on her lap, Zac and Cissie being welcomed by all the neighbours and chatting away like old friends.

Oh, yes. This is what it should be like. This was peace. They'd planned games for both children and adults when everyone had eaten their fill. The men had struggled and sweated but between them had managed to drag a piano outside, and they were going to have a proper knees-up with singing and dancing. Cissie had offered to bring out her gramophone later on. And, of course, Jake had promised to play his guitar and sing when he got back.

Ah, Eva released a deep, contented sigh. This was the beginning. A new life for them all. Whatever the future held, it could only get better.

★ ★ ★

At the same moment that Eva was surveying the Banbury Street party, two American soldiers were perched on the edge of a fountain in the square of a small French town in the middle of liberated France.

'Never mind victory. I sure as hell can't wait to get back home.' The sergeant in his once smart uniform — now somewhat the worse for wear after a year's fighting in France — smoothed down his hair and placed his cap at a jaunty angle on his head. 'These Froggy girls aren't what they're cracked up to be. Think they'd be darned grateful to be liberated an' pay us in kind, wouldn't ya?'

'Is that all ya ever think about?' The black GI sitting next to him frowned at his companion in disgust. Saul Williams had prayed nightly that he'd be transferred to a different squad. After all, forces were constantly being rearranged. But no. Fate seemed to have decreed that he should remain under Chuck Masters' command.

They had been among the infantry assault on the first day of the invasion of the occupied French coast and had been met with a hail of enemy fire as they'd fought their way up the beach, trying to avoid the wooden spikes, barbed wire and buried mines that had only been partially cleared. Utah Beach hadn't been quite as well defended as others, but it was still hell on earth. Chuck, it had to be said, had led his squad fearlessly, obeying every preordained command. When one of his men fell next to him, he'd pushed on without looking back.

But Saul couldn't leave the young GI. He had a bullet in his leg and, given the chance, would survive to fight again, but would surely be killed if he was left where he was. So Saul had risked his own life to get the youngster to relative safety before he somehow managed to meet up with the rest of his squad in the utter chaos.

They'd fought on. The high hedgerows and marshy nature of the land behind the coast had made for vicious battles. Ambushes were frequent, nerves jangled at every moment. It might have been easy to get lost and confused. They battled on through war-ravaged, shell-pocked towns and villages, sometimes building by building, dodging bullets, creeping up and lobbing grenades into machine-gun posts. Saul was good at that. He seemed to be blessed with natural stealth, and, as Chuck put it, his 'nigger' skin gave him added camouflage. He didn't like killing people. But it was kill or be killed.

Days turned to weeks. The Allies had pressed on against fierce resistance, slowly nibbling away. Villages began to fall. They heard horrific stories of innocent people — the elderly, women and children — being taken out and shot in reprisal for action by the French Resistance, or captured SOE operatives being brutally tortured. It had all brought tears to Saul's eyes, but Chuck always appeared unmoved. All he was interested in was saving his own neck, Saul considered bitterly.

Whenever they'd been part of a force that liberated a town or village, and the residents came out to thank them with gifts of wine or valuables or whatever they had, Chuck took everything that was on offer. Saul, on the other hand, delighted in dishing out cigarettes or candy and seeing the gratitude on the faces of those who'd suffered so much under the occupation. Once, when separated from the main division, their squad had freed a besieged farmhouse on its own. Chuck had at once taken up the offer of the old farmer's own bed for the night. Saul had slept with his fellow GIs in the barn. He'd hardly been surprised when on guard duty later that night, he'd seen Chuck lurch drunkenly outside, no doubt having worked his way through several bottles of the farmer's wine. But at least, as far as Saul knew, he'd had the decency to stagger outside before he threw up.

They'd been there at the liberation of Paris back in the previous August, although the worst of the fighting had been over by the time they arrived. While they were still stationed in the French capital, Chuck had taken himself off several times to the delights of the Bois de Boulogne — hangout of the local prostitutes. Saul hoped he'd get a good dose of the clap and be put out of action. Serve him right. But he never did, so he must have used the protection the US Army handed out to every soldier.

'Yeah, an' why not?' Chuck's hated voice snapped Saul back to the present.

'Ya know why not.'

The whites of Saul's large eyes glinted in the evening light that streamed across the square. He hadn't forgotten; the memory of that night in London made him feel sick with shame.

But his sergeant obviously hadn't forgotten either. He thrust his nose almost into his subordinate's face. 'I told ya before, ya mention one word an' I'll bring some charge against ya.'

'Huh. We're not gonna be in the army much longer. I'll go back to London, tell the authorities. I'm not gonna lie for you no more.'

'Ya do that an' I'll say it was you, an' then ya'll hang for it. An' I know where your family live, remember. Pity if their house burnt down an' them inside it. So ya just remember to keep your big mouth shut! No one's gonna believe a nigger over me. Ya not even supposed to be in my company. So shove off. I'd watch your own back from now on, if I was you!' He jumped to his feet and swaggered away across the square.

Saul clenched his full lips together, his heart enraged. He was never meant to be a soldier. He was a quiet man. Loved his mam and his dad and his sisters. How the hell had he got tied up with Chuck Masters? He rued the day they ever met.

14

'Hello, Bridie, love. Nice to see you. Wanna come in for a cuppa? Not too tidy, mind.'

Eva had been surprised to discover Bridie on her doorstep, since it was the first time her new friend had accepted her open invitation to pop round whenever she liked. Eva was still in her curlers and slippers as she wasn't expecting to go out, but Bridie would have to get used to taking her as she found her. And somehow she didn't think Bridie would mind one jot.

'Don't you be worrying about that,' the Irishwoman beamed, following as Eva beckoned her down the hallway. 'Just thought I'd get out the house for a few minutes while Jane's asleep. Sure, I don't know how my poor Ron stands it, staring at the four walls like that. He can't walk that far, so he can't. And it's getting even worse as he gets older.'

'You ain't got no wheelchair for him, have you?' Eva's kindly face pleated in concern as she indicated for Bridie to sit down at the table.

'They gave him an arm and a leg and a crutch all those years ago, and reckoned that was enough,' Bridie grimaced. 'But he could really do with a wheelchair nowadays. So now we're settled, I guess I can go through all the rigmarole of applying for one. Certainly can't afford to buy one ourselves just now, although things are easier now Zac's working. So grateful we are to your

Stan and Jake for getting him that job at Price's.'

'And how's he getting on?' Eva called over her shoulder, popping out into the scullery to light the gas under the kettle.

'Loves it, so he does,' Bridie replied as Eva reappeared. 'It was really good of that Belinda to listen to his needs and give him a test at packing rather than — what was it? — night-light wicking. Even cleaner work, and he's so neat and tidy that his hands became expert at it in minutes. He only needs to be shown a couple of times and he's got it. He says there's so many different ways that different candles are packed, it makes it interesting for him.'

'Yeah, lots to learn,' Eva agreed. 'Not as easy as it sounds. That's what our Gert did when she worked there. Got a bit boring sometimes, but on the whole, she quite liked it. So how does Zac like working with a load of women?'

'Sure, don't the older ones mother him, and he seems to have a bit of a laugh with the younger ones. Giving him confidence to be doing a job and doing it well, so it is.'

'I only hope it lasts, then,' Eva sighed, carrying in the kettle and pouring hot water into the teapot onto the same leaves they'd used for breakfast. 'Some people are saying Price's won't last with all the electric now. Or it'll get smaller, at least. But we'll have to see. But I've been thinking, we've still got my old mum's wheelchair at the back of the outhouse in the yard. Been out there ten years, but it might be OK. I'll get Stan to have a look at it for you.'

'Oh, sure, we'd be more than grateful! You're a

good friend, Eva.'

Eva felt herself blushing and flapped her hand dismissively. 'Well, I can't promise it'll be usable, but we'll see. And I'm afraid I can only spare a few drops of milk for your tea,' she concluded, passing her friend a cup of wishy-washy liquid.

'This rationing's enough to drive you to drink,' Bridie agreed. 'If there was enough of the stuff to be had, that is. All those celebrations a few weeks ago, and now what? Bacon ration cut from four to three ounces, and cooking fat halved. And soap cut down, too, unless you've a babby, so at least we should be able to muddle through with Jane.'

'I know.' Eva shook her head. 'Next thing is they'll be putting flipping bread on ration.'

'I wouldn't joke about that if I were you.'

'What!' Eva was horrified. 'You don't think they'll ration bread, do you? Not when it ain't been rationed all through the war? Even if it is this disgusting National Loaf stuff.'

Bridie shrugged ruefully. 'Who knows? Sure, the country isn't going to get back on its feet in a few weeks. And what with Mr Churchill resigning, who knows what'll happen to us next? I don't understand why Mr Attlee refused his offer to continue the coalition until after we've beaten Japan.'

'Wanting to force an election, my Stan reckons. Still in charge, though, ain't he, Churchill? And you must've heard his speech the other day. Said they're calling it a caretaker government or something. And that's what Mr Churchill promised to do. Take care of us.'

'Well, sure, cutting our rations when they're

meagre enough already doesn't seem too much like taking care of us to me. Much as I admire the man as much as anyone does.'

'Well, he'll get my vote when it comes to the election. Bound to win, though, ain't he? But life ain't gonna be easy for a while, I suppose. At least we ain't got to worry about no bombs no more, mind. It's just people like our Milly what's got someone still fighting against the Japs what's still got something to worry about.'

'Still trying to take that island, Okinawa, aren't they, the Allies? Been going on for weeks. One of the worst battles in the Pacific, they're saying.'

'Yeah, they are. I think it's mainly Yanks, but a lot of our boys are involved, too. Anyway, my Stan reckons once Okinawa falls — all these strange blooming names — the Allies'll be straight in to flatten the rest of Japan proper. You'd think that after seeing Dresden, the Japs'd blooming realise they're beaten and give in.'

'They're a strange people, so they are. Brainwashed into believing they should die fighting rather than surrender, even when the odds are totally against them. And have you heard about these young kamikaze lads they're calling them? Crashing their planes onto the Allied warships. Or at least trying to. They say they're virtually all shot down before they can do their worst. I don't know. All of it such a waste of young lives.'

'Yeah.' Eva gave a deep, wrenching sigh. 'Our Mildred ain't heard from her Gary for a while. She don't say nothing, but that's our Milly for you. Putting on her usual happy face. Yeah, terrible thing, war.'

170

'Well, I'll be praying to Our Lady that her young man comes home safely,' Bridie said, standing up. 'It's been nice having a chat even if we don't have as much to be happy about as we might've done after all the celebrations. Thank you for the tay, and for all the babby clothes and things you got for us.'

'Not at all,' Eva smiled, seeing Bridie to the front door. 'And I'll get the menfolk to take a look at that wheelchair for Ron.'

'Thanks, Eva. It'd make a real difference to him. See you again soon. And feel free to pop round to us, too, whenever you want.'

'Thanks, Bridie, I might take you up on that,' Eva winked. 'Ta-ta, then, ducks.'

Bridie turned to wave as she covered the few yards to her own front door. A good sort was Eva Parker. Bridie had the feeling that if she knew the truth, she'd be horrified at what had happened, but no way would she turn against them as others had. Bridie hated lying to such an honest soul. Not only did it go against her beliefs, but it would be such a relief to confide in someone outside the family. But for Cissie's sake, her lips remained sealed.

★ ★ ★

In the front room of Number Twelve, piano music was floating from the gramophone. Cissie was standing, one hand resting on the back of the chair, as she began the exercises to warm up her muscles. The time-honoured routine started with a *demi-plié*, full *plié*, rise and lower in each position with the appropriate *port de bras*, then turning to repeat on the other side. A series of *battements* followed, working through *tendus*, *soutenus*, *retirés* and *frappés*, all performed *en croix*. One of Cissie's favourites was *battement fondu*, a sinking or bending of the supporting leg while performing a *développé* with the other. Years of training, of precision, of control, allowed her to carry out the movements with intuitive perfection, and yet every cell of her mind and body was lost in concentration. Concentration that blotted out the anger, the bitterness and frustration. The pain.

Illogical resentment speared into her brain each time the record came to the end and it whirled round and round, the needle gliding over the soundless grooves in the centre. Cissie stepped across to replace the stylus at the beginning, her teeth gritted. How dare it interrupt the soft enchantment that swallowed her torment and allowed her to be free, to breathe again? But a second later, the gentle, inspiring tones of the music were filling her head once more, and she let herself sink into the passion that was her salvation.

There was a rough order to follow, building to the more extended, more difficult exercises. *Grand battement en croix*, raising the working leg to the front as high as it could go, then lowering it back down to fifth position. Repeat to the side, closing behind, repeat to the back, and then again to the side, closing in front. As always, back like a broomstick, hips square, legs turned out from the hip and straight as a die. Weight over the little toes of the supporting foot, working foot pointed and turned out as it soars through the air. Free arm fluid as it swoops through the accompanying *port de bras*, head turning, inclining or rigidly straight. Pulling her into some glorious world where nothing existed but grace and beauty and achievement, all else forgotten.

Damn. The music had ended again. She needed to get stronger. Her leg wasn't reaching the height it used to. Her hips needed to regain their old flexibility, the muscles in her back no longer of steel. *Battement cloche* would stretch them out, her leg swinging back and forth with the momentum of a bell. She'd change the music, a different rhythm. Perhaps something stronger would help.

On again, pushing and pushing. Her hips still didn't feel right. It *had* to come back, that sensation that she could fly, that her legs could reach any height she demanded of them.

Grand battement en rond. That was always the test. Raise the working leg to the front, rigid as an arrow, to hip level or higher. Then sweep it, fully extended and at the same height, all the way to the side and then through to the back. That transition from *seconde* to *derrière* was the ultimate struggle, as was the return.

Yes, it was good. But it wasn't good enough. Not for the principal dancer of the Romaine Theatre Company. Perhaps her mum was right. That she wasn't ready yet. But she *needed* it, to be herself, to be whole again. And this chair was useless. She needed a proper *barre* to work on. To be able to stretch her joints, to get back to where she was. And maybe *then* she'd find peace.

There was only one answer. She would finish the punishing regime she was putting herself through. She would wash and change. And then she would go to the call box and telephone the studio. If there was a class or rehearsal in progress, they might not hear. There might be no one there. The company toured the capital, after all. It didn't have its own permanent theatre. But as soon as she could, she'd be back in the studio. She had to be. Or else she'd go mad.

15

'Cissie!'

'Oh, you're back!'

'We've missed you! Are you better now?'

A chorus of welcome greeted Cissie as she walked into the dance studio. Her former colleagues, most of them female, left off their preparations for the class and hurried over to hug her, some with only one shoe on, the ribbons neatly about the ankle, others with the ties of their wrap-over cardigans trailing to their knees. A lump rose in Cissie's throat at the warmth of their friendship. She'd missed them so much more than she'd realised.

'It's so good to be back,' she managed to tell them, trying to conceal her deep emotion. And then guilt snapped at her heels as she said, 'And yes, I'm much better now, thank you.'

But was it truly guilt, or was it shame at the lie that dug its teeth into her? But she had to lie. Not everyone might understand, and she didn't want to feel shunned by anyone, not in this, the only place where she might find salvation.

'Ah, Cissie, *ma chérie*, it is so good to have my little star back!' Monsieur Clément, the dance master, strutted across the studio. The girls at once stood back, allowing him to reach Cissie. His face, with its oiled and twirled moustache, was beaming like a polished apple. He took Cissie's hands, brought them up to his lips and then kissed her on both cheeks for good measure. '*Mon Dieu*, you still look a little pale. You must only do a little work at the *barre*. We must build you up slowly. We do not want any torn muscles that will take months to heal.'

'I've been doing a lot of work at home,' Cissie assured him. 'So it's not as if I'll be starting from scratch. But I've only got the back of a chair, not a proper *barre* to work with. And I haven't got much room, either.'

'Well, you are returned to the right place.' Monsieur Clément nodded his head like a puppet. 'But I will not allow you to overstrain yourself before you are ready. Now, *mes jeunes*, prepare yourselves for class. *Vite, vite!*' he commanded, clapping his hands.

'So where did you go to get better?' one girl, Jo, asked as Cissie went with them to finish changing. 'An aunt of mine was sent to a sanatorium on the Isle of Wight. But she was there three years.'

'I was lucky they caught mine early. They sent me to Devon. On the edge of Dartmoor. It was beautiful. The air was so clean, it smelt different. That's why I got better so quickly.'

The lies tripped off Cissie's tongue so easily that she inwardly cringed. But then she spied Sean emerging from the gents'. Dear Sean, whose idea the deception had been when she had been so broken.

'Sure, isn't it my little bird!' he grinned, coming over and lifting her from her feet. 'Wasn't I over the moon when I heard you were flying home.'

Yes, that was just how she felt. That she was

coming home to the nest where she felt safe and secure. There were only four other male dancers. All the rest were girls. But every one of them wanted to welcome her back, all except one, who just nodded at her.

Cissie didn't care, though. She was there to dance, to let the old euphoria froth up inside her, to transport her to that other world where nothing else existed.

The class went on for nearly two hours with a couple of short breaks — and Monsieur Clément constantly ensuring she wasn't overdoing it. When they finished at the *barre* and came into the centre, it was as though Cissie's soul broke free. Her body swayed and bent and lilted like a flexible doll, arms floating through the air when a *grand port de bras* was incorporated in an *enchaînement*. She twirled across the studio in a string of *posé* turns, spun in a whirlwind of elation as she executed eight *ronds de jambe en tournant* and soared like a bird with the three *grands jetés en tourant* that she could fit across the diagonal of the studio.

Monsieur Clément clapped his hands, his face split in a grin of adoration. ' *Ma petite* Cissie, you have lost nothing of your grace. But that is enough. You will please go to the *barre* and do some gentle exercises to calm the muscles down while the rest of us continue. After our long break, perhaps you will stay to watch our rehearsal? It will help to exercise the mind and the spirit.'

Cissie didn't protest. Despite her work at home, it hadn't been quite the same, and she knew she had done enough on her first day back. She went

177

off meekly to the *barre*, her heart drumming with happiness. For at last, she was home.

★ ★ ★

'Sure, you're as good as ever.'

When the class was over, Cissie waited with Sean as he changed his shoes and pulled on some clothes over his dance wear. They were a little apart from the others, who respectfully kept their distance. They all knew Cissie and Sean had a special relationship and needed some time together.

'And *are* you fully recovered now?' he asked, raising a sceptical eyebrow. 'It hasn't been that long.'

'Long enough. And I *needed* to come back.' Cissie felt her pulse accelerate. She *had* to ask. 'And you're sure no one knows?' she quizzed him, lowering her voice.

'Not even Monsieur,' Sean assured her under his breath. And then his flecked, green eyes fixed on her face. 'You know, we could've done what I suggested. Said it was — '

'And who would've believed it?' Cissie gave a wry smile that spoke also of amusement and fondness. 'You're an angel and a good friend, Sean. But that wouldn't have been right.' Sean blinked at her, almost sadly. But before he could say anything, she went on, 'I understand Deirdre's been partnering you while I've been away?'

'She has so. And that probably accounts for the sour expression on her face. None too pleased to see you back, I don't suppose. She's good. But she's not as good as you and she knows it.'

'Yes, she was the only one who didn't give me a hug.'

'Ah, my two little doves.' Monsieur Clément interrupted their conversation as he padded up to them. 'I wish to talk to you. It will take two or three weeks to build up your stamina, I think, Cissie. But come to class every day and I will decide how to work you back into the performance. Perhaps I will create for you a solo that will be beautiful but not too tiring.

We will put our heads together, no? I promise we will revive *Tristan and Isolde*, but not yet. I think first, a *pas de deux* a little less strenuous when I feel you are ready. I am thinking 'Rhapsody in Blue' perhaps?'

'Oh, yes.' Cissie nodded thoughtfully. 'That's a lovely piece of music. It'd be a bit different.'

'And a little more *moderne*, perhaps,' the dance master beamed. 'So, we have a plan. *Bon.* Now then, Deirdre, come here if you would,' he called across the studio.

Cissie watched the other dancer come over to them. She didn't look too happy. But Monsieur Clément reached out and took her hand to silence her.

'Deirdre, you have been wonderful filling in for Cissie. But she and Sean belong together. There is magic in their dance. So, when she is returned to full strength, she will dance with him again in our main *pas de deux*. But do not worry. I create a new role for you, yes? You will still be a principal dancer, but I will choreograph solos for you instead. Now, off you go. Rehearsal begins in one hour.'

179

He trotted away, chivvying the chorus dancers as he made for the door. Cissie turned back to Sean, feeling happier than she had since . . . She'd begun to think she'd never be happy again. But perhaps she would, after all.

'Shall we be getting something to eat in the café round the corner?' Sean asked.

But before Cissie could answer, Deirdre poked her nose forward, face as dark as thunder. 'I suppose you think that's fair?' she spat.

Cissie blinked at her, shocked to the core, as Deirdre spun on her heel and stomped away. Cissie stared after her, disbelieving. The girl should think herself lucky. At least she hadn't been . . .

'Take no notice of her,' Sean advised. 'Can't I see the little green monster inside her?' he attempted to joke. 'Sure, she'll come to her senses when Monsieur creates something wonderful just for her. Come along now, and let's find what we can to eat.'

Sean put his arm around Cissie's waist as he directed her towards the door. But Cissie could feel Deirdre's eyes boring into her back. A shiver of unease slithered down her spine.

* * *

Two tall young men, accompanied by an older, slightly shorter fellow, turned the corner from Stanmer Street into Banbury Street. The older chap wore an old flat cap, while the two youths were bare-headed, but all three were dressed in workman's clothes. It was lunchtime one warm Saturday in June, and two of the three had

180

removed their jackets and carried them slung over one shoulder.

'See you Monday if not before, laddie,' Stan called as Zac turned into Number Twelve, and he and Jake went on to Number Eight.

Jake followed his father inside. He would definitely see Zac before Monday! Once he'd swallowed whatever Eva had rustled up for dinner, he was going to call on Cissie and ask if she'd like to go for a walk in the park. Mildred was on shift, so it would just be the two of them, and he couldn't wait. They'd become good friends in the six or seven weeks since her family had moved in. He wouldn't push her, but he was hoping that, in time, they could become more than that. And his heart beat harder at the thought.

'Hello, love. Hello, Jake,' Eva greeted them as they walked straight into the back room. 'Have a good morning?'

'Yeah, fine, thanks, love. Mmm, something smells good.'

Indeed, Jake's nostrils, too, flared as the aroma of some sort of stew wafted in from the stove in the scullery. Rationing hadn't improved and obtaining ingredients was still difficult, but his mum seemed to have learnt some tips from her new friend, Bridie, and her cooking had improved. Her old friend, Nell, had apparently been a good cook, too, but none of it had rubbed off on Eva at the time. In those days, she'd been too busy with their young family and caring for Old Sal, Stan had confided in his son. But now she had more time on her hands and they were all benefitting.

'Oh, Jake, there's a letter for you, love,' Eva

announced as she carried in the large saucepan of stew. 'Up on the mantelpiece. Looks like it could be from the fire brigade.'

Jake gulped down his heart that had jumped up into his throat and then banged against his ribs when it slotted back into its rightful place. It had been weeks since he'd written in, asking if he could train to be a full-time fireman when he reached the minimum age of eighteen in July and reminding them of how he'd been a runner for the brigade while the war was still on and had helped tackle blazes caused by the flying bombs. Now, the envelope fluttered in his shaking hands and he had to force himself to tear it open.

The typed words leapt about on the page as he strove to focus on them, sweat oozing uncomfortably from every pore.

This was it. His future. His eyes scanned the lines, his brain not taking them in, and then he went back to re-read them properly.

'Well?' His mum's face was beaming expectantly at his shoulder. 'You gonna keep us in suspenders all day?'

Jake couldn't answer. A lead weight had landed heavily in his belly, and he silently handed the letter to Eva. Her face was still bright as she read the letter, but the smile slowly faded from her lips.

'Oh, Jake,' she breathed, aching for her son. 'I'm so sorry, love. I know what it meant to you.'

A deep frown folded Stan's forehead. 'Why, what's it say?'

'They say they're sorry but they ain't taking on no one new,' Eva summarised, her voice portraying all the disappointment she knew her son was

182

feeling. 'It says the fire brigade'll be contracting now there ain't no more bombs. And even though it was a reserved occupation, some full-timers went to fight anyway, and when they're demobbed they'll have to try and find jobs for them first. Oh, but look here, Jake.' Eva tried to sound enthusiastic. 'They've said they've put your name on a list and'll let you know if anything comes up in the future. So all ain't lost yet, love.'

Jake gave his mother a wan smile. He knew she was trying to restore his hopes, bless her, but it wouldn't work. All his aspirations for the future had been torn to ribbons. He wanted to make something of his life. Like his elder brother, Kit, had done. And now it had been taken away.

'Oh, well.' He gave what he hoped appeared as a casual shrug. Deliberately tamping down his frustrations, he stepped into the scullery and out of the back door into the yard to shut himself in the lav. He needed a few moments to compose himself. He knew his mum and dad would share his disappointment, but for him it was more than that. Assisting the fire brigade had ignited a passion within him. Now his dreams lay shattered at his feet.

He would have to put on a brave face. Despite his feelings of defeat, he would have to pull himself together. He was almost eighteen. A man. Time to act like one.

So, what now? He certainly didn't want to work at Price's for the rest of his life. And it seemed to them all that Price's long-term future was uncertain anyway.

When Jake went back indoors, Eva was serving out the stew and ladled an extra large portion onto Jake's plate. He hid a wry smile. His mum's way of expressing her sympathy.

'I don't really want that much, Mum,' he said gently, scraping some back into the pan.

'You've got to eat, love.'

'I know, Mum. But a normal portion. I'm not that hungry.'

'So, you're gonna have to rethink things, son.' Stan's words were calm. Rock solid. 'Any ideas? Police, perhaps?'

Jake sucked in his lips. He knew his dad wanted to help, but first he needed to get over the emptiness that weighed inside him.

'Probably be the same story there,' he sighed. 'Anyway, it's not the same. And I wouldn't want to be dealing with criminals all the time. I'll have to reconsider my future now, I guess.'

'Well, you're young enough, so you've plenty of time.' Eva wagged her head. 'So eat up. Jam roly-poly for pudding.'

'With lumpy custard, just the way I like it?' Jake teased, fighting his way out of his dark mood.

'That's my boy,' Stan chuckled as Eva shook her head, not the least affronted. 'So, got any plans for this afternoon?'

Jake at once felt his optimism return, washing away the misery inside him. 'Yes. I thought I'd ask Cissie if she'd like to go for a walk in the park,' he answered, a blush scorching across his cheeks. 'It's such a lovely day,' he added, hoping he sounded nonchalant.

He caught Eva and Stan exchanging glances, but all anyone said was, 'Yeah, we must make the most of the good weather,' as they went on eating.

Jake couldn't wait for the meal to be over. If anything could soothe him, it would be seeing Cissie. Hopefully, he could get her out on her own, without Zac. Or without her parents, since now that he and Stan had repaired Old Sal's wheelchair, Ron was able to be taken on outings, too. And then there was the baby, of course.

Oh, Jake had everything crossed that his heart could be lifted by spending a couple of hours alone with the girl who both intrigued and enthralled him. Despite her initial coolness that he'd put down to caution now he knew her better, he'd found himself caught up in some glorious, mysterious web whenever he was with her.

'Is Cissie in?' he asked half an hour later as he stood on the doorstep of Number Twelve, excitement unleashed inside him. 'I wondered if she'd like to go for a walk in the park.'

'Oh, didn't Zac mention it?' Bridie looked mildly surprised. 'She's been back at the studio all week. Twelve till six, and tonight she's watching the performance. She'll be back on stage herself in a couple of weeks, so she will, five days a week. So she'll only be around on Sundays and Mondays, I'm afraid.'

Jake felt a sudden emptiness take hold of his heart. Not today, then. But he should be happy for Cissie, going back to what she loved.

'Well, I hope she's enjoying herself,' he managed to say without sounding too down in the mouth. 'Perhaps she'd like to come out tomorrow if the weather holds.'

'Oh, I'm sure she would,' Bridie smiled back. 'Her old dance partner's coming to lunch, but

185

you can all go out together afterwards. Haven't seen him for ages, and he comes from the same part of Ireland as me, so don't we always have a lot to talk about.'

Jake's hopes crashed down about him. First the letter from the fire brigade, then learning that he'd only be able to see Cissie on Sundays and possibly on a Monday evening, and now the worst of all. He had a rival, and someone from a world that was her life and that he could never hope to aspire to.

'Oh, well, I'll look forward to tomorrow, then,' he lied between clenched teeth. 'Thank you, Mrs Cresswell.'

He turned away, his heart dragging. Of course, he still wanted to see Cissie, but he'd just have to admire her from afar and keep his feelings to himself. But to see her with this other chap would be torture. Perhaps he'd find something else to do instead. Call on his mates, maybe. Go and kick a football around in the park. More fun than having his heart ripped out.

But try as he might to extricate himself from his tangled emotions, he felt drawn to Cissie Cresswell by some unbreaking, invisible thread.

16

Mildred wheeled her bicycle out onto the pavement and clicked the front door shut as quietly as she could so as not to wake the others, pausing for a moment to breathe in the new day. Although it was fully light, the hour was yet too young for the sun to have shown its face, but the still air promised a fair if cool July morning.

Mildred loved being up so early at that time of year, not minding one bit being on the first shift. The streets were quiet and unhurried, a peaceful prelude to the hustle and bustle that the rush hour would bring a little later. Only a few people were already preparing for the day ahead, for the first bus Mildred would be conducting was one of those transporting the earliest workers of the day to their place of labour.

Today, though, could be somewhat different. Whether or not it was Mildred's imagination, she thought she could sense excitement buzzing in the air. It was election day, and there would be many who wanted to cast their vote first thing in the morning on their way to work.

As Mildred pedalled to the corner of the street, she caught the familiar clippety-clop of horses' hooves on the tarmac and the tinkle of glass bottles. The milk cart turned into Banbury Street, the bay mare walking alone and coming to a halt on its own outside the first house, while the milkman took a bottle from the back, whistling between the gaps in his teeth.

'Morning, Norman,' Mildred called softly from the opposite side of the street.

Norman looked around, ceasing his unrecognisable tune, and his old face wrinkled into a gummy smile. 'Morning, Milly, love. You on earlies? I wanted ter get me round done extra early so I can go ter vote. I guess yer too young.'

Mildred nodded with a rueful smile and left him to put the full bottle on the doorstep and collect the empty one. At least she'd be able to vote when she came of age, unlike up until the end of the first war when no women at all had the right to vote. But it was still crazy, she considered as she made her way towards the bus station. People under twenty-one weren't allowed to vote, and yet they were old enough to be conscripted to go and fight for their country, and possibly give their lives in the process. People like her Gary.

She hadn't seen him since he'd left Britain two years ago, and hadn't even heard from him for some while. It wasn't entirely unusual not to receive anything for ages and then for several letters to arrive at once. She wrote to him every week, but she knew that many of her scribbles never reached him since he often complained that she hadn't written. She supposed they were flaming lucky if anything got through at all, given the circumstances. But the niggling doubt that something had happened to him gnawed away at the back of her mind all the time, even though she tried desperately to put it to one side.

The island of Okinawa had finally fallen three days ago, giving the Allies a base from which to start attacking the main islands of Japan, pounding Tokyo and other important cities into submission. It was all over the news. Had Gary played a part in it, gliding about beneath the waves and torpedoing Japanese warships? Mildred supposed he must have done. But submarines could be blown up, too. And there was something called depth-charging, wasn't there? But surely if anything like that had happened, she would have been told pretty quickly? And that was what she clung to.

It was so long since she'd seen him, mind, that every time she put pen to paper, it was almost like writing to a flipping stranger. Would what he'd been through have changed him? And how well had she known him in the first place? Certainly, their relationship wasn't like that between her mum and dad, who seemed to share one soul. Perhaps they could see that, and it was why they hadn't been keen on her getting engaged. She'd defied them, sincerely believing at the time that she was in love, but had she secretly been unsure, deep down inside?

She'd felt back then that she really needed more time. But time was something they hadn't had. And Gary had been so imploring, and she hadn't wanted him going off to war knowing she'd turned him down. It would have been cruel. But might it have been a case of being cruel to be kind? For now that she'd had two years to think about it, she wasn't entirely sure she still loved him and she felt trapped, whether she liked it or not. She just prayed that she'd fall in love with Gary all over again when he came home. If he came home. Of course, she wanted him to. She wanted every soldier, sailor or airman to return. But could she bring herself to hurt Gary if she found he wasn't the one for her, after all?

Oh, why was everything so complicated, and why did she feel pulled this way and that? She frowned to herself as she cycled onwards, deep in thought and grateful that there was very little traffic on the road to worry about. A flash of colour on the pavement opposite caught her eye and drew her from her ponderings. It was the woman who ran the flower stall round the corner, struggling along with a massive basket of bright blooms in each hand, and another strapped to her back. She must've been to the market at the crack of dawn, better now in July than in the depths of winter. Mildred took one hand off the handlebars to wave, and the flower seller nodded back with a cheerful smile.

Must be a blessed hard life for her, Mildred mused, outside in all weathers with nobody to help her, as far as she knew. And the poor woman probably didn't make much at the end of it. To top it all, the war had made flowers harder to come by, with growing food much more of a priority. Mildred had heard that in the West Country, they'd dug up all the fields of daffodils and thrown the bulbs into the hedges to make room for cabbages and potatoes and what have you instead.

But keeping up morale had been part of the war effort, too, of course. And that included fresh flowers, even if they were a luxury. A bit like — what was it Cissie had called it? — CEMA or something? Entertaining civilians or factory workers at home to help keep their spirits up.

Cissie's theatre company was concerned that now the war in Europe was over, CEMA was shutting down, although something called the Arts Council was apparently taking its place. But if the company's subsidy from CEMA wasn't replaced by one from this new institution, they'd have to work doubly hard to bring in the punters. Not Cissie's words, of course, but that's what she'd meant as they'd sauntered through Battersea Park together on Monday. Because of her shift pattern, Mildred had the three days off at the start of the week. Knowing Sunday and Monday were the equivalent of Cissie's weekend, she'd called round to ask if she fancied going out for a breath of fresh air in the park. And Mildred had an ulterior motive for doing so, too.

'You must be pleased to be back at work, though,' she'd gently prompted Cissie as they strolled across the grass, hoping to steer the conversation in the direction she wanted.

'Oh, yes.' Cissie sounded full of enthusiasm. 'It was a bit tough at first. Even having done a lot of practice at home, I hadn't built up my stamina enough. Doesn't take long, though, once you're back in the stride. I feel pretty much back to normal now. And Monsieur Clément — that's our dance master — he's choreographing a new piece for Sean and me. To 'Rhapsody in Blue'.'

'Ah, no, don't tell us,' Mildred giggled. 'Think I know that one. By your friend, Gershwin, ain't it?'

'As it happens, yes, it is!' Cissie laughed back. 'You're learning.'

'Yeah, not as daft as I look, me. A bit on the jazzy side, ain't it?'

191

'Just a touch. But that's what I like about our company. We have the freedom to do all sorts of things.'

'Yeah, I can see how much you love it.' Mildred tipped her head to one side as she contemplated Cissie's expression. 'You know, you're looking a lot happier now you're back dancing. Is it something to do with this Sean fella? Even came to Sunday lunch at yours recently, didn't he?'

'Yes, Sean's a good friend. He and Mum get on like a house on fire. They're both from County Tipperary, you see. Oh.' Her face suddenly stretched. 'You didn't think . . . Sean and me?' She broke off, shaking her head with a small smile. 'Oh, it's nothing like that. Sean doesn't, well . . . Don't get the idea all male dancers are like that, because it simply isn't true. But Sean's not like me and you, let's say. You know,' she concluded pointedly.

No, Mildred didn't know. A perplexed frown puckered her brow and then her eyes widened as the penny dropped. 'Oh, you mean . . . ?'

'Sean's kind and sweet and gentle. But there could never be any more than friendship between us. You see, he doesn't have an eye for the ladies, if you understand me. He, well, he prefers other men. You're . . . you're not shocked?'

'Er, no. Just surprised, I guess. I mean, I've heard of it, but never known anyone . . . But it's illegal, ain't it?'

'Only if you're practising, shall we say. Sean just admires from afar.'

'Oh.' Mildred couldn't think of anything else to say and, once again, was bewildered by Cissie, who seemed to take some things for granted and yet, in other ways, was so sensitive. But more than anything, Mildred was swamped with relief. She knew Jake held a torch to Cissie. He'd not said anything outwardly, but it was obvious. And he'd been proper down in the dumps since he'd clearly got the wrong end of the stick about this Sean chap. Now Mildred could put him right about it.

And she had done so with great glee when Jake had got in from work that evening. Optimism had bloomed on his face.

'Oh, well, then, d'you fancy going to the flicks tonight, Mill? Anything on you'd like to see?' he'd asked at once, almost without a pause to think. 'We could ask Cissie if she'd like to come with us.'

'Want me to play gooseberry, do you?' Mildred had teased.

No. Cissie and me'd be going just as friends,' Jake had replied awkwardly. 'We could ask Zac as well, to make up a foursome. Be rude if we didn't, anyhow.'

Mildred smiled to herself now as she applied the brakes to turn in at the bus depot. They'd had a good evening, the four of them, and Mildred felt proud that she'd set the ball rolling for Jake. There was hope for her little brother's love life yet! She just wondered how her own affairs would turn out.

She secured her bike in the bicycle rack, bidding good morning to her colleagues as they all trooped into the office to clock on. Drivers had to collect keys and conductors their ticket machines. Mildred chatted to her workmates as they waited patiently in the queue. They were a mix of older men who'd been over the age of conscription and women who'd taken over the jobs of the younger men who'd been called up. Mildred hadn't seen any of them for a few days, of course, but catching up properly would have to wait until their break.

'Here, have you seen Bev?' Mildred gazed around anxiously before consulting her watch. Time was creeping on.

Their bus was due to leave soon, and so far it didn't have a driver! Bev had never been late, and Mildred imagined she'd come running up at any second. But by the time it was Mildred's turn at the desk, there was still no sign of her. 'D'you know where Bev is? Me driver?' she asked, starting to panic.

The clerk at the desk looked up at her and then called across to the manager. 'Miss Parker's asking about Bev Grainger, Mr Grimwald.'

The older man came over, his expression serious. 'I'm sorry, Miss Parker, but I'm afraid I had to let Mrs Grainger go.'

Mildred frowned at him, uncomprehending. Bev was a good driver and always on time. Mildred didn't understand. 'You given her her cards? What'd she done to deserve that?'

'Absolutely nothing. But some of the men who worked here before have been demobbed and want their jobs back, and I'm obliged to re-employ them.'

'What! Did you hear that, girls?' Mildred raised her voice to get the attention of the other women still in the office. 'They're giving our jobs back to the men! I know I ain't been doing this as long as some of you, but there's those here what's risked

194

their blooming lives all through the Blitz to keep the buses running, and now they're giving us the sack!'

A disgruntled murmur hummed through the room, with many a cross muttering. But Mr Grimwald held up his hands to silence them.

'I really am sorry, ladies. But it's a directive from the government, so there's little I can do about it. I'm sure I can speak for the public when I say we're all really grateful for what you've all done throughout the war. But men are being demobbed who have families to support, so you can see the sense of it. Now, I can assure you that we're considering each case carefully. And everyone who leaves will be given a good reference if they are indeed seeking employment elsewhere.'

'Leaves? Given the push, you mean!' Mildred scoffed.

'In some cases, I'm afraid it might come down to that, Miss Parker. But some may be pleased to leave. While you were off the last few days, Mrs Grainger volunteered to go. Her husband's coming home next week, and he's got a good job to go back to, so she was happy to leave. Now, everyone, you have buses and passengers waiting, so may I suggest you get on with it?'

'Huh, while we've got jobs to go to, you mean?' Mildred grumbled, picking up her ticket machine and money bag. And slinging the straps over her shoulders, she stalked out towards the bus garage.

'It had ter happen, Milly,' one of her friends acknowledged with a sigh.

'Yer must've seen it coming, love,' said one of the men.

195

Yes. Mildred knew very well she had seen it coming. But it seemed outrageous now it had actually started happening. It was so unfair when so many women had given their all to the war effort. Not just in public transport, but in munitions factories, the services and all manner of ways. But jobs for the lads who'd risked their lives in the fighting also seemed fair. Mildred could see that, too.

Nevertheless, a white line of anger surrounded her pursed lips as she weaved her way round the other vehicles to her own waiting bus. She just prayed she wouldn't be one of those to be *let go*. Her family weren't exactly destitute, but they weren't well off, either, and she liked to pay her way. She'd probably find some other sort of employment, but the thing was, she loved her job on the buses and couldn't imagine doing anything else.

So what might she be forced to turn her hand to? Her sister-in-law, Hillie, Kit's wife, had four younger sisters. What were they doing?

The youngest was at grammar school and the next one up was at art college and planning to go on to train as a teacher. One of the older ones was a Land Army Girl. She'd always been animal mad and was hoping to study to be a vet when things settled down. The other one was a nursing sister at the famous Queen Victoria Hospital in Sussex where they specialised in pioneering plastic surgery for burn victims, notably pilots who'd been shot down during the war.

Now Mildred couldn't imagine herself working on a farm or as a nurse. Either stinking manure or blood and vomit. No thanks! Even if she didn't dislike animals and her sympathies for the patients were as strong as anyone else's. And she knew she wasn't bright enough to be a teacher, so what the hell could she do if she was forced to give up being a clippie? She hadn't much liked working in a shop, which was what she'd done before going on the buses, and she hated the idea of being cooped up in an office. Above all, she wasn't going to work at blooming Price's like her sister, Gert, had all those years ago!

Bitterness was rumbling away inside Mildred's head as she rounded her own bus, and she took a step backwards at the uniformed figure perched on the open platform, apparently waiting for her. Seeing her approaching, the man got to his feet and held out his hand.

'Hello. You Mildred Parker? I'm Oscar Miles, your new driver. Pleased to meet you.'

Mildred peered up through narrowed eyes at a disgustingly handsome, if a trifle gaunt, face that met her gaze with a cautious smile. Mildred scowled back, ignoring his proffered hand as she stepped up onto the platform.

'Wish I could say the same,' she said haughtily, reaching up to change the destination scroll. 'Hadn't you better start her up if you're gonna do my friend's job properly and run on time?'

The fellow blinked at her, then, with a resigned sigh, walked round to the front of the bus and swung himself up into the driver's cab.

Mildred glared down the rows of seats at the outline of his back as the engine growled into life. Oscar. What sort of a bleeding name was that? A bit posh for a flaming bus driver, wasn't it?

As the bus pulled forward, joining the queue of

197

vehicles waiting to turn out onto the road, Mildred's lips bunched into a rebellious knot.

★ ★ ★

Eva shuffled up to Number Eight and put her
heavy shopping bags down on the pavement while
she opened the front door.

She'd had to queue again for ages to get enough
food for the four of them to last the weekend,
and her legs were aching from standing still for
so long.

She'd blooming well had enough of it over
all those years. Two months it had been since
Germany had surrendered, and things weren't
getting no better. Worse in some ways. It was
even rumoured the government was sending food
abroad to formerly occupied countries including
Russia, as well as to Germany itself. But people
there were literally starving, whereas at least Eva
could just about feed her family, even if it did take
some effort. And, when all was said and done, she
supposed most German civilians were as innocent
as those who'd had to suffer in Britain.

Eva found herself lost in thought as she lugged
the shopping down the passage and into the
kitchen at the back. Before she'd gone to do battle with the rationing queues, she'd stood waiting
in another one, except that it had moved a lot
quicker. Since all people had to do was officially
identify themselves and then cast their vote.

But during the wait, she'd overheard some alarming discussions among other voters. Churchill an
old man, must be worn out. Great leader in time

of war, but wasn't it time for a change? Did they want to go back to the poverty and lack of jobs they'd had under the Tories before the war? If you think we had it bad, what about the poor devils up north? Wasn't it time Labour had another chance of being in power? They've hardly had a look-in. And do you remember the Beveridge Report? Labour seemed quite keen on that. Wouldn't it be a fine thing if it came about? Imagine a free health service for all, just for starters. Wouldn't get that under the Tories, I'll be bound. If you vote Tory, you'll be voting for the party, not Churchill. He wouldn't have the same sort of say he'd had during the war.

As Eva put the shopping away, she felt her hackles rise. They were going to have to wait three long weeks for the election results to be announced so that the votes from personnel still serving overseas could be included. After the comments she'd heard in the queue, Eva dreaded what the outcome might be.

She was a working-class woman, not like some of the toffs she worked alongside in the WVS. Yet her loyalty to Mr Churchill was unshakeable. She was sure he'd back the proposed new welfare state, even if the idea had initially received a lukewarm reception from the Tories. But that had been back when they had a war to win, which was surely more important at the time? And whether directly or indirectly, Churchill had kept all her family safe throughout the war. All they needed now was for Mildred's Gary to come home in one piece. The boy wasn't exactly what Eva had wanted for Milly, but Milly had been adamant she loved him, so for her sake, Eva prayed for Gary to come home safely.

So absorbed was she in her ponderings that the knock on the front door made her jump. Oh, she wondered if it was Bridie. If she wanted to push Ron round to the polling station in the wheelchair, with Zac at work and Cissie having left for the studio by now, there'd be nobody to mind the baby. Bridie couldn't push the pram as well, and it wouldn't be safe for Ron to hold Jane on his lap with only his one arm as they manoeuvred up and down kerbs and across roads.

Eva's heart lifted. She'd be more than happy to oblige. Jane was a placid little soul, and there was nothing Eva liked more than children. Much as she was pleased that Kit and Gert had both moved on and were making a success of their lives, she regretted that her five grandchildren didn't live on the doorstep, and Jane would make a good substitute for an hour or so.

When Eva opened the front door, however, she found not Bridie but a telegram boy on the doorstep. Fear at once stampeded through her, making her heart hammer. Her brain immediately flew to all her chicks. But surely there was no reason why any of them should be in trouble. Gary, then. Oh, Lord. How the flaming heck could she break any bad news to Milly? But the telegram was addressed to her, not Milly, and Gary had put Mildred as his next of kin with his father being long dead and his mother estranged. So that wouldn't be it.

There was only one thing for it. Open the envelope. The only time Eva's hands had shaken like this was when the V1 had fallen on Price's, and she felt her mouth go dry. But when her eyes managed to focus on the thin brown paper, her terrors were swept away so instantly, she felt faint.

Rob home stop ring me stop

'Any reply, missis?' the boy asked.

Eva's face lit up like one of the neon lights that shone out brightly in the West End again. 'Nah!' she beamed back, going to shut the door.

'Good news, then, missis?' the boy persisted almost cheekily, and then Eva realised what he was waiting for.

'Just a minute,' she said, bustling inside to get her purse, and then handing the boy a thrupenny bit.

'Thanks, missis,' the boy nodded, and ran off.

Eva didn't hesitate for a moment. Purse still in hand, she shut the door behind her and hurried round the corner to the telephone box. Never mind about the shopping. Her Gert's hubby was home! Time to celebrate.

17

'OK, then, love. See you, then!' Eva raised her voice above the pips and then the line went dead. No point putting in extra pennies when they'd made all the arrangements. Oh, life was truly beginning to look up, and Eva made no attempt to conceal the smile on her face as she left the telephone box and headed back to Banbury Street.

'Hello, Eva!' she heard someone call. 'I was just coming to see you.'

Eva turned round and saw Hester Braithwaite hurrying to catch her up. Well, at least she'd have someone to share her news with. Hester wasn't a terribly close friend. In fact, they'd been almost enemies at one time. But Eva appreciated that Hester had swallowed a great deal of pride in the past, and had suffered in her own way. She'd lived at Number Three opposite with her husband Charles, a senior manager at Arding and Hobbs, although they'd moved out before the war. Eva and Hester had kept in touch, though, and were friends of a sort. However, on Eva's part, it was more because Gert and Hillie had remained good friends with Charles and Hester's daughter, Jessica, and had corresponded by letter throughout the war while she'd been stuck out in Nigeria.

'You're looking very pleased with yourself, I must say, Eva,' Hester greeted Eva in her usual tight-lipped way.

'That's 'cos our Gert's hubby's home at last.

202

You remember him? Rob? And they're all coming up to stay at Rob's parents' house next weekend for a welcome home party,' Eva beamed back. 'So I rang Hillie, and she and Kit can come up with the children on the Sunday, so we can have a proper old knees-up.'

'Oh, that is good news.'

Hester's reply was polite, but sadly Eva detected a little envy in it, too. So she tried to suppress her own elation as she went on, 'I'm sorry. There's me wittering on when it must be hard for you with Jess and Patrick and the children so far away.'

'That's what I wanted to speak to you about,' Hester frowned. 'I had a letter from Jessica this morning. Now the war's over, she wants Charles and me to go out to Nigeria and meet Patrick's family before they come back home. I can't speak to Charles about it until he gets in tonight, and I just needed someone to talk to.'

'Of course, dearie.' Eva could see that Hester looked a bit nervy and put a sympathetic hand on the woman's arm. 'Come back to mine, and I'll squeeze a cuppa out of this morning's leaves.'

'Thanks, Eva. You're a good friend,' Hester answered, falling into step beside her.

'Hmm, going to Africa,' Eva murmured, thinking aloud. 'I can understand why you feel nervous about it.'

'Nervous isn't in it,' Hester moaned, wringing her hands. 'They wanted us to go with them when they had the tribal ceremony out there after they were married. You remember? That was back in thirty-six. I was too frightened to go. Didn't fancy such a long sea voyage, and then all that strange

203

food. I managed to put it off, but then they wanted us to go with them when they went back in thirty-nine. But just think, if we had gone with them, we'd have got trapped out there, too!'

'Well, you didn't.' Eva paused outside Number Eight to fish her front-door key out of her purse. 'And if you had, well, it'd have been a sight safer than London! The Nigerians did a lot to support us during the war, and a lot of their young men joined up and died fighting in the Far East. Yeah, you should be honoured to go. But what we doing standing here on the doorstep? Come on in.'

Eva opened the door and stood back to let Hester go in first. Always liked to show Hester she had manners. It was a sort of rebound action from when Hester had looked down on her. Engrained so deep that she still couldn't quite throw it off despite herself. But it had come as a huge shock to Hester and Charles that their daughter had fallen in love with an African tribal prince — even if he was such a lovely chap and a highly respected, qualified dentist to boot. And Eva couldn't help but appreciate Hester's present concerns.

Nevertheless, she disguised a sigh as she followed Hester along the passageway to her own back room. She'd try to prop the other woman up a bit. Because that was what Eva Parker did. But she'd far rather have been popping round to Bridie's, or across the street to Ellen Hayes, to share her own good news. But that would just have to wait.

★ ★ ★

204

Oscar Miles skilfully reversed the bus into its parking bay at the depot. Empty now of passengers, Mildred had watched him through the glass that separated the driver's cab, wanting to pour scorn on his ability and willing him to make a mess of it. But she had to admit to herself — grudgingly — that he carried out the manoeuvre perfectly, turning his head from side to side as he used the mirrors to line the bus up dead straight.

Just for a second, Mildred experienced a twinge of admiration, but she instantly quashed it. He must be in his late twenties or thereabouts, so had probably driven a bus for a couple of years or so before he'd been called up. And maybe he'd been a lorry driver in the army or something, so he jolly well ought to know what he was doing. But whatever his driving pedigree, she wasn't going to give him the satisfaction of congratulating him on his prowess.

He hadn't even turned off the engine before she jumped off the open platform at the back of the bus and hurried towards the office to hand over to the relief crew. They'd already had a short break after the rush hour was over and the timetable became less frequent, which allowed them a little respite between runs. But now it was considered their lunch hour, even though it wasn't yet midday.

Mildred went straight to the ladies' and afterwards washed off the grime from handling money and inky tickets all morning. Then she made her way purposefully to the canteen where dinner was being served. It had been a lifesaver during the war when food had been so scarce. And still was with supplies and food rationing not having improved as yet. She was grateful to sit down at the long table with a good plate of something resembling Lancashire hotpot and join her mates who were gradually coming off duty.

'So, what d'you think of it, then?' she demanded, spearing her fork into the stew. 'I don't want to give up me job if I can help it.'

'Me, neither,' Freda Green agreed, bobbing her head. 'But if the government's said we have ter, then we do.'

'Well, I'm the same as Mrs Grainger,' Iona Pauncefoot declared. 'My husband's been promised his job back at Head Office, and I'll be quite happy not to have to work any more. My mother looks after the children, but she's getting on and I think it's a bit much for her.'

'It's all right for you if you've got a husband,' Mildred frowned between mouthfuls. ''Specially if he's got a good job to go back to. But it ain't so good for those of us what ain't. I mean, I can see the point of it for men what's got families to provide for. But for those of us what still need a job, it ain't really fair. Not till we've found something else, anyway.'

'You gonna speak up fer us all then, Milly?'

Mildred drew in a deep, thoughtful breath and held it, closing her teeth over her bottom lip. She knew she could be outspoken when she wanted, but she wasn't sure she could make any difference in this situation.

'I could have a word with the union rep,

I suppose,' she answered, screwing her lips together. 'I could at least suggest we could each get to say if we'd be happy to leave or not. That'd be some sort of reasonable compromise, I guess. But I'll speak to Mr Grimwald first and see what he has to say.'

The group of women nodded their heads in agreement, and then got on with the business of eating. Mildred was still mulling the situation over in her mind when Freda dug her in the ribs.

'There's yer new driver,' she whispered in Mildred's ear. 'Looks like he's coming over. He can drive my bus any day! Bloody good-looking if you ask me.'

'Oh, shut up,' Mildred snapped. 'Probably already spoken for. And don't look at him. Then he might go somewhere else.'

Mildred locked her gaze on her food, hoping and praying that Oscar Miles would get the message and go away. Her stomach rose in rebellion when he put his tray down on the table and sat down opposite her.

'Do you mind if I join you, ladies?'

A bit late to ask, Mildred silently scoffed, and could have throttled Freda when she smiled up at him angelically and said, 'No, course not.'

Oscar took a sip from his mug of tea and then picked up his knife and fork. 'I hope you'll forgive me for taking your friend's job,' he apologised, looking directly across at Mildred. 'But it is my right, and I'm not the only one. There'll be thousands of transport workers being demobbed who want their jobs back. And factory workers and all sorts.'

'Yeah, but not driving *my* bus.'

'I'm sorry you feel that way, Miss Parker. But it's really not my fault. I could ask Mr Grimwald to swap me to someone else's crew if you object to me personally. But you're likely to get teamed up with someone who's been demobbed in the end.'

'If I manage to keep me job,' Mildred retorted acidly.

'If you keep your job, yes. But look around. There's already a few of us who've come back. Faces you won't recognise. And there's going to be a lot more.'

Oscar's gaze swept about the canteen before coming to rest resolutely on Mildred's face again, and somehow she felt compelled to stare back. His eyes were an arresting, uniform chestnut that seemed to bore steadily into hers with a deep intensity she couldn't escape from. And, curiously, didn't want to. But she wasn't going to let him get the better of her just because he had nice eyes.

'Well, I just hope you're gonna tell me you need the job 'cos you've got a wife and kid to support,' Mildred challenged him. 'Otherwise it don't seem fair to have got Bev thrown out.'

His eyes didn't leave her face but darkened to a near black, and hard lines deepened about his mouth. 'Don't forget your friend volunteered to leave,' he reminded her brusquely. 'And for your information — not that it's any of your business — no, I don't have a wife, but I do have a frail mother and a younger sister to provide for. I hope that satisfies your criteria,' he

208

concluded tersely.

Mildred felt herself suitably reprimanded and knew that colour was flooding into her cheeks. But she wasn't her big-hearted mother's daughter for nothing. 'Yeah, it does,' she conceded, her voice softer. 'But I'll be fighting to keep me own job if someone tries to make us leave.'

'That's your prerogative, of course. And hopefully it won't come to that and there'll be enough jobs for everyone who wants one. But I hope we can work together OK in the meantime. However, I'm sure you'd rather enjoy your lunch with your friends, so I'll leave you in peace.'

He went to pick up his tray, but before he could get to his feet, Freda piped up, 'No, don't mind us. Been a bit short of decent male company the last few years.'

Mildred tried to kick Freda gently under the table, but her foot only found air. Damn, she was going to have to put up with this la-di-da fop over dinner as well! She noticed, though, that Oscar Miles had the grace to blush slightly and hesitate for several seconds before he replied awkwardly.

'Well, if you're sure. The other men I see weren't particular friends from when I worked here before the war. Those I was friends with, well, we were all conscripted in different directions and we lost touch.' And then he lowered his eyes and muttered under his breath, 'Of course, some of them won't be coming back at all.'

He shot Mildred a dark glance before digging his fork into his portion of the stew, but that was as far as it got. He didn't appear to have much appetite, pushing the scant cubes of meat about his plate without anything actually reaching his mouth.

It made Mildred feel a prick of guilt, and since nobody else seemed to be able to think of anything to say, she felt obliged to do so herself.

'Yeah, it's hard, ain't it? Me fiancé's out in the Far East on subs. I ain't heard from him in a while, so I'm hoping no news is good news.'

'Well, I do hope he comes home safely,' Oscar said, looking up. 'Must be horrible for you. Seeing chaps like me coming home.'

There was a sharp edge to his voice, which wasn't lost on Mildred. 'Yeah, it is,' she admitted. 'But it's still good to see people coming home in one piece, whoever they are. Suppose I've been lucky, only having one person to worry about. Me brother-in-law was wounded slightly and went back to fight in France, but he's OK and must be coming home soon. Me older brother's got an important job on the railways, so he was exempt. And me other brother's only eighteen next weekend, so he was too young.'

'You must've been pleased he was never called up, then.'

'Yeah. But he was a firefighter. Unofficial, like. A runner for the brigade, but he helped put out fires and all. Wanted to be a fireman, but it's the same blooming story. They don't need so many firemen now the war's over. He works at Price's Candle Factory, but he don't want to stay there. Don't know what he's gonna do, now.'

Mildred wasn't sure why she was telling Oscar Miles, of all people, about her family, but it seemed to have put the conversation back on an even keel. The other women found their tongues again, especially Freda, whose eyelashes suddenly took on a life of their own.

When the meal was over, Oscar offered round a packet of cigarettes, and even Mildred deigned to accept.

'Right, we've got ten minutes,' Oscar announced, consulting his watch. 'See you back on the bus, Miss Parker,' he nodded at her, and made his way towards the gents'.

'Cor, ain't he gorgeous?' Freda swooned at his departing broad shoulders.

'A bit posh to be driving buses, though, don't you think?'

Iona queried in her usual condescending way.

Yeah, he is, Mildred thought to herself. Bit of a mystery, Mr Oscar Miles. But what did it matter to her? She could maybe tolerate him as her driver, but that was about it, as far as she was concerned. She'd be pleased when the shift was over and she could go home and spend the rest of the afternoon with her mum.

* * *

'See you tomorrow, then, bright and early, Miss Parker.'

Oscar gave a tentative half-smile as they clocked out. Mildred had to admit to herself that she really had no grounds to object to him personally, and her own lips curved at the corners in return.

'Yeah. And you can call us Mildred if you want.'

She saw him raise a sceptical eyebrow. 'Why not, if you'd allow me? And Oscar's a lot less formal than Mr Miles. And I've answered to Sergeant Miles for such a long time that Mr Miles doesn't sound right any more.'

'Oscar it is, then. Not a name I'm used to, mind.'

She couldn't believe it when his mouth broadened into a grin. 'My father's choice, I'm afraid, God rest his soul. Think yourself lucky having such a lovely down-to-earth name.'

'Yeah. Me mum's Evangeline, though, but she makes sure everyone calls her Eva.'

They stood for a moment, smiling at each other, before Mildred dragged herself away.

'See you in the morning, then,' she called over her shoulder.

But an instant later, Oscar had caught her up. 'How do you get here if we're running the first buses?' he asked. 'A pretty girl like you walking the streets when it's so quiet . . . ?'

'Nah, got me bike,' Mildred assured him with a chuckle. 'Harder to catch, me.'

'Ah, right. I'm pleased to hear it. Well, take care of yourself, then. I'm off to vote on my way home. I imagine you're too young.'

Mildred at once snatched in her breath as the hairs on the back of her neck bristled with indignation. OK, she was too young to vote, but did she look like a child? Oscar Miles immediately went down in her estimation again. She could maybe put up with working with him, but she certainly didn't want to be friends!

She strode off towards the bicycle rack, and didn't look back.

18

Private Saul Williams hesitated on the corner of the London back street, nervous sweat seeping from every pore of his dark skin, despite the cool July afternoon. Was this the right place?

It had been well over a year and so much had happened since.

But he'd bet his last American dollar it was.

In his head, he'd retraced his steps on that night a million times. Normally he probably wouldn't have been able to. It had been just one more darned evening to kill among the tension of manoeuvres down in what the British cutely called the West Country. Something big had been afoot, and it didn't take a genius to work out that it was going to be the invasion of occupied France.

It was almost impossible to relax, nerves jangled as they'd awaited the order for the big push. So when the squad had been granted a seventy-two hour pass, some of them had decided to jump on the first train up to London. Maybe they'd find sufficient entertainment there to take their minds off what was in store. And for Saul and others of his race, it meant more freedom. Black GIs weren't supposed to mix with the locals, but in the capital, nobody seemed to care.

That night back in May the previous year, Saul's heart had sunk when Chuck Masters had announced he was coming with them. 'Got to keep an eye on ya black bastards,' he'd pretended to joke. But Saul knew he meant it. Except that it was more the other way round.

Chuck liked the ladies, and Saul knew he thought he'd have a better chance of a one-night stand in London than in the local towns and villages of Devonshire. The train had arrived in time for them to check in at a boarding house they'd been recommended before the pubs opened. As soon as they had, Chuck had started drinking heavily straight away, going from one pub to another on the hunt. As the evening wore on and he wasn't having much luck picking up a willing girl, he'd become more and more drunk and abusive. He was unpopular with his squad, and the other soldiers had made themselves scarce. But Saul — God knew why — had stayed by him. God-fearing and teetotal, he supposed he must have wanted to keep Chuck out of trouble. Chuck might be Saul's sergeant, but they hailed from the same small town in Alabama, and Saul supposed he must have felt some sort of responsibility towards him, even though it put him in such an awkward position.

By the time Chuck was almost legless and declaring that he wanted to find a brothel instead to satisfy his needs — Soho was the place, wasn't it? — he was so drunk that Saul had been relieved when he'd persuaded him that they should return to the boarding house. He only managed to do so by suggesting they go straight to Soho the next evening. Quite what would happen then, Saul didn't know. But he'd probably wash his hands of Chuck and go off with his fellow GIs instead.

But with what happened later that first evening,

his relief had turned to guilt, a guilt that had consumed his every waking hour since. It had torn at his soul, so painful that he'd wished one of the bullets that had raked across the sand as they'd landed on the French beach code named Utah would blast into his chest and end his misery. It hadn't. While many others fell, both he and Chuck Masters had fought on unscathed, liberating towns and villages until Hitler had been defeated.

Life meant nothing to Saul. He might have been floating through France on a cloud, so oblivious was he to any danger. The memory of that night in London had never left him. His own shame and horror at what had happened, at what he'd been helpless to prevent, had sharpened his perception, forming a crystal-clear record of events. And that was how he'd found his way back to the street Chuck had lurched into, drunk and brimming with alcohol-fuelled anger, despite Saul's protestations and efforts to direct him back to the boarding house where they were staying.

Yes, he was sure this was it. The image he had formed in his head was exactly the same as the one that presented itself to him now. They'd been there in the blackout, of course. But a bright, three-quarter moon had drifted overhead, and though the sky had been banked with clouds, whenever they parted, the street had been bathed in silvery, liquid light. A few houses on the right, then a small park. And opposite was the bomb site, still waiting to be cleared. The bomb site where . . .

Jeez. The bile rose into his throat, and he had to take a determined hold on himself. What the hell was he doing here, in this place that filled him with self-disgust? But something had compelled him to come. Exactly what, he couldn't say. But deep in his gut, he knew it was the right thing to do. He could never forgive himself if he didn't at least try to make amends. Though he knew it simply wasn't something you could ever make amends for.

Some boys were playing among the rubble of the bomb site, digging for any trophy, a piece of shrapnel, some lost remnant of the lives of the people who'd once lived there, since it looked to Saul as if it had been a residential street. He picked his way over the debris, his heart thumping as he relived those dreadful moments.

'Hey, guys, can ya help me, please?'

The boys, five of them, looked round at his voice. Their eyes widened at the sight of a black American in the familiar GI uniform. It wasn't something they'd seen around here too often, though, and Saul cursed the colour of his skin. He hadn't wanted to draw attention to himself. That was why he'd chosen today to come. Election Day. He'd hoped everyone would be too distracted by voting fever to take much notice of some Yank making enquiries. But he'd been wrong. Generally speaking, the British didn't hold the same prejudices as many Americans still did — particularly in southern states such as his own. But he realised with unease that he stood out like a sore thumb. Nothing was going to put him off, though.

'Yeah, what d'yer want?' demanded one of the boys, possibly the ringleader, Saul thought, by the way he swaggered forward. He reminded Saul of

Chuck, and it made him shudder. 'It'll cost yer.'

Saul's full lips broke into a forced smile, revealing teeth that seemed to gleam like tombstones. 'What d'ya prefer?

Chocolate bars or candy? Or maybe gum?' He reached into the ample pockets of his uniform to retrieve a few of each but swiftly held them on high as the boy tried to snatch them from his hands. 'Ya answer my question first. I'm looking for a girl — '

'Oh, yeah?' the boy sneered, glancing at his mates, who sniggered behind their hands.

But Saul was determined not to be intimidated. 'Yup, a girl. About eighteen or nineteen. Only so high, very small build. Moves very gracefully. Yeah, that's what I remember most about her.' Saul frowned to himself, trawling his memory. The moonlight shafting across her face. 'Long neck, long, dark hair. Pretty face. Lives around here some place. Walks home on her own late at night.' But what he couldn't say, what would have seared into his tongue, was the word for what had been done to her.

The boy in front of him now pulled a face. 'Yer know some girl like that?' he leered lopsidedly over his shoulder at his mates. But he was answered by a chorus of shaking heads. 'There. D'we get our payment now?'

Saul sighed and brought down his hands to offer up the sweets. He doubted these kids would've told him even if they'd had any ideas as to who the girl could be. It was going to be like looking for a needle in a haystack, but he was driven by some inner compulsion to push on.

Presumably the girl had been on her way home at that late hour, and Saul remembered which direction she'd been heading in before Chuck had started chasing her. Saul walked down the street to where three houses still stood at the far side of the bomb site. The first one was clearly unoccupied and possibly bomb-damaged by its half-destroyed neighbour. Saul didn't get an answer to his knock on the next door, and at the last one, an elderly man shook his head in reply to Saul's question.

The street ended at a T-junction. Which way? Saul could only guess. But he had all afternoon and the evening, too. He'd go so far along on one side and then try the other way. But there were side streets galore. The girl could live anywhere, if indeed she still did. It was hopeless, but he had to try. He'd give himself the rest of the day and tomorrow. And if he'd had no luck by then, he'd go back to base and give up.

It seemed a modest but respectable area. Apart from the boys on the bomb site — and after all, boys would always be boys — he encountered no scruffy urchins playing on the streets. The houses were in neat terraces, attractive with little front gardens, dating possibly from the very beginning of the century — or the Edwardian period, as Saul had gathered the English called it. Somehow it pleased him to think the girl lived here rather than in one of the East End slums he'd heard about. Hitler had done a good job at slum clearance, he'd heard someone joke — in bad taste as far as Saul was concerned. But even here, there was the odd gaping hole where a house or two had been blown to smithereens. Bizarrely, it reminded Saul

219

of his grandmother and her missing teeth.

He stopped and asked a young mother with a pram who'd eyed him suspiciously, an older woman carrying her shopping, and anyone else he passed. But the answer was always the same as when he knocked at each house in turn.

'Could be anywhere, dear,' a sympathetic old lady told him as she peered out from behind her front door. 'But I was just putting the kettle on if you'd like to come in.'

Something twitched inside him. He could do with a cup of tea, but it worried him that the old lady was so trusting or maybe lonely that she'd ask a complete stranger into her house. And he was wary from his home where any innocent act by a black person could be turned against them, so he replied politely, 'That's very kind of ya, ma'am, but I'd best get on.'

'That's a pity, young man. But I wish you luck.'

Luck? He'd need more than luck. He'd need a miracle.

He turned into yet another street. Jeez, it was such a labyrinth that he was no longer sure he could find his way back. The place was getting busier as people were coming home from work. Saul sighed and consulted his watch. He was tired, hungry and thirsty. He'd just try this road, and then attempt to retrace his steps.

A prim-looking woman in her forties or thereabouts opened the door to the fourth house down, gazing accusingly at him over her horn-rimmed spectacles.

'Yes?' she demanded, making Saul feel awkward and rather stupid as he gave out the spiel he'd repeated so many times that afternoon that it had become mechanical. What was the point? his brain thought while his lips moved of their own accord. She wouldn't know anything. It was a lost cause.

Something, Saul wasn't sure what, flitted across the woman's face. Just for a split second. Saul's heart rose on a crest of hope. And then the woman's expression hardened before she shook her head and all but slammed the door in his face.

Saul stood on the step, a deep frown creasing his broad forehead. Did she know something? Recognise his description? Something jerked in his chest. Was he getting near?

With renewed vigour, he began knocking systematically on each door. Some faces were blank. Others curiously veiled over. They knew something. She was here. Somewhere. Saul could feel it in his bones.

'Sorry. We've only lived here a few months. Doesn't ring a bell. Try next door. The old busybody knows everything. Or thinks she does.'

Saul smiled his thanks and turned away. Next door was the last house in the street on the corner. Ah, well. He might as well drag himself up the short front path to speak to this busybody neighbour, though he doubted he'd get any joy.

The girl who opened the door was of such a similar age to the one he was seeking that Saul almost recoiled and had to steady himself. He could see instantly that it wasn't her, but just for a second . . .

He smiled shakily as he repeated his description, watching as the girl's eyes widened and then settled steadily on his face as he finished.

She didn't speak, her cheeks draining of their colour. Saul held his breath, pulse hammering as he waited. The girl hesitated, glancing down the street as if checking that nobody was in earshot, her mouth half open as if trying to formulate some words.

'Who are you, then?' a voice demanded from inside, and a woman's head appeared round the door behind the girl.

'Good evening, ma'am,' Saul smiled politely, hoping the quiver in his words wasn't obvious. 'I'm trying to find a young lady I met somewhere near here a year or so ago.' And he described the girl for the umpteenth time.

He couldn't believe it when the woman's face fairly sparked with distaste, setting some sort of panic rampaging through his body. Did she immediately dislike him because of his colour, like so many people did back home? Or — ?

'Oh, I know who you mean!' she spat viciously. 'You don't want anything to do with her, the little strumpet, I assure you!' And with that, she yanked the girl, her daughter presumably, inside and slammed the door.

Saul stood there. Poleaxed. Unable to move. He'd been beginning to think he'd imagined the whole affair. That being with Chuck Masters that night had been but a nightmare in his sleep. But now he knew he was right. The girl existed. But he knew nothing about her. And maybe Chuck wasn't so far off the mark. Walking home alone, late at night. Maybe she wasn't of good repute. But whatever her circumstances, she hadn't deserved

222

what had happened. And perhaps it wasn't the same girl the woman was referring to, anyway.

Saul turned away, his head a swirling vortex of emotion. He needed to think, to consider. He needed to get back to the cheap boarding house where he'd taken a room for the night. Get some sleep. Maybe come back tomorrow and see what else he could dig up.

He rounded the corner of the street back the way he'd come. He was so lost in thought that when he felt a sharp tap on his arm, he nearly jumped out of his skin. He looked down to see the girl he'd spoken to so briefly at the last house. Where had she sprung from? Surely he'd have heard her running up behind him? But then it dawned on him that it was a corner house and she'd slipped out of a side gate from the back garden.

'If it's the same person, I can tell you a bit more,' the girl said urgently. 'She and her family lived next door until a few months ago. She'd just had a baby. And she wasn't married. No sign of a steady boyfriend, even. Everyone shunned her. You can imagine what my mum was like towards her. Well, they were driven out, moved away. But I think . . . ' She glanced nervously over her shoulder, but then fixed her gaze on Saul's face. 'One night, there was a terrible commotion. My bedroom's at the front, so I saw. She was a dancer, you see. So she used to come home late after the performance. But that night, she hadn't shown up. Her family went out to look for her. Calling her name. That's what woke me up. They must have found her eventually and brought her back. I was still awake and went to look out of the window.

She was in a right state, crying, could barely walk. I remember thinking she looked as if she'd been attacked. I mean, I couldn't see that well. It was dark, except for when the moon came out. And soon afterwards, some policemen arrived. Anyway, nine months later, the baby came along. I think I was the only one on the street who felt sorry for her. We'd been sort of friends, you see. But . . . the baby couldn't have been yours. It was . . . very white. Look, I'd better go before my mum catches me. Her name was Cecily Cresswell. Cissie for short. If you find her, say hello to her for me.'

And then the girl was gone. Like a sprite. Leaving Saul reeling. Cecily Cresswell. A dancer. It all added up. Made sense. And the poor kid . . . Oh, Jesus, it was far worse than he could ever have imagined.

He staggered off down the street.

★ ★ ★

'That's fabulous news!' Stan and Jake chorused that evening when they got in from Price's. 'Rob home, at last!'

'Well, you can imagine our Gert's cock-a-hoop,' Eva crowed back. 'I can remember what it was like when you got back from the first war, Stan. Had to pull us down from the ceiling, I was that blooming happy.'

'Missed me charm and me good looks,' Stan grinned, catching her about the waist.

Eva flapped him away. 'Give over,' she laughed. 'So they're all coming up to stay at Rob's parents' next weekend. They're having a welcome home party for him there on the Saturday afternoon. So I've invited everyone here on the Sunday for your birthday, Jake. We'll have a bit of a knees-up. I rang Hillie, and they can come and all.'

'Oh, that's great, Mum, thanks! Works out quite well, 'cos I was planning on going out with some of my mates on the Saturday night.'

'Cor, me little brother eighteen,' Mildred teased. 'Proper grown-up.'

'Huh, not that it'll do me much good, not with the fire brigade not wanting me,' Jake grumbled. 'Not sure what I want to do with my life now.'

'Well, at least you've got this party to look forward to. That should cheer you up,' Mildred said pointedly.

'Yes,' Jake muttered half-heartedly. And then a sudden light shone into his thoughts. 'Tell you what. If it's going to be for my birthday as well, can I invite Cissie? Don't see much of her now she's back dancing.'

Eva made a deliberate effort not to exchange knowing glances with either her daughter or Stan. They could see Jake held a torch to young Cissie.

'Course you can, love,' Eva beamed. 'In fact, I thought it'd be nice for all her family to come along and meet all of ours.

Don't seem to have none of their own.'

'Thanks, Mum. That'll be great,' Jake said nonchalantly.

'Right, well, that's settled, then.' Eva's brow folded into a frown and she scratched her head. 'Better start working out how the blazes I can feed everyone, mind.'

'Easy. Ask everyone to bring something,' Mildred chimed in. And then she turned to Jake with a wink and whispered under her breath, 'Be better than anything Mum'll rustle up.'

Jake couldn't help but smile at the mention of Eva's lack of culinary skill. But the thought of Cissie coming round had lifted his heart even more.

* * *

Cissie sprang up onto the platform at the back of the bus, returning the conductress's smile as she went to sit down on the long sideways seat. It wasn't that the bus was full. Just the opposite, in fact. But over the past few weeks, she'd become friendly with the clippie whose bus she'd caught most nights and was looking forward to chatting with her.

'Yer looking chipper tonight, ducks,' the older woman beamed. 'Performance went well, did it?'

'Oh, it always has to,' Cissie told her earnestly. 'If it doesn't, you can get a bad reputation, or people won't come back again. But, no. We've had some good news. We've managed to book Wimbledon Theatre for three months, starting the first of August. Often, we only get town halls or whatever. So to have a long run at a proper theatre is very welcome.'

'Yer gonna get digs there, then? By the time yer get a train from Wimbledon ter Clapham Junction, yer could miss the last bus, and it wouldn't do fer a pretty kid like you ter be walking all that way alone late at night.'

A dagger sliced beneath Cissie's ribs, shattering

226

her joy at performing Monsieur Clément's flowing, fluid interpretation of 'Rhapsody in Blue', and performing it to perfection. It was only when she was dancing that she felt alive again. Alive, vital, *worth* something. And now the kindly woman's well-meaning words had destroyed the peace that was slowly melting the ice that had frozen solid inside her that night on the bomb site . . .

She had to force the shadow of a smile to her face. 'Yes, they're arranging digs for those who want them, so I probably will,' she muttered. And suddenly she was back, lying on the rubble in the dark, shame and pain flaming into her spirit and body as if trying to rip out her insides. She felt stifled, head spinning as if she'd pass out, and she ran a desperate hand around the neck of her cardigan.

'Here, you all right, love? Yer've gone all pale.'

Cissie panted out heavily a couple of times as the inside of the bus swam back into focus. 'Yes. Yes, thanks, I'm fine. Still a bit hot after the performance.'

'Well, yer ain't got far ter go once yer get off, have yer?'

Cissie managed another small smile. 'No, thank heavens. Just round the corner. I'll be home within a minute.'

Yes, that was another good thing about Banbury Street, she thought to herself. Buses stopped almost at the end of the road, and she only had to walk past a few houses to her own front door. And, of course, the street lights were back on, which made her feel a lot safer.

It had been a good move in more ways than

one. Everyone had fallen for the white lie, hook, line and sinker. It was a lie that hurt no one, but one that had saved her sanity. Banbury Street had offered them a fresh start, and where else would they have found such generous, kind-hearted people as the Parkers? Eva, who'd taken them under her wing in her chaotic, loving way; Mildred who was merely a younger version of her; kind, quiet Stan. And then there was Jake.

Oh, Jake. He was lovely. She could sense how he liked her. And she liked him. But . . . oh, God, she could never bear for a man to touch her in *that* way ever again. Even if it was someone she loved. It wouldn't be fair to give Jake the wrong idea. No. Better to stamp it out right from the start.

So perhaps moving to digs for three months was just what was needed.

19

Cissie sat on the kerb outside Number Eight, knees drawn up beneath her skirt to protect her modesty. Her eyes were closed, face tilted towards the afternoon sunshine that kissed her skin with a soft bloom. Summer seemed to have arrived, at last. About flipping time, she could hear Mildred saying, and the memory brought a soft smile to Cissie's lips.

Ah, Mildred. What a good friend she was proving to be. They might only have known each other a few months, but they'd felt like bosom pals almost from the start. Strange really, considering how different they were. And yet perhaps that was why. Cissie wondered if one day she could trust Mildred with the truth. It would be a release to share it with someone from outside her family.

Mildred's young nephews and her niece were engaged in a game of hopscotch chalked out on the pavement. Gert's three boys were, of course, erupting with excitement to have their daddy back home for good, their exuberance reflecting in their high voices as they played. Cissie let the happy sounds wash over her. Through the open front door of the house behind her, the joyful noise of Jake's birthday party going on inside wafted onto the street. The warm sun was easing the tension in Cissie's heart, and the distinctive smell of baked, dusty tarmac filled her nostrils. For the first time since . . . since *it* had happened, she almost felt content.

In her head, the music began to play. She was flowing, bending, to 'Rhapsody in Blue', but then her mind drifted to *Tristan and Isolde*. They were reviving it at rehearsals, ready to add into the show at Wimbledon Theatre. It was nearly six months now, and her body was strong enough to cope with the extra vigour required for the controlled intensity of strict classical ballet and the demands of the pointe work. But to dance it again, to lose herself in her art, would help bring her peace and restore her sanity.

'Hello. You had enough of my boisterous family, then?'

Cissie opened her eyes and squinted up at the familiar form silhouetted against the glaring light. Her face spread into a smile as Jake squatted down on the kerb beside her.

'Oh, I think your family are all lovely,' she assured him. 'I'm so glad I've had the chance to meet them all. Now I'll know who they are when you talk about them. And I think it's great the way you're all so close.'

'I reckon we have Mum to thank for that.' Jake gave a wry chuckle. 'There was only her and her mum. Her dad had swanned off when she was little. So she wanted things to be just the opposite for us.'

'Well, she's certainly achieved that. Mind you, she's so outward-going, I think she'd have created an extended family one way or the other, even if she hadn't had so many children herself. And she seems as thrilled as Gert is to have Rob back home.'

'Yes, Mum lives for us children,' Jake agreed, bobbing his head up and down. 'But, talking of Rob, I think I told you that before the war, he was senior clerk at a major branch of his bank. Well, the deputy manager's about to retire, and they've told Rob he's in line for the job. Anyway, he says he might be able to get me a job as a junior clerk if I'm interested.'

'Oh.' Cissie cocked an eyebrow and glanced at him sideways. 'That'd be different from being a fireman.'

'Yes, I know.' Jake released a pent-up sigh. 'But that doesn't look on the cards now. I'd really only been hanging on at Price's as a stopgap before the fire brigade. So I'd never really considered anything else before, let alone office work.'

'But would it be just office work, or would you be dealing direct with members of the public, as well?'

'I don't know. I think it'd depend on exactly what was on offer. But I was always good at arithmetic at school, and I enjoyed it, too.'

'Well, I think you're very sensible to consider your other options. There's no harm in waiting to see exactly what comes up, is there? You can't judge until you know.'

'How very wise. And thanks again for the tie. It'll be perfect if I do start work at the bank.'

'My pleasure. I'm glad you like it. It's hard to know what to get people when there's not much around. I had plenty of clothing coupons, but there wasn't much choice, of course, when I actually went to buy it.'

'Well, I think it's perfect.' Jake smiled at her,

231

springing to his feet. 'It's chaos inside,' he grunted, jabbing his head towards the open front door. 'Think I'll grab my guitar and sit out here with you and play. If that's OK with you, of course. Don't want to spoil your quiet moment.'

Cissie twisted her neck to gaze up at him. 'No, I'd like that very much. I've only heard you play a couple of times, and it was super. I love any sort of music.'

While Jake popped inside again, Cissie turned her attention back to the street that already felt like home. Ellen Hayes was coming back with little Lily who was pushing a toy pram. She waved cheerily across at Cissie.

'Been to the park, Mrs Hayes? Lovely day for it.'

'Yes, it is. We're coming over to join the party a bit later. Eva asked us.'

'I think she's invited the whole street!' Cissie laughed back, and watched as Mrs Hayes helped her daughter lift the doll's pram up the steps to their front door.

'Nice lady, Mrs Hayes,' Jake commented, reappearing behind Cissie with his guitar and lowering himself down beside her.

'Yes. My mum's become good friends with her, too. It's so good to have such nice neighbours.'

Jake paused for a second or two as he tuned the strings on his guitar. He might have been wrong, but he thought he'd caught a hint of bitterness in Cissie's voice. But then, so many of her former neighbours had died when the V1 had fallen on Islington that she'd be bound to feel angry about it for the rest of her life, so it was no wonder really.

Beside him, Cissie was determined to bury her rancour, though it was caused by something entirely different from what Jake had imagined. But that was all in the past, she told herself. She had a new home now. A new future, with new friends like the Parkers, especially Jake and Mildred. Above all, she was back dancing, performing on stage where her soul belonged.

Jake had started playing, strumming gently on his guitar. It was a beautiful instrument with a mellow tone, and Cissie admired the dexterity of his long, artistic fingers. It wasn't often she had the opportunity to study the small orchestra of the Romaine Theatre Company, but when she did, she was always enthralled and fascinated by their talent. She couldn't imagine knowing exactly where to hold down the strings with each finger. It was a mystery to her. All she knew was that the music penetrated her inner being, soaked into her mind, overwhelming her soul until every muscle itched to dance, to translate into movement whatever emotion the melody inspired in her heart.

Listening to Jake crooning softly beside her, it was impossible for her imagination to keep still. Behind her closed eyes was the image of a dancer interpreting every note. Jake was a talented musician, but his voice was even better, soft, lyrical, full of expression. Not just singing, but *performing*, making each note *mean* something. Touching her heart.

Now he was singing 'When You Wish upon a Star', his voice low, like velvet. Cissie's head was swinging to the slow rhythm, calm, relaxed, excited, all at once. It was all so harmonious, sitting there in the quiet afternoon sunshine, that when Jake came to the end and moved seamlessly on to 'Summertime' from Gershwin's musical, *Porgy and Bess*, Cissie was helplessly overcome. She found herself on her feet, swaying to the mesmerising melody. Her dancer's spirit was captivated, entranced, as her arms began to stretch and float, forming shapes in the warm, golden air, her long neck bending like a weeping willow waving in the breeze. Her feet trailed behind the swooping of her body that rippled and flowed, enraptured by every rise and fall of the music until Jake lifted his voice to the final crescendo and faded the tune to an enchanting, tender close.

Cissie was holding a finishing pose in *attitude grecque* and slowly drew herself from the bewitching dream. She glanced round, suddenly embarrassed, heat raging into her flushed cheeks. But the children were still playing hopscotch and nobody had been watching her dancing in the street. Except Jake, whose eyes were studying her, unblinking and intense.

'That was beautiful,' he murmured. 'I can't wait to see you performing on stage.'

Cissie gulped hard. 'You're pretty good yourself. Maybe you ought to audition for a slot in our new show.'

Jake gave a nervous laugh as he stood up and lifted the guitar strap from over his shoulder. 'No. That sort of life wouldn't do for me. I just enjoy playing for myself and my friends, and my monthly stint at the pub. It's unusual to have anything other than someone thumping out a tune on a pub piano, so I get a bit of a kick from that.

But as for a career, I don't think so. I'd rather see if Rob comes up with anything at the bank.'

Cissie smiled and nodded, awkwardness still niggling at her. The sooner she went back inside and rejoined the party, the better. But as she stepped past Jake, she felt his hand rest on her shoulder. She turned back, saw the depth of emotion in his eyes, his head moving towards her, his lips soft and sensuous.

Panic flared through her like a fire storm. She turned away, pulse exploding at her temples, and had to stop herself stumbling as she stepped briskly across the pavement.

* * *

'Ah, there you are. Any objection if I join you?'

Mildred was sitting on a bench outside the canteen. Heavy, thunderous rain had fallen the previous day, cooling the high temperatures of the last couple of weeks. Now the sun shone fitfully from a blue sky punctuated by plump, grey clouds, and Mildred was enjoying its intermittent warmth before she went back to work.

She lifted her gaze to Oscar's tall, lean figure, casually drawing on her cigarette and blowing out the smoke through pursed lips before she replied. 'You got as much right as me to sit here,' she shrugged.

'Thanks,' Oscar answered, his voice tinged with sarcasm. 'I wouldn't ask, only there's nowhere else to sit outside, and it'd be nice to get some fresh air before we get back to work.'

Mildred shifted slightly as Oscar sat down beside

her. She'd learnt to tolerate him over the month or so they'd been teamed up together. He was a good driver, and considerate, too, always waiting if he saw someone running for the bus stop. Perhaps they'd just got off on the wrong foot.

Nevertheless, there were a few awkward moments while Oscar lit up his own cigarette. 'What d'you think of the election results, then?' he asked at length, as if wanting to break the silence.

Ah, the results of the election. The only thing anyone was talking about that day. The completely unpredicted landslide victory for Labour who'd hardly ever been in power and then only with a minority government.

'Unbelievable,' Mildred bristled back, since the unexpected outcome had indeed come as an unwelcome shock to her. 'We wait three flaming weeks just to learn that Churchill's been forced out. And after he won the war for us.'

Oscar arched an eyebrow. 'Well, not quite personally,' he interjected. 'But maybe it *is* time for a change. People don't want to go back to how things were under the Tories before the war. They've suffered so much hardship and now they want real progress, and they think they'll have a better chance of that under Labour. All those things that've been discussed — a universal pension scheme, sickness benefit and even financial help with a second child — might have a better chance of coming about with a new, fresh government. And the idea of a national health service is amazing.'

'Churchill would've given us all that, too,' Mildred retorted.

'I'm sure he would. But poor chap must be exhausted. Let's give the new parliament a chance, eh?'

'I suppose you voted for them — '

'As it happens, no, I didn't.' Oscar's tone was annoyingly calm and rational. 'But we've got to accept it. It was done entirely democratically, after all. Especially delaying it those three weeks so that all personnel still serving abroad could cast their votes, too. People like your fiancé. Have you heard from him yet?'

'Yeah, I have as a matter of fact. Most of it was censored out, though.'

She wasn't going to tell Oscar, mind, that what was left could almost have come from a stranger. Gary had written that he loved her and was looking forward to coming home. But it was the way he'd put it. Factual, passionless.

'You must be putting great store in this Potsdam Declaration, then,' Oscar interrupted her thoughts, referring to the recent ultimatum given to Japan jointly by America, Britain and China.

'What, you think threatening the Japs with utter destruction like the world's never seen before — or however they put it — if they don't surrender straightaway is gonna make a blind bit of difference?' she scoffed. 'The Japs'll fight on to the bitter end, and it's probably just a bluff, anyway.'

Oscar pushed out his bottom lip. 'I wouldn't be so sure about that. There's huge amounts of hush-hush stuff going on with top scientists and engineers. Never know what they might come up with. Some massive bomb far greater even than the V2, maybe.'

237

'And how would you know?' Mildred scorned.

'My father was a physics laboratory assistant,' Oscar answered simply. 'He didn't talk a lot about his work, but he said there were incredible things going on. And that was some time before the war started. So nothing would surprise me.

Think of the bouncing bomb. You wouldn't have thought that was possible.'

'So how come your dad was a scientist and you're just a bus driver?' Mildred demanded somewhat testily.

'An assistant scientist,' Oscar corrected her, and then he went on to explain, 'My father was a clever man, but he lived on a different planet, almost. One that didn't include practicalities like planning for the future. So when he died suddenly, I had to get a job pretty quick at a time when jobs were at a premium. I did whatever work I could find for a while. And then when I eventually ended up driving a bus, I found I rather liked it. So here I am back again. For now, anyway.'

Despite herself, Mildred realised she was being drawn into Oscar's story. Besides, it was another quarter of an hour before their bus was due to leave the depot, and she didn't fancy the idea of sitting there in silence for that long.

'So, didn't you have no job before your dad died?' she asked vaguely, trying to hide her interest.

Beside her, Oscar shook his head. 'No. I was in my first year studying engineering at university. I didn't have enough qualifications or experience to get the sort of job I wanted, but I had to support my mother. And my little sister was only six at the time. There's a big gap between us, you see.'

'Couldn't your mum go out to work, then?' Mildred asked almost accusingly.

'No.' Oscar gave a rueful sigh. 'She had rheumatic fever as a child and it left her with a weak heart. It was a wonder she survived two pregnancies, but the strain of having Georgie —

Georgina, that is — virtually left her as an invalid. She can manage to keep house, but that's about it.'

Flipping heck, Mildred thought, and she was sure she could feel those two little telltale spots of red embarrassment blooming on her cheeks. There she was, blaming Oscar for wanting his job back and giving him the cold shoulder, when he'd given up a dream career to support his mum and little sister. Maybe Mildred had misjudged him, and she felt overcome with guilt.

'Oh, I'm sorry to hear that,' she said, aware that her tone had softened. 'And what about your sister? How old's she now?'

'Sixteen. And before you ask, she's still at school. She got a scholarship, and I wanted her to have the chance of a proper education until she's eighteen at least. Maybe beyond, if she does well enough.'

'When you had to give up education yourself.' Mildred's voice was almost hushed. 'That's very noble,' she couldn't help saying, though it made her feel even more embarrassed. 'I hope she knows how lucky she is to have a brother like that.'

She heard Oscar give a short, awkward laugh, and was amazed how pleasing the sound was. 'I didn't see I had any choice,' he told her. 'Not

239

when she was little. And then, when I got called up, my army pay was more than I was earning as a bus driver.'

'Really? I'd have thought — '

'I'm one of the few who can say the war did me a favour. Apart from sending me to places where I could've been blown to bits, of course,' Oscar said wryly. 'When I told them I knew a bit about engineering, they put me in the Royal Engineers. I managed to survive in one piece — well, just about — so now I'm hoping that with the engineering experience I gained in the army, I might be able to rescue my career, after all. As the country gets back on its feet, it's going to need engineers.'

'So your job back here driving buses is just a stopgap?'

'Possibly. But keep it under your hat, please.'

His meaningful look caught her eye, and she felt a confusing tingle of excitement. Oscar Miles had trusted her enough to take her into his confidence, despite her initial hostility towards him. Blimey, he must like her, or recognise that she had good, steady common sense. And old-fashioned principles that wouldn't allow her to betray him.

'Yeah, course,' she nodded. 'But we can't sit here all day. Time to get the bus on the road. Can't keep our passengers waiting,' she half joked with a tentative grin.

They had to go back inside to the office before the last leg of their shift, and Mildred knew she just had time to pop to the ladies' before they set off again. But something made her glance fleetingly over her shoulder at Oscar's retreating broad back. Yes, Freda was right. He was a fine-looking

240

fellow, and there was more to him than initially caught the eye, too.

Perhaps Oscar Miles was OK, after all.

★ ★ ★

'Hello, Mum, I'm home!'

The front door of Number Eight crashed open, and although Eva had been listening out, the resounding bang made her jump. Right from the cradle, Primrose had been the noisiest of Eva's offspring, and six years of living with her chaotic eldest sister, Gert, and her three equally noisy boys, hadn't improved her ways.

I must be getting old, Eva thought — briefly — to herself. But joy expanded in her chest like a balloon. Primrose, her baby, had come home for good, now that she'd just left school and the war was over so that there'd be no more bombs falling on London. It was the beginning of a new phase in Eva's life — or perhaps a return to the past when her life had revolved around caring for her brood and making them feel loved and secure. It still did, of course, but much of her time during the war had been taken up with her work with the WVS, too.

'Hello, sweetheart!' Eva's arms were opened wide, ready to hug her youngest daughter as she blundered in through the kitchen door, her rosy face glowing. 'Had a good journey?'

'Yeah, course,' Primrose grinned as she launched herself into her mum's embrace. 'Trudy ain't come with us, mind. Playing tennis with her posh school friends.'

241

'Hello, Mum!' Gert called, shouldering her way in through the door and dragging one eight-year-old son by the earlobe. 'Told you not to tease your brother, didn't I?' she reprimanded. 'Now go and give your granny a kiss.'

Whatever it was young Tim had done was entirely forgotten as the rest of the family filed into the kitchen, which was at once filled with laughter and happy voices. Gert's husband, Rob, pushed his way in, suitcase in one hand and string bag in the other.

'Don't you think you'll be needing these?' he asked, pulling Primrose's leg with a cheeky smile.

'Oh, yeah. Sorry, Rob, forgot in all the excitement.'

'So which room would madam like them in?'

'Oh, you!' Primrose laughed at her brother-in-law. 'Presumably I'll be back in with Milly, Mum?'

'Well, the house ain't grown, so, yes, you daft brush,' Eva chuckled back. 'Mill's not too happy at having to share again. And you'll have to remember to be quiet 'cos she's on shifts.'

'OK. I'll take me things up, then,' Primrose answered and, taking her luggage from Rob, lugged them back out into the hallway and up the stairs.

'Fat chance of that, her being quiet,' Gert grimaced. 'Worse than my three put together. Why don't you lot go out in the yard and knock Jake's old football around for a bit? Phew!' she sighed, slumping down on one of the kitchen chairs as the boys charged outside. 'An hour in the back of the car and they're like jack-in-the-boxes. Maybe we should've come by train, after all. But now us civilians are allowed a little bit of petrol again, even if it is rationed, it made it more of an occasion to get the car on the road again. But what I'm going to do with the boys now the school holidays have started, I really don't know.'

'Gonna have your hands full, that's for sure!' Eva sympathised. 'Got that rec round the corner, ain't you?'

'Yeah, but they can't spend the entire holiday there. And I've got work for them to do in the garden. Still got to grow a lot of our own veg. Rationing's not gone by a long chalk.'

'Well, at least I can make you a cuppa after the drive. Do sit down, Rob. Making the place look untidy.' Eva winked at her son-in-law, considering for the umpteenth time that Gert had been so lucky to have won his heart.

'Dad and Jake not back from work yet?' Gert asked.

'No, but they won't be long,' Eva called from the scullery, where she was putting the kettle on the gas. 'Still same hours as when you used to work there.'

'Well, I might have some news for Jake that'll mean he won't have to work on Saturday mornings again,' Rob put in.

'I've only been back at the bank a week, but I'm definitely going to have Mr Breakwell's job when he retires next month, and there's going to be a lot of changes. I've talked to my superiors about Jake and they're very interested in him. He'd have to start at the bottom and work his way up, but there's going to be plenty of opportunity for an intelligent young chap like him.'

243

'Well, that's good news,' Eva said, coming back in. 'It's what he needs to take his mind off not being able to get into the fire brigade. And off a certain young lady who's caught his eye.'

'What, that dancer girl?' Gert raised her eyebrows in questioning. 'Cissie, ain't she? Well, I'm not surprised. Pretty kid.'

'Yeah. But the only time they can see each other is Sundays. And though they seem to get on really well, I reckon she's too tied up with her dancing.'

'Yes, but they're only very young, Eva,' Rob commented wisely. 'A more pressing point is what you're going to do with Primrose. She can't just swan around for the rest of her life.'

'Yeah, I know. But I've had an idea. She's always liked clothes and things. Now you remember the Braithwaites what used to live opposite, don't you, Rob?'

'Well, of course,' Rob answered. 'Gert's always kept in touch with Jessica over the years.'

'Well, I saw her mum, Hester, recently,' Eva informed them all. 'They're planning on going out to Nigeria while Jess and Patrick and the family are still there. So before they go, I thought I'd ask if Charles might be able to find Primrose a job in the fashion department of Arding and Hobbs.'

'Cor, Mum, you're a genius!'

'Well, when clothes start coming off points, whenever that'll be, there's gonna be good business in fashion, I reckon. Everyone's gonna want new clothes after this make-do-and-mend lark we've had for so many years. And then with Mildred loving her job on the buses, everyone's gonna be really happy.'

'And when Gary comes home,' Gert added, catching her bottom lip between her teeth. 'The Japs can't go on fighting forever. They say they're all but beaten.'

'Well, I hope so, Gert, love. I hope so.'

Somehow it felt to Eva that a heavy, grey blanket had descended over her happiness at having her Primrose come home. It was only two days since the shock election results, the same day Japan had been given some sort of ultimatum in something they were calling the Potsdam Declaration. Nobody knew exactly what this threat was, but Eva felt in her bones that it must be pretty serious.

She just hoped Mildred's Gary came home from it all in one piece. She didn't know what it would do to Mildred if he didn't. Although had she detected some cooling in Mildred's feelings towards Gary, or had she just imagined it? Oh, dear. You never stopped worrying about your children even when they were grown-up, did you?

Eva fixed her usual, generous smile on her face. 'How long's that blooming kettle gonna take to boil?' she demanded.

20

'So, you're off this afternoon, then?'

'Yes. All packed and ready to move into the digs tonight. We've got the theatre to rehearse in tomorrow, and then we open on Wednesday night.'

'It's gonna feel real strange without you, even if you've only been here a bit.'

Mildred and Cissie were sitting at a table by the pavilion in Battersea Park, enjoying a mid-morning cup of tea. With it being the start of the school summer holidays, the grass areas — those that hadn't been dug up as vegetable allotments — were noisy with children letting off steam. The boating lakes were back in full swing, and a general feeling of well-being permeated the warm air. The war was over, in Europe at least, and life was slowly creeping back towards normality.

'I'm going to miss you, too.' Cissie could feel tears forming in her eyes and had to gulp down the lump swelling in her throat. 'I've always been so wrapped up in my dancing that I've never had a friend quite like you. It's wonderful.' She couldn't resist reaching across to squeeze Mildred's hand before she went on, 'But it is only for three months, and I'll be coming back every Sunday and staying overnight, so I can see you then.'

'Yeah, but only if me shifts let me,' Mildred complained. But then her face brightened a little. 'I know someone else who's gonna be pleased he can still see you on Sundays, mind. And that's

246

our Jake. Proper taken with you, he is. So, tell me, truthfully, what d'you think of him?'

Cissie felt a jolt in her chest at the bluntness of Mildred's question, and her heart suddenly raced on. Mildred was staring fixedly at her, head tipped enquiringly to one side. Oh, Lord. Mildred was such a genuine, open person that Cissie wanted so much to tell her everything. But the tangled knot inside wouldn't let her. Filled her with the fear that it might drive Mildred away, and she didn't want that. But Mildred deserved the truth to an extent. And so did Jake.

Cissie lowered her eyes to her half-empty cup. 'I do like Jake very, very much,' she admitted. 'He's sweet and kind, and we've got our love of music in common. But I can't lie.

I'm just not ready to have a man in my life yet. It's not that I've got my eye on anyone else. And whenever I do want to find someone, I'll be looking for someone just like Jake. But I don't know when that might be, so it'd be wrong of me to encourage him as anything other than a friend. If he's looking for romance, he needs to look elsewhere, I'm afraid.'

'At the moment, I don't think he wants to look elsewhere. I reckon he'll wait for you, however long it takes.'

'No.' Cissie's voice cracked, for wasn't she ready to break? A beacon seemed to flare inside her at the very thought of Jake, but she knew a physical relationship could never be. The very idea made her cringe. Better to make that clear now, though she felt a piece of her heart tear. 'Tell him that as long as I'm dancing, which I'm hoping will be for

247

a very long time, there's no room in my life for romance.'

She heard Mildred draw in a hissing breath through her teeth and swivelled her eyes towards her friend. She hoped Mildred wouldn't notice the tears she could feel trembling on her lashes and was relieved when Mildred merely shrugged her eyebrows.

'Pity,' she sighed. 'I could see you and Jake making a proper go of it.'

'I know. And I'm sorry,' Cissie all but whispered. But talking to Mildred was so easy that she couldn't help voicing the thought that was circling in her head. 'Ironic, isn't it? There's me with someone who's keen on me when I don't want a relationship, and you wanting your Gary back when he's on the other side of the world.'

She watched, overwhelmed with surprise, as Mildred leant back in her chair, steepling her fingers in front of her chin. Mildred always seemed so bright and happy-go-lucky, but Cissie was starting to see there was a much deeper side to her. A hidden thoughtfulness that only occasionally rose to the surface.

'To be honest, I'm not so sure now,' Mildred began tentatively. 'I've never said it to no one else, and promise you won't tell a soul?'

'No, of course not.' Cissie shook her head in confusion.

Mildred gave a sharp nod before she went on, 'You see, Gary and me didn't really know each other that well. He was fun, and I hadn't been living back here long, so it was great to have someone to go out with. And he didn't have no family, so . . . I think I felt a bit sorry for him. I mean, don't get us wrong, I really liked him. And when he got called up and asked us to get engaged before he went, well, I thought it'd be cruel to say no when he was going off to war. And I mean, he still might not come back. But . . . he's like a ghost in me head now. I worry about him like you would a friend, but it don't feel right. That if and when he do come home, I'm supposed to be walking down the aisle with him. So, I don't know. It all just keeps going round in me head, and I don't know what I'm gonna do.'

She shifted her gaze towards Cissie, blinking slowly, and her shoulders sank in a profound sigh. The tiny muscles in Cissie's smooth forehead twitched into a frown.

'So, we're both feeling a bit unsure, then.'

She saw Mildred nod slowly, and a sudden, fathomless compassion took hold of her heart. Compassion mingled with guilt, since Mildred had been totally honest with her, while she had only spoken half the truth. But, for now, all she could do was lean forward and wrap her arms about Mildred, a hug that Mildred returned, holding her tightly. Two friends, two aching souls. And when it came down to it, it was all because of the war. Not that Mildred knew the truth behind her own story. Could Cissie tell her one day?

At that moment, she really couldn't say.

★ ★ ★

Mildred pressed the bell by the bus platform twice in succession to let Oscar know that all the

249

passengers were safely on or off and that he could drive away from the stop.

Not that there were huge crowds about. It was August Bank Holiday Monday, and the hands on Mildred's watch showed her that the bus was dead on time. Half past nine on a dank evening following earlier heavy thunderstorms. Overall, it wasn't feeling like a very good summer at all, but there was still time, Mildred told herself optimistically.

Just for a very short stretch, their bus route coincided with that of a tram before they diverged again. Mildred was still ringing up tickets along the aisle when Oscar slowed the bus in order to make the turn. Just as they were moving forward again, Mildred happened to glance up and, in the evening gloom, spied some idiot launch himself from the tram Oscar had waited to pass and then spring across into the bus, hanging onto his trilby hat and with his unbuttoned raincoat flapping perilously.

Mildred spun indignantly on her heel and marched down to where he'd plonked himself on one of the sideways seats. 'Oi, what d'you think you're doing?' she demanded. 'That was bloody dangerous! Don't want no accidents on *my* bus. If anything'd happened, me and me driver could've been in trouble.'

'Cor blimey, proper little ray of sunshine you are, love,' the fellow grunted none too quietly. And then he raised his voice even louder, 'Here, you lot, have you heard? Just announced on the wireless. Few hours ago, the Yanks dropped a bleeding great bomb on the Japs. Something or other — shima. One of their biggest cities, and

250

this here bomb's so powerful, it's wiped out the whole bloody place.'

'Oh, yeah?' Mildred snorted. 'Pull the other one. And keep your voice down — and mind your language when you're on *my* bus.'

'Sorry, miss, but don't shoot the messenger. It's true, I tell yer,' he said in a more moderate tone. 'They said it was two thousand times more powerful than those flaming V2s of Hitler's. Imagine that. Destroyed everything for miles.'

A murmur began to rumble through the passengers, and some of them swivelled round in their seats to question the man. Used to keeping her balance as the bus moved along — Oscar driving more smoothly than Bev used to, she had to admit — Mildred clamped her lips together as people began to emerge from the sudden news and started muttering their reactions.

Flipping heck, was all Mildred could think for several seconds, she was so stunned. Looking down the rows of seated passengers, it was like watching a film. A separate world she wasn't really part of, as she was swept up in the thoughts that swirled in her head.

Utter destruction. Those had been the words in the Potsdam Declaration, hadn't they? Is that what the threat, the ultimatum had meant? Bloody hell. Destroyed everything for miles, the chap had said. An entire city in one fell swoop. People. Women. Children. Was it really that bad? Was such a thing possible? It seemed incomprehensible.

Mildred gazed down the dimly lit bus to the driver's cab, which was, of course, in darkness. Her mind flipped back to her recent conversation with Oscar. He'd believed almost anything was possible, and yet at this moment, he was ignorant of this momentous news. If it was indeed as the passenger had made out. But there'd been millions of flaming bombs dropped in this blooming war. So surely it must have been something pretty special to have its own announcement on the wireless?

Another half-hour yet before she and Oscar had a ten-minute break, and then the final run of their shift. Mildred realised that her heart was pulsing with frustration. She needed to talk to Oscar. He was the only one she knew who could make sense of all this.

And then it hit her like a ten-ton lorry. Only now had she thought of Gary. The passenger, who seemed happy to be the centre of attention as his fellow travellers quizzed him, had said the Yanks had dropped this bomb. But her Gary was out there somewhere. Had it affected him at all? Had he played a part? Surely, not. Not in his submarine. He'd be OK. That was all right then, and she dismissed him from her mind.

She consulted her watch again as Oscar drew the bus to a halt by the next compulsory stop, and she jolted back to reality. Nobody was waiting to get on, but every passenger was engrossed in conversation.

'Here, stop gassing, everyone,' she called out. 'You sure none of you want to get off here before I ring the bell?'

★ ★ ★

Cissie and Sean were sitting with some of the other dancers in a café round the corner from the theatre. It was Monday evening, so they'd had their two days off, the first since opening the show at its new venue. Now they were congregating, ready for rehearsals to begin again the next afternoon before the evening performance. At the boarding house where some of them were lodging, there was no communal space other than the room where breakfast was served, and the landlady had shooed them out.

Though she was chatting with her friends, Cissie's mind wasn't entirely on the conversation. Her thoughts were drifting back to her overnight stay with her family in Banbury Street from where she'd only just returned. It had been lovely to be with her mum and dad, Zac and even the baby again. They had no news to report, except that Jane, now six months old, had learnt to roll onto her back when she was put on her tummy in the playpen. It was the first time Cissie had seen the well-used cage that had arrived, strapped to the roof of the car, when Rob had brought Eva's youngest daughter, Primrose, back to live with her parents again.

Cissie had pretended to show an interest in Jane's development, but she didn't really care. The metallic taste of bitterness had been sharp in her mouth, watching her family struggle to make ends meet and having to accept hand-me-downs and charity from every direction. If it hadn't been for Jane's arrival, there would still have been her mum's much-needed wage coming into the house. Thank goodness dear Jake and Stan had managed to find a job for Zac at Price's. He didn't earn a lot, but every penny counted.

Cissie herself could probably have earned more if she'd gone into an office job of some sort. But her parents had let her follow her dream to become a dancer. She had been determined to make them proud of her and, with utter dedication, had danced her way to the top for them. The *Tristan and Isolde pas de deux* had been the pinnacle, and her heart flew to the heavens now that she was performing it again each evening. The opening night on the Wednesday had been another triumph, and the auditorium had been packed ever since.

But at certain moments, she couldn't stop her mind from jumping back to that very first time she and Sean had danced it before a public audience back in May the previous year. She had been boiling over with excitement and nerves as she'd waited in the wings, but the instant the music had struck up, all that had vanished.

She had been lost in a dreamlike world from the opening bars when she stepped with acted uncertainty into the spotlights, hands crossed over her heart. On reaching centre stage, she paused in *croisé derrière* position, extending her right arm and glancing over her shoulder to watch Sean appear from the wings and come to stretch his arms along the length of hers. Then the *petits pas de bourrée courus* on pointe as she led him in a circle to return to centre stage, where he supported her in *attitude*, helping her to turn a slow circle on her left pointe while performing *petits battements sur le-cou-de-pied* with the right. They moved together as one, through waltz steps and *ports de bras*, their bodies lilting and swaying, yet never for one second relinquishing the balletic control practised for so many years that it had become instinctive. The traditional moments of coyness followed, leading to an explosion of *grands jetés en tournant* as they chased each other in teasing across the stage, coming together in a dramatic lift before the final, protracted series of *pirouettes* and *arabesques*. She twirled in Sean's hold about her waist, ready to end, to the audience's delight, in another lift from which he dropped her into a stunning fish dive and finally lowered her gently to the floor and sank down beside her in balletic embrace.

The applause had been deafening. She had breathed it in with joyful pride in her heart as she had dropped into one curtsey after another, waiting for the clapping to die down and catching Sean's smiling face.

'You were incredible, so you were,' he'd beamed at her as they made their way backstage, and the singer waiting in the wings for the next act congratulated them both on a wonderful performance. 'You really ought to apply to Sadler's Wells,' Sean went on. 'Snap you up, so they would.'

'You weren't so bad yourself,' she'd grinned back. 'As for Sadler's Wells, well, they're sent all over the place, on the road all the time, living in awful digs and performing in leaking theatres and aircraft hangars and what have you. And I've heard the *madam* there is a bit of a tartar. Besides, I like the variety and the freedom we have here. Where else would they choreograph a piece like

255

that for me just because I happened to mention I loved the music?'

'Sure, you're right there,' Sean had said, disappearing towards the male dressing room. 'Better get changed for the grand finale. Not that it'll be a patch on us, so it won't!'

He'd given her his bright, twinkling Irish wink as he turned away, and she'd hurried into the chaos of the female dressing room, the music still roaring in her head. The other dancers surrounded her as she changed, wanting to know how it went. They'd heard the clapping from there, so it must have been good. And all her concerns over whether it had been a wise choice of music had been dispelled.

'Wagner could not help being German,' Monsieur Clément had replied with a shrug when she'd questioned his idea. 'And he has been dead sixty years. And this is a variety theatre, not Covent Garden. Most of our clientele will not even recognise the music, let alone know who wrote it!'

If the cheering and clapping that night had been anything to go by, he'd been right. Cissie's only disappointment was that her family hadn't been there to share her triumph, but, of course, back then, her mother had been working at the nursing home and was on duty until eight o'clock that evening.

'We'll all come tomorrow instead,' her father had promised with an adoring smile. 'And then the first night nerves'll be over and you'll give the performance of your life.'

She'd imagined the beloved faces of her parents and brother smiling down at her from the box Monsieur Clément had promised. But the joy of dancing this beautiful piece, knowing her family were in the audience, hadn't happened. At least, not until several weeks later when physically she'd felt sufficiently recovered. But it hadn't been the same. How could it be after what had happened? And even now, though her soul took wing when she was on stage, afterwards the elation was always tainted with bitterness and anger. She was beginning to wonder if she could ever be the same person again.

'Shush, you lot!' the café owner's voice pierced her dark thoughts. 'Sounds like there's something important on the wireless.'

The babble of voices quickly died away as he turned up the volume on the radio behind the counter. The monotone flared across the tables, and everyone paused to listen. Faces slowly took on serious, shocked masks as the news unfurled, and silence hovered for some moments when the announcement was over.

'Jesus, Mary and Joseph,' Sean whispered when heads began to shake in disbelief. 'Does it take something like this to make the Japs surrender?'

'Surely they will now?' someone else asked as low voices began to murmur softly again.

Cissie said nothing, but her head was spinning like a whirlpool. Would the world ever be the same after this? Would it end the war against Japan? What did the future hold for any of them?

Perhaps her own troubles weren't so desperate, after all.

★　★　★

At Number Eight Banbury Street, the radio was turned off. In the kitchen, Jake was playing some popular tunes on his guitar, and Stan and Eva joined in as he sang. Happy and laughing together, they decided not to wait until Mildred came home from her shift and went straight to bed without turning the wireless on again.

While they slept peacefully in their beds, the entire world was shocked by the news.

21

Saul Williams slung his rucksack on his shoulder and waited his turn to step down from the carriage compartment. Once on the busy station platform, he strode out, slipping past the other passengers and then aching with frustration when he had to queue to get through the barrier. There was no time to lose.

It was Saturday 11th August, and the expectation in the air was almost palpable. Saul imagined it must have been the same back at the beginning of May when it was known Hitler was dead, and the nation had been waiting with bated breath for Germany to surrender.

Saul had been in France, where the atmosphere had been different. To witness towns and villages that had been living under the terror of Gestapo reign for years suddenly liberated was joy itself. But that was immediate, freedom exploding only as Allied forces marched in, confirming that the hated retreating occupiers would not return. The citizens of France ran to cheer their liberators, hug them, kiss them. But London on this Saturday morning was holding its breath.

Everyone in Britain who hadn't heard the radio announcement the previous Monday evening had woken the following morning to the news that the United States had dropped what was called an atomic bomb on the Japanese city of Hiroshima. Of huge military significance, the whole place had

259

simply been wiped out in one massive explosion that had caused the very air to catch fire. There was virtually nothing left. The morning papers had featured photographs of a vast, mushroom-shaped cloud spiralling overhead, a tornado of death that nothing could escape.

This was the utter destruction Japan had been warned of in the Potsdam Declaration. Even though it had happened on the far side of the world, the news had been shocking, whatever you thought of the Japanese. But still they wouldn't give in. It wasn't until America had dropped a further A-bomb on Nagasaki three days later, and Russia had declared war on Japan the same day, that Japan had taken a further day of deliberation before it finally announced its intention to surrender under the terms of the Declaration.

Saul felt shot through with shame and sadness that his mother country had felt obliged to do this terrible thing in order to save further bloodshed. The same horror and guilt he had felt because a fellow American had perpetrated the heinous crime that he himself had been helpless to prevent. But at least it looked as if the inhuman act of destruction had achieved its aim and was bringing the global conflict to an end. There could be no good whatsoever in what Chuck Masters had done.

A horrible, cloying disgust still ate into Saul's insides like a cancer. Even more so now that he'd learnt the poor girl had produced a child as a result, or so it seemed, and that she and her family had been driven from their home because of it. And now she had a name to make it seem even

260

more real.

He was sure it was her. He could sense it deep inside his raw soul. He felt such a coward, and there was no way out of this hellish agony, except to carry out his plan. To allow his good Christian upbringing some atonement for his failings. Even then, it wasn't a way out, just a way to let himself breathe when he'd been suffocating all this time. But it would still haunt him until the day he died.

But time was running out. There had been speculation among the ranks that if the Japs didn't give in soon, America might want to pour more troops into the fray. That instead of being transported home from the US base where they were being held, they might be sent to the Far East to fight yet again.

As his comrades discussed the situation, Saul kept his thoughts to himself, letting his heart thump away in his chest as a cold sweat broke over him for the thousandth time. Now that Japan was about to surrender, he definitely wouldn't be around here for much longer. He *had* to find her. Make recompense in whatever way he could. Not that he would ever feel unburdened.

He tapped the bulge in the breast pocket of his uniform. It was still there. Every goddammed English pound he'd been able to draw from his army pay. He measured his failure by its fatness as it grew, week by week.

Discovering her name had made her seem real, and he'd taken every darned pass he could to come to London in search of her. The scruffy, backstreet boarding house where he stayed had become a second home. The landlady, despite her curlers and slippers and the fag dripping from the corner of her red-painted lips, always kept for him all the newspapers she could lay her hands on. She wasn't sure exactly why he wanted them, but he was a good customer, and he always paid up front.

'Morning, Saul! You back again?' she greeted him when he knocked on the front door. 'Guessed yer might be coming, so I kept Room Four free for yer. All made up wiv clean sheets,' she lied, since the bed had only been slept in for one night by a very clean young woman. No sense in making work for herself, but she'd changed the pillowcase as it smelt faintly of telltale perfume. 'You drop yer fings upstairs, an' I'll have a cuppa waiting for yer in the dining room. An' I'll put out all the newspapers for yer, an' all.'

'Thank you, ma'am,' Saul answered politely as he loped up the stairs two at a time. He wasn't a fool. The place was a dump, and the landlady wouldn't have kept a room for him if she'd had the chance to let it. But it was cheap, and he didn't have time to waste finding somewhere else. Besides which, the woman was useful, collecting so many newspapers for him. Newspapers and the odd theatre programme any of her other guests left in their rooms.

Five minutes later, he was working his way through the pile she'd accumulated for him over the past fortnight since his last visit. There were only two theatre programmes, flimsy things since paper was such a precious commodity. But both were from plays, which wouldn't be of any help.

Onto the newspapers then. Saul's broad chest

fell in a deep sigh of frustration. They were all full of the two atomic bombs, plus speculation over Japan's intention to surrender. And rightly so. This must be the most important and profound news of the twentieth century. But it didn't help Saul. Nevertheless, he scoured every theatre-related column, searching for a dancer by the name of Cecily Cresswell. But it was hopeless. And what if she hadn't gone back to dancing after having the baby? And even if she had, maybe she was just some chorus girl who mightn't even be named in a programme. But something drew Saul on as if a string was attached to his chest. There'd been something so special about the way she'd moved, visible for just those flickering seconds of moonlight. She was no chorus dancer, he was sure.

He leant back from the table and stretched his long arms out towards the ceiling. He'd have to resume his search of the London theatres, buying any programmes he didn't already have. He had an old map of London, and had been systematically working his way through the streets, marking off every theatre he'd been to and noting it down on a sheet of paper. He'd covered all of central London, so now he'd need to cast the net wider, but in which direction? He really didn't know.

And this could be his last chance. They could be leaving the base any day, transported by train to one of Britain's ports, maybe back down to Plymouth where they'd arrived, and onto a troop ship bound for home. Leaving a festering sore in Saul's heart forever.

Oh, well, he might as well go through the last of the papers before he set out on his mission.

The landlady had, as always, made a surprisingly neat pile as she collected them, so that they were in reverse date order. Now Saul was working his way backwards over a week previously, but he was beginning to lose heart and started flipping over the scanty editions with just a cursory glance. Was it really worth the effort? It was beginning to seem pretty pointless.

He transferred the next thin newspaper into the 'read' pile almost without looking at it. And then a flush of heat washed down through him like boiling water in his veins. Had something jumped out in the subconscious part of his mind, his brain latching onto some familiar words among a whole jumble of print?

His big, strong hand shook as he retrieved the paper, the pupils of his mahogany eyes flaring wide, making it difficult to focus. But there it was, leaping out at him from a sea of wavering letters. Her name. Cecily Cresswell.

He gulped. Blinked. His whole body trembling and his stomach suddenly turning vicious somersaults. He must be mistaken. It wasn't possible. But there it was. In black and white.

His eyes shifted to the beginning of the short article, quickly scanning the lines. *The Romaine Theatre Company opens its run at prestigious Wimbledon Theatre with a triumphant variety show.* Wimbledon? Jeez, where the darnation was that? He'd never heard of it. But he could soon find out!

He was breathing hard, forcing himself to concentrate. The short piece mentioned a couple of singers — apparently well known, though their

264

names meant nothing to Saul — a comedian, and a wonderful chorus of singers and dancers. However, the journalist concluded that the highlights of the evening were the two enchanting *pas de deux* by the company's leading dance principals, Sean O'Leary and Cecily Cresswell. One was in a more modern style, being an interpretation of Gershwin's 'Rhapsody in Blue', while the other was a classical ballet to Wagner's Overture to *Tristan and Isolde*. The two differing pieces displayed the extreme versatility of these two accomplished and talented *artistes*.

Below the article was a telephone number for the theatre's box office, and here Saul's mind came to a stunned standstill. He continued to stare at the paper, but the print had blurred into an indecipherable haze of hieroglyphics. For a good minute, not a muscle in his body moved as he waited for the tumble of crazed thoughts in his head to land into some sort of order.

Was he completely mad? Wouldn't the best thing be to walk away from the whole sorry affair? He could go back to the States and forget it ever happened. But could he live with himself for the rest of his days, knowing that he could have at least apologised to her for being unable to stop it? The pain of his guilt would grind him down to nothing if he let the opportunity slip through his fingers now.

Of course, what if he was wrong? What if it wasn't her, after all? In a way, he hoped it wasn't. But if it was . . . Jeez, he felt as if his heart was being torn in two. What if her memories of what had happened that night were blurred, and she accused him of being the . . . the . . . He couldn't even bring himself to think the word. The baby, if it had been conceived that night, couldn't be his, of course. The girl he'd met had said it was white. But what if Cecily Cresswell had been so confused — after all, she'd looked virtually unconscious — that she believed he'd assaulted her as well? Then he'd be hanged.

Chuck was right. No one would believe the protestations of a black GI. But death would be less cruel than the torture he was living, day in, day out.

There was only one thing he could do. He turned his back on the sensible side of his brain and, in a blind, unseeing fog, ripped the article from the thin sheet of paper and blundered out to the front door. Where was the nearest telephone box? If there weren't any tickets left for that evening's performance, he'd go anyway. Wait by the stage door and find out if it really was her.

And then what?

At that moment, Saul didn't know. But what he did know was that if he did nothing, he'd hate himself forever.

22

Mildred hummed softly to herself as she turned into Banbury Street and let her bike slow to a halt as she freewheeled across to Number Eight. The shift pattern had changed during that momentous week, and she was on earlies again. She'd finished at two o'clock on that Saturday afternoon. The sky was grey and overcast, and it was decidedly chilly for early August, but at least it wasn't raining. And something bright and sunny was singing in Mildred's head. It was unexpected, but it was warm and happy, and filled her with a deep inner contentment she hadn't felt in a while.

She let herself inside Number Eight, propping her bike in its habitual place against the wall in the hallway.

'I'm home!' she grinned, popping her head round the door to the kitchen. 'And how's me little banker brother?' she asked in a light, teasing tone as she bounced into the room.

Jake glanced up from poring over the books he had spread out on the far end of the table. 'I'm never going to be a banker proper. And I haven't even started working at the bank yet, as well you know,' he chided playfully. 'But Rob's lent me these books so I can get an idea before I start.'

'Always knew me second clever son could make something more of himself,' Eva declared, shuffling in from the scullery in her slippers.

'Gonna knock a football around in the park

later, though, ain't you? With your mates from Price's?' Stan said, emerging from behind his depleted newspaper. 'Gonna be great when we can go and watch some decent football matches again soon, ain't it?'

'Will you be back in time for tea, love?' Eva asked.

'Er, no, probably not, Mum. Not sure what we'll end up doing afterwards.'

'OK, love. Only gonna be bread and cheese and a bit of pickle, anyway.'

A frown twitched on Mildred's forehead. Sounded to her as if Jake was being a bit evasive. She was going to need to be economical with the truth herself in a minute but couldn't quite summon the courage just yet.

'Where's Primrose?' she asked instead.

'Upstairs, going through her clothes, deciding what to wear for her interview on Monday. Not that she ain't got much to choose from. But if she wants this job in the womenswear department, she needs to look her best.'

'Flaming lucky Charlie Boy Braithwaite got her the interview before he and his missis go off to Africa,' Stan chipped in.

'Yeah, I know. Must be feeling brave, even if it is to see their daughter.' Mildred nodded hard. 'Still a bit scary, mind, if you ask me. But I liked Jessica. What I remember of her, anyway.'

'Yeah, nice kid,' Eva agreed. 'You ready for a cuppa, then, Mill? Or d'you want to change out your uniform first?'

'I'll change first, Mum. Only . . . ' She paused just for a second, letting the warm flush wash

268

through her. 'I mightn't be in for tea, neither. You know I mentioned me new driver? Chap called Oscar?'

'Yeah, and you was none too happy about him, neither.'

'Well, he's OK really.' Mildred tried to act casually. 'He looks after his invalid mum and his little sister. He said he's got some things to do this afternoon. But, after that, we'll both be at a loose end, so we're meeting up later. Maybe going for a drink or something. Can't be late, though, being on earlies. Even if Sundays ain't as early as weekdays.'

She prayed the pink spot she could feel in each cheek wasn't too visible but watched as her parents exchanged glances. She forced a chuckle as she tried to throw off the awkward moment.

'We're just friends,' she protested with a laugh she hoped sounded natural, and to save herself any further embarrassment, turned swiftly out of the room.

Yeah, that's all they were. Friends, she told herself firmly as she danced up the stairs. Oscar was bloody attractive, but he was also kind, intelligent and had a wonderful way of reasoning things out that she liked. A bit like her elder brother, Kit, who had the ability to see all sides to a situation and then rationalise them. She recognised the same quality in Oscar, and she had to admit, she found it rather appealing. So when he'd asked her if she fancied doing something with him later on, she'd jumped at the chance.

Primrose was standing in front of the old, mottled mirror when Mildred went into the bedroom they now shared. Her youngest sister was twisting this way and that in order to contemplate her reflection from all angles. Cor, she didn't half look like their mum, Mildred considered. Even more so than Gert, herself and Trudy, who all took after Eva. Frizzy, auburn hair, scattering of freckles on her round face, slim at the moment but with wide hips she'd doubtless grow into, and broad, stocky shoulders. Rationing had slimmed their mum down, but she was still plump, with a generous bosom. At fourteen, Primrose's chest was only just starting to gain womanly curves, but she'd no doubt be well endowed, too, when she was older.

'What d'you reckon?' she asked Mildred now, smoothing her hands over the navy serge skirt that hugged her hips. 'It's me old school uniform, and it's getting a bit tight.'

'Yeah, but I think it's just right for an interview. D'you want to borrow me red cardigan? It's really smart and it'll brighten it up a bit.'

'Oo, can I? Ta ever so much, Mill. I really want this job.'

'Yeah, course you can borrow me cardi. Only I want to wear it meself this afternoon. Meeting a friend from work later.'

'Well, don't get it dirty, then,' Primrose teased and spent the next few minutes changing back into her bright, floral dress that strained over her budding breasts, and an old cardigan that was so small for her that the sleeves were halfway up her forearms and there was no way she could do it up.

Mildred shook her head as Primrose skipped out of the room, and then listened as she thumped down the stairs. Perhaps she should go through

270

her wardrobe, such as it was, and find a couple of things for her younger sister to wear. But first she needed to decide what else she was going to wear herself this afternoon. Like Primrose, she'd grown from a child into a woman during the war, only earlier on, of course, when she'd still been living with Gert. Once clothing had gone on coupons, it had been hard to keep up with her growing stature. Gert had generously lent her some of her attire, but Mildred still had very little to dress herself in.

As the weather was hardly what she would have expected for August, she decided to wear her oftmended petticoat beneath a pink gingham blouse with the cardigan on top, and a plain, straight skirt. No pleats or gathers or flaring panels, of course, and the hem only just below her knees — the only kind of fashion permitted with the scarcity of material. She hadn't been able to get hold of any stockings since she couldn't remember when, so it would have to be short white socks with her usual brogue shoes. She did have a pair of sandals from when she was still growing, but now her toes hung over the ends, and besides, it was too cold for bare feet. And she hardly imagined that Oscar would take too much note of her footwear. The schoolgirl look of lace-up shoes with short socks was so commonplace that it was taken for granted nowadays.

So why was she thinking that she wanted to look her best just for a walk in the park with Oscar? She was engaged to Gary and was only waiting for him to come home. Japan was going to surrender any day, so it might only be a couple of months before they were reunited. And yet she knew that this innocent little outing with Oscar had triggered something sweet and tender in her heart.

★ ★ ★

Happiness pattered in her chest as, later that afternoon, Mildred found herself bowling along towards Battersea Park. She'd walked the same route a thousand times in her life, but never before had she been so intrigued by the delicious emotion that churned in her breast. Not even in those far-off days when she'd been going out to see Gary.

Oscar lived the other side of the river, somewhere off Chelsea's King's Road, meaning the park was a mutually convenient place to meet. They'd arranged a rendezvous at the bandstand. If they were lucky, there might be some musical entertainment. If not, they could take a walk along the park's roads and pathways as it didn't close until dusk. Or maybe they could go and get a bite to eat somewhere.

The delight that suddenly began to waltz inside her when she caught sight of Oscar took Mildred by surprise. Dressed in grey flannels, a shirt open at the neck and a fawn jumper that had worn somewhat thin on the elbows, he looked relaxed and casual, and so much more approachable than in his stiff uniform. His eyes lit up when he saw her and his face stretched in a broad, handsome smile.

'Mildred!' he greeted her, stepping forward. 'I wasn't entirely sure you'd come.'

'Wasn't you?' she grinned back, endeavouring

to ignore her pulse that had begun to beat wildly. 'Why wouldn't I meet up with a friend?'

Oscar gave an enigmatic shrug and didn't answer as he pointed to a sandwich blackboard in the bandstand. 'We're in luck. There's a concert at six o'clock. So we've got just over half an hour to kill,' he said, glancing at his watch, 'if we want to be back in time to get a decent seat. Shall we see if the pavilion's still open and grab a cuppa?'

'Oh, I only just had one before I came out. But if you want one . . .'

A small smile returned to Oscar's face. 'So did I, actually.

So . . . shall we take a walk around and then come back?'

'Yes. Yes, I'd like that,' Mildred agreed, only afterwards wondering why she'd said *yes* instead of her usual *yeah*.

They set off at a stroll, ambling down the central avenue away from the bandstand. Young families and older children out alone were beginning to make their way towards the gates on their way home for tea, while couples of all ages and other older groups were still enjoying the fresh air and calm the park had to offer.

'What did your family think of your coming out to meet me?' Oscar asked when they'd been exchanging nothing but pleasantries for some minutes.

'What, with me being engaged to Gary, you mean?' Mildred shrugged one shoulder. 'Don't stop us going out with a friend, do it? And I don't always wanna go out with the girls from the depot. None of them are quite me cup of tea, to be

273

honest. 'Cos I was evacuated to me big sister, Gert's, during the first half of the war, I didn't really have no proper, close friends when I came back here. Got one now, mind. She's a dancer. Moved into our street a few months ago, and we've really hit it off. Only she's doing a stint at Wimbledon Theatre. Staying in digs but coming home for Sunday and Mondays. So I'll see her tomorrow afternoon after our shift.'

'What sort of dancing?' Oscar enquired with what appeared genuine interest. 'Perhaps we should get tickets to go and see her. Georgina — you know, my sister — I'm sure she'd love to go, too. The three of us could go together. It'd be too much for my mum, though.'

Mildred glanced sideways at Oscar, feeling the breath flutter at the back of her throat. The more she saw of him, the more she liked him.

'Think a lot of your family, don't you?' she asked.

'Doesn't everyone?'

Mildred screwed up her nose. 'Not sure they do. Lots of people like being with their friends better.'

'Hmm, I lost touch with most of mine when I had to leave university to take care of Mum and Georgie. I was never one for having lots of friends, anyway. And then . . . ' He seemed to break off in some mysterious reverie before dashing his hand almost angrily across his eyes. 'I always preferred more intimate relationships,' he went on, but with a crack in his voice that made Mildred frown. 'And then the war came along, and now I'm back. Without a proper friend to my name.

Apart from you, that is.'

There was something in his tone that made Mildred think he was suffering some sort of mental anguish, and any uncertainty she'd felt about coming to meet him was swept away.

'Well,' she went on, wanting to steer the conversation in a different direction, 'if you want us to go with you and your sister to see me friend dancing, we'll have to take me brother, Jake. He's gone right soft on Cissie. That's her name, Cissie. Surprised he ain't gone to see her already, but I think he didn't want to look too eager and frighten her off.'

The memory of the conversation when Cissie had told her she wasn't ready for romance tweaked at Mildred's heart, but was instantly dispelled by the attractive little smile Oscar gave again. 'Tell me about your family, then,' he invited her.

'Lucky we got half an hour, there's so many of us,' Mildred chuckled back. 'Only I'm not sure that'll be long enough. Well, there's Mum and Dad, of course. Dad's always worked at Price's, but Mum's never worked much. Too busy caring for us lot, but she's done WVS work in the war. Then there's the eldest, Kit. He's sub stationmaster at a town in Kent, so he was never called up. Married with two children. His wife's Hillie, me sister Gert's best friend.'

'And Gert's the one you were evacuated to?'

'Yeah, I mean, yes, that's right. Lives in Stoneleigh in Surrey. Got three boys. Her hubby worked in a bank before the war, but now he's back and he's got Jake a job there, too, starting next month. Then there's Trudy what's really bright. She's

275

staying on with Gert 'cos she's at the local grammar school. And the youngest's Primrose. She's just come back home to live, so I've gotta share me room with her again,'

Mildred concluded, rolling her eyes.

Oscar gave a soft laugh that sent a shiver down Mildred's spine. 'Well, if they're all as funny and charming as you, I can't wait to meet them.'

Mildred's heart tripped and began to beat faster as she realised she'd love to introduce Oscar to her family, too! And it wouldn't be like when she'd sidled into the house with Gary for the first time, worried they wouldn't approve. Except that now she was engaged to Gary, they might wonder what she was up to. Her eyes scanned the grass area in front of them, searching for a way out from her thoughts.

'Oh, well, actually you might meet Jake sooner than you think,' she announced as her gaze fell on a group of young men running round after a ball. 'He was coming to play football with his mates from Price's. Looks like them over there. Come on.'

She hurried forward to where a casual game was being played, using two impromptu goals marked out with jumpers dropped on the ground. Mildred squinted as her gaze travelled over the individual players, but Jake wasn't among them. That was odd. And then she remembered Jake's evasiveness earlier. What was her little brother up to?

When Mildred turned round, Oscar wasn't immediately behind her. She waited for him to catch up, frowning not just because Jake wasn't with his pals, but also because Oscar appeared to be limping slightly. Unless she was imagining it, of course.

'Oh, false alarm,' she told him, ignoring what she had or hadn't noticed in his gait. 'He must've gone home already. Funny I didn't pass him, mind. Must've gone another way.'

'Never mind. Another time,' Oscar said, seeming to hide a grimace.

'Yes, well.' Mildred was still perplexed. 'Anyway, we've got time to do a circuit round the lakes before the concert starts.'

But she noticed Oscar purse his lips, a bashful expression on his face. 'Actually, would you mind if we go back the way we came? Old war wound playing me up a bit.' He sucked a breath in through his teeth and then gave that attractive laugh again. 'No, I'm not joking. Sicily 1943. We were based in Malta. Getting pounded like there was no tomorrow. Until we were ready to invade. I was lucky. At least I made it back.'

Mildred watched him blink, noticing the swooping of his long, dark lashes as his words sank in. Oh, Lord, was he a war hero to boot? How could a girl fight that?

'Well, I'm glad you did. Make it back, I mean. Does it trouble you much?' Mildred asked, her words ringing with sympathy. 'Only I didn't notice you limping before.'

'No, you probably wouldn't. Most of the time you see me I'm sitting down, driving a bus. And it does only decide to play me up occasionally. Otherwise, I'd have been invalided out instead of going on to fight another day. Or build more makeshift bridges and what have you, in my case.'

Mildred found herself smiling back as she nodded. 'Well, I'm pleased it ain't too bad,' she told him. 'Me brother-in-law, the one what works in a bank, he was wounded in Sicily, too.

And course we can go straight back. D'you wanna hold onto me?'

'No, thanks, I can manage if we don't go too fast,' he answered, gesturing a decline with his hand. 'Wouldn't do to be arm-in-arm with an engaged lady.'

'OK, then. Means we'll get a good seat for the concert, too.'

'And then, afterwards, maybe we'll try and get something to eat before we part company.'

Mildred nodded at him. 'Yes, I'd like that,' she said. And as they walked slowly back towards the bandstand, she felt some curious seed begin to germinate somewhere deep inside her.

23

The lights went down. A soft hush descended on hundreds of chattering voices. Whispers faded. There was a short silence, punctuated by a couple of echoing, subdued coughs. The small orchestra struck up, its cheerful notes reverberating in sizzling expectation. A short overture, and then the audience stilled in excited anticipation as the velvet curtains slowly opened.

Saul's heart was racing. He was surrounded by so many people who were clearly wrapped in delight as the show commenced, while he . . . while he knew that whatever transpired that night would seal his fate. Nervous sweat trickled down his face. He hoped nobody in the darkened auditorium could see.

He'd been more than impressed when he'd arrived at the theatre to collect his ticket from the box office. When he'd asked his landlady how to get to Wimbledon — to the theatre to be precise — he'd been pleasantly surprised to learn that it was among London's top ten, despite being a reasonable bus or train journey from the capital's centre.

When he'd found his way there in time for the evening performance, he'd admired the curved front steps, and then had been dumbfounded by the massive auditorium with its scarlet and gilded decor. Although he'd visited other London theatres, he'd never been right inside, so maybe they were all like that, but he didn't know. Certainly, there was nothing like it in his provincial home town in Alabama. But Wimbledon Theatre seemed to Saul a magical world and he was pleased that the girl who'd been so dreadfully wronged that terrible night was at least at the top of her career and not dancing in some sleazy backstreet nightclub.

He'd been lucky to get a seat in the stalls, not too far from the front. He needed to see the girl's face. To know if it was really her. And if it was, she held his future, his life, in her hands.

The opening number was cheerful and jolly and uplifting. There were two lead singers with a chorus of singers and dancers in brightly coloured costumes representing the old Wild West, which made Saul feel curiously at home. He became even more relaxed as he peered at each dancing girl in turn. None of them triggered the memory he was expecting. Relief and disappointment poured through him in equal measure. He was wrong, after all. Fate, destiny, call it what you will, had decided it was but a wild goose chase. He'd have to put the whole sorry business behind him and settle down to enjoy the show. If he could. For that uneasy niggle persisted in his chest.

The piece ended to enthusiastic applause. The compère came on stage to welcome the audience and announced that the opening act was, unsurprisingly given the lyrics, the title song from the Broadway musical hit, *Oklahoma!* , performed by kind permission of someone Saul had never heard of. The writers, composers or producers, presumably. And then the compère made his first joke of the evening by referring to the colossal fee the company had needed to pay for the privilege.

The second act was announced as something less rousing. The stage was dimmed so that a replica street light could glow softly in the gloom. Another female singer in a trench raincoat moved into its amber glimmer to give a haunting rendition of 'Lili Marlene'. Her deep, rich voice touched something inside Saul's heart. So engrossed was he that at first he didn't notice the figure emerge from the wings. When he did, he had to stifle a gasp. But the solo dancer moving so expressively to the song was fair-haired and, though slender and graceful, was taller and not of such a petite frame as Saul remembered. No. It wasn't *her*.

A magician was next. Clever, but not Saul's cup of tea. Music and rhythm was what he liked best, so when a fiddle player, an older gent, stepped up to the microphone to deliver a medley of lively Irish tunes, Saul found his foot tapping on the floor. Even better, the main chorus then returned with a hearty version of 'Chattanooga Choo Choo' to which the dancers clicked away in a merry tap routine. Saul felt a gentle balm of contentment soothing his restless spirit. The evening wasn't bringing him the trauma and anxiety he'd expected. Instead, he'd found himself thoroughly enjoying the spectacle.

He settled back in the seat as a male singer appeared on stage to the introductory bars of 'Apple Blossom Time'. Three dancing couples slid into the background as a moving accompaniment. The same ones as before. That was going to be it, then. Cecily Cresswell must be the blonde soloist of 'Lili Marlene'. Not the girl he was looking for. He'd come to the end of the road.

And then, suddenly, his whole body juddered. His heartbeat ratcheted up in his chest as another dancing couple stepped out from behind the others, poised for just a split second before they began. An electric charge fizzed through the air, scorching Saul's brain as they broke into dance with such fluidity and grace that it set his head spinning. The girl's costume was loose and flowing, falling about her tiny frame in a cloud and echoing the bending and lilting of her body. That long neck, the tilt of her chin. Her dark, straight hair, caught back from her face at the top of her head, fell about her shoulders in a shining curtain of silk, whipping about her form as she twisted and twirled. Just as it had on that semi-moonlit night.

It was her. It was Cecily Cresswell.

Fire raged through Saul's flesh. He felt sick, dizzy. Stifled. Ran his hand frantically around his collar. He had to get out! But he was trapped, enclosed on either side by spectators. He'd just have to sit tight. He was choking, about to pass out. Black stars in front of his eyes. The figures on the stage grew smaller. Fading. As if in a dream.

By the time everything swam back into focus, the act was over and another had begun. Saul sat, unseeing, unhearing, hardly aware of his surroundings. He had found her. Could he find the courage to carry out his plan?

Finally the compère announced that the first half of the show would end with the act they had all been waiting for. The audience had already caught a glimpse of Sean O'Leary and Cecily Cresswell. Now they would perform the first of their two *pas de deux*, to Gershwin's 'Rhapsody in Blue'.

Pain and guilt tumbled inside Saul's head as this time he succeeded in forcing himself to watch. She was ethereal, like a sprite. Dazzling, bewitching. Pure. Yet he had witnessed the evil thing that had been done to her. And he couldn't stop the tears that dripped down his cheeks.

When the lights came up for the interval, he stumbled out to the gents', furiously splashing cold water over his face. When someone clapped him on the shoulder, he nearly jumped sky-high.

'Bet yer can't wait ter get home,' a stranger's voice came to him out of a fog. 'Couldn't've won the war without you Yanks. Thanks, mate.'

Saul managed to arrange his face into a smile. People mustn't know. He nodded. And made his way outside.

His frail hold on his emotions was ready to snap, but he forced himself to watch the second half of the show, breathing heavily to keep calm each time she appeared on stage. He was sure the evening must be drawing to a close as act followed act. And then, somehow, he must hold his nerve to do what he'd come for.

The second *pas de deux* was announced; Saul could barely breathe. It was to some piece by Wagner, according to the compère, who made some quip about forgiving him for having been born German. And what did it matter anyway now that we'd won the war?

A victory cheer filled the auditorium so that

the pair of dancers arrived on stage to vigorous applause even before the music began. Saul could appreciate the difference between this, which he assumed was classical ballet, and the more modern, freer movements of the earlier dance. This time, Cecily Cresswell was dressed in traditional costume — a tutu Saul overhead someone comment — but in a soft peach rather than the white he believed ballet dancers normally wore. For much of the time, she was spinning on her tiptoes, and when she wasn't, her feet were pointed, her legs lifting in impossible positions, arms floating like lilies on a pond. Saul's tears flowed unchecked.

The show concluded with another fast-paced number,

'Boogie Woogie Bugle Boy', in which the entire cast performed. Cecily and her partner had obviously rushed off for a quick costume change since they reappeared halfway through to lead the dancers. The finale ended on a rollicking note and the performers took their bows. But it was Cecily Cresswell who received the loudest, most deafening whoops and cheers from the audience and at whose feet a mat of thrown flowers landed.

When the final curtain call was over and the applause reluctantly died down, Saul waited patiently in the queue to file out of the theatre, though his heart was pounding like a battering ram. The cool of the summer evening was welcome when he stepped outside, calming his burning skin. He drew deeply on the air, dragging it into his lungs. He must do this thing. Was it right? Would it open up the wounds for her? Or would his coming forward allow her the satisfaction of justice?

All Saul knew was that if he didn't do this now, his heart and soul would lie empty and withered in his breast forever.

He would never break free. And so, with his heart rearing in his chest, he made his way to the stage door.

★ ★ ★

'Ah, my little stars, you were all wonderful tonight, as always,' Monsieur Clément proclaimed outside the cramped dressing rooms. The dancers were emerging into the narrow corridor, changed and ready for home. Some were aiming for their digs round the corner, while others were heading directly for their permanent homes towards central London. It was, after all, Saturday night, and they weren't due back at the theatre for class and rehearsals until Tuesday morning. 'Enjoy your rest, but do not forget to exercise your muscles,' the dance master instructed.

Cissie was one of the last to appear, buttoning up her cardigan, just as Sean was coming from the other dressing room. Spying them both together, Monsieur Clément turned to them, his face aglow with admiration.

'And you, my two little doves, you were *superbes*!' He brought his bunched fingertips to his lips and launched a pretend kiss into the air. 'The company is so lucky to have you.'

Cissie felt her cheeks flame with embarrassment. It was lovely that Monsieur Clément praised his dancers. He pushed them hard and could be sharp with anyone who didn't put their heart and soul into their work, but he was always ready to give credit where it was due. As far as Cissie was concerned, though, she was only immersing herself in her passion for her own sake. For while she was concentrating on giving only her very best, there was no room to remember.

'I will see you all sharp sharp on Tuesday, then,' Monsieur Clément concluded with a smart clap of his hands and, giving his quick little grin, turned to strut away down the corridor.

Cissie watched him go, giving an amused shake of her head. She was lucky to be working with such an endearing dance master. But as the other female dancers squeezed deferentially against the wall to let him pass, she caught Deirdre glancing at her with a sour scowl.

'*Superbes!*' she mimicked under her breath, pulling a face at Cissie before turning her back with a deliberate jerk of her shoulders.

Cissie's jaw dropped for but a second. She went to step forward to give Deirdre a piece of her mind. The girl had been permanently promoted to soloist, which she might not have been had it not been for Cissie's prolonged absence. So why should she still hold such a jealous grudge against her?

Before Cissie had a chance to open her mouth, though, she felt Sean's hand on her arm. 'Sure, she isn't worth it,' he whispered in her ear and laced an affectionate arm about her waist.

Cissie instinctively drew back. At one time, she would have thought nothing of Sean's gesture, but nowadays . . . When they were dancing together, she didn't think twice about his hands about her waist or supporting a leg. But in any other circumstances, physical contact made her cringe, even though she knew it was perfectly innocent, especially given Sean's persuasions. She cursed herself for it. Dear God, would she ever feel normal again?

'Yes, you're right,' she murmured, making a big effort to pull herself together. 'So, what are you doing the next couple of days?' she asked, relieved to think of something to change the subject.

'Booked meself a little trip to the seaside, so I have,' Sean grinned back as they followed the others towards the stage door. 'Sure, it's grand to see all the miles of barbed wire being taken away.'

'OK. Have a nice time, then. And don't eat too many ice creams or fish and chips. Monsieur Clément won't be happy if you put on too much weight.'

They were still laughing together as they emerged into the lamplit street. As usual, a small crowd had gathered around the stage door, waiting with programmes and pencils at the ready in the hope of getting a signature or two. Cissie noticed that Deirdre was already signing away with a simpering expression plastered on her face.

'I'll leave you to your adoring fans, then,' Sean said with a knowing half-smile. 'Prefer to escape them meself.'

'Not sure I can get away with it,' Cissie chuckled back. 'Have a good trip.' And then as a group of admirers recognised her and pushed forward, she nodded a goodbye to Sean and began signing her autograph. It was, after all, what was expected, part and parcel of her job. She smiled politely, asked people their names and put *Love from Cecily C*

287

followed by kisses to complete strangers. Accepted their praise with modest thanks.

After several minutes, the fans began to disperse, expressing their gratitude and happily clutching their prizes. It was so rewarding that people appreciated her performance to such a degree that they were prepared to hang about at the stage door, but at the end of the week's run, Cissie was tired and just wanted to get back to the digs, where tea and sandwiches awaited, and then climb into bed. The next morning, she'd be catching the train to Clapham Junction to be with her dear mum and dad, and Zac and the baby. She hoped her dad had been all right and not had one of his turns. She knew that sometimes her mum struggled to deal with him alone.

She was relieved when she had signed what seemed to be the last programme extended eagerly towards her and was able to turn away, duty done. It was only then that a figure stepped towards her out of the shadows. The light GI uniform stood out in the gloom so that Cissie could see that the Yankee soldier was of average height and, although not exactly stocky, was certainly well-built. He wasn't holding out a programme, so what did he want? Cissie's forehead squeezed into a frown.

The fellow reached up to remove his cap. In the shaft of light from the open stage door, Cissie saw that he was dark skinned, the whites of his large eyes gleaming out of his face. Eyes that were desperate.

Eyes she was sure she'd seen before.

How the hell had he found her? No, it couldn't

be. This was just one of thousands of black GIs still here in Blighty. But his face speared into that memory she'd battled so hard to bury in the secret depths of her mind. And she knew.

She rocked on her feet. Opened her mouth, but the scream died in her throat. She felt herself falling into darkness. The air about her turned red, red with fury and hate and terror, as the memory came back like some slithering evil.

The man's eyes bore into hers, searching. She reared away from him, a horrible coldness breaking over her as she emerged from the veil of shock, and festering rage boiled up inside her.

'Get away from me!' she hissed through clenched teeth, forcing her numbed legs to move her body away from him.

But his hand caught her arm, stinging into her flesh. 'Please, miss, if ya won't talk to me, at least take this. It's mighty little, but it's the best I could do.'

Cissie's eyes flashed at him like rapiers. But as her senses trickled back, she was aware that he'd let go of her and instead had reached into his breast pocket and was holding out a fat envelope. Though her soul blackened with anger, her hand moved forward to take the item from him. She glanced down. It was so stuffed full of banknotes that it couldn't be sealed.

Money. Did he think money could compensate for what he'd done? She went to tear the notes from the envelope and throw them back in his face. But, somehow, in one of the most appalling moments of her life, she managed to find the courage to remain calm and dignified. An image of her parents, her poor father, struggling to make ends meet, jumped into her mind. And someone having to stay at home to care for the baby the bastard had given her instead of going out to earn a wage had made matters so much worse. This money could make a difference to them.

Reason clawed its way through her anger and pain. The individual that stood before her, cap in hand, hadn't been the one. Punched to the ground and kicked, knocked unconscious, he'd been as powerless as she had been to stop the thing that had been done to her. She plumbed the depths of her memory.

There'd been arguing, his deep voice had been appalled, and in her head swam the wavering image of the black GI being dragged away, blundering and protesting, by the *other* one.

It felt as if a stone had lodged in her throat, and she had to force her voice to function. 'If you want to talk, meet me at ten o'clock tomorrow morning,' she grated. 'There's a café just round the corner.' She pointed briefly in the right direction, and watched as he nodded sharply.

'I'll be there, miss. Without fail. And . . . thank you.'

She could see his face was taut as he lifted his hand to the side of his head in the indication of a salute and then disappeared into the shadows. Would he come? Would she find the strength to go there herself? Just now, there was a knot locked solid in her chest, and a faint, desperate sound escaped her lips.

She looked up. And felt she would break, as

suddenly, from out of nowhere, Jake materialised in front of her.

★ ★ ★

Jake found himself perched on the edge of the seat with joyful excitement and had to force himself to sit back comfortably. He hadn't told a soul that he was going to the theatre to watch Cissie that night. He'd even secreted his best shirt and flannels, carefully folded, in the drawstring bag that normally contained his football boots, so that his family wouldn't question why he was going off to play footie in his best clothes. Instead, he made his way to Wimbledon, got himself something to eat in a café and changed in the toilet, before going in search of a small bunch of flowers that was now tucked under his seat.

That evening was going to be the most exquisite of his life and he didn't want to share it with anyone else, not even his family. He knew Cissie was going to be amazing. His heart had felt all tangled up in itself when she'd performed that impromptu dance in the street on the afternoon of his birthday party. How stunning would she be in the stage spotlights, dancing to an orchestra?

He'd been to the flicks loads of times, of course, but never to a theatre. The ticket hadn't come cheap, but it was going to be worth every penny. He'd been open-mouthed as he'd entered the auditorium. The rich drapes, the gilded work, the complete grandeur of the place overawed him. And the atmosphere was totally different, a sort of electricity buzzing in the air. And perhaps it was because the war in Europe was over, and Japan was expected to give its unconditional surrender any day, that jubilation was about to burst out, accentuating delight in whatever form it took.

The squeaks of sound as the orchestra tuned up, the lights dimming. The breath quickened in Jake's throat. Any moment, he would see the girl who had unwittingly wrapped herself about his soul. The orchestra struck up and Jake could barely contain himself.

She wasn't in the opening act, but it didn't matter. The whole thing was mesmerising and, if anything, the wait brought his nerves to fever pitch. 'Lili Marlene' then, a magician and a medley of Irish tunes played expertly on a fiddle. Jake was in his element. It was with Irish music that he'd been introduced to the guitar, of course. The theatre reached out to him like an ephemeral dream that encompassed his very being.

A couple more acts, and then there she was, gliding in front of some other dancers with Sean as her partner, interpreting the singer's performance of 'Apple Blossom Time'. She was like an angel, ethereal, her long hair swinging loose down her back. Jake had never seen anything so beautiful, the loveliness of her lithesome figure filling his heart. Oh, he knew from Mildred that she wasn't ready for romance. But he loved her so much, wanted to be with her, protect her, care for her, that he would wait for however long it took.

He itched for her next appearance, and when the compère at last announced that the first half would finish with Cissie and Sean dancing to

'Rhapsody in Blue', he found himself holding his breath in anticipation. He gasped as the music started and she floated onto the stage, enchanting, wondrous, and he knew then that he loved her with a passion beyond his understanding. His heart was skittering about, totally absorbed by this delicate, fragile, endearing creature.

It was over all too soon, but after the interval, she appeared in several acts, to take the lead briefly either as a soloist or with Sean. Jake's breath became trapped in his throat when the second *pas de deux* was announced. It was pure classical ballet this time, Cissie spinning impossibly on her toes and turning in Sean's supporting hands about her waist. Jake was utterly bewitched, as if under a spell. Which he supposed he was.

When the entire show was over, Jake sat for some moments, his heart glorying and lifted high on a wave of utter wonderment. He only got to his feet when he realised with embarrassment that he was blocking the row of spectators waiting to exit the auditorium. He mumbled an apology and joined in the exodus from the theatre.

But for him, it wasn't over. He was going to the stage door to surprise Cissie and present her with the flowers. He prayed she'd be delighted to see him. But if she only wanted to be friends for now, he didn't mind. They were both young and he understood how her dancing and the theatre were her life.

He waited almost breathlessly outside the stage door. Other dancers emerged first. The entire evening had dazzled him, so it would be a superb memory to collect some other autographs. And perhaps Cissie would be happier to think that he'd come to enjoy the whole event, which he had, rather than having eyes only for her. And so he held out his programme to the girl he recognised as the one who'd danced to 'Lili Marlene'.

'Is Miss Cresswell coming out, d'you know?' he couldn't stop himself from asking.

The blonde dancer's face twitched with annoyance. 'I expect so,' she snapped as she handed back the signed programme.

'Amazing to think she was off for so long with her ankle and yet she's back to dancing like this,' Jake went on, taken aback by the girl's attitude and wanting to soften the conversation.

'Ankle?' the girl almost scoffed. 'She hurt her ankle last year and was off for a few weeks, but then she was off for months because she had TB.'

Jake jerked back in surprise. TB? He shook his head in confusion.

'She had TB? Are you sure?' he mumbled. 'I thought —'

'I should know. I filled in for her while she was away, and now all I get is one flipping solo.'

'Er, oh,' Jake stuttered. 'Oh, I must've heard wrong. Never mind. Thanks for your autograph, er, Deirdre,' he said, glancing at the programme, but his voice faded in a trail of bewilderment.

Off with TB for months? So what was this story about Cissie's ankle? It didn't make sense. Jake stood back, his emotions fraying at the edges. The world seemed to fall away as he spied Cissie coming through the stage door with Sean at her side. They spoke a few words and then Sean slunk off into the night while Cissie stepped forward to meet the group of admirers wanting her autograph, a radiant smile on her face.

Jake couldn't bring himself to join them. What was going on? He'd always felt that there was some mystery about the Cresswells, but he'd forced it to the back of his mind, his feelings for Cissie had been so strong from the very beginning.

Now, suspicion and dismay tore through him. Those times when they'd gone up to central London first to see Big Ben lit up again, and then later on VE day, he'd constantly asked Cissie if her ankle was holding up. Had she been lying to him all along? And . . . why?

He waited, his heart numbing with pain, as the fans dispersed. The flowers slipped unnoticed from his fingers. What could he say to her? What words could he find?

And then something extraordinary happened. A GI, clearly of African descent Jake had noticed in the audience, stepped forward and grasped Cissie by the arm. She glared at the Yank, eyes blazing, and they exchanged a few heated words. Then the Yank gave her something, a small package, an envelope, maybe. She took it, her face like granite, spoke briefly again and pointed to the corner of the street. The American nodded, gave a half salute, and then strode off into the darkness.

For a second or two, Jake was stunned. What the blazes . . . ? But the overwhelming need to protect his love flared out and he sprang to Cissie's side.

'Jake!' Her eyes widened in shock and something he wanted to believe was relief.

'Was that chap bothering you?' Jake snapped, burning with rage. 'I'll knock his block off — '

'Jake, no!' Cissie's grip was tight on his arm. 'No, truly, he's not bothering me. It's just someone I knew. Once. It's all right, believe me.'

She was staring up at him, desperate and pleading. The muscles around his heart had contracted as he struggled to hold his shattered thoughts together. Was she lying? Again?

'What the hell's going on?' he demanded. 'Who was he really? And what's all this business about being off for months with TB?'

He watched as Cissie's mouth fell open. 'W-what? H-how did you know?' she stammered.

'That other dancer, she told me. So why have you been lying, Cissie?'

She remained motionless, and even in the dim light he could see her face turn to paper.

'All right,' she murmured, her voice low and intense. 'Go home, Jake. I'll see you tomorrow. And I'll tell you everything. I promise. But . . . I need you to trust me.'

Trust? Could he trust her after this? But yes, of course he could. He nodded, and she gave a half-smile as she turned and walked away, leaving the magic of the evening shattered at his feet. His instinct was to go after her, see her safely back to her digs, but somehow he knew he wasn't wanted. Besides, another girl from the cast had come up and linked her arm through Cissie's and they'd turned the corner out of sight. Perhaps Jake should at least run after them and give Cissie the flowers, but . . . where were they? Damn, he must have dropped them. They must be somewhere.

But as he searched the pavement and the little gathering dispersed, they were nowhere to be seen. And he was left, confused and alone, in the street.

★ ★ ★

From the corner of her eye, Deidre had observed the scene with Cissie with burning curiosity. First this handsome young chap — at least he appeared handsome in what light there was — had asked Deidre for her autograph when it was clear it was Cissie bloody Cresswell he was really interested in. Then some sort of altercation with a black GI that had ended with Cissie accepting a small package from him.

It was really strange. The young man obviously knew Cissie in some way, but seemed to think she'd only recently damaged her ankle. And he was definitely taken aback when she'd said Cissie had been off for many months with TB. So taken aback that he'd dropped the flowers he was carrying, which he'd doubtless planned to present to Cissie. But then he sprang after her when he saw her arguing with the GI.

How very odd. Deidre wriggled her lips venomously as she mulled it over in her mind. She must be able to use this little nugget to her advantage. Maybe even get Cissie dismissed from the company so that she herself could regain her place as principal dancer. And then she'd be the one getting all the praise and the flowers again!

Deidre went to stamp on the little bouquet on the pavement. Oh, dear, did it get trodden on? But then she changed her mind. It would feel like a triumph to take Cissie's flowers and let everyone think they were for her. Oh, what joy!

A sly smirk lifted the corners of her mouth as she checked no one was looking before snatching up the posy. Now, she really needed to give this some thought. And she hurried off to her own digs which were in the opposite direction from Cissie's, the wheels of her mind spinning deviously.

24

Cissie sat at the table in the café, conscious of the blood trundling nervously through her veins. She aimlessly stirred the hot drink in front of her. The one cube of sugar the café owner had allowed her had done nothing to disguise the bitterness of the coffee that she suspected consisted entirely of chicory. Wartime rationing and substitution were still in force.

She'd tossed and turned the whole night with scarcely a wink of sleep, her brain going over and over the event that had destroyed her. She couldn't for the life of her conjure up a picture of her attacker's face. Yes, it had been dark, and yes, she'd barely been conscious after the way he'd smashed her head on the ground. But how could she not have an image of him in her head? Had it been shock, some sort of self-defence mechanism that had blanked it from her mind? All she could remember as her senses had slowly drifted back was the wild expression of the black GI as he fought to come to her aid while the *other one* was restraining him and pulling him away, to leave her broken and shattered on the ground.

Her head ached from digging into her empty memory. All she could find there was anger and suffering. But what she knew for certain was that the GI who'd turned up the previous evening like a bolt from the blue had done his best to protect her, even if his efforts had been in vain.

Would he have the courage to meet her again? God knew she'd had to scrape the depths of her own soul to drag herself here. She almost wondered if she'd imagined the whole affair. But she'd slept with the bundle of banknotes under her pillow, and now they were tucked safely in the inner pocket of her handbag.

The bell over the door jangled, and she glanced up. Her heart buckled. It was him.

She stiffened, unable to move, as his large, expressive eyes swivelled about the café. It was a small place, and he spotted her at once. She thought she might pass out as he came to stand before her.

'Morning, miss,' he began in a low, strained tone, giving that half salute again and removing his cap. 'May I sit down?'

Cissie's voice stuck in her throat, and she had to nod her consent, her pulse drumming a savage tattoo at her temples.

'Thank ya, miss.' He pulled out a chair with guarded, deliberate movements before slowly lowering himself onto it. 'And thank ya for seeing me.'

Cissie gulped, and forced herself to meet his searching eyes.

'W-who are you?' she croaked hoarsely. 'And what d'you want?'

The fellow lowered his dark brown eyes. 'My name, I's ashamed to say, is Private Saul Williams of the United States Army. An' I don't want nothing. Except to say I couldn't go back home without trying to find ya, an' saying how mighty sorry I am that I couldn't save ya that night. No, sorry ain't in it. I's nothing but a contemptible coward, an' I've hated myself ever since.'

The hard lines about Cissie's mouth slackened. This man, whoever he was, seemed genuinely remorseful. But she couldn't help retorting, 'And I've felt dirty and ashamed ever since, too.'

This Saul Williams's smooth forehead was suddenly scored with deep furrows. 'I understand that, miss. An' I'd give my life if I could change what happened. An' I ain't asking for forgiveness. No siree. 'Cos I know ya can't give it. But what I can do is give ya the name of the man who did that to ya so ya can get justice.'

Cissie jerked back in the chair, her heart vaulting painfully. That was what she craved, wasn't it? But the enormity of it was too much to take in so quickly.

'H-how did you find me?' she quizzed him, fighting her emotions that were all topsy-turvy and upside down. Could she trust this chap who could, after all, be a complete stranger and not who he said he was at all?

'Wasn't easy,' he explained, spreading his hands. 'When Germany surrendered an' we were eventually transported back to the United Kingdom, I went back to where we were that night, an' tried to retrace our steps. Took me a while an' then I found the street with the little park an' the bomb site an' all. I seemed to recognise it, an' it just had to be the place. I knew which direction ya was headed an' figured ya must've been heading home. So I started knocking on doors. Spreading out down side streets in all directions. I was that close to giving up, an' then I struck lucky. A young kid, must've been yar next-door neighbour, told me ya might've been the girl I was looking for. She . . . she told me why ya had to move away. An' she told me yar name an' said ya's a dancer. So every time I got a pass to come to London, I trawled through all the theatres till I found ya. Was in a newspaper review I saw yar name in the end. But I couldn't be sure till I saw yar face on stage last night.'

Cissie's gaze had been riveted on her cup of bitter coffee while Saul's voice had droned on. It was the mix of southern drawl and sing-song lilt that she recognised *from before*. She'd jolted when he'd mentioned he knew why she'd had to move away. So, he knew about Jane, did he? She was grateful when he didn't dwell on it, and waited for him to finish.

When he did, the awkwardness returned, cramping her belly. It was easier to listen than to talk herself. So sudden, such a shock. She didn't know what to say. The cogs of her mind sluggish and senseless.

'So . . . now you're willing to tell me . . . who the other man was?' she asked him after several moments of silence.

Saul dipped his head sharply. 'Sure am, miss.'

Cissie pursed her lips, struggling with her crippling agony. Did she really want to know? To relive the pain? Or leave it buried? She could feel the man's eyes on her as she digested his words.

'By the laws of the United States Army, he'll hang for what he did,' Saul barely whispered.

Cissie's glance shot up, locking on his. Yes, that's what she'd been told. The bastard who'd . . . assaulted her — she still couldn't say the foul word — deserved it. He'd wrecked her family's lives, and her own. The consequences had ruined her future. What nicer lad than Jake could she ever meet? She wanted to get close to him, but she couldn't. She could never love a man in the full sense of the word after what had happened.

She suddenly filled up with suspicion. 'How do I know you're telling the truth?' she demanded. 'For all I know you've just got some other grudge against the man you're going to name and you want him out of the way. And then the real culprit gets off scot-free while an innocent man is hanged.'

Saul took an enormous breath, his wide nostrils flaring. 'I's telling the truth, miss, 'cos I'll go to prison for perverting the course of justice. For some years, I figure. But I can't live with myself no more.'

Cissie's eyes narrowed. 'So why didn't you come forward at the time? I went to the police, you know. And they called in the American Military.'

'Yeah, I know. They made extensive enquiries. But I's ashamed to say I kept my mouth shut 'cos I was scared. Scared of his threats towards me.'

'Threats?'

'Yes, miss,' Saul answered, and Cissie could see from the expression on his face that he was desperate to explain himself. 'I know him of old, ya see. We come from the same small town, an' I never liked him much. But he ended up as my sergeant, an' he had a pass to come up to London at the same time. The whole squad did. But it was more him hanging around us than the other way round, even though strictly speaking blacks and whites aren't supposed to hang out together. I could see he was getting drunk an' abusive, an' we Americans are supposed to be good an' upright. The others could see which way the wind was blowing, too, an' disappeared off. So I was left trying to keep him out of trouble on my own. But it was difficult with him being my sergeant an' all. An' . . . ' Saul paused, his voice ragged. 'Ya know he knocked me down. I fell back an' cracked my head on a brick or something. I lost a bit of time, an' then when I came to . . . I realised what had happened. An' he threatened to say it was me if I reported it. He said no one would believe a dirty nigger over him. An' I didn't want to hang for something I didn't do. Ya see, I didn't know if in the confusion an' the dark, ya'd have realised that it wasn't me who did it. I mean, I didn't know then ya was going to have a child because of it. A white child. But, anyway, that's not proof that I didn't do it as well.'

Cissie looked at him steadily, holding his gaze for some seconds before nodding. 'But I know you didn't. I remember you trying to stop him. How he punched you and you fell back. And then he kicked you several times as well. You were lying still, unconscious. And then straightaway after he . . . you were trying to help me, but he was pulling you away. I know you weren't to blame at all.'

'Thank ya, miss. It's good to know ya believe me. So can we go to a police station right now, and I can hand myself in? But just one more thing, miss. He threatened my family back in Alabama. Blacks an' even poor whites don't have no rights back

304

home, ya see. So will ya make sure the authorities know to keep an eye out for them, please?'

Cissie snatched in an unexpected gasp. Against all odds, she believed what this fellow was saying. The other . . . creature sounded a really nasty piece of work and deserved to be punished. But did Saul Williams deserve to go to prison? Did his family deserve to be put in danger? For what if for some reason his story wasn't believed despite her own evidence? She'd been warned at the time that such cases were sometimes very hard to prove. If the monster was tried and then acquitted, might he not seek revenge? And what about Jane, for surely it would mean that he'd learn he had a daughter?

Oh, God, Cissie felt torn apart. Anger rose in her like a riptide. Of course she wanted the brute to be punished. But that meant . . . that another human being would be hanged on her say-so. Didn't that make her as bad as him in some way? And what if it all went wrong and Saul Williams was convicted instead, despite her own testimony? Things could get twisted by a good lawyer, she'd been warned. And did she want to go through a protracted court case, live the trauma all over again? Be humiliated, probably have to be in the same room as *him*?

A strangled groan wrenched from her throat. She didn't know what to think, her brain deadened by an unaccountable numbness.

'W-would he do it again, d'you think?' she heard her trembling voice ask.

She saw Saul blink at her in surprise and it was several moments before he replied. 'I can't answer that question, miss,' he spoke at last, his words slow and heavy. 'Back home, he was never in no trouble with the ladies. Always found what he wanted. But here we were stationed inland from Plymouth, on a wild open place called Dartmoor. The ladies there weren't so accommodating, shall we say. An' we knew where we was headed. France. An' we figured we'd be like cannon fodder when we went. None of us expected to survive, an' I guess that ate into all of us. We'd done all the training, an' then it was just the waiting. It could get to ya, miss. I reckon some of us just managed it better than others. An' he was mighty drunk that night. So I don't know, miss. I'd like to think it was a one-off, but a one-off too many.'

Cissie had bowed her head as she listened, thoughts racing about inside her skull and bursting to escape. This had all come too suddenly. And too late. If Saul Williams had come forward at the time, when outrage and the desire for justice still burned in her breast, it might have been different. But now that she was starting to get on with her life — not put things behind her, since that was impossible — but at least to move forward, did she really want to open up the chasm of her despair once again?

She raised her eyes to Saul, caught between anger and doubt. 'To be perfectly honest, I don't know what to think,' she sighed, amazed at herself for opening her heart to this stranger. 'I'd like to see him punished. Of course I would. And I appreciate your tracking me down. It must've taken some courage. But what if we go to the police and it all goes wrong?

I don't want to get you into trouble.'

'That's a risk I's willing to take — '

'But I'm not sure *I* am. Let me think about it. As it is, you can walk away from this with a clear conscience. And you're right. I can't forgive you. Because there's nothing to forgive.'

She watched, intrigued almost, as his prominent eyes glittered with tears. 'Ya don't know what it means to hear ya say that,' he choked. 'I'll still never forgive myself, but . . . Ya need time to think this over. Let me . . . D'ya have a paper an' pen on ya?'

Cissie gazed at him and shook her head. The next instant, Private Williams pushed back his chair and went up to the counter to speak with the café owner. He evidently begged a scrap of paper, wrote on it, folded it into four, then wrote something slightly longer on the outside. He politely thanked the man standing behind the counter, then returned to the table, holding out the note to Cissie.

'That's my name, army number an' my family home back in Alabama. An' inside . . . ' he faltered, 'is the name of the man ya might want to bring to justice. I's not sure right now what I want to do. I can only thank ya for talking to me, Miss Cecily, if ya'll permit me to call ya that?'

Cissie stared at him, suddenly overcome with a sadness that astounded her. This poor man had suffered almost as much as she had. 'Of course,' she half smiled back. 'And it's Cissie. To friends. And thank you for the money. It wasn't necessary, but it'll be very useful.'

Her body, her mind, everything stilled. She felt

307

scoured of all emotion now. Empty. Unable to absorb anything more. She looked at the folded paper, so white against the dark brown fingers that held it. Slowly, Saul lowered his hand and placed the note on the table in front of her, before turning and walking out of the café.

Cissie sat, stunned, almost in a fever stare, waiting for the world to fall back into place around her. Gradually she felt the strain empty out of her in a weary torrent, but it wasn't over. She'd promised Jake the truth. And he deserved it.

Hauling herself to her feet, she picked up the piece of paper. She read Private Saul Williams's details on the outside. But she couldn't bring herself to unfold it. That would make it too real. So she stuffed the note down to the bottom of her handbag and made for the door.

25

Cissie walked through the hallway towards the kitchen, her jaw set firmly. She'd left the café in a daze, her legs feeling unsteady. She was grateful that her colleagues had already set out in whichever direction they were headed, since at that moment she didn't feel she could enter into any coherent conversation. But as she'd sat in the compartment for the short train journey, her reeling senses had gradually settled. She decided to walk from the station at the other end rather than catch a bus. It would give her more thinking time. And as she made her way through the Sunday morning streets, her resolve began to strengthen.

'Ah, Cissie, sweetheart!'

Bridie looked up at once from peeling potatoes at the table and stepped forward to hug her daughter. Ron was sitting in his chair, and his face lit up like the sun to see his special girl. Wrapped for a moment in her mother's arms, Cissie's throat closed up. Her dearest family, who'd endured so much because of her.

'Mmm, you had a good week?' Ron asked as she went to give him a kiss.

'Yes, I have.' Cissie made sure her smile was radiant. 'In fact, the show's doing so well, I was given a bonus.' She opened her handbag and taking out the bulging envelope, placed it on the table. 'There!' she crowed triumphantly.

Bridie gazed down at the package, her jaw

sagging in astonishment. 'Sure, that must be a small fortune, so it must.'

'Well, we're sold out for the whole three months,' Cissie explained. It wasn't a complete lie, after all. There were indeed very few tickets left. The bonus idea was fabrication, of course. She might reveal the truth in time. But for now she needed to sleep on her encounter with Private Saul Williams, and she wanted her parents to have the money straight away.

'It'll come in handy for some things for Jane,' she continued, giving her mother a knowing look.

Bridie nodded her head. 'If that's what you want. But I'll be buying some material out of it to make you a new frock, so I will. Haven't we got enough unused coupons to paper a wall. Talking of which, I pooled our rations to buy a joint for today. A hand and spring, so it'll do a few days into the week, as well. I've only just got back from Mass, so I haven't put it in the oven yet, and I didn't know what time you'd be back.'

'So I've got a couple of hours, then? Only I wanted to spend some time with Jake.'

The words rolled around in her mouth like gravel. She saw the little smile on Bridie's face. Her mum would have gained the wrong impression, but it couldn't be helped.

'Off you go, then. Zac's taken Jane round the block in the pram to try to get her off to sleep. Grizzly, so she's been. Think she's teething.'

'OK, Mum, thanks. See you later.'

Cissie turned from the room, her feet suddenly dragging. But she needed to talk to Jake, and it was now or never. She left her handbag in her room. She didn't even want to think about the paper scrunched up at the bottom.

When she knocked on the door to Number Eight, she was half relieved and half fearful when it was Jake who answered it. She couldn't read the expression on his face.

'Jake,' she said, and he nodded a silent greeting. Oh, Lord. 'Jake, about last night,' she went on in a rush, abandoning the words she'd rehearsed. 'It's a long story. Can we go somewhere quiet? To the park?'

'Yes, of course. I'll just tell Mum I'm going out.'

Cissie waited, chewing her lip. But Jake returned within a minute.

'I reckon they all think there's something romantic developing between us,' he said wryly, pulling the door shut behind him. 'I wish there was. At least, I think I do. You were phenomenal last night, you know. I fell in love with you all over again.'

They'd reached the end of the street and had to concentrate on crossing the main road. With private cars starting to emerge again, traffic was generally becoming heavier. It made a good enough excuse not to reply. For Jake's words had been a spike in her side.

'I really loved the show,' he enthused when they'd reached the pavement on the far side and were walking along Cambridge Road. 'I didn't tell anyone I was going 'cos I wanted it all to myself. To savour the moment. I've never been to a live performance before; it was amazing.'

'I'm glad you enjoyed it.' The platitude tripped easily from Cissie's tongue, denying the angst that

311

churned inside. She was thankful when Jake went on to comment on the various acts. His praise was gratifying, yet it felt as if they were both tiptoeing round the reason they were there.

By the time they walked in through the Sun Gate entrance to the park, Cissie's pulse was gearing up. They'd dropped into an awkward silence that Cissie filled by searching out a bench somewhere quiet. It wasn't easy with it being a summer Sunday and so many people flocking to the park. She finally spotted an empty seat under a tree away from any roadway or path, where they could talk without too much distraction.

'So, you want to know what was going on last night,' she began, fighting to hold together the tortured splinters of her heart.

'Well, yes.' Sitting beside her, Jake sounded equally as awkward. 'I was worried about you, with that fellow.'

'As it happens, there was no need to be,' Cissie assured him. 'But you deserve the truth. You've been so kind. Only . . . I hope it won't make you hate me.'

'Hate you?' Jake protested. 'Why should I do that?'

Cissie stole a sideways glance at him. 'Because I've been lying to you. We all have. My entire family.'

She saw Jake frown, and her heart wanted to cry out. 'With good reason, I'm sure,' he murmured, closing his fingers around her hand.

She instantly pulled away. 'Judge that for yourself when I've told you everything. The thing is . . . ' She hesitated, but now the moment had come, she

312

felt unbelievably calm about it. Resigned, weary of the lies, perhaps. She clasped her hands in her lap, staring resolutely at them. 'The thing is,' she repeated, 'we never lived in Islington. We weren't bombed out. We were driven out from where we lived. By nasty remarks, people calling us names. Well, me mainly. We had rubbish stuffed through our letter box. Poison letters. I even had stones thrown at me in the street.'

'What!' Jake's eyes flashed with anger.

But Cissie shook her head. 'It was my own fault, really. They didn't understand. Because I didn't want to tell them. I felt so ashamed, humiliated. Guilty, even though it wasn't my fault. It's ... really hard to talk about. So ...' She turned back to Jake, gently placing her forefinger over his lips. 'Please don't say a word until I've finished. I know you'll be shocked and angry. But I hope you won't think too badly of me, because I value your friendship.'

'No, I won't think that!'

She could see the fire in his eyes and gave the hint of a wry smile before she folded her hands in her lap again, fixing her gaze on them. 'Well,' she began, bowing her head further,

'Jane isn't my sister. She's mine. And the reason we were hounded out was that our neighbours thought I was a fallen woman. But it wasn't like that, at all. If it had been, it might've been easier.'

She felt Jake shift beside her, but he kept to his word. Her heart shrivelled, but she had to tell him. Everything. So she began with what happened that night, how her parents had come to look for her when she hadn't arrived home, and found her

313

crawling from the bomb site. How her mother had called in the police, who in turn had called in the US Military, who'd treated the matter with grave severity. But all to no avail. How she'd later discovered she was pregnant, but rather than give Jane up to the authorities, Bridie had persuaded her to keep the child and she and Ron would bring it up as theirs. But with their neighbours not knowing the truth and being so horrible, they'd decided to move on and make a fresh start where nobody knew it was she who'd had the baby and not Bridie. By saying they'd been bombed out, they'd hoped to gain people's sympathy rather than hostility. And how, out of the blue, Private Saul Williams had turned up the night before and given her the name of her attacker. How she believed what he said, but dreaded to think what the consequences could be.

'And now I don't know what to do,' Cissie concluded in a whisper.

She heard Jake draw in a deep breath and then release it in a long, heartfelt stream. She couldn't bear to look at him. Didn't want to see the distaste on his face, so waited silently for his reply while her heart knocked against her ribs.

When he finally spoke, Jake's words weren't what she'd expected. 'So, at the theatre, they didn't know what had really happened, either?'

Cissie shook her head. 'No. Only Sean. We have a special relationship, you see. He even offered to marry me, bless him, and say the baby was his. Not that anyone would've believed it. So he came up with the idea that I'd developed a mild case of TB and had to go away to recuperate. I said I'd been in Devon because I knew there was a sanitorium from when I was evacuated there at the start of the war.'

'Yes, that's what the girl I was talking to before you came out said. The fair-haired dancer. The one who did a couple of solos.'

'Oh, Deirdre,' Cissie scoffed. 'That doesn't surprise me. She doesn't like me because she filled in for me while I was away and reckoned she should keep the role when I came back.'

'She certainly seemed surprised when I said you'd been away because of your ankle. So why did you tell us something different?'

'Oh, that was because of Zac. If we'd kept to the TB story, he might've let the cat out of the bag. Forgotten that I was supposed to have been away for months. And apart from Sean, he'd never see anyone from the theatre, so it seemed the safest thing.'

'Oh, I see. And what about the baby? Why did you let your mum persuade you to keep her? Isn't she a constant reminder of what happened?'

Cissie felt the familiar stab of pain in her side. 'Yes, she is. But she's still half mine. And she's the only grandchild Mum and Dad are ever likely to have. Zac, well, he never even realised I was pregnant. I never got really huge like some people do, and I wore loose clothes. Zac doesn't understand about things like that. But most of all, Mum was once the nurse in a big children's home, and she didn't want her grandchild abandoned to somewhere like that. And she's always been so good about everything, supporting me becoming a dancer when I could've earned more money elsewhere. And she was marvellous when Jane was

315

born. Delivered her, helped me through it all. I couldn't deny Mum the chance of being a grand-mother. Because, after what happened, I could never let a man near me again. Even if I loved him.' She forced herself to steal a glance at Jake, and her soul fragmented as she saw the pain writ-ten on his face.

He swallowed hard.

'Not even . . . if that someone was prepared to wait?' he croaked. 'To take things as slowly as you wanted?'

Cissie felt cruel shards of glass in her heart as she shook her head. 'No. But what I need now is to decide what to do. I'm not sure I even want to know the bastard's name, let alone face him in court. Go through it all again. Be publicly humil-iated. We've already had to move on once. We don't want to be forced to do it again. And my career could be ruined if the truth got out. And do I really want to send my daughter's father to the gallows?'

Misery tightened into a desolate fist inside her and Cissie turned her head to look steadily at Jake. She could see his eyes were pools of anguish and a deep frown raked across his forehead. He opened his arms as if to draw her to him, but she instinctively backed away.

'Jake, I'm sorry,' she muttered as her insides lurched.

She waited, listening to him give another deep sigh. She knew she must have hurt him terribly, so she was surprised by his next words.

'Don't say that. None of this is your fault. But I can't decide for you. Only you can do that. But what I do know is that you need to take your time. And shouldn't you talk to your parents about it?'

Cissie gave a brief shake of her head. 'No. I don't think so, anyway. I don't want to bring the pain of it back again unless I have to. I think Mum's still so angry that she'd encourage me to go back to the police. But she hasn't met Private Williams. She wouldn't understand that I'd be worried it'd go wrong for him. And Dad . . . He blames himself that he wasn't able to protect me. He still has funny turns from the first war. A type of shellshock. An upset like that could bring on a serious episode. No, Jake.' She turned to him, grasping his arm so that he'd look directly at her. 'You're the only person I'm telling about Private Williams. I'm not even telling Sean. He'd just fly off the handle. No. You're the only one I trust to keep a level head. To help me decide what to do.'

Jake pulled in his chin as the enormity of the situation washed through him, thoughts racing about in his head. All he wanted was for Cissie to be happy. To recover from the terrible ordeal that had broken her life. Her revelation had been a massive shock to him, although at least he knew now why she felt she could never properly love a man. He was the only one she trusted to help her make this huge decision. Her words were like arrows darting about in his brain. It was all too much.

'Look, Cissie,' he said on a long exhalation of breath. 'We're both of us only eighteen. And this is . . . too big for us to handle on our own. I'm pleased you felt able to confide in me, but . . . There is one other person we can trust.

317

You mightn't think so, but then you don't know her like I do. And sometimes it helps to talk to someone who's just that bit removed. And she has the most remarkable ability to see through things.'

Cissie blinked slowly. 'I'm . . . not sure,' she murmured. 'Who?'

Jake's mouth curved with compassion. 'Someone closer than you think. Best wait until tomorrow, though. She'll be on her own. But for now, seeing as we're here, shall we go for a stroll? Seems a pity not to.'

He stood up, holding out his hand. Cissie got to her feet, doubting, perplexed. Unsure. But she found her hand moving forward, and Jake's fingers closed gently over hers. It felt safe and warm and secure.

* * *

Eva's fingers had been resting softly against her lips. She'd sat, quietly listening while Cissie emptied out her heart. She'd been knocked sideways by the revelation, although in some ways, she wasn't surprised. She'd always felt the family were hiding some sort of secret. But she hadn't expected this.

She felt herself stumble through every emotion, just as she knew the poor kid and her family would have done. Shock, horror, anger, frustration, sadness. Followed by admiration for their courage. She could see unshed tears collecting in Cissie's eyes as she finished her story. Eva's warm, golden heart brimmed over, and she hurried round the kitchen table to hold Cissie's trembling form against her.

318

'There, there, luvvie,' she crooned. 'That's right. Have a good cry. It's what you need.'

She waited patiently, Cissie's tears ripping her to shreds. It was bloody awful what the girl had been through, and it wasn't over yet. Jake had landed her with a flaming big responsibility. She was flattered by his faith in her, but was she up to it? But that's what you did for your children, wasn't it? *Anything.*

She knew, though, that no one cried forever, and Cissie's sobs gradually eased. The girl pulled back, sniffing, and rubbing her fingers over her tear-ravaged cheeks.

'Oh, Mrs Parker, what am I to do?' she gulped.

'Call me Eva, ducks.' Compassion was etched into Eva's lined face. 'And for now, you do nothing. Though it seems to me you've already got all the pros and cons worked out. You don't really want to open up a can of worms. Justice might seem sweet, but it'd come at a bleeding great price.'

Cissie gave a wry grimace. Yes, Jake was right. His mum had hit the nail on the head.

'Yes.' Cissie swallowed down the last of her tears. 'But . . . what if he did it again? I'd hate to think of someone else going through the same thing when I could've prevented it.'

Eva leant back, tipping her head to one side as she contemplated the tension on Cissie's face. 'You know, love, sometimes in life you have to be a bit selfish. Think just of yourself. I think in your heart of hearts, you just want to put it behind you. Pick up the pieces of your life as best you can, and get on with it. But you need time to make up your mind for sure. My advice to you is to carry on as normal. I think that's what this Private Williams chappie understood. That's why he wrote them details down for you like he did. Took him a year to work out what he wanted to do. He wanted to give you the same choice. So dry your eyes, and I'll put the kettle on. But I'm always here if you want to talk to me again. About anything.'

'Oh, Eva.' Cissie's shoulders slumped as the fight drained out of her. 'I think you're right. I'll try and put it out of my mind for now.'

'That's right. You'll know when you're ready to make that decision.'

'And you didn't mind me coming to talk to you? You won't tell anyone else what I've told you, will you?'

'That's one thing Evangeline Parker can do. I'm a bloody awful cook, and I'm not much better at sewing. But I know how to keep me gob shut.'

Cissie couldn't stop a wan smile appearing on her lips. 'Thank you, Mrs Parker, I mean, Eva. It's just that I really don't want Mum and Dad knowing about Private Williams. That I had the option of . . . well, you know. Not unless that's what I decide, and then they'll have to know.'

'No need to worry. Really. As far as I'm concerned, you never came through that door today.'

'Oh, thanks, Eva. I do appreciate it. And you're right. I do feel better for talking to you.'

'Feel even better with a cuppa inside you. And let me see if I can find a biscuit to go with it,' Eva winked as she trotted off towards the scullery.

Cissie watched her go. What a wonderful woman

she was. Because of her, Cissie was already feeling that the twisted threads of her life were beginning to unravel.

26

Mildred shoved open the kitchen door, humming as she did so. And then leapt back with a choking gasp.

'Cor, Mum, you didn't half make me jump!' she cried, her palm reaching protectively to her throat. 'It was so quiet, I thought you were all out celebrating.'

'You heard the news, then?'

'Course I did. It's all over the place. And I heard before you did, probably. The newspaper boys were already calling out about it when I was on me way to work and you were still fast asleep. *Japan surrenders!*' she mimicked. '*Read all about it!*'

Eva shook her head with a chuckle. 'Yeah, fantastic news, ain't it? Mind you, took the Japs bloody long enough, didn't it? You'd've thought one of them bleeding bombs was enough, without waiting for a second one, and *then* they waited a few days to make it official.'

'Strange lot, the Japs. Don't seem normal to me. But never mind. It's all over now,' Mildred crowed. 'We can all sleep easy in our beds. Can I have a dripping sandwich or something? I'm starving.'

'Course you can, love.' Already on her feet, Eva reached for the unappetising loaf on the table and began to saw off a slice for her daughter.

'So where's everyone else?' Mildred questioned,

flinging herself into a chair. 'Why ain't you out celebrating?'

'Have been. We heard it on the wireless first thing. They repeated the announcement what that new Prime Minister of ours, Attlee, made at midnight when we was all tucked up in our beds. And a nice surprise to wake up to the news that today's another public holiday, and all. But your dad and Jake and Zac still went into Price's to make sure they could have the day off. When they got back, they decided to go and watch the State Opening of Parliament. Never had the chance before. Took Primrose with them, but I didn't wanna go. It was chucking it down. Went round to Bridie and Ron's instead.

Ain't been back long.'

'Well, I wonder what the others are up to now.' Mildred began to ladle dripping from the chipped enamel fat-cup onto the chunk of bread. 'All right for some. Some of us have had to work, even if it is a flipping public holiday.'

'You wanna cuppa to go with that?'

'Yes, please, Mum. If you're putting the kettle on.'

'Yeah, I am. Could murder a cup meself. Bridie gave us one, but it was so weak, it was like bleeding dishwater. Between you and me, I'm sure it ain't just rationing. They can't afford much, I don't think. But you never hear them grumble.'

'Think you're right,' Mildred called out as her mum disappeared into the scullery. 'Things are better now, mind, with Cissie back at work. She won't get the evening off, neither. The show must go on, and all.'

323

'Yeah.' Eva gave a pensive nod as she shuffled back into the kitchen, her slippers scuffing along on the worn quarry floor tiles. 'Kettle was stone cold, so it'll take a minute or two to boil,' she muttered absently, since the words on her lips were far from those going round in her head. It was only the day before yesterday that Cissie had come to confide in her, and Eva was still in shock. Poor bloody kid. But she wouldn't tell a soul. Not even her Stan, who she shared everything with. The only other persons outside the Cresswell family who knew the truth were this Sean fellow and Jake. Eva's heart bled for her younger son. She could tell he was absolutely smitten, but Cissie had explained how she couldn't bear the idea of a man touching her in *that* way ever again. So could there possibly be any future in their relationship?

And Jake wasn't the only one of her offspring Eva was worried about. She knew more than anyone that Mildred's happy-go-lucky, carefree mask hid a far deeper, more troubled soul.

'Well, you must be overjoyed with the news,' Eva declared, putting a beaming edge to her subtly probing question. 'Means Gary'll be coming home soon.'

She noticed that Mildred's lips twitched. 'Not for a bit, I don't suppose,' Mildred answered. 'The Japanese surrender won't actually be done and dusted till the beginning of September. So they'll be keeping troops and the navy on alert till then. Didn't you read all of it? Or wasn't it all on the wireless?'

'Oh, erm, no,' Eva had to admit. Her Mildred, though, was becoming quite the learned one,

324

wasn't she?

'And then they've got to get back,' Mildred went on, biting delicately on the last of the bread and dripping rather than stuffing it into her mouth, Eva noticed, as she would have done just a couple of months previously. 'It's a hell of a long way to go by sea, even going through the Suez Canal. And then they've got to come right the way from the far side of the Med. So it'll be ages before Gary's back even if he left tomorrow.'

'Yeah, I suppose so.' Eva turned back towards the scullery as the kettle started to whistle. Since when was their Mildred such a clever clogs?

Eva took her time making the tea, the problem chewing at the back of her mind. For how could she broach the subject while making it seem uncontrived?

'Well, here we are,' she said, coming back into the room with the teapot. 'Used all the milk ration till tomorrow, but there's a bit of sugar left.'

'Right, ta, Mum.'

'So what you gonna do for the rest of the day, then?'

'When I've had this, I'm gonna change and then I'm meeting Oscar at the other side of the bridge at half past three. Gonna go and join in all the celebrations, me and him. 'Specially now the rain's cleared up. Never see nothing like this again in our lifetime. Least, I hope we don't! They say people'll have fireworks and all sorts. Music and dancing in the streets. And later on, lots of public buildings are gonna be lit up. Course, we can't stay out too late what with having to be up at the crack of dawn for our shift, worse luck.'

Eva drew in a wary breath through pursed lips. How could she put it without making it sound too obvious? 'You see a lot of this Oscar, don't you?' she said mildly.

But Mildred merely shrugged. 'So? Why shouldn't I? We're just mates. I like being with him. He's clever. Knowledgeable about stuff. Doesn't mind explaining things to me that I don't understand. Makes us feel like I could be clever, too.'

'Well, you are clever, love. Cleverer than what I could ever be. I've even noticed you've been talking posher since you've known him,' Eva observed cautiously.

'D'you think so?' Mildred's face lit up with pride.

'Yeah, I do. And I don't know what Gary'll think about it when he gets back.'

'Gary? Well, I don't care what he'll think. And I'm not gonna live like a flaming nun till he comes home. Anyway, he's hardly written to me over the past few months, so why should I care?'

Eva pulled in her chin. 'You are engaged to him, love, remember.'

'I know. But I'm not a hermit. Besides, I thought you and Dad were never that keen on him.'

'Well, it was all a bit rushed,' Eva agreed, biting her lip. 'But you did promise him.'

'Yes, well, I'll see what happens when he gets home. And I'm not stopping going out with Oscar.'

Eva blinked at her daughter, thoughts flying about in her brain. Mildred could be as stubborn as a mule. Just as she'd been when she'd announced she and Gary were getting engaged in the first place. In some ways, Eva was secretly pleased. This Oscar sounded a much better catch. But she could see trouble ahead. In the meantime, though, perhaps she should try and be a bit more open-minded.

'So, good-looking is he, this Oscar?' she asked with a twinkle in her eye.

Mildred stared at her for a second. 'Yes,' she nodded carefully. And then she threw caution to the wind as she grinned openly, 'Actually, he's bloody gorgeous!'

A smile flashed across Eva's lips at her daughter's obvious enthusiasm, but then she asked in a serious tone, 'So you sure you're just friends? Seems to us you quite fancy him. And you say he's footloose and fancy-free? So,' Eva hesitated for no more than a heartbeat, 'if you didn't already have Gary, would there be something in it?'

The jubilation slid from Mildred's face and she lowered her eyes. 'I don't know, Mum,' she sighed. 'From my side, yes, I think there probably would. But I don't know about Oscar. He's such a gentleman, I don't think he'd let his feelings show. Not when I'm engaged to Gary. And why would he fall for some ignorant little cow like me when he's so posh and clever?'

'For the same reasons Rob fell in love with your sister. 'Cos you're good and kind and funny. And you ain't ignorant. You just ain't had the chance of a good education. And you want to learn, so with him as your teacher, well. And let's face it, being a clippie for two years when there's a war on and having to deal with all sorts is an education in itself.'

Mildred's eyebrows wriggled. 'Yes, I suppose

so. And I mean, Oscar obviously likes being with me. And I love being with him. So . . . Oh, I don't know what to think.'

'Well, I think you should go out and enjoy yourself with him. It's not every blooming day a world war comes to a complete end. And if anything starts developing between you, then you should let it. As a mum, all you ever want is to see your children happy.'

Mildred met her mother's steady gaze. 'D'you really think so, Mum? That I should let me feelings for Oscar show?'

'Yeah, well, at least then you'd know how he feels. And you'd know if *you* really feel something for him, too. Now, when you've had that, go and make yourself look your best for him.'

At Eva's words, Mildred popped the last piece of bread into her mouth and, getting to her feet, washed it down with a slurp of tea. 'Thanks, Mum,' she nodded. 'Should've spoken to you sooner, you wise old owl.'

'Oi, not so much of the old!' Eva called at her daughter's retreating back as she went out of the door. Were they words of wisdom she'd imparted? She hoped so!

But those words stayed in Mildred's head as she hurried across Albert Bridge at the appointed hour, butterflies fluttering in her stomach. Her heart flipped over when she spied Oscar waiting for her, looking even more handsome in his civvies. Well, what the heck. The last twenty yards or so, she ran towards him, arms outstretched, so that he was pretty well obliged to open his own arms wide to catch her. Oh, it was so good to feel him against her, his strength as he lifted her off her feet and swung her round.

When he set her down again, she grinned up at him breathlessly. He looked astounded, but then he started laughing as he shook his head at her.

'Mildred Parker, you're crazy!' he chuckled. 'Nearly knocked me over!'

'Well, you don't celebrate the end of a world war that often!' she told him, her face split in a joyful smile. And then she added for good measure, 'And I can't think of anyone else I'd rather celebrate it with!'

She threw him a cheeky glance. He could either think her whirlwind greeting was because of the celebrations or because she had feelings for him. Hopefully, she was sowing a seed and then could see what his reaction would be.

Well, in for a penny, in for a pound. She grabbed his hand and pulled him forward. 'Come on, let's catch a bus up to Trafalgar Square and see what's going on there!'

She saw an answering grin spread across his face. He glanced down at their joined hands but made no attempt to pull away as they walked towards the bus stop.

Mildred thought it was the most wonderful afternoon of her life. The morning's rain had completely dried up and people were singing and dancing in the streets. It wasn't nearly so packed, though, as it had been on the two VE Days, and it all seemed a bit watered down by comparison.

Mildred supposed it was because the war in the Far East had affected far fewer people. It was only if you had someone fighting out there, as she had, that you really felt involved. And after all, it wasn't Japan that had dropped all those flaming bombs on London and all the other towns and cities in Britain. Also, it was three months now since Germany had surrendered, and the euphoria had died down. Nothing much had changed. Rationing was still in force — in fact, in some instances it was flipping worse — and the nation had been warned the austerity could go on for years. And Gawd knew how long it would be before this new welfare state the new Labour government had promised would come about.

On their way home, she and Oscar had discussed it over a meal of soup and home-made rolls in a quirky little café he knew in Chelsea's King's Road. The rolls were so much nicer than anything you could buy in the shops, and the soup tasted delicious. It was a fitting end to the celebrations, even if it hadn't, generally speaking, been as boisterous as the VE Days. And Mildred knew she'd enjoyed it more because she'd spent it with Oscar.

'I've had a smashing time,' she said as he paid the bill and they left the café. 'Thanks ever so much.'

'Just a pity we need to get some shut-eye before our early shift tomorrow,' Oscar answered ruefully, 'or we could've stayed out later. I'll probably be in bed before Georgie.'

'Won't you be worried about her?'

'No, no. She's with a group of school friends, so she'll be OK. She's a bit scatty, but when it comes to it, she's got her head screwed on. And one or two of the parents have gone along, too. And Mum was going to a neighbour's in our block of flats, so she won't have been on her own, either.'

'My mum was on her own this afternoon. She'd been in with our new neighbours, the ones I told you about, but me dad and me brother and sister went to watch the State Opening of Parliament this morning. Their only chance ever 'cos they'd normally be at work. But I expect they'll have got back soon after I left.'

'Certainly been a lot going on recently,' Oscar observed. 'The end of the war, the election, new government, the celebrations — '

'Well, I'm so glad I spent these ones with you,' Mildred interrupted him, Eva's words coming back to her as they reached the corner with Beaufort Street that ran into Battersea Bridge and her way home. 'It's OK. I can walk back on me own from here. And thanks again for a super time.'

She turned to him, and before her courage waned, she rose up on tiptoe and placed a quick peck on his cheek. She stood back, smiling and holding her breath. How would he interpret it? A polite kiss from a friend swept up in the joy of the occasion, or something more?

Oscar looked somewhat taken aback. But before he had a chance to react, Mildred danced away. 'See you in the morning!' she called back to him, laughing and waving as she skipped down the street. Well, she couldn't give him a better hint than that, could she?

Now, she'd have to wait and see.

27

'So, Deidre, *ma petite*, what was it you wanted to speak to me about in private?'

Monsieur Clément indicated that the girl should sit down in the chair opposite the desk in the office of the producer who had gone off to a meeting with the new Arts Council. He himself sat down in the producer's seat and leant back, contemplating the expression on the dancer's face. He couldn't quite make it out. But what he knew of old was that she could be difficult to handle sometimes.

'*Oui?*' he prompted when she didn't begin at once.

'Well,' she said hesitantly, 'I'm not quite sure I should be telling you this, but I thought you ought to know.'

Ah, the English had an odd way of beating about the bush, *n'est-ce pas?* Monsieur Clément thought to himself. And now he could put a name to the look in Deidre's eyes. Devious.

'If you think it is something that could affect the company, then you should tell me, *ma chère*,' he encouraged her, already on his guard.

'It could be if it became common knowledge,' Deidre answered. And now he could detect the smugness in her voice. The vindictiveness. *Oui*, that was the word.

'What could?'

'Well, it's to do with Cissie.'

Monsieur Clément, so used to scrutinising tiny movements of the body, saw her straighten her shoulders, and he was sure she was trying to hide a spiteful smile. He sat forward slightly.

'Go on.'

It seemed that Deidre didn't need telling twice now that she considered she'd hooked him in. 'It was last Saturday, at the stage door after the performance,' she said, launching delightedly into her story. 'It was really strange. A black GI went to speak to her. She obviously knew him and they had a bit of an argument. And then he gave her something. A small package. A bulging envelope, I think, though it was hard to see properly. But it all looked a bit suspicious to me.'

'Is that all? Did something else happen then?'

'Not really. Not with him. He went away. But then something else did happen.' She wriggled forward and dropped her voice conspiratorially. 'There was another chap as well, in civvies. He spoke to me while he was clearly wanting to speak to Cissie. Anyway, he said to me wasn't Cissie brilliant when she'd only just returned from her ankle injury. Well, I naturally thought he'd just got it wrong. I mean, her ankle was way back last year. At that point, it wasn't obvious to me that he knew her, so I just said no, she'd been away recovering from TB, and he was really shocked. And then he saw the argy-bargy with the GI and ran over as if to protect her. The GI was already leaving, but then Cissie spoke to this other chap, and it was as clear as day that they knew each other well. So, I think, from his reaction about the TB thing, that she'd been lying to him. And

333

if she has, maybe she's been lying to us all along as well. I mean, what proof do we have that she was ever ill at all? I know she said it was a mild case, but I never saw her coughing or anything. She just suddenly disappeared. So what if she went off dancing somewhere else? Not in London, else we'd know, but in some other place? She just went off, leaving you in the lurch — or you would've been if you hadn't had *me* to fill in. Or, worse still, what if she went off to have a baby, and it was that GI's? The timings would be about right. That could've been money for the kid he was giving her. If it got out that our principal dancer had had an illegitimate kid — and by a darkie at that — the press'd have a field day! It could ruin the company. So I reckon you should give her the push before it's too late.'

Monsieur Clément had been listening to her animated report with his eyes lowered to his clasped hands, but now his gaze shot up to the girl sitting opposite. She'd clearly relished telling him, and now she stopped and waited, a triumphant smirk plastered across her face.

Monsieur Clément watched her for some moments, wanting to make her sweat. Slowly, taking his time, he eased himself back in the chair again. His hand went thoughtfully to his chin, and then he twiddled his moustache, first one side and then the other. If there was anything in what Deidre was saying, it could possibly damage the company if it became public knowledge. The war, and particularly CEMA's backing, had done wonders for the world of dance, ballet in particular. It had brought it to the attention of the common man, when before it had been considered an entertainment only for the upper classes, and now all levels of society wanted to watch it. But classical ballet also held a certain traditional ethos with it, and having a child out of wedlock wasn't part of it. It wouldn't ruin the company, but it could bring some bad publicity — if it was true, of course. But it could ruin Cissie. She could be heckled nightly at the stage door, and he'd hate that for her. His little star might even leave, and he wouldn't want that, either. No. He could see that he was going to have to deal with this very carefully.

'*Ma chère mademoiselle*,' he began with a small smile, 'I am thinking that you have a very vivid imagination, which is, perhaps, not so bad in an *artiste*. But I myself rang the sanatorium and spoke to Cissie, so I am afraid your conclusions are incorrect. Whatever her relationship is with these two men, of course, I cannot say. But the fact is, *Mademoiselle* Deidre, that good though you are, she is a better dancer than you, and her private life is her own affair. You must understand, *ma petite*, that I have now lived through two world wars. In the first, I was a young man and I fought for my country in the trenches. I saw the most terrible things. Afterwards, I came to London to dance and escape the pitiable state my poor France had been left in. But my heart was still there, and it bled to see my country overrun by the Germans once again. The stories of what the Nazis did to my countrymen have sickened me. People I know. So, you see, this small thing you have brought to me,' and here Monsieur Clément flapped his hand

335

dismissively, 'is of no significance. I know you are jealous of Cissie, even though I have made you a soloist. But if I hear that you ever make any derogatory remarks about Cissie or the company, you will be dismissed. And do not forget that I know a lot of people in the dance world, and I could make it difficult for you ever to dance again. On the other hand, if you were to transfer to a different company of your own free will, I will give a good report of you. There are many big cities in this country with plenty of opportunities, and I should be willing to help you make the move. Now, please, leave this office and consider what I have said. Let me know your decision, and I can start making enquiries for you.'

Monsieur Clément had watched Deidre's face slowly lengthen as he'd spoken. Yes, he was tired of all the evil in the world and was overjoyed the war was over. All he wanted now was to concentrate on his art for as long as he was able. Men were gradually being demobbed, and it would be marvellous if the company could find some good dancers among them. If the outcome of this meeting with the Arts Council was favourable, the company could afford to take them on. They'd had a few good youngsters in the war, sixteen and seventeen-year-olds who'd then been conscripted. If some of them could come back, he'd be delighted. But he was sure nobody could ever match the chemistry between Sean and Cissie.

Ah, poor little flower. Whatever had really happened to her? He had to admit that he'd sometimes wondered. But he wasn't one to pry. It wasn't his place. And he could surely be forgiven the little white lie about the telephone call. He had a very soft spot for Cissie, as the English said. But he'd taken the greatest satisfaction from watching Deidre leave the office, her face like thunder.

Ah, well, she only had herself to blame. Now he could get on with the real business of the day. Rehearsals.

★ ★ ★

'Oh, isn't it exciting!'

The young girl was almost jumping up and down, grinning broadly at her new friend. Mildred smiled back. Yes, she was bloody excited, too, but she didn't want to let it show too flipping much. Georgina Miles might be only three years or so her junior, but she wanted to appear far more grown-up on her first proper evening out with Oscar — even if his little sister was in tow!

The foyer at Wimbledon Theatre was fizzing with anticipation as the spectators flocked in. So many voices bubbling in joyful expectancy, the atmosphere electric. Cor, no wonder Cissie loved being part of it all, Mildred thought as she gazed about in awe. It was like a different blooming world. Dazzling. So — what was the word? Yes, sophisticated. You'd never find Gary setting foot in a place like this. Even if many of the people weren't exactly toffs, they had certainly made the effort to dress up for the occasion. You didn't get nothing like this when you went to the cinema. The audience there filed in almost anonymously. Here they nodded and smiled and even spoke to fellow strangers. It seemed that gathering in the foyer was a sort of happy ritual.

'You two stay here and I'll go and get a programme,'

Mildred realised Oscar was saying in her ear, obviously wanting to make himself heard above the hubbub without having to shout. For just that second, Mildred tingled with delight at his closeness as his breath gently fanned her cheek when he spoke. She'd love it if . . . if he could be that close to her more often.

'Make sure you don't get picked up,' Oscar went on. 'Two prettiest girls here.'

He winked as he turned away, and Mildred's excitement grew. She felt . . . well, she couldn't really say what she felt as Oscar was swallowed up in the crowd, just the back of his head visible as he joined the queue for programmes. But there was definitely something warm curdling in Mildred's stomach.

She brought her head back to face Georgina, smiling at the younger girl's flushed cheeks. She didn't half look like her brother, even if he was so much older than her. Georgie was as beautiful as Oscar was handsome. Same generous mouth that seemed permanently curved upwards at the corners, same firm jawline, although slightly more pointed in Georgie. Above all, those expressive, warm brown eyes that could darken with gravity one moment and twinkle mischievously the next.

'Yes, it is,' Mildred finally replied to Georgie's comment. 'I ain't never . . . I mean, I've never been to a live theatre before.'

'What! Living in London and never been to the theatre?' Georgie's eyes nearly popped out of her head.

'Nah, never. Been to the flicks hundreds of times, but never the theatre.' Mildred didn't want to explain that in her circles it was considered a bit above them. Only posh people went out to the thee-ay-ter, although Rob had taken Gert a few times before they'd got married and moved out to their Surrey suburb. Mind you, Rob's family were several steps up the class ladder from the Parkers. 'I suppose you've been loads of times?' Mildred asked, trying to hide her thoughts and feeling somewhat envious.

She was surprised when Georgie pulled a face. 'Not really. I haven't been since before the war. Oscar and Susan took me a couple of times, so I'm really looking forward to this.'

Mildred lifted an enquiring eyebrow. She'd instantly warmed to Georgie and wanted to learn as much as possible about the family. 'Who's Susan?' she asked, imagining she must be a cousin or family friend.

'Susan?' Georgie answered casually. 'Oh, Oscar's wife. Didn't he tell you?'

Mildred froze, her mind reeling. Wife? Oscar had a wife? Mildred's world suddenly caved in. Had . . . had he been lying to her all along? She was preparing to face the music and break off her engagement for him, when all the time he was married?

Her heart lurched as Oscar came back, waving a thin programme at them and smiling triumphantly.

'There,' he said, handing it to Georgie. 'Only one allowed per party, I'm afraid. Don't mind if

Georgie looks at it first, do you, Milly?'

'Erm, no,' Mildred muttered, attempting to put a faint smile on her face while calling him *you bastard* in her head.

'Oh, come along. We're going in.'

Oscar ushered Georgie and Mildred in front of him as the audience began to filter through the doors.

Oh, so he thinks being polite and bleeding chivalrous makes everything all right, does he, Mildred silently scorned. How could he trick her like that?

But she damned well wasn't going to let it spoil her evening! Cissie had been lucky to get these tickets, even if Mildred and Oscar had needed to swap shifts to use them.

They'd been short-notice cancellations, just the three. Jake had already seen the show, they all knew now, and so had Ron, Bridie and Zac, Eva jumping at the chance to babysit Jane. When Cissie had given her the tickets, Mildred had offered them to her mum and dad and Primrose first, but much to Primrose's annoyance, Eva had insisted Mildred went with Oscar and Georgie. Milly was Cissie's special friend, after all, Eva said, and the rest of them hoped to get tickets for a later date.

Now, as they entered the auditorium, Mildred stifled her gasp at its beauty. She wasn't going to let Oscar think she was some uncultured ignoramus. When they took their seats, she made sure Georgie sat between them. She didn't want to sit next to that lying trickster.

When the music struck up, though, her bitterness melted away in her delight at the performance. She was entranced by every act, and when Cissie was on stage, her spirits soared. She'd thought Cissie would be good, but her performance was enthralling. She moved across the stage so easily, like flowing silk, a dream, while her body lilted in all sorts of beautiful and yet seemingly impossible movements. The music, the costumes, the singing and dancing seemed to wreathe themselves about Mildred in a kaleidoscope of enchantment. It was all blooming fantastic!

When the interval came, by the time she and Georgie had queued to use the ladies', it was time to resume their seats. The second half of the show was, if anything, even more overawing than the first, and when the applause finally died down after several curtain calls, Mildred felt sad and deflated. And not just because the evening was over.

They were having to do an early shift the next morning to make up for the one they'd swapped. So Mildred had explained to Cissie that they wouldn't wait at the stage door to meet her afterwards. Instead they made their way directly to Wimbledon Station, Georgie chatting nineteen to the dozen as they went. She'd linked her arm through Mildred's so that Oscar was obliged to walk a few paces behind them. Thank goodness for that, Mildred seethed. She felt she didn't want to talk to Oscar ever again!

'That was brilliant!' Georgie cried now. 'Worth waiting for. I was evacuated to a village in Wales, you see, at the beginning of the war,' she explained to Mildred. 'It was nice in the country, but there wasn't much going on. Susan had been looking after Mummy, but then, of course, I had to come back to take over. The bombs had stopped then, anyway. The Blitz ones, I mean. But with Oscar away in the army, there was no one to take me to the theatre, and I couldn't go on my own. So you and Oscar can take me lots now!'

Mildred had been glad of the girl's chatter, but at the mention of Oscar's wife again, she felt bloody angry. She'd be sorry not to see Georgie any more. She was a nice kid, and Mildred would have liked to be friends. But how could she if she wasn't going to see Oscar again, the lying bugger?

She was so flipping furious, though, that she might as well have it out with him right now. Walking behind them, Oscar had evidently not been able to hear their conversation, so now Mildred spun round to face him.

'Yes, Georgie told me about your wife,' she said accusingly, her teeth gritted.

She glared up at Oscar, her eyes blazing. In the gloom from the street lamps, she saw Oscar's face darken. As well it might!

'Georgie, you know I don't like anyone talking about Susan,' he reprimanded, his gaze darting across at his sister.

'No, I don't suppose you do,' Mildred retorted.

She noticed a frown flicker across Oscar's face. 'No, of course, I don't,' he mumbled. 'It's too upsetting.'

'Huh, upsetting? Well, I'm pretty upset, too!'

'What?' Oscar's frown deepened as he shook his head. 'I don't understand. Why should you be upset? It wasn't your wife who was killed in the Blitz.'

342

Mildred's jaw dropped open in horror. Flaming Harry!

Oscar wasn't *married.* He was *widowed.* She'd put her bleeding great foot in it, hadn't she? If she'd ever wanted the ground to open up and swallow her, it was now.

'Oh, my God, Oscar, I'm so sorry!' she blurted out, tears of shame and remorse burning in her eyes. 'I didn't — '

'So, you thought . . . ' Oscar interrupted. 'Well, no wonder . . . I suppose Georgie didn't explain.'

'Oh, I'm sorry, Oscar,' Georgie squeaked. 'I would've done, only it was when you were getting the programme and then we had to go straight in, and in all the excitement, it went out of my head.'

Mildred was holding her breath. Such a horrible misunderstanding. How could she have doubted Oscar like that? Could he ever forgive her? But then she heard him release a quivering sigh.

'No, it's my fault,' he said, closing his eyes for a moment. 'I should have told you about Susan before. But I really do find it so hard to talk about her.'

For once in her life, Mildred was at a loss for words. 'I-I can understand that,' she managed to stammer. 'And I am blooming sorry. I added two and two and made five. It . . . it won't change anything between us, will it?'

Relief broke over her as Oscar turned to her with a smile unfurling on his lips. 'No, of course not.'

Oscar held out his hand. Mildred took it, and

she felt him squeeze her fingers as they walked on down the street. Beside them, she heard Georgie give a cheeky little squeal.

28

Cissie lay on her back on the old picnic blanket, gazing up through the canopy of green leaves to the clear blue sky above.

On the whole, August had been a cool month, but today the sun had graced her with its presence, making her feel warm and relaxed. A gentle contentment was seeping into her flesh, and she was beginning to feel that just a small part of her was starting to mend.

On her birthday the previous year, it had felt as if her whole life had been smashed apart. The wound had been so fresh and raw, the investigations by both the civil police and the US Army police were drawing unsuccessfully to a close — and she'd known for sure that she was pregnant. She'd tried to deny it at first, telling herself it was the shock that had made her late. But morning sickness, sore, swelling breasts and a general lethargy had forced her to admit it to herself.

She'd told Sean first. He was the only person at the theatre company who knew what had really happened. Her absence of a couple of weeks after the *event* had been explained away by her twisted ankle. Dance had been the one place where she could temporarily forget, and even that had been taken away from her.

Dear, dependable Sean had hatched the plan, his open-minded understanding helping her

345

through. Telling her mum and dad had been the worst part. Ron had roared like a lion, banging his clenched fist against his head. He hadn't been able to protect his darling girl, he'd groaned aloud, and Cissie had found herself comforting him rather than the other way round. And Bridie? Well, she'd looked horrified at first. But then her Catholic soul had kicked in. Life was a gift from God, however it had come about. And she would go to the end of the earth to support her daughter and her unborn child.

Who'd have thought that, a year on, the whole family would have found a new life? Cissie knew it was mainly down to the Parkers with their down-to-earth, caring hearts. Telling Jake and Eva the truth had been such a release. She would tell Mildred, too, one day. But not yet. When the time was right.

And then there was Saul Williams. She still had the scrap of paper. She hadn't unfolded it yet. Read the name of her attacker. Of Jane's father. His life was in her hands. She had that power over him. And that knowledge had given her strength.

The distant sounds of happy laughter drifted into her reverie, becoming more distinct and drawing her attention. She locked her thoughts back in their box and brought herself back to the present. She turned on her side, propping herself on one elbow. Her mum, Zac, Sean, Eva, Stan, Jake, Mildred, Primrose and Trudy, who'd come to stay with her parents for a couple of weeks, were all playing a makeshift game of cricket with a tennis ball and an old bat of Stan's. Behind her head, Cissie knew that her dad was sitting in the wheelchair, keeping an eye on Jane who was asleep in her pram. And all around them, people were enjoying a Sunday afternoon in the park.

Mildred waved and came over, dropping onto the rug beside her.

'You awake now, then?' she asked in her own flippant way.

'Yes. Must've dropped off,' Cissie fibbed, as really and truly she'd pretended to be asleep because she'd just wanted a few moments to herself. 'Sorry.'

'Don't be sorry. It's your birthday party. Smashing idea to have a picnic in the park.'

'Seemed a shame not to, with it being a nice day. And you've all been so kind. Thank you ever so much for the perfume.'

'It was only eau de cologne.' For once, Mildred seemed a bit awkward, making Cissie chuckle to herself. It wasn't often Mildred appeared bashful. 'Was the best I could afford. Or get hold of. Be nice when we can get decent stuff again. Wonder how long it'll be before things start coming off ration.'

'Yes, hardly been anything so far,' Cissie agreed. 'But when you think about it, could be years before things get back to normal.'

'That's what Oscar says, worse luck.'

'Pity he couldn't join us,' Cissie put in. 'Looking forward to meeting him.'

'Yeah, so's me mum and dad. But he's returning a favour for someone at the depot. Easier to do it on his official day off. Sends his apologies, mind.'

'Apologies accepted,' Cissie smiled back. 'You've not met his mum yet, either, have you?'

'Haven't been to the flat yet, no. Just met his sister the other night. Didn't all half enjoy it. You're bloody good, you know.'

Cissie felt a rosy hue warming her cheeks. 'I'm glad you all enjoyed it,' she mumbled in embarrassment. 'And it isn't just me. I reckon the whole show's pretty good.'

'Yeah, Oscar and Georgie thought so, too.'

'And . . .' Cissie glanced sideways at her friend. 'You're going to give up your fiancé for him?' she asked gently.

She saw Mildred bite her lip. 'I don't suppose Gary'll get home for a few months yet,' Mildred said thoughtfully. 'But if things are still going the same way with Oscar, then, yes. I just feel so happy when I'm with him, far happier than I ever did with Gary. I can really see a brighter, better future with him. Of course, I'll have to let Gary down gently, but I'm not gonna waste me life on some childish crush.' She broke off, wriggling her lips. But then she seemed to dismiss the subject from her mind as she turned the tables on Cissie. 'So what about you and Jake, then?' she quizzed her.

Cissie felt the little knot tighten in her chest. With all her new-found friends around her, the tensions inside her had eased a little. But she was such a long way off the path to normality that she didn't think she could ever find her way back.

'Jake's a lovely fellow,' she began cautiously.

348

'Maybe one day, I'll be ready for romance, but it'd be unfair of me to get his hopes up over something that might never happen. Much better for him to look elsewhere.'

She felt her heart rear up against her own words. She was very, very fond of Jake. Maybe she was even falling in love with him. She imagined him taking her in his arms, and the sensation was all-encompassing. But it could never go further than that, and it was breaking her. She'd explain the real reason to Mildred. But not today. She didn't want to spoil her birthday by digging up something so horrible. And maybe it would be better to keep the past buried.

So she turned to Mildred with a happy smile. 'Jake's present was so thoughtful, though.'

'Yeah, a seventy-eight of *Swan Lake*, wasn't it? By some Russian bloke?'

Cissie couldn't help but laugh. 'Tchaikovsky, yes!' she giggled. 'And it's an album of three seventy-eights so there's six extracts. I can listen to them over and over again.'

'Bet you'll be on your feet dancing to them, and all.'

'Yes, probably,' Cissie grinned back. 'And I do wish Jake all the best,' she went on more seriously. 'Hope he really enjoys it when he starts work at the bank next week.'

'Yeah, so do I. He so wanted to be a fireman, and it's a lot different from that.'

Cissie nodded, not sure what she could say next. If only she'd met Jake without what had happened to her, things might have been very different, and it was tearing her in two. But she was saved any further torment, for now at least, as the band of merry cricketers finished their game and came over to join them.

'Ain't it about time we had that picnic?' Primrose complained.

'Isn't it,' Trudy corrected her. 'I hope you talk better than that when you're serving customers.'

'Yars, of course I do,' Primrose mimicked. And then went on, 'Anyway, where's the food? I'm bleeding starving.'

'Don't you bloody well swear,' Eva reprimanded her, panting up behind.

There was a brief moment of exchanged glances, and then everyone fell about laughing. Cissie felt herself caught up in the joyful sound. Her family. Her best friends.

Was she coming home, at last?

★ ★ ★

'So how's your brother getting on at his new job?' Oscar wanted to know.

It was their long break at work, and they were sitting outside on the bench, having a cigarette and enjoying an unusually hot day in September. But who knew how soon the autumn would be upon them and their breaks would have to be spent indoors.

'Well, he's only been there a couple of weeks, but he says he's really enjoying it,' Mildred replied, blowing out smoke. 'Between you and me, I think he's more suited to it than being a fireman. I mean, I know he had the experience of it in the war and he'd set his little heart on it. But he ain't ... I

350

mean, he isn't like me. He's proper brainy, like Kit and Trudy. So I think he'll be a lot better off in the long run,' she mused, taking another deep draught on her cigarette. 'Funny how things can work out for the best in the end.'

'Well, I'd agree with you there.' Oscar caught her gaze and she saw his expression soften. 'Think how we locked horns when we first met. And look at us now. You know, when I first came back from the war, I wanted to go straight into engineering. But it wasn't that easy, so I came back here instead. If I hadn't, I wouldn't have met this wonderful, funny, passionate, beautiful, caring, clever — yes, clever — young woman and — I reckon I can say it now — fallen in love with her glorious auburn hair and her scattering of freckles,' he murmured, running his finger tip down her nose. 'And her lovely, smiley mouth . . .'

This time, he outlined her lips with a touch like gossamer, sending ripples down to the tender spot between her thighs. Oscar leant closer, tipping her face upwards with a finger under her chin. Mildred held her breath, gulping at the intensity in his eyes as his lips brushed so sweetly and gently against hers. Unlike Gary's demanding kisses, this was so delicate, awakening something inside she'd never felt before. It was the first proper kiss they'd shared, and when it was over, she was left breathless and giddy.

She realised then that she'd closed her eyes. When she opened them again, Oscar was gazing intently at her, one eyebrow raised rakishly.

'So, did you like that, Miss Parker?' he asked

with a twinkle in his eyes. 'Y-you know I never meant this to happen, but — '

Mildred placed her finger against his lips. 'Yeah, I know. But I'm glad it has. Made us realise that what I had with Gary, well, it wasn't right. Not for me. I felt sorry for him, not having no family. He was a bit brash, to be honest. Wanted people to do whatever *he* wanted. Not kind and gentle like someone else I know. So it really has worked out for the best for me.'

She watched as Oscar's mouth curled upwards at the corners. 'Yes,' he nodded with a little perplexed shake of his head. 'You know, after Susan, I never expected to fall in love again. We met at school, you know, so she'd been part of my life for so long. She was beautiful, intelligent, caring, bubbly. Just like you. So it's a miracle I found someone else to love just as much.'

'So does this mean I really will have to take you home to meet me family soon?' Mildred asked, feeling her cheeks redden.

'Yes, I guess it does,' Oscar chuckled. 'And I'll have to take you to meet my mum, too. But I'll have to introduce the idea to her slowly. She might get overexcited and that wouldn't be good for her. But, oh, look at the time! Only got five minutes before we're off again.'

'We can't keep meeting like this,' Mildred laughed, jumping to her feet.

'Actually, we might not for much longer. I've seen a job I'm going to apply for. With an engineering firm. Here in London. If I get it, you might need to find a new driver.'

'As long as he or she's better than you!' Mildred teased, and together they hurried inside the depot.

* * *

Eva stood behind the trestle table with her WVS comrades, waiting for the special trains to rumble into the station. She'd done her best to smarten up her uniform, sponging it down and giving it a good press. For all she knew, this could be the last time she ever wore it.

The special trains were bringing lads returning from the Far East. They weren't the ones who'd stayed on to the bitter end. Oh, no. Those ones wouldn't be home for another couple of months or so. There'd be thousands upon thousands of those. Organising their transportation home would be a nightmare. Even Eva could appreciate that.

No, these trains were bringing those who'd been wounded earlier on, but who'd recovered enough to endure the journey home long before the Japs had surrendered. They'd been transported on a hospital ship that had docked in Portsmouth the previous day. Those still more seriously incapacitated had apparently been dispatched to hospitals first under medical escort. Those arriving at Waterloo today were the more recovered, the walking wounded, en route to convalescent homes or to be discharged and demobbed. After the journey in the crowded trains, they'd be hungry and thirsty, and the WVS ladies would be waiting with their tea urns and piles of sandwiches.

They hadn't long got everything ready before they heard the familiar rattle and groan of a train inching along the nearest platform, followed by the grinding of brakes and hissing of steam as the engine came to a halt and the carriages all clonked to a standstill. There was whistle-blowing and shouting, all echoing beneath the station's huge domed roof, and the sound of compartment doors being flung open. Men's voices, some louder than others, calling instructions, and a general clatter and clamour.

'Right, here they come, ladies!' the WVS centre organiser called, and Eva stepped up to the plate with her fellow volunteers.

For the next half-hour, all was bedlam, even though the hundreds of soldiers and sailors formed orderly queues for the WVS tables. The women had each been allocated a role. Eva's was to hand out the enamel mugs of tea that someone else had poured and instruct each man where to leave his empty vessel when he'd finished.

Eva was pleased to see that a lot of the men looked almost fully recovered, with their injuries not visible. Others, poor beggars, looked awful, their faces gaunt and yellow. Must've been ill, Eva reckoned. She'd heard of nasty diseases such as dysentery that were rife in the Far East and could take months to get over. Maybe even some of the poor sods had survived the building of the Burma Railway. The way the Japs had put thousands of Allied prisoners of war to slave in the jungle in blistering heat and under horrendous conditions, at the mercy of God knew what diseases, with little food and savagely beaten when they'd become

354

too ill to work, well, it defied words. It was as bad as the Nazi concentration camps. Worse in some opinions. Those who were lucky enough to survive when the railway was finished had been forced to endure another two years of brutal treatment before they were liberated, and only now was the true horror of their imprisonment coming to light.

Eva forced the thoughts from her mind. These men needed a jolly face to welcome them, not a long one. 'There you are, ducks,' she said cheerily to each chap in the queue for the table as she handed out the tea.

'Cor, ain't it nice ter see a cheerful face!' one cheeky private grinned back at her.

'Even better ter be back on bloody British soil again!' someone else declared, and was instantly given a cheer of approval. 'And better still if yer give us a kiss, darling!'

''Ere, she don't wanna kiss you! She wants ter kiss me!'

'Oi, give over,' Eva bantered back.

The line of men gradually moved forward. Eva guessed they must have been divided into groups on the train as mainly soldiers on crutches or with an arm in a sling filed along next. The voyage home must have taken several weeks, so their wounds must have been pretty flipping bad not to have fully healed by now, Eva assumed. Some of her WVS colleagues had been given the task of physically helping those who needed it. There were some amputees, but not in the numbers Eva had seen after the first war, thank Gawd. And she didn't see any like poor Ron, who'd lost both an arm and a leg.

The time flew by, the stream of dirty mugs being washed and reused finally stopping so that they were ready and waiting for the second train, while Eva furiously buttered slices of bread for hundreds more sandwiches. And then it began all over again.

Visible, burnt and twisted skin, eye patches. Two holes where once there'd been a nose. Heads that had obviously been kept shaven to allow long, curved wounds to knit together. One or two still bandaged. A lacerated face.

Poor bloody souls, Eva thought. It could put even your loved ones off you. Or stop you ever finding a girl if you didn't already have one. Especially hard for the younger ones. Some seemed no more than kids.

The chappie standing in front of her now, for instance, wasn't old. Early twenties maybe. A deep scar ran down his forehead, crossed an eye that stared, open and vacant, and carried on across his cheek to his jaw. Beneath his Navy uniform, one shoulder appeared lifted as if still in pain.

Another poor bleeding blighter. Eva gave him a sympathetic smile. He ignored it, took the mug and moved on without so much as a grunt. Well, who could blame him? Something struck deep inside her. So why did she notice this fellow in particular?

Her whole body turned rigid with shock. Oh, good Gawd. He hadn't recognised her, she was sure. But she knew who he was.

'Come on, Parker. What's the matter with you?' she heard the centre organiser bellow in her ear.

She shook her head to bring herself back as she

356

handed out the next mug. Then she glanced over at the sailor again. He had his back to her now, but yes, she was right.

It was definitely Mildred's Gary.

29

'I always think we're so lucky to have such a great big park right on our doorstep,' Jake observed as he and Cissie wandered along one of the meandering paths around the waterfall section of Battersea Park's gardens. He'd been delighted that she'd agreed to go for a stroll with him, even though it was a dank, drizzly afternoon. It was still mild, though, and the dampness had brought out the smell of wet earth and vegetation that was just beginning to die back at the end of the summer season.

'Mind you,' Jake continued, 'I don't suppose I thought like that when I was a kid. I just took it for granted then. We were up here almost every day. Or at least it seemed like it.'

'Yes, it is lovely.'

Thinking as one, they stopped by the main cascade, watching the silvery water splashing down the rocks and into the pool at the bottom. Different ferns with feathery or shiny leaves crowded the edges in various shades of green, giving a magical atmosphere as if fairies or elves could fly out from them at any moment.

Cissie felt the stillness of the moment wash through her. 'There was a park,' she almost whispered, her lips seemingly moving on their own. She was suddenly overtaken by a strange sense of detachment, as if a voice inside her was compelling her to speak and she was merely its mouthpiece.

'Near where we used to live,' it went on. 'On the street where I was ... attacked. It was tiny, though. Not like this. I never went down that street again. So it's nice to have this place just round the corner. It's hardly Devon. You know, where I was evacuated. But it does give you space to breathe.'

Her own words had astounded her. How simple she'd found it to speak to Jake about what had happened. When she was with him, she no longer felt lost in the shadows. She turned her head to look at him, a small smile slipping onto her lips. She saw a tiny frown flicker across his brow, and his eyes seemed to deepen with understanding.

'I'm so glad we moved here,' his expression prompted Cissie to say. 'And not just because of the park, or making a fresh start. If we hadn't moved here, I'd never have met you. Or your family.'

She watched as a gentle softness came over Jake's face. Her own muscles stilled. It really was as if a sudden peace was starting to cleanse her heart of its agony.

She saw Jake swallow, his Adam's apple moving up and down his slim throat.

'There's a rec just a couple of hundred yards from where Gert lives,' he gulped, as if grasping at something to say. 'A good size, but nothing like this. But not much further away, there's Nonsuch Park. That's massive. Henry the Eighth had a palace there. It was supposed to be so beautiful, there was to be nonesuch other like it. That's how it got its name, apparently. But in Elizabeth the First's reign, it was owned by the mistress of some nobleman and she had it demolished and the materials sold to pay off her gambling debts, or something like that. Anyway, the grammar school where Trudy goes is on the far side of the park. I could take you there. Easily done in a day on the train. Well, Rob commutes in every day to the bank, of course. I'm sure they'd love to have us for Sunday lunch.' He stopped, realising he was gabbling. So he finished with a wry laugh, 'I'm afraid Gert's not a much better cook than our mum, though.'

Cissie's smile grew wider. 'I think I could put up with that. It'd be nice. But, Jake.' She reached out, putting a restraining hand on his arm. 'Getting to know your family better. It won't change anything between us. I like you. Very much. And I feel . . . I could love you. But only ever as a brother. I could only ever love *any* man as a brother. And . . . I'm sorry for that.'

She felt the shard of pain at the hurt she saw on Jake's handsome young face. But then a rueful smile tugged at his lips.

'But that can't stop *me* loving *you* as a man loves a woman,' he croaked.

Cissie knew she was putting them both through torture and groaned inwardly. But she must dissuade him, though it was breaking her heart. 'No, Jake,' she said. 'You must look elsewhere. There'll be some other lovely young lady out there far more worthy of you. And anyway, you hardly know me. We're both so young — '

'I know you well enough to know that I'll always be there for you,' he insisted. 'A close friend, if nothing else.'

'Well, I should like that very much.' Cissie smiled back, feeling more comfortable. 'Good friends should always stick by each other.'

Jake gave her a long, searching gaze. 'And . . . can good friends hold hands?' he asked tentatively.

'I don't see why not,' she answered, remembering how they'd held hands once before, here in the park, after she'd told him everything. It had felt good and safe then, and she was sure it would do again. 'In fact, I'd rather like it, too.'

She held out her hand and Jake took it, grasping it firmly as if his touch was sending her a message. She could trust him, she knew she could. He wasn't like . . . whatever his name was.

And did it matter what *his* name was? It was just a jumble of letters on a scrap of paper. What had happened couldn't be undone. But right now she knew she didn't want to rake up the past, bring back the memory in all its hideous clarity. Wouldn't knowing *his* name make it all seem so real again? Real and vivid, rather than the nightmare that was starting to fade and blur into the past with the new contentment that was filtering into her life? With Eva and Mildred and their family. With Jake? There would always be that door that could never be unlocked. But knowing *his* name could only make matters worse. Act as a focus to bring back the pain and the anger. Surely it would be better never to know. But having that piece of paper could only taunt her, torment her. And suddenly she knew exactly what she must do.

As she and Jake turned back towards Banbury Street, hurrying now as the drizzle thickened and became light rain, his strength seemed to pump into her through their joined hands. Grim determination grew inside her, but while her resolve increased, so did the sense of relief at having made the decision. Unwittingly, Jake had helped her claw her way out of the dilemma that had been ripping her apart. And she would always love him for that.

Later that night, when the rest of her family were asleep, she retrieved Saul's scrawled note from its hiding place and crept out to the scullery. She took a baking tray from the oven, placing it ready on top of the stove. Then she took up the matches and lit one of the gas rings.

Only for an instant did she hesitate. Was she doing the right thing? Would she regret it? And then she thought of Jake. She wanted to love him, but she knew she could never love any man. Knowing the name of the evil weasel who'd done this to her would never help. It must be better this way.

She held the corner of the paper in the flame. Saw it scorch at the edges for a split second before it caught alight and she dropped it onto the metal tray to watch it curl and burn and turn to ashes.

There. No going back now. It was done.

★ ★ ★

Mildred pushed open the front door and propped her bicycle in its usual place in the hallway. When she'd left that morning for her early shift, the late September air had been cool enough for her to need a coat over her uniform. Now she hung it up on the hook on the opposite wall.

'Hello, Mum, I'm home!' she called cheerily. She wasn't going back out to see Oscar again, but she couldn't wipe the smile off her face these days. She woke up each morning feeling like the cat who'd got the cream. And she knew why.

She turned round as she heard Eva come out of the back room. The smile died on her face. She could see from her mother's expression that something was wrong.

'Here, Mum, what's up?' she asked, putting her own joy on hold. It was probably nothing.

'Love, you've got a visitor.' Eva's voice was low, and she glanced anxiously back over her shoulder as if she didn't want whoever was waiting in the kitchen to hear her. 'It's . . . Oh, love, it's Gary.'

The happiness she'd felt over the past weeks drained from Mildred's heart and a cold dread took its place. Gary! It couldn't be. She wasn't expecting him home for another month or more at the earliest. Hadn't had time to gear herself up to telling him it was over. Oh, why had he come back to spoil everything!

But she supposed it wasn't his fault. She'd just have to deal with it as best she could. Steeling her courage, she stepped determinedly forward.

But Eva put out her hand. 'Before you go in, love,' she said gravely, 'I need to warn you. He was wounded. His shoulder . . . and his face. It ain't pretty. He says that's why he ain't wrote much recently. Couldn't bring hisself to tell you. It was a while ago. Before the war ended. That's why he's home a lot earlier than what we thought.'

Mildred's blood froze. Injured? Bleeding hell, that wasn't in the script! She'd planned on telling Gary that their engagement had been a mistake. That with him going off to war, her acceptance of his proposal had just been a spur-of-the-moment thing. That she'd had time to think — and realise he wasn't for her. That there were plenty of girls out there who'd want a good-looking fellow like him.

But now . . .

She stared at Eva, blinking her eyes wide in horror. What in Gawd's name was she going to do? She felt bloody sick in her stomach as she gulped hard and forced herself to slide past Eva and go through the door.

Gary was standing by the fireplace with his back to her, gazing into the empty grate. From behind, he looked just the same, if a little thinner. She recognised the stocky build, the slightly hunched shoulders. The blond hair that was clipped short in a Navy cut. He didn't appear any different. And then he turned round.

Mildred had to stifle a gasp. Thank Gawd her mum had warned her. The deep, jagged gash that had been gouged out of his face ran down his forehead, crossed his eye socket and didn't end until his jaw. The eye looked strange, and she wasn't sure if it had any sight in it. Flaming heck.

'Milly.'

Gary's voice was flat, no longer the devil-may-care, jocular tone she remembered. She swallowed, scraping herself from her shock. Could feel the tremor of each painful heartbeat.

'Gary,' she heard herself say. 'Welcome home.'

There was a hard silence between them, and then Gary stepped towards her, his arms outstretched. Mildred wanted to back away, her flying pulse making her feel faint. But she must stand firm. She didn't want him thinking his face had put her off him. Didn't want to make the poor sod feel even worse about himself than he doubtless already did.

The next instant, his arms closed around her and he buried his head in the crook of her neck. She could feel him trembling as heaving sobs racked his body, and she instinctively returned his embrace, holding him close, comforting him. Though the very core of her screamed out in protest.

'Oh, yer dunno how I dreamed of this,' he mumbled in her ear. 'Coming home to yer is all what kept me going. I knew yer'd still love us, scar and all. There's not many yer can rely on like you, Mill. I love yer so much. I knew yer wouldn't let us down.'

Mildred held onto him. What the heck was she going to do? This was just some stupid bloody dream. She'd wake up any minute and laugh it off. Wouldn't she?

At last, Gary stopped shaking so violently and he pulled back. She saw tears glistening in his eyes, making the injured one look even more peculiar. His cheeks were wet, and a rivulet had formed in the deep crevice on the scarred side. But the terrible, distraught look on his face gradually slackened, driven away by a watery smile as he reached into his pocket and pulled out a tiny box.

Flaming Nora, no! Mildred wanted to pull away, but every muscle locked down as Gary took her left hand and slid the ring from the box onto her third finger. Mildred stared at it. Crikey Moses, she couldn't move.

'There. Didn't have no ring before, did yer? So now we've done it proper like. Got it in the Philippines. It ain't a proper ruby, but it is real gold. D'yer like it? I got it before this happened,' Gary explained, gesturing towards his face. 'But yer do still love us, don't yer?'

Bloody hell. How could she answer that? Because she didn't. She loved Oscar.

'So how did it happen?' Mildred was relieved to hear someone ask. She glanced round. It was just her and Gary in the room.

'We was in a small port. On the edge of the jungle,' he answered, his words choked again. 'On some poxy little Jap island. Just us. Took it in watches ter guard the sub. Had me back against a tree, but a Nip still managed ter jump us from behind. Aiming fer me throat, I reckon, but he missed 'cos I clocked him just in time. Got me shoulder first, and then me face as we fought. But I got him back. Got me own knife in his guts. Slashed him right open. At least I survived. And it got us home early. And back to me girl.'

Mildred's stomach flipped over. There was something in Gary's voice. Bitterness, hatred. She could understand all of that. And she could imagine the scene. His fear as he stood on guard. A Jap sneaking out of the jungle behind him. She'd seen things like that at the flicks. Must have been terrifying. And then wondering what on earth his face was going to look like.

'I'm sorry me letters weren't great,' she realised Gary was apologising now. 'Didn't exactly feel up ter writing much. And I wanted ter surprise yer.'

'Well, you've certainly done that,' she murmured.

'Yeah, given yer a bit of a shock, ain't I? Sorry about that. But I've got a nice surprise for yer, and all.' He suddenly grinned, making the scar stretch across his cheek. 'I've been ter the Registry Office. Arranged fer us ter tie the knot on yer birthday next month. Just time ter plan a party. And fer us ter find somewhere ter live. Ain't that great? Oh, Mill, I can't wait! Thinking about this is what kept us alive. I'd've given up if it hadn't been fer knowing you was waiting fer us.'

Mildred watched his expression light up. And then he took her in his arms again, hugging her tightly. Bringing his mouth down desperately on hers. She could scarcely breathe, her heart deadened. She'd promised, hadn't she? Could she break him now? Destroy him by turning him down? It was all arranged. Done and dusted, as far as he was concerned. What would it do to him if she refused him now? He needed her. Had lived only for her. And who else would have him with his ruined face?

Her soul crashed to the ground, splintering like broken glass. The good, kind, generous, compassionate heart that was Mildred Parker stood firm. It was too strong for her other being, the one that craved love for herself. That loved Oscar. She couldn't resist it. Couldn't fight it. Though she knew her life would be ruined, an empty, bottomless void that could never be filled, she nodded back.

30

A wild frown slashed across Stan's face. 'You sure that's what you want, girl?'

Mildred rolled her head agonisingly on her neck. 'No, I'm not bloody sure. But what else can I do? It's the right thing, isn't it?'

'Depends how you look at it,' Eva interrupted, crossing her arms over her heaving bosom. 'And what about this Oscar fella? You was so keen on him, you was going to bring him home to tea. You gonna let him down instead?'

Mildred drew in a deep breath to calm herself. How could she convince her parents if she wasn't sure herself? She wanted them to support her decision, not question it.

'Yeah, I don't want to, but I'll have to. Oscar'll be OK. He'll find someone else easy enough. He's so good-looking, but he's kind and clever, too. I'm sure it'll be for the best in the end. I'd be far too beneath him really for us to have been happy.'

She forced a shrug, trying to convince herself, if nothing else. But Eva came back fiercely.

'Don't you ever say that. You're as good as anyone. But I won't have you throwing away your life on someone what's not right for you. Nell did that, and look where it got her.'

Mildred clamped her jaw. She knew her mum must be upset to mention her old friend, Nell. The story was shrouded in mystery. Mildred really had

368

no idea what it had all been about. She felt it was a secret her mum would never reveal.

'Well, I don't know about that, but what I do know is that Gary needs me,' she protested, her chin thrust out stubbornly. 'You saw how he was. He's changed. His confidence's been knocked for six. He's got no one else. And can you imagine how he feels with his face like that?'

'Yeah, but having sympathy for someone's not a reason to marry them!'

Mildred released a sigh of exasperation. 'I know, Mum. But I loved him very much before. I don't see why I won't love him again. And this . . . this fling with Oscar, it was good while it lasted. But it might well not've worked out in the end.'

Mildred gave a small, wistful shake of her head as she battled to hide the pain inside. She did love Oscar, but spending her life with him was probably just some stupid pipe dream. He was too far above her. He probably wouldn't have still wanted her once he'd seen the sort of family she came from. It'd never have worked out.

Would it?

She pushed the idea firmly to the forgotten recesses of her mind. 'Nah, it'll be much better this way,' she said with a sad smile.

She saw that Eva's lips were pushed forward in a mutinous pout, but when Mildred glanced at her dad, he was nodding, his head moving slowly and thoughtfully up and down.

'Well, if it's really what you've decided, I know you won't change your mind, so I'll give me consent,' he said steadily. 'And I'm proud of you, Milly, doing what you think's the right thing. So unselfish. Just like your mother, even if she won't admit it.'

'Thanks, Dad.' Mildred gave him a hesitant smile. His words had helped her make up her mind. Definitely. 'Mum?' she asked in a small voice.

Eva hesitated, her eyes meeting her daughter's. 'All right. But I hope you won't end up regretting it.'

'I won't. I know I won't,' Mildred assured her. But deep down in her heart, she could only pray she was right.

★ ★ ★

'No, you can't marry him!' Oscar's eyes were aflame. '*I* love you. And *I* want to marry you!'

Mildred stared at him. Oscar wanted to marry her. Her face crumpled and she was unable to stop the tears spilling down her cheeks as his words sank into her distraught mind.

'Oh, Oscar.' She forced his name out in a squeak. 'I love you, too. And I'd've said yes. But . . . it's too late. I was promised to him first. And he needs me. If only you'd seen him —'

'Needs you?' Oscar's voice was a bitter laugh. 'And don't you think *I* need you? After Susan, I never thought I'd find someone to love again, and then I met you. Don't put me through all that again, I beg you.'

Oh, Gawd, how could she do this to him? To both of them? A torrent of broken emotions welled in Mildred's breast as she watched Oscar's taut face tighten further. But she had to push the

370

agony aside.

'I'm so sorry, Oscar, I can't tell you,' she croaked. 'But put yourself in Gary's place. His face is ruined forever. He's lost the sight in one eye. People'll either stare at him in the street or turn away. He'll be made to feel like a flipping leper. And he's got nobody else. No family. None of his old mates want to know, and the ones what he made in the Navy won't be back for a while, and when they are, they're not going to want to know neither. So he needs my help.'

Oscar arched his eyebrows in exasperation. 'But surely you can help him without *marrying* him?'

'Please, Oscar, don't make this harder than it is,' she groaned, wringing the words from her throat. 'Have you looked in the mirror recently? Any girl'd fall for you. And you're kind and clever. But Gary, he's . . . well, he's not like he was, even without his poor face. Always used to be so sure of himself, but now he's just the opposite. I can see his moods swinging backwards and forwards. Only happy for a minute, and then sad and doubting himself. If I turn him down now, I reckon it'll push him over the edge.'

'And you reckon you can live like that? On a knife-edge all the time? No. I won't let you throw your life away.'

Mildred saw Oscar's eyes snap challengingly, and though her heart shattered, she held his gaze until his shoulders finally sagged in a dejected sigh.

'Well, if I can't change your mind, at least let me congratulate you.'

He stepped forward, and before Mildred knew it, she was crushed in his arms. His hand entwined in her auburn curls, dragging her head back so that he could bring his mouth down on hers, hard, desperate, bruising her lips. It wasn't what she'd expected from him, but she knew his kiss was born of yearning and frustration and love that matched her own. She let it sweep through her, encompass her, for she knew it was all she would ever have of him.

When he finally let her go, she could see his eyes were deep and intense with pain.

'I'll always love you, Mildred Parker,' he grated almost inaudibly. 'For being the funny, strong, caring girl who insisted on doing what she thought was right. Even if she was wrong.'

Mildred gulped. Felt she was drowning in an ocean of sorrow. 'You'll find someone else,' she managed to whisper.

'But she won't be you.'

'No. She'll be better than me. B-but we can still be friends, can't we?' she asked, seized with panic.

A shuttered look suddenly veiled his expression. 'Friendship can take many forms,' he answered enigmatically.

'And I'll always consider you a friend. A very special one.'

He bent his head, brushed a soft kiss on her forehead. Turned. And walked away.

Mildred watched him go. And felt the brutal sorrow tear through her heart.

★ ★ ★

'Right. We ready for the off, then?' Stan asked, glancing round at the family members who'd come to the house first and had squeezed into the kitchen of Number Eight. 'You look a picture, sweetheart,' he added, turning to Mildred. 'And happy birthday again, love.'

'I'd've liked it better if it'd been a church wedding like what Kit and Gert both had,' Eva couldn't resist grumbling. 'But you do look lovely.'

Mildred couldn't stop the slight blush that coloured her cheeks. They'd had plenty of clothing coupons going spare, and Eva had found the money to splash out on a new outfit for her daughter, a tailored suit in soft cream wool with a matching pillbox hat that set off her halo of auburn waves to perfection. Now Eva pinned onto her daughter's lapel one of the brooches Abraham had left her.

'There,' she said, blinking away a tear. 'An extra little present.'

'Cor, thanks, Mum. It's beautiful. And thanks for the reception and everything, as well.'

'What?' It was Eva's turn to blush. 'A few sandwiches and jam tarts at the pub? Not exactly a feast. I could've afforded more if it'd been available. You all know now that old Abraham left me a little nest egg. It's been nice to have something to spend some of it on. And what else would I be doing with all that money? Or that posh jewellery? Apart from giving you each a piece to keep.'

'Will you, Mum? Cor! But I reckon you should let Mr Braithwaite see the rest of it when he gets back from Africa,'

Primrose piped up. 'I'm sure he'd know where

373

to get the best price.'

'No time for all that now,' Stan interrupted to usher them all along. 'Milly mustn't be late for her wedding.'

Everyone moved towards the door and then filed out into the street. Stepping out onto the pavement, Mildred took a deep breath. This was it.

Next to her, Stan turned from locking the front door behind them all. 'You absolutely sure about this?' he whispered in her ear.

The words *lamb to slaughter* flitted across her mind in large, red letters. But it'd be all right in the end, wouldn't it? Gary was OK deep down. They'd make a go of it.

So she fixed a dazzling smile on her face and nodded. 'Yes, course, Dad.'

Everybody else was waiting at the Registry Office. Altogether, there was Mildred's elder brother, Kit, and his wife, Hillie, who'd come up for the day from Kent by train, though they couldn't stay too long as Kit needed to be back at the station by five o'clock. It was a Thursday so they'd taken the children out of school, and one of Hillie's younger sisters, Trixie, had managed to come, too. She'd been Mildred's closest childhood friend, although she was a couple of years older.

Gert was there, of course, with her three young boys, sworn to be on their best behaviour. Gert wasn't going to miss her sister's wedding for the flaming world! Rob couldn't take time off now he was deputy manager of the bank, but he'd allowed Jake a few hours off provided he worked through his lunch hour on a few days to make up the time.

Even Trudy had been allowed a day off from the grammar school. She was doing so well, her teachers thought she could easily catch up. Cissie had successfully begged Monsieur Clément to let her off class and rehearsals that day. Zac couldn't get time off his work at Price's, but Ron and Bridie had come along with baby Jane. Even Ellen Hayes from Number Three was among the guests, though she had to be back in time to collect Lily from school.

Nobody from the bus depot was coming. Mildred hadn't told them why she needed a few days off. Was that the result of her guilt at giving Oscar the push when everyone knew they'd become so close? She'd have to tell them as soon as she went back, of course.

With no family or friends, Gary had no one to witness or celebrate his tying the knot.

Mildred's heart skipped a beat when she caught sight of him. He hadn't seen her arrive and was partly turned away from her. He had yet to be officially demobbed and was dressed in his smart Navy uniform, bell-bottom trousers making him look taller than he was and the tunic with its distinctive white-braided square collar sitting on his shoulders. Mildred could only see the undamaged side of his face, and the love she'd once had for him seemed to unfurl inside her again. He wasn't Oscar, but when she'd nursed Gary back to the man he used to be, she was sure they'd find true happiness together.

He turned round, and his face broke into a grin when he saw her. She didn't see the scar, the sightless eye. She saw the handsome face it had once been. Only for a second did another face flash across her mind, as dark as Gary was fair. But she hurled it away. She had made her choice.

She stepped forward resolutely and took Gary's hand.

31

'So, how was it?' Cissie dared to ask. 'The honeymoon?'

'Three nights in a boarding house in Bournemouth? Not much better than the room we've rented round the corner. But yeah, it was OK. Quite a treat for us to see the sea. Well, for me, anyway. Bit like coals to Newcastle for Gary. But it was warm enough for us to sit on the beach to have our fish and chips every day. Warmest October since 1921, they say.'

The wedding had been on the Thursday, and this was the following Monday morning. Mildred wasn't due at the depot for her shift until after lunch. The Romaine Theatre Company's run at Wimbledon Theatre didn't finish for another couple of weeks, so Cissie would be going back to her digs later that afternoon but had the morning free. Gary had gone off to be officially demobbed, so the two girls had decided to take a stroll in the park while the October weather still held. It wasn't quite as unseasonably hot and sunny as it had been the last two weeks, but it was still pleasant enough for the time of year.

'Yes, it's nice to have a bit of an Indian summer, isn't it?' Cissie agreed. 'Sets you up better for the winter ahead.'

They were crossing the bridge that separated the Ladies Pond from the main lake, and stopped to look down on the water. Cissie felt a hot flush of nerves. Mildred hadn't exactly answered her question. It had been playing on her mind ever since Mildred had announced that she was still going to marry Gary, even though Cissie knew it was Oscar she truly loved. Mildred was her best friend, and she wanted to be sure she was happy. She couldn't imagine . . . or maybe she could, and that was what had rekindled her own dread.

She swallowed hard. 'That wasn't quite what I meant,' she began again in a small voice. 'About the honeymoon. I meant more . . . the wedding night.'

'Oh.' Mildred's voice landed flatly. She remained silent then, and Cissie began to curse herself for asking. But Mildred rested her arms on the rustic bridge, gazing down onto the soft ripples on the Ladies Pond. 'It was OK,' she answered quietly. 'Hurt a bit, but Gary was quite gentle. Least I think he was. Got nothing to compare him with, have I? All a bit embarrassing, but I guess I'll get used to it. I just closed me eyes and . . . I imagined it was Oscar and that made it easier.'

Her last words were choked and, beside her, Cissie knew she was fighting back tears. Cissie put her hand on Mildred's arm, and Mildred looked at her for a moment with a rueful, watery smile before turning back to contemplate the pond.

'You . . . don't regret it, then, do you?' Cissie ventured.

She heard Mildred sniff. 'Nah. Knew I'd done the right thing when I woke up one night with Gary's hands round me neck trying to throttle us.'

'What!'

'He was dreaming of that Jap what did for him.

Thought I was him. I slapped him and he woke up. Broke down and cried like a baby in me arms. I'll make him better, and we'll have a good life together. And me and Oscar, we'll still be friends. Got to be if we're working together.' A small, wry laugh escaped her throat.

Cissie's eyebrows dipped in the shadow of a frown. She couldn't think of anything to reply, and joined Mildred in staring sightlessly at the water.

Stillness settled on the two friends. It was quiet that autumn morning in the park, nobody else around. The only sound was that of birdsong and the water splashing from the little fountain just below them. A strange calmness filled Cissie's heart. Now was the time.

'You and me, neither of us can have what we really want, can we?' she murmured.

It was a moment before Mildred spoke. 'What d'you mean?'

Cissie gulped. 'You, you really wanted Oscar, no matter how much you've tried to persuade yourself. And me . . .' She broke off, drowning in a tidal wave of emotion. 'I could love Jake. I really want to. But I can't. I could never give myself to him in that way. You see . . . ' Her heart was beating furiously, but she had to say it. 'I was raped. And Jane's not my sister. She's my daughter.'

She heard Mildred's audible gasp. Then silence. A sinking sensation in her belly.

'Oh, my Gawd,' Mildred breathed at last, for once in her life struggling for words, and her brow swooped fiercely. 'Y-you poor little sod. That's . . . that's bloody terrible. So that's why . . . you and Jake . . . ?'

Cissie nodded, her eyes still fixed on the small lake. It was easier to speak if she wasn't looking Mildred in the eye. 'I told Jake. I had to. To explain why I could never love him in that way, even though my feelings for him are so strong. And I told your mum. She was brilliant about it. And Sean knew from the beginning. But that's it. Nobody else outside the family knows.' She paused. It felt better now she'd done it. The excruciating churning in her stomach had stopped. 'That's why we came to live here. A new start.'

'So, you wasn't bombed out at Islington, then?' Mildred's question was deep with understanding.

'No. But we were hounded out from where we lived. People didn't know the truth, you see. And Zac doesn't understand. He still thinks Jane's his sister. And we want to keep it that way.'

'Cor, blimey. It's a lot to take in. But no, I don't blame you or nothing for lying to us.'

'Thank you. But you see now why we're like two of a kind. Only I'm not strong like you, Mildred. I can't face my demons like you have.'

Mildred turned to face her, drawing her round. 'You will one day. And you are strong. Mine was me own decision, but yours . . . And you say you could never love Jake properly. But never's a long time. But, whatever happens, I'll always be here for you, kid.'

Cissie brushed away the tears that were starting to trickle down her cheeks. 'And I'll be here for you.'

They laced their arms about each other, holding tightly. Silently. Without moving. Standing in a pool of pain and waiting for it to drain away.

'You Mildred Lockwood?'

'Yeah, that's me,' Mildred answered, surprising herself at responding to her married name so quickly. 'And you are . . . ?' she asked as a young chap breezed towards her.

'Frank Arrowhead. Sharp an' as straight as. Pleased ter meet yer, darlin'.'

He thrust his hand towards her. She took it, narrowing her eyes warily.

'But I still don't know who you are.'

'Oh, didn't no one tell yer?' he said, cocking a surprised eyebrow towards the depot offices behind them. 'I'm yer new driver.'

'Me what?'

'Yer new — '

'Yeah, I heard you the first time,' she snapped. 'So where's Oscar?'

'Oscar? That's a bleedin' posh name. But I don't know nuffing about no Oscar, love. I'm just pleased ter be back home safe an' have me old job back. Oh, I hear congratulations are in order. Just tied the knot, ain't yer? Lucky fella — '

His words petered out as Mildred turned and fled into the offices. What the hell was going on?

Mildred pushed her way past her colleagues queuing at the desks. The clerk looked up in irritated surprise, opening his mouth to speak, but Mildred didn't give him a chance.

'Where's Oscar? Oscar Miles, me driver?' she demanded. 'Is he off sick? On leave?' Yes, that must be it. Only got six days holiday a year, but no reason why he shouldn't have taken one of them. Or maybe his mum was ill or something. She didn't enjoy the best of health, he'd said.

'Ah, Miss Parker,' Mr Grimwald, the manager, called over. 'Or Mrs Lockwood, should I say? Congratulations on your marriage — '

'Never mind about that.' Mildred cut him short as she strode across towards him. 'Where's Oscar?'

The older man looked confused and spread his fingers. 'He's gone, of course. Gave in his notice a week ago and left while you were on your honeymoon. Got a job with some engineering company. Said he didn't want anyone knowing. But I assumed he'd told *you*.'

Mildred stared at him in disbelief. Oscar gone. Without telling her. Nah, must be some mistake.

'Well, I knew about the job,' she said, her lips like rubber. It was a half-truth, after all. She knew he was applying for it, but not that he'd got it. 'And he probably told us when he was starting, only with all the excitement of me wedding, it went in one ear and out the other!' she attempted to joke. 'Oh, give us his address, would you? It'd be nice to keep in touch.'

'Give you his address?' Mr Grimwald sounded affronted. 'I can't do that, I'm afraid. Not without his permission. Why, don't you know where he lives, then?'

'Oh, well, no,' she stammered. Oh, Jesus, she *had* to persuade him. And to sound casual. Maybe if she could convince him what good friends they were, how well she knew Oscar's family background, Mr Grimwald might believe it was just some sort of oversight. 'I've met his sister, Georgie. We all went to the theatre together. Looks just like him, she does, only about half his age. He was going to take me to meet his mum. She's an invalid and can't get out much. Only we never got round to it.'

'Well, I'm sorry, Mrs Lockwood, but I really can't go handing out people's addresses, you know.' Mr Grimwald looked at her over the top of his horn-rimmed spectacles. 'He knows he can contact you here, if he's a mind. Now, I suggest you get off to your bus. It's due to leave in two minutes, I believe. That's if you want to keep your own job.'

Mildred jolted out of her shock. 'Yes, of course, Mr Grimwald. Thank you.'

Why the hell had she said that, *thank you*? she thought as she turned away. She had nothing to thank him for. The words had tripped off her tongue of their own accord while the rest of her mind was whirring in horror and shock. She had no way of contacting Oscar. And he . . . Had she hurt him so much that he never wanted to see her again? After all the things he'd said.

About being in love with her? Had that all been a lie?

Oh, Oscar, I'm so sorry. I didn't mean to hurt you so much. Will you ever forgive me? Will I ever see you again?

She hurried back out to the garage part of the depot. Frank Arrowhead was lounging against the side of the bus and pushed himself away when he saw her coming.

'Come on, darlin'. Don't wanna be late on me

first shift back.'

Mildred looked at him daggers as she jumped up onto the bus's platform. Cold. Numb. She felt lost, as if half of herself had fallen away. For, somehow, she knew she would never see Oscar again.

32

'Well, we're off to Mass,' Bridie told her son, keeping her voice low so as not to wake Cissie who was asleep in her room next door. 'If Jane wakes up before Cissie does, you can be giving her a Farley's rusk soaked in milk. I've left the packet on the table, see? And you know where the milk is.'

Zac nodded slowly. 'Milk and rusk,' he repeated. 'Yes, all right, Mum. I'm good with Jane, aren't I?'

'You are so. Or we wouldn't be leaving her with you, so we wouldn't.'

'Help your mother get this contraption outside, will you?' Ron asked, jabbing his head at the wheelchair. 'And then help me get outside and into it, so I don't have to strap on the crutch.'

'Yes, Dad. Of course I will,' Zac grinned back amiably, and at once went to help his parents.

He felt so proud that he was trusted to do all manner of things nowadays. He'd felt so much better since they'd come to live here. The house wasn't as nice and there was a back yard instead of a garden. But you didn't catch people whispering behind your back or calling you names in the street. He couldn't understand why they'd suddenly started doing that. But here, everyone was nice to him. He wasn't afraid to go outside. In fact, he looked forward to it.

He really liked his job at the candle factory, as well. He missed Jake not being there, even though he worked in another part and only used to see

Jake at lunchtime. But he had Mr Stan to walk to and from the factory with every day, and he looked forward to that. He could even find his own way there now, and had done so on the day of Mildred's wedding. And there was a girl in the packing shed he liked the look of. He didn't really understand why men and women loved each other, but he did feel all funny when he saw her. Perhaps they could get married one day, like Mildred and her sailor. Only thing was, his words refused to come again whenever he saw the girl. That made him cross with himself, because he knew he'd been talking much better recently. That was because of coming to live in this new place, too.

He waved his mum and dad off down the street through the autumn drizzle and went back inside. His mum came from a different country and went to a different church called Mass. His dad only went once in a blue moon. He'd had to convert when they'd got married. Zac didn't really know what that meant. He thought it was something to do with getting better, but he wasn't sure. All he knew was that his mum went to Mass every week and usually took baby Jane with her. She used to take him when he was small. But when he was learning his catechism and everything for his First Communion, he was ribbed by the other boys for being so slow, and the priest cuffed him round the ear regularly. When his mum found out, she didn't make him go any more. There was a new priest by the time Cissie was doing her preparation, and she did make her First Communion. But apparently she never went to Mass when she was evacuated as there wasn't the right sort of church in Tavistock, and she refused to start going again when she came home. It was the only time Zac had ever heard Cissie and their mum rowing. But Cissie had stood her ground and had never been to Mass since. So Zac supposed their mum was going to have a last try with Jane.

Today, though, had been different. Jane had been crying in the night. Zac had heard her. Teething, Mum had said. But when the time came to leave for Mass, Jane was fast asleep in her cot, and Mum didn't want to disturb her. Usually Dad liked to hobble to the newsagent's for a paper while they were out, but this morning, Mum had persuaded him to go to Mass with her. It might be raining, but it would be a good opportunity. She wouldn't have the pram to push, so she could push the wheelchair instead.

Back in the kitchen, Zac sat down at the table and rested his hands in his lap. His chest swelled proudly at having been left in charge. He would wake Cissie up if he really needed to, but he was determined he wouldn't. The run at Wimbledon Theatre had ended the previous night, just a few days before the end of October, giving the stage crew a couple of days to take down and pack up all the scenery and so forth. The company had held a big party to celebrate their success. It had gone on into the small hours, but the landlady at the digs where Cissie and some of her colleagues had been lodging had still wanted them out by nine o'clock. So when Cissie had arrived home in Banbury Street an hour or so later, she'd been so tired that she'd gone to bed shortly before their mum and dad had set off for the second Mass of the day.

Zac sat in the chair, his eyes wandering about the room as he wondered how to make the most of the situation. He could turn on the wireless, but that might wake Cissie up, so he didn't want to do that. Everything was neat and tidy. He'd scrubbed the saucepans until they gleamed only the night before, and he'd already cleaned out the kitchen cupboard that morning. There wasn't a speck of dust anywhere. Even he could see that.

What, then? He drummed his fingers on the table. Aha. There was the book Jake had got him from the library. He wasn't all that good at reading. Cissie liked books. She'd read a story called *Jane Eyre* once. She'd told him what it was all about. It sounded really good, so he tried to read it himself.

But the words were so hard to work out that it didn't make any sense to him.

Jake liked reading, too, and he'd suggested Zac try an adventure story that might be easier to read. He knew an author who wrote such books for older children that Zac might like and got one out of the library for him. Jake was right! Zac found he could read it without any problem, and it was a super story. He couldn't wait to find out what would happen next to his new friends!

A couple of chapters, though, was as much as he could cope with in one go. So he meticulously placed the bookmark at the open page and closed the book. Hmm, now what?

Ah, yes. Cissie would probably be awake soon and she'd be hungry. He could cook her some bacon. He'd never cooked it before, but if he could be trusted to keep an eye on the baby, surely he could cook some bacon? He'd seen his mum do it hundreds of times.

First you had to melt some fat in the frying pan. He carefully lit one of the gas rings, blowing out the match and setting it to one side to cool completely before he put it in the bin. Next he got the fat bowl from the cool cupboard. Now, how much? Better too much than too little. So he scooped all of it from the bowl, leaving just some jelly-like stuff at the bottom.

Right. The mound of fat in the pan would take some time to melt, so he turned up the gas underneath and returned from the scullery into the kitchen. He'd just read another page or two while he was waiting.

Oh, this was exciting! They'd just gone down to the seaside and were going into a cave that they were sure smugglers were using. The further they went in, the narrower and darker it got, but fortunately they'd remembered to bring a torch. One of the girls was really scared, but the boys told her it'd be OK. The smugglers wouldn't be there in the daytime. But then the torch began to fade. The battery must be running out. But they'd just go on a bit further. Suddenly, their dog's hackles began to rise. What were hackles? Never mind. Then the dog growled softly. Was someone there after all? Zac simply had to know! And he read on.

It wasn't until a crackling, hissing sound reached his ears that Zac lifted his head from the book. He sniffed the air. That didn't smell right. Oh, the fat must be melted enough by now. He'd better put the bacon in.

He opened the door to the scullery. Hot fat was spitting out of the pan and some of it was catching fire in the gas jet. Smoke hovered over the cooker, and flames were dancing all about the frying pan. Even as Zac gazed on, rigid with shock, the fat inside it flared up in an arc of orange and yellow and red.

Zac's jaw dangled open. That wasn't supposed to happen. It never did when Mum was cooking. He needed to do something about it. He'd have to clean the pan again before Mum and Dad got back. It was all black and sooty now. But first he had to stop the flames. You put fires out with water, didn't you? On the *Pathé News* at the pictures, he'd seen films of firemen in the Blitz squirting water from hoses over burning buildings. That must be what he needed to do. So he filled a jug with water from the scullery sink. And tipped it over the burning pan.

The explosion made him fall back so forcefully that he crashed through the door to the kitchen and landed on the floor. His eyes widened in horror at the fireball that was engulfing the scullery. Scarlet, glowing sparks were raining down on the quarry tiled floor. Some newspapers by the back door waiting to be torn up into squares for use as toilet paper smouldered and began to ignite. Flames were licking about, up the walls. His mum's tea towel and oven gloves were smoking, tiny flames beginning to sparkle. While Zac lay stunned on the kitchen floor, another blinding flash dazzled him, and when he opened his eyes again, the whole scullery was ablaze, and the paint on the open door near his feet was starting to bubble and scorch.

Zac's senses suddenly snapped back into action and he scrambled backwards, screaming for his sister.

★ ★ ★

Cissie was on stage, dancing, wrapped in that euphoria that rocked her only when she was performing, the music, the lights, the costumes. Sean was smiling at her as she executed a series of *posé* and *pas de bourrée* turns diagonally across the stage towards him, ending in a *pirouette* into fifth *arabesque*, supported in his hold about her waist. She gazed up at him, triumph gleaming in her eyes. But the smile had gone from his face. He was staring at her, his eyes stretched as wide as saucers, shouting, yelling . . .

She realised someone was shaking her so hard that her head was wobbling on the pillow. She blinked herself awake. Zac was screaming incoherently at her, obviously terrified out of his wits. What on earth — ?

It was then that she smelt it, an acrid whiff wafting into her nostrils. Her brain clicked into focus. Something was wrong. And then through the open door behind her brother, she saw a pale, grey mist drifting along the hallway. Dear God. Smoke!

She leapt out of bed. Grabbed her dressing gown but didn't stop to put it on. No time to think. She grabbed Zac's arm and dragged him back out into the hallway. In those few seconds, the smoke had increased and was pouring from the kitchen, and she could see flickering flames of incandescent orange darting about the table and sideboard. She slammed the door shut. Her action caused a puff of dense smoke to billow into her face, making her cough and wheeze, but then it seemed to be holding it back a little. Cissie grasped Zac's arm again and pulled him out into the street.

Oblivious to the rain, she drew an enormous breath into her lungs, making her throat burn. And then she screamed with every ounce of her strength. Like she'd never screamed before. 'Help! Help! Fire! Fire!'

She'd never yelled like it. Her lungs hurt and she thought they'd burst. But she kept on yelling. Someone must come soon!

And then she saw Jake dash out of his house and fly towards her.

'I saw smoke and flames from our back yard,' he shouted, skidding to a halt beside her.

'Yes. There's fire at the back,' she squealed. 'I don't know what happened. I was asleep in the front.'

'Dad, call for the fire brigade!' Jake yelled over his shoulder at Stan, who was scurrying up behind him. And then, his face working frantically, he demanded, 'Is anyone inside?'

Cissie was so stunned, she stared at him blankly and so he shook her hard. It instantly brought her back to her senses. 'N-no. Mum will have taken Jane to Mass with her, and Dad always goes for a newspaper —'

'Oh, thank God —'

'N-no,' Zac put in urgently. 'Dad went to Mass

with Mum and they left Jane asleep upstairs.'

'What!'

Cissie and Jake met each other's horrified gaze. Panic cut through Cissie's heart. Jane! Her daughter.

'Dad, get an ambulance, too!' Jake screeched down the street after Stan, who waved his arm as he skidded round the corner towards the telephone box.

'Which room?' Jake demanded.

'Front bedroom. In her cot.'

Oh, God, what was Jake doing? He was racing back to his own house. *No! You can't abandon me now!* Cissie was jumping up and down on the pavement. She had to save her child! And she sprang blindly towards the front door.

A hand was at once on her arm, pulling her back. Jake was by her side again, wrapping a soaking, dripping towel about his head and face to form a mask, a second towel in his hands.

'Zac, d'you know what happened?' he growled so fiercely that Zac was jolted into a sensible reply.

'I-I was frying bacon — ' he stammered.

'Is the gas still on?'

'Y-yes, I — '

'Damn,' Cissie caught Jake swearing under his breath. And then he disappeared inside, swallowed up in the black, demonic smoke.

Cissie's knees were buckling beneath her. Her child, and the man she loved. Oh, dear God, what if . . .

Her mind was frozen. The rain was coming down hard now, dripping down her face, her long hair wild and plastered to her head, her nightdress so drenched it was transparent as it clung to her fragile frame.

'There, luvvie, let's get this dressing gown on you,' Eva said beside her now, and she made no movement as the older woman slipped the garment about her shoulders.

They stood there together in the rain, gazing at the burning house. Every nerve screwed in anguish. For both had a child inside.

It seemed an eternity but was perhaps scarcely more than a minute before a shadow took shape low down in the smoke that was now gushing from the front door. The figure of a man, his head swathed, crawled out of the now blackened door frame. He held a bundle up towards Cissie's waiting arms, a bundle that was wrapped in a wet towel. As soon as she'd taken it, Jake rolled onto his side on the pavement, coughing and spluttering and gasping for breath.

Clanking of bells, then. Chaos. Fire engine. Men in uniform, shouting. *Shut off the gas.* Run out hoses that wriggled and sprang to life. Spurting water, hiss of steam. More bells. A white van. Man in white coat.

He took the bundle from Cissie's arms and ran with it to the ambulance.

★ ★ ★

'Oh, Jake, I can't tell you how grateful I am. Really I can't.'

Cissie was sitting by Jake's bed in the charity hospital. Rain was still clattering down outside, making up for the Indian summer at the start of the month.

'It's all anyone would've done,' Jake said modestly. 'And I had a bit of training behind me, so I knew what to do. If I hadn't, I might've inhaled a lot more smoke. But, as it is, they're going to discharge me tomorrow. Just as well. Two nights in hospital's about as much as I could stand.'

'Oh, that's good news. About being discharged, I mean.'

But Jake merely shrugged. 'Far more importantly, how's Jane? I hardly dare ask, but is she going to be all right?'

He was utterly relieved when Cissie nodded. 'Thanks to you, yes. They're going to keep her in maybe a week or so, just to be sure. It could leave her with a bit of a weak chest, but Mum'll know how to keep an eye on her. It might've been very different if you hadn't got to her so quickly. Or if she'd been in the back room above the fire.'

'Mmm.' Jake gave a jerky, rueful nod. 'And is the house very badly damaged?' he asked cautiously.

'Well, not as badly as it might've been,' Cissie answered with a sigh. 'It was mainly confined to the kitchen and scullery. The ceilings in there partly collapsed and some of the joists were charred and'll need replacing. But the rest of the house is mainly smoke damage. I mean, all the walls will need stripping back and repapering, maybe replastering in places. And all the paintwork will need redoing. Well, replaced here and there as well. Just as well the landlord never got round to repainting the place like we asked. He's hardly too pleased, as you might imagine.'

'Did he have the place insured?'

'Fortunately, yes. He's even said we can move back in when it's all done. But only if we promise faithfully never to leave Zac unsupervised again.'

'Well, that's understandable.'

'Yes, but it was good of him to accept that it was an accident and that Zac wasn't really to blame. Oh, that reminds me,' Cissie said, reaching into her handbag and withdrawing a folded piece of paper. 'Zac made a get well card for you.'

'Oh, that was kind of him,' Jake smiled, taking the makeshift card and looking down at it. 'Not a bad drawing. Do thank him for me, won't you? But tell me, where are you all living now? I mean, the house will be uninhabitable for a while.'

'Oh, your mum's come to the rescue there, as you might imagine.' Cissie gave a chuckle. 'I'm sharing with Primrose in the back bedroom at your house, sleeping in Mildred's bed now she's no longer there. And . . .' She hesitated, pulling a grimace. 'I'm afraid Zac's on a mattress on the floor in your room.'

To her relief, Jake merely shrugged. 'That's OK. We've all got to pull together when things go wrong. And what about your mum and dad?'

'They're with Mrs Hayes across the street. She's got a front parlour she doesn't use much. It's a bit awkward for Dad, having to go up steps to the front door. And the lav's in the semi-basement. Indoors, mind. But at least Dad's sleeping on a sofa, but poor Mum's having to manage on an eiderdown on the floor. So we're just hoping the house gets repaired as soon as possible.'

'Well, I can help at weekends. Not the structural stuff. You need a proper builder for that. But I could lend a hand with the redecoration.'

Cissie felt the familiar pull on her heart again. Jake was such a good young man. 'That's really kind. Your dad's offered, too. We might well take you both up on it, but it depends on the landlord and the insurers, of course. And your mum's been terrific. She's been helping Mum wash all our clothes and bed linen and everything in her kitchen to try and get rid of the smell of smoke. My gramophone and records survived, thank goodness. And, fortunately, Mum had put that money from Saul Williams I told you about in her bedroom, so that was OK. But a lot of our other things are beyond it. But Eva's so generous, she's said she'll buy us anything we can't afford. We'll pay her back in time, of course, but she says there's no need. She said the money came from our house in the first place, so it's only right it goes back there. I really don't know what she meant, but we're ever so grateful.'

'Ah.' Jake nodded wisely. 'I know what she means. The older couple who lived there before you and that Mum took care of, they left her a small legacy. They had no family, you see.'

'Ah, yes. I remember now. She said the china and things left at the house had belonged to them. Good-quality stuff it was. All lost now, of course. But she didn't mention a legacy. Really deserves it, though. I think she's amazing.'

'So do we all. Even if she can't cook!' Jake laughed now. 'Maybe I'll try and stay in here a few extra days after all. The food's much better than at home!'

Cissie was glad to have something to smile at. The fire could have been a lot worse. An awful lot worse. She couldn't get out of her head what might have happened.

'I'd better go and see Jane now,' she said. 'It's only due to you that's she's still alive.'

'Tell you what, though. It's made me realise that perhaps I'm better off at the bank in the long run. I was damned scared going in there, knowing the gas was still on.'

Cissie's heart turned a cartwheel at the memory. 'And I was pretty scared watching you go in. It made me realise what Jane means to me.' She lowered her eyes, dropping her voice and reaching out to take Jake's hand. 'And how much *you* mean to me.'

She watched as his fingers closed about hers. They looked so right together. But . . .

'It doesn't change anything, though,' she croaked. 'I still don't think I could ever — '

'Then I'll wait.'

'You could be waiting a long time.'

'I'm a patient man.'

Cissie lifted her head, felt his smile twist the knife in her side. She swallowed.

'I'll see you back home tomorrow, then. It'll be nice living under the same roof for a while.'

She returned his smile, then got to her feet and walked down the ward and out through the doors. She wished the fire had changed things, but it hadn't. The bitter agony, the fear, would never leave her.

'Cissie!'

She was so engrossed in her own painful world

that she hadn't noticed Mildred coming towards her along the corridor.

'Hello, Mildred!' she answered, her mood brightening at seeing her friend. 'You come to see your hero of a brother?'

'Not half. Bloody hell, what a to-do!' But then Mildred tipped her head, fixing an enquiring gaze on Cissie's face.

Hero, eh? Did that mean Cissie and Jake might get close now? But she felt it wiser to keep that thought to herself.

'Certainly is,' Cissie agreed. 'I don't know how I'd have felt if anything had happened to Jane. Or to Jake.' She felt the sharp pain in her chest again and forced it aside. 'And how about you?' she asked quickly, wanting to change the subject. 'How's married life treating you?'

Mildred puffed out her cheeks. 'Oh, Gary and me, we'll be OK. It's only been a couple of weeks, but we're rubbing along fine. He's got a job interview on Thursday. Not much of a job, but it'll boost his confidence. And it'll mean we can move somewhere better. Mum says she'll help out when she's sold that jewellery, but we'd rather be independent. So I really hope Gary gets the job, for his own sake if nothing else.'

'Oh, so do I, then.'

'Yeah, thanks.'

'And . . . Oscar? Have you heard from him?'

Cissie saw Mildred's face fall. 'Nah. Keep me eyes peeled for him, mind. If Gary gets this job, when he's at work and I'm not on shift, I'll go round Chelsea, just in case I bump into Oscar. Or maybe Georgie. Don't suppose I'll ever see either

of them again, though. Still, I got Gary, ain't I?'
She couldn't disguise the sadness in her voice,
even though her face was smiling.

Cissie gave a tiny nod. 'Yes. The war has a lot to
answer for, doesn't it? I mean, beyond all the obvious. You wouldn't have married Gary if he hadn't
been hurt. Probably wouldn't have got engaged to
him in the first place if he hadn't been going off to
war. And I wouldn't have been . . . Well, without
the war, a certain Yankee soldier wouldn't have
been where he was. There must be so many people whose lives will never be the same again.'

'Yup. But there's nothing we can do about it.
We've just got to make the most of it, kiddo,' Mildred ended, forcing brightness into her wistful
tone. 'Anyway, I'd better get in to see me brother
before visiting ends. Bit of a dragon, Mum said,
the ward sister.'

'Yes. See you soon, then. I'm popping up to the
children's ward to see Jane.'

'Glad she's OK. TTFN, then,' Mildred replied
and went in through the doors to the men's ward.

Cissie turned and walked the opposite way down
the corridor. She was going to see her beautiful,
darling little daughter.

Epilogue

Six years later — Summer 1951

Cissie was tying on her pointe shoes, tucking in the loose ends of the pink ribbons. It might only be a rehearsal, but you always had to be properly presented. It was all part of the dance ethos.

She was still passionate about her art and still preferred to stay with the same company. She enjoyed the variety it offered, Monsieur Clément developing fresh material all the time, and life had been so much pleasanter since Deidre had left out of the blue all those years ago.

Cissie went over to the *barre*. They'd done the usual class in soft shoes, so that their muscles were nicely warmed up and stretched. But the blocks were new — an unusual occurrence — and she wanted to mould them to her feet a little before the rehearsal began. She'd darned the toes to make them last longer. Supplies were far better now than during the war, but old habits died hard.

'Right, are we ready?' Monsieur Clément bustled into the studio. 'Ah, Cissie, *ma chérie*, I have something for you. The office have just given it to me.'

The dance master held out an envelope to her. Cissie frowned as she took it. Why should she receive a letter at the studio? That was very odd. And the stamp was unfamiliar. Her hands began to shake as some sort of realisation filtered through to her brain. *Miss Cecily Cresswell, c/o The Romaine Theatre Company, Wimbledon Theatre, London, England,* the scrawled, childlike writing said. The envelope was creased and worn, as if it had passed through many hands before it got to her. Which it probably had. Someone had obviously made quite an effort to trace the company to where it was now. It was all really strange, but her heart began to thump as she looked at the postmark . *Alabama, USA.*

The paper stung into her fingers, burning them, and she dropped the envelope onto the floor with a little cry. Monsieur Clément's head jerked back. Then he stooped to pick up the letter and handed it back into Cissie's trembling grasp.

'C-can I have a moment, please?' she stammered as crucifying horror circled her heart. She'd struggled for so long to try and put it all behind her. But . . . Could it be that Jane's father had somehow managed to trace her? Somehow forced the connection out of Saul Williams after all these years? What if — oh, heaven forbid — he'd found out he had a child and wanted to take her? Jane was still being brought up as her sister, but the idea of her being taken away was unbearable.

'Of course, my little one,' she heard Monsieur Clément agree at once, his voice low and understanding. 'I hope it is not bad news.'

Cissie stumbled on unsteady legs back to the bench and lowered herself onto it. The envelope juddered in her hands as she tore it open. A thin sheet of paper was folded inside.

Something smaller fell out and fluttered to the

floor as her eyes scanned the untidy writing of the letter, the same as on the envelope. Slowly, the words began to take shape and form themselves into some sort of meaning.

Dear Miss Cresswell,

I hope this letter will reach you. I don't know who you are, but my son has asked me to send the enclosed to you. He says you are very clever and will understand. When he gets out of prison, he says it will be over and he can start his life anew. Because he is a black man, he was given a longer sentence. At least, that is what we believe. But he says it doesn't matter. Justice will have been done. I don't know what he means, but I hope you will.

Verity Williams

Cissie stared at the letter, her mind locked in confusion. No, she didn't understand. Was this Saul Williams's mother? It must be. But what . . . ?

She bent to pick up the scrap of flimsy paper from the floor. It was a newspaper cutting, small, just two inches square, perhaps, and dated three months earlier. The print was tiny and difficult to see. But she must decipher it. *Manslaughter Conviction*, the headline read in slightly larger letters. Cissie squinted to make out the rest.

Last week, garage mechanic, Saul Williams, was convicted of the involuntary manslaughter of general store owner, Charles Masters. It appears that when Mr Masters brought his automobile in for servicing at the garage where the convicted man is in employment, Williams failed to adjust the brakes properly. The vehicle later went off the road at a notorious bend while traveling at high speed, it is concluded due to brake failure. Masters was killed instantly in the crash. The automobile was said to be his pride and joy and he never permitted anyone else to drive it. Masters left no family. Williams was sentenced to . . .

The corner of the cutting had obviously been fingered so much before it was posted that Cissie couldn't read how many years. Maybe it was three or eight, or something different altogether. She could imagine Saul's mother agonising over the cutting, mourning the temporary loss of her son. Maybe rocking herself back and forth, a big, black, handsome woman, with a colourful scarf wrapped around her head and tears rolling down her cheeks.

Cissie realised that she, too, was crying as it dawned on her what the truth must be behind the newspaper report. Dear Saul. He was sending her a secret message, wasn't he? He'd waited all those years to find a way to deal with — what was his name? Cissie didn't want to remember. But Saul had found a way in the end, to carry out justice himself but without losing his own life in return.

Yes, now she understood. Nobody else in the entire world did. Just her and Saul. That was obviously how he wanted it to be. And she would keep it that way.

Jane's father was dead. And she'd had nothing to do with it. Nothing to feel guilty about. But he'd got what he deserved, had been punished in the same way the law would have done.

Cissie sat on the bench in the studio that was the centre of her life, letting the shock flow out of her. What had been done to her could not be undone, but knowing the perpetrator was no longer around to do the same to anyone else was a supreme relief. That justice had been carried out without her having to relive it all, face him in court. She'd so often wondered if she'd made the right decision, but it no longer mattered, thanks to Saul.

She checked the envelope and the letter again. No address for her to write back and thank him. Perhaps he knew that was the best way and had guessed that she'd either lost or destroyed the piece of paper he'd given her all those years ago, since she'd never been in touch. And he was right. It was the best way. But they both *knew*. And that was enough.

Slowly, as Cissie watched Monsieur Clément walking round to speak with each of his dancers in his own inimitable way, making sure all his *little flowers* were content, a peace she hadn't felt for seven long years began to trickle into her spirit.

She'd wanted for so long to put all the sorry business behind her, but the doubt that she'd made the wrong choice had always persisted at the back of her mind. But now it was over, and she could start to live again.

Thank you, Saul. You have set me free.

405

'Is everything all right, Cissie?' The caring voice of the dear dance master brought her back to the present. To a world that suddenly seemed flooded with light and hope.

'Yes,' she said as a wondrous sense of release began to unfold inside her. 'Sorry to keep you waiting. What are we going to rehearse first?'

Monsieur Clément clapped his hands and everyone sprang to their feet. 'Today we begin something new!' he announced with a twinkle in his eye.

Something new. Yes. A new future.

Cissie crunched the letter and the newspaper cutting into a ball and went over to deposit them in the waste bin. As she turned back to begin this new adventure, someone else dropped an apple core and a banana skin on top. There. It was history.

★ ★ ★

'Oh, I love coming here!' Jane cried, bouncing up and down with excitement. 'Can I go on the Big Dipper?'

It was a Sunday afternoon in July, and the happy group were sauntering along The Parade in Battersea Park's Pleasure Gardens. Some of the park was still given over to allotments. Not exactly part of the Dig for Victory campaign since the war had been over for six years, but the idea was the same, to help feed the local population while food supplies were still struggling. Thirty-seven acres of the park, though, had been given over to the Festival of Britain, not the cultural side of the celebration of all good things British — that was on the South Bank area — but the side where people could simply relax and enjoy themselves.

Stan and Ron had gone off to one of the many tearooms and snack bars for a cup of tea, while Eva and Bridie, Mildred and Jake, Cissie, Zac and Jane were continuing to wander around the new attraction. They'd already stopped to watch the Guinness Clock as it chimed each quarter of an hour and the doors would open to reveal the dancing toucans, the Mad Hatter would catch a line of fish, the zookeeper would rise up under his umbrella to ring his bell and the sun's rays would whirl dizzily over all the proceedings. It wasn't the first time they'd seen it. While the adults found it amusing, Jane was still enthralled by all the moving components.

'No, you can't be going on the Big Dipper,' Bridie told her. 'You're too young. But, sure, isn't the Peter Pan Railway more the right size for you. Cissie, will you be taking your sister?'

'Yes, of course. Come on, Jane,' Cissie beamed, holding out her hand. The child skipped to her side and a warm sense of serenity rippled up Cissie's arm as their fingers met. She'd felt a calm joy gradually building inside her these last few weeks, ever since she'd received the letter. Jane was all hers now. Half of her didn't belong to some vile monster across the ocean. And as luck would have it, she was the image of herself and bore no trace of her father. The child was something good and wholesome. To be loved.

'I'll come with you,' Jake offered, and Jane grinned up at him, her free hand grasping one of his. She hopped along between the two adults like a jack-in-the-box as they crossed over to the little railway.

They sat with the child between them as the train trundled along the track. Out of the corner of her eye, Cissie watched Jake with her daughter. He was so good with her. He'd been caught up in the first wave of the new National Service Act and had served abroad for eighteen months. But he'd been back since the previous autumn, returning to further his career at the bank and had built up a strong relationship with young Jane. He was like a big brother to her, and it was something else that Cissie admired in him.

In the six years since Cissie had confessed the truth to Jake, he'd kept his promise. He'd always been there for her, but had never tried to push her into a relationship. Now, as she secretly observed him, Cissie couldn't help notice his generous mouth stretched in a wide and yet caring grin as he looked down on Jane, his kind eyes dancing, his hair faintly tinted with copper in the summer sunshine. Gone was the lanky lad who despite his youth, had risked his own life to save Jane's. Instead, here was a grown man with broadened shoulders and strong arms poised to grab hold of Jane if the train jolted too hard. Arms Cissie suddenly yearned to feel around her.

Such a sparkle of pleasure had begun to twinkle in her heart, growing steadily day by day. She'd tried to deny it. Even now she was holding it back. But watching Jake, she could feel it burning into the core of her being. It really was time to let go of the past.

When they came back to where Eva and Bridie

were waiting, they found that Zac and Mildred had gone off to enjoy the thrill of the Rotor. They'd been on it before a few weeks ago, and Zac had been so fascinated at being pinned to the rubber wall of the drum with nothing but centrifugal force to hold him there that he'd been going on and on ever since to have another go.

'What d'you fancy next, Jane?' Jake asked the little girl. 'The boating lake, maybe the merry-go-round in the funfair — '

'What about the Grotto?' Jane squealed with delight. 'Some of my friends from school have done that and they say it's great!'

'The Grotto it is, then,' Jake chuckled at her enthusiasm. 'Coming, Cissie?'

'Thanks, Jake!' Jane shouted, running on ahead.

'We told Milly and Zac we'd go along to the Grand Vista and find somewhere to sit,' Eva informed Jake as he and Cissie hurried after the child. 'We'll wait for you there.'

'OK, Mum. See you later on,' Jake called over his shoulder.

The Grotto wasn't far away, and they soon found themselves passing through the rocky entrance. On the far side, more boulders rose up, with a silvery cascade of gushing water rushing down over them. Off of it led dark caves, each representing one of the four elements.

Inside all was gloomy and mysterious. Jane squeaked with mock fear, but Cissie shuddered involuntarily. There was still that dark place in her heart, and she was glad Jake was beside her. She scarcely realised, but the next moment, she was clinging onto his arm, her body pressed closely against his. She felt him stop still for an instant. He turned, and in the shadows, she could see him smile at her. And then they moved on.

But Cissie didn't let go. Something she couldn't explain wrapped itself around her. It was good holding onto Jake. It was as if a tiny, flickering flame inside her was starting to flare out. Something she no longer felt afraid of.

'Can we go on the Tree Walk next, please?' Jane begged when they'd emerged back out into the sunlight. 'Oh, please.

Just one last thing?'

Cissie was about to reprimand her, but Jake replied with a chuckle. 'All right, young lady. But then that's enough for one day.'

He grinned across at Cissie and winked. Cissie felt a sudden rush of elation. Oh, yes. The Tree Walk. She'd been up there before, among the fluttering leaves. It was a bit like being a bird. There were other things up there to amuse children — a miniature village, a dragon and other beasties — and lots of other people, too, of course, but for Cissie it was the sense of being above the world, away from all troubles and cares, that intrigued and delighted her.

She took Jake's arm again as they strolled along the elevated walkway. He turned to her with a look of pleasant surprise, a translucent smile glowing in his eyes. It reached down inside her, and she felt her cheeks blush an excited peach.

Suddenly, an all-encompassing euphoria took hold of her.

She was free, at last. She could be who she was meant to be. Not just a dancer, but a young woman who was free to do all the things she wanted to. Free to love.

A delicious, astounding wonderment made her turn Jake to her. She put her hands on those strong shoulders and lifted herself on tiptoe so that her lips could reach his. They were warm and moist, sending a glorious shiver down her spine.

She felt Jake's arms come tentatively around her, holding her gently against him as his mouth responded to hers. Just for a few seconds. And Cissie knew her body had been awakened.

'What have I done to deserve that?' Jake gulped as they pulled apart.

Cissie looked up at him, entranced, intoxicated. 'Nothing,' she smiled. 'You've just been you. All these years. You've waited long enough.'

Jake's sapphire eyes opened wide. And then narrowed. 'D-d'you mean . . . there could be some future for us?'

Cissie smiled back at him, almost breathless. This was Jake, who she'd loved for so long. Who she'd missed terribly when he'd been away on his National Service. And now, at last, that black cloud that had hung over her for so long like an executioner's axe had drifted away. Taking its place was an intense harmony, an overwhelming need. It was a new, utterly wonderful sensation, and her heart soared on invisible wings.

'Yes, I think so,' she whispered.

'We'll . . . take it slowly.'

'Yes.' And then she suddenly felt she could burst. 'Oh, Jake, I do love you. I always have. But I'm ready now. And I'm so happy.'

'Oi, you love birds, move along now. You're

holding us all up,' a voice interrupted from behind.

Cissie stifled a giggle, and as Jake threw his head back in a joyful laugh, he grabbed her hand.

'We'd better catch Jane up, anyway,' he told her as they hurried forward.

'Yes, I think we better had,' Cissie agreed. And they had a future to go in search of now, too. A future of peace and happiness, and a love that could be fulfilled.

For now, at last, she was free.

★ ★ ★

'Oo, that was great, Milly! Can we do it again?'

Mildred rolled her eyes. He was OK, was Zac. Childlike and easy-going, bouncing around her like a blooming overgrown puppy. But she seemed to be getting lumbered with him more and more since . . . well, *since*. It was OK sometimes, but she wanted to build up a life of her own and she couldn't get on with it with him in tow, even if he was so soft. It really could get a bit wearing at times. Just like now.

'Well, I'm not queuing for another flaming half hour,' she told Zac firmly. 'And our mums'll be waiting for us and wondering where we've got to. Let's go and find them, and then maybe we can get an ice cream.'

'Oh, yes,' Zac grinned, instantly pacified. 'I like ice cream.'

'Come on, then. Oh, look. There's the others coming.'

'D'you think Jane will want an ice cream, too?'

'I expect so. I don't see why we can't all have

412

one. Oh — '

Mildred pulled herself up short. Jane was skipping alongside Jake and Cissie in a little world of her own, head rolling from side to side in time to each bound. It wasn't that which made Mildred's mouth drop open. Jake and Cissie were holding hands, dancing along in a flurry of laughter of their own. Then they paused, and blimey O'Reilly, they kissed! Not lengthily, but a bit more than just a peck on the cheek. A few seconds later, they stopped again, and this time — flipping heck — they was really at it, arms round each other, lips clinging like blooming lovers on the big screen!

Well, it was about bloody time, Mildred smirked to herself. Jake had waited long enough. Never had eyes for nobody else. Never even been out on a date. And Cissie, well, Mildred could understand how she felt. No wonder it'd taken years to get over what'd happened to her. But now it looked as if things was looking up.

Mildred wondered vaguely if something had happened to cause the change in Cissie. She certainly looked jolly happy just now! Mildred was so pleased for them both. They was made for each other. She couldn't begrudge them coming together at long last. She'd have to keep it to herself, though, that she was blooming jealous. But things didn't always turn out the way you planned, did they? Oh, well.

No good crying over spilt milk, she chided herself as she called out to the love-struck couple. They looked across when they saw her and waved. Jane ran towards her like a bullet, and when Cissie and Jake caught up, Mildred noticed the scarlet rising in both their faces.

'You two having a good time, then?' she couldn't resist teasing.

They exchanged an embarrassed glance, then looked back at Mildred with nervous laughter. She shook her head, grinning from ear to ear.

'Come on, then. Let's find Mum and Bridie. Then we'll get an ice cream.'

'Ice cream?' Jane repeated. 'Oh, yes, please.'

They all fell into step, making their way towards the Grand Vista. Mildred hid her smile as Jane told her excitedly all about the Grotto. As the child chatted away, Mildred furtively observed her brother and Cissie. They deserved to be happy.

It wasn't quite so crowded here as by the Big Dipper, Funfair, Far Tottering and Oyster Creek Railway and all the other attractions. But there was still a jolly lot of people milling around. Mildred's eye was caught by a tall man wheeling a little boy of about two in a pushchair. The child was dead to the world, totally oblivious to all that was going on around him. Mildred smiled at the happy image, and then her gaze lifted casually to the man.

Her heart stopped. He was just the same — strong jawline, generous mouth, eyes like polished chestnuts. His face was a little more lined, a tiny fleck of premature silver in the hair just above his temples, even though he must be only — what? — thirty-four or five? Her brain was too stunned to work it out exactly.

Her eyes dropped back to the slumbering toddler. He was the image of his father. So he'd made

414

a life for himself in the end. When you loved some-one as much as Mildred still loved him, you had to be happy for them. But her heart cried out in pain.

'Oscar,' she croaked, stepping over to him.

Her gaze travelled back up to his face and saw the wary astonishment in those glorious eyes. He swallowed hard.

'Mildred.' His voice was low and thick. They stared at each other for a moment, shocked, unsure.

'How are you?' she felt her mouth say. 'Enjoying the fair?'

'Not really my cup of tea, but the engineering's interesting.'

Oh, yes. 'So you made it into engineering, then? Is it going OK?'

'Yes. Everything I'd hoped.'

But she knew that neither of them cared a fig about flipping small talk.

'I searched for you, you know,' she couldn't resist saying as all the hurt rushed back. 'All over Chelsea. I couldn't believe how you just left like that, knowing I had no way of contacting you.'

'I'm sorry. I thought it was for the best. A clean break.'

'Yes.' She nodded. What did it matter now? It was nice to see him, though, even if her heart was breaking. She ought to turn away —

'How's married life?' she heard him ask. 'How's Gary?'

Oh, if only he hadn't asked! It might've been best if he didn't know, but she couldn't lie. 'He died,' she answered, surprised at the wistful sadness in her words. 'Got depressed. Couldn't live with himself looking like that when he used to be so proud of his appearance. Threw himself under a tram.'

'What!' The shock and horror was clear on Oscar's face. 'Oh, Mildred, I'm so sorry.'

'No need to be,' she said, trying to make herself sound jaunty. 'Your little boy's lovely. What's his name?'

'Gregory.'

'That's nice.'

'After Gregory Peck. Georgie's idea, of course. But then, he is her son. She's here somewhere. With her fiancé. Did things the opposite way round, but that's Georgie for you. Gregory was tired and getting grizzly, so I said I'd walk him round while they went on the Water Flume or something. Dare I ask, did you and Gary have children?'

'No. It never happened. And you?' she managed to ask without choking on her welling tears.

'Me?' Oscar sounded surprised. 'No. I never remarried. I could never get over a funny, clever girl with laughing blue-green eyes and a mop of red hair who captured my heart when I thought I'd never feel like that ever again.'

Their eyes met. The years melted away. A multitude of jumbled emotions tumbled in Mildred's breast. She was free. And Oscar was free.

She watched, unbelieving, joy rising up inside, as Oscar let go of the pushchair handle and opened his arms wide. A moment later, she was locked in his embrace, feeling his heart beating against hers, his fingers entwined in her hair, his mouth coming down firmly and hungrily on hers.

It robbed her of her breath, and when she pulled back, there were stars shining like diamonds in her eyes. Oscar was laughing, that lovely sound she'd missed so much.

'This must be the best day of my life,' she crowed.

'And mine!'

Mildred shook her head in glorified confusion, and then caught sight of the others who'd stopped to watch her, curiosity written on their faces.

'Everybody, this is Oscar,' she announced gleefully. 'Oscar, this is me — I mean, my brother, Jake. And this is my best friend, Cissie. You know, the dancer we went to see. And her brother, Zac. And this is Jane.'

Everyone nodded and smiled and greeted each other. Mildred stood back, overcome, and then, as she glanced around, spotted Eva and Bridie sitting in the front row of the deckchairs by the Fountain Lake.

'That's my mum over there. Would you like to come and meet her?'

'Nothing would give me greater pleasure,' Oscar grinned back.

★ ★ ★

Cor, this was nice, Eva thought to herself, languishing in the comfortable deckchair. Managed to get in the front row so they had the best view over the Fountain Lake at the southern end of the Grand Vista. Water splashed and tinkled from a series of differently shaped but symmetrically placed fountains in the large, oblong pool. At the other

417

end, a huge intricate screen reminiscent of the old Crystal Palace provided a lacy background to the playing fountains and was flanked on either side by an openwork obelisk.

Eva stretched her neck and twisted her head round to look towards the other end of the Grand Vista behind them. Sitting down as she was, she couldn't see the other shallow, rectangular pool, but she could see the top of its two pyramid-shaped fountains. At the far end rose two dark red gothic towers, and Chinese gothic arcades ran along the two long sides of the pool as well. Eva didn't know why everything needed to have this oriental feel to it, but everything was bright red and blue and white with flashes of yellow and gold all glistening in the sunshine, so it was all rather bright and jolly.

Eva swivelled back round and turned to Bridie, who was lounging in the deckchair next to her. 'This is just the ticket, ain't it?' she said lazily. 'Kids off enjoying theirselves and us sitting here with nothing to do. Whoever'd thought they'd build pleasure gardens like this right on our doorstep? I mean, I can take or leave the blooming funfair, but these here fountains and the new flower gardens are lovely. And the buildings are a bit odd, but I do like all the bright colours they've painted everything in. Makes a nice change after all the drabness we had during the war, don't it?'

'Sure, it's all a bit gaudy for me,' Bridie replied. 'Like a park to be a park, so I do. I like all the bright flowers, but I like the green trees all around better. Reminds me more of home.'

'Will you ever go back, d'you think?'

'That I will, one day. Don't think I want to meet me Maker without seeing the old country once more.'

'Cor blimey, that's a bit morbid, ain't it?' Eva chuckled. 'Anyone'd think you was on your last flaming legs.'

'Well, doesn't time pass so fast. Look at all that's happened since we met. Yet doesn't it seem like only yesterday.'

'Oh, I dunno. And we've still got bloody rationing, ain't we?'

'Yes, but it's getting better, so.'

'Bread and spuds and flour, that was the worst, wasn't it?' Eva nodded vigorously at the memory. 'And to think they wasn't rationed till *after* the war.'

'That was partly the weather, mind.'

'Yeah, that's true,' Eva conceded. 'But it was still a shock after everything else.'

'And clothes are off coupons now. Sure, that's helped your Primrose with her little dress shop, has it not?'

'Yeah. Never thought our Primrose'd set up her own business. Or that Trudy'd go to university and end up teaching in a grammar school herself.'

'Sure, life moves on,' Bridie agreed. 'We've got lots of good things we never had before. Old-age pension —'

'Yeah, and for everyone. Not just for people what worked at somewhere like Price's what had its own scheme.'

'Unemployment and sickness benefit.'

'Oh, and the National Health Service. Great

that is.'

'And don't forget Family Allowance. Not that it's any good for us with Jane. Only for the second child and however many more you might have.'

'Yeah, Stan and me could've done with that in our day.' Eva paused and sniffed. And then took another deep breath. 'Lived through a lot together, you and me, in them six years since you came to live here, ain't we? Remember that bloody awful winter?'

'Never forget it.'

Both women bobbed their heads up and down in unison. They thought so alike, it was no wonder they was such friends, Eva mused. Strange really, if you thought about it. If Nell hadn't gone all those years before and was still living at Number Twelve, she and Bridie would never have met. And Eva wouldn't have had another secret to keep locked away.

Bridie had eventually told her about Jane. But Eva never let on that she already knew. That Cissie had already confided in her.

And she kept quiet about that Saul Williams, too. It was only her and Jake what knew about him, and she wasn't telling no one else. Knew how to keep a secret, did Eva. Always had.

'D'you think you'll ever tell Jane the truth?' she asked delicately.

She saw Bridie wiggle her lips. 'I guess we'll have to one day,' the Irishwoman sighed. 'When she's old enough to understand. But not that her father was a dirty rotten . . . well, you know. I expect we'll say Cissie had an affair with a GI, who then gave his life on the D-Day beaches. We

420

left the father's name blank on the birth certificate so we'll have to make one up, so we will. But we'll cross that bridge when we come to it. We'll just have to hope she understands why Ron and I brought her up as our own. It's not as if Cissie abandoned her or anything, after all. Oh, just look at them all coming now, all laughing and enjoying themselves together.'

'Here, look!' Eva's eyes nearly popped out of her head and she jabbed Bridie in the ribs with her elbow. 'Cissie and Jake. Hugging each other. And . . . and kissing! Blooming heck, now if that's not two people in love then I don't know what it is!'

'Oh, sweet Jesus, Mary and Joseph.' Bridie crossed herself in joyful excitement. 'Isn't it about time Cissie felt herself healed and gave into her feelings for Jake. And Jake such a lovely young man. A miracle, so it is!'

The two mothers and friends gazed delightedly at their offspring who were making their way towards the lake. Cissie and Jake were arm in arm, Cissie occasionally resting her head on Jake's shoulder or turning her glowing face to receive his kiss, while Jane hopped along beside them.

A moment later, they were joined by Mildred and Zac, and all five were coming towards them, laughing and joking. +Suddenly, Mildred stopped to talk to a man with a small child in a pushchair. Eva's heart lurched. Poor Milly. She'd have made a great mum. But would she ever get the chance? It looked as if Jake and Cissie were all set now, and Eva couldn't have been more pleased. All six of her children were making their way in the world. All six except Milly. And Eva worried about her.

But then the most extraordinary thing happened. Milly seemed to be deep in conversation with this stranger. And the next second, she was in his arms, kissing him.

Eva audibly gasped. And then held her breath. Mildred knew this man. He was no stranger. There was only one person it could be. And after all these years. Bleeding hell.

Eva waited. Watched as Mildred seemed to be introducing the fellow to the others. Cor, handsome as a film star as far as Eva could see from that distance.

And then the little troop was coming towards the two older women. There wasn't room for the pushchair among the deckchairs, so the man picked up the child so gently that the little fellow didn't even stir as he flopped against his daddy's shoulder. Oh. Eva's heart plummeted as Mildred came to stand in front of her.

'Mum, this is Oscar,' Mildred gasped breathlessly. 'And the little one is Gregory. His *nephew*,' she added pointedly.

Eva caught her breath. Nephew. This handsome vision before her was Oscar. The child wasn't his. And from the look on Mildred's face, Oscar was free. Milly seemed about to burst she was so flipping happy. And just behind her, Jake and Cissie were entwined about each other as if they'd never let go.

Eva nodded as she took everything in, a smile blossoming on her face. It had taken six flaming long, horrible years of heartache and pain, every second of which she'd lived and suffered with these two children of hers. But now she knew everything was going to be all right. She couldn't wait to find her Stan and tell him the fantastic news.

But for now, she must contain her joy. 'Very pleased to meet you, I'm sure,' she said to Oscar Miles. And she held out her hand.

Acknowledgements

Once again I must thank my wonderful agent, Broo Doherty, for her belief in my writing and for placing yet another of my novels with the lovely team at Aria Fiction. It is always a delight to work with you all.

Anyone who has read my previous story, *The Candle Factory Girl*, will know that I lived in Banbury Street as a small child. The era of *The Street of Broken Dreams* is, however, much nearer to the time of my own residency, so the book is, if anything, even closer to my heart. So I owe huge thanks to my parents for making their home in this unassuming street, little realising that, many decades later, it would provide the setting for not one, but two of my historical novels. Strange how life works out!

My parents provided inspiration for this book in other ways, too. Something my mother told me once when speaking of her wartime memories gave me the idea for Cissie's story. My father served on submarines in the Far East during that terrible time, and some of his stories led to Gary's tale in this novel.

A major passion in my life has always been dance in any form, but, in particular, classical ballet. I studied under Miss Doris Lightowler Knight for many years, and we remained friends up until her death. She was a huge fan of my historical novels and knew that one day, I intended to write a story about a dancer. Indeed, her recollections of being a dancer in a repertory company during the war was the inspiration for The Romaine Theatre Company. Thank you so much, Miss Knight, for all that you taught me and for so many years of friendship.

I wish that both you and my parents were still alive today to witness your parts in this novel.

As always, my greatest gratitude goes to my husband whose patience, support and understanding over my writing have known no bounds, and also to you, my dear readers, who make it all worthwhile. If you enjoyed this story and are kind enough to leave a review on your preferred platform, I should be extremely grateful. And, of course, if this is the first of my novels you have read, there are plenty more for you to lose yourself in. Why not head across to my website at www.tania-crosse.co.uk and take a look? And don't forget that you can follow me on Twitter @ TaniaCrosse or on Facebook @TaniaCrosseAuthor. I shall look forward to seeing you there!

Again, very many thanks, and happy reading!
Tania

We do hope that you have enjoyed
reading this large print book.

Did you know that all of our titles
are available for purchase?

We publish a wide range of high
quality large print books including:
Romances, Mysteries, Classics
General Fiction
Non Fiction and Westerns

Special interest titles available in
large print are:
The Little Oxford Dictionary
Music Book, Song Book
Hymn Book, Service Book

Also available from us courtesy of
Oxford University Press:
Young Readers' Dictionary
(large print edition)
Young Readers' Thesaurus
(large print edition)

For further information or a free
brochure, please contact us at:
Ulverscroft Large Print Books Ltd.,
The Green, Bradgate Road, Anstey,
Leicester, LE7 7FU, England.
Tel: (00 44) **0116 236 4325**
Fax: (00 44) **0116 234 0205**

Other titles published by Ulverscroft:

A PLACE TO CALL HOME

Tania Crosse

Thrown together by tragic circumstances some years previously, Meg and Clarrie's hard-won friendship eventually brought them both some sense of peace. But how deep do their feelings run, and how long can their happiness last? The outbreak of war brings a new set of concerns and emotions, especially with the arrival of the evacuees who come to share their home and lives. Can they unite to form a bond powerful enough to sustain them through the darkest days of war? And what will happen when an enemy from Meg's past comes back to haunt her?

NOBODY'S GIRL

Tania Crosse

The boom years immediately after the Great War bring nothing but happiness for wealthy industrialist Wigmore Stratfield-Whyte and his wife Clarissa — until tragedy robs them of their greatest treasure. Many years later, a horrific fatal accident brings young Meg Chandler, a spirited farmer's daughter, into their lives. Meg wants nothing to do with them, but Clarissa is drawn irresistibly towards the bereaved girl and will move heaven and earth to help her. Will Meg allow Clarissa into her own shattered life, and can the two share a future happiness together? And will Meg's new acquaintances bring her the contentment she craves — or seek to destroy her?

TEARDROPS IN THE MOON

Tania Crosse

Rose Warrington could not be happier surrounded by her family and friends on her sixtieth birthday. But on the same day, Archduke Ferdinand is assassinated in far-away Sarajevo, leading to the outbreak of The Great War. Rose's spirited younger daughter, Marianne — having taken a vow of chastity some years earlier — sees the war as an opportunity to prove herself as capable as any man. She joins the First Aid Nursing Yeomanry as an ambulance driver in war-torn France and it takes all her strength to face its horrors: there are tragedies lying in wait for those she loves, and her girlhood vow will be challenged and tested.